Southern Temptation

Sue Langford

Copyright © 2024 Sue Langford
All rights reserved.

To the readers who love spice, sexy accents, the hot men and the romance that never leaves your soul.

Southern Temptation

Charleston Series, Volume 7

Sue Langford

Published by Sue Langford, 2024.

Find someone who's a home and an adventure all at once -
Anonymous

Chapter 1

"Right this way Kelly," the tour guide said as she looked out at the view.

The cliffs were even more amazing than she expected, but the boy she saw out there was catching her eye more than the view. When he stepped on the bus and came and sat down beside her, Kelly was almost stunned.

"Liam," he said as she looked at him.

"Kelly Ryan," she replied.

"Don't tell anyone I snuck on okay," Liam whispered. Kelly smirked.

"You live here. Why would you want to be on a tour bus with a bunch of tourists?"

"I hadn't been out here in a while. I wanted to come." He smirked and looked at his phone, seeing a message from his friends:

She can't be that cute. Come on.

He smirked and looked at Kelly. "How much longer are you here?"

"Kinda here on a tour. I head home next weekend."

"8 days?"

Kelly nodded. "Why?"

"Do you have a phone here?" Kelly smirked. She pulled her phone from her bag and opened it, handing him the phone. "Call me tomorrow. I know a much better place to show you anyway," Liam said as they made their way to her hotel. "You're staying here," Liam asked.

"For tonight. Why?"

"What's left that you haven't seen yet," Liam asked.

"A complete stranger is asking me that?"

He smirked. "Castles?"

"I stayed an extra week past the tour. I wanted to go…"

"Then you have a week left of fun."

Kelly nodded. "Something like that."

He smirked. "Come with me. Dinner," he said.

"Liam. I don't even know who you are let alone your last name. I'm not going anywhere."

"Liam Murphy. I live all of a 10-minute walk from here. The pub is right there," he said.

"Fine," Kelly said with a smirk ear to ear as she watched the sexy stranger make his way to the bar and order them each a drink.

That was how it all started. Her first Guinness, her first Irish pub. When her phone buzzed at midnight, she smirked:

How was your day baby? I can't wait to hear all about it. See you next weekend. – Dad

"Put the phone down and come," Liam said.

"Where," she asked.

He got Kelly her first shot of Jameson's and couldn't help staring. Maybe it was the dark hair, the blue eyes, the smile ear to ear, or maybe it was the giggle that had him smitten, but he didn't want her to leave. They made it back to the hotel not long later and he was determined to walk her to her door.

"I really am fine," Kelly said.

"Promise me that you won't kick my backside to the other end of the planet," he said.

"Meaning what," Kelly said.

He kissed her. One kiss was all it took. One. "I'll come get you in the morning. I'll bring a full Irish breakfast," he said.

"I guess," Kelly said. Liam kissed her again and leaned her against her hotel room door. Just as he was about to ask her if he could come in, her phone rang again. "Tomorrow," she said.

He nodded and kissed her. "I'll be here early."

That was all it took. Every minute that she'd spent in Ireland was right beside him until he had to take her to the airport in Dublin. "Promise me that you call when you're home. I'll fly out. Just don't vanish on me," Liam asked.

"We're have a world away Liam."

He kissed her, picking her up, and wrapped her arms around him, sitting down on the bench outside. "I don't want you to leave."

"I have to. I start college in two weeks Liam."

"Then stay."

"I can't."

He kissed her again, devouring her lips. "Promise me that this isn't the end," he asked.

"I have to go."

"Kelly."

"What?"

"This isn't over. Promise me that it isn't."

"I have to…"

He kissed her again. "Promise me."

She nodded and he slid something in her pocket. "What's that," Kelly asked.

"My address. Home phone and cell. Don't lose the number. I saved it in your phone."

Kelly smirked. "Alright," she said.

He took a picture of them with her phone then another with his. "It's not over. Never will be," Liam said. She kissed him and he walked her to the gate. She checked her bag and after one more kiss, she walked out to board the plane and vanished from his life.

LIAM REMEMBERED THAT day like it was yesterday. It had been on a constant loop since she'd left at 18. Now, he was 28. Ten years she'd been stuck in his memories and his dreams at night. Ten years he'd wished that she'd never left. He'd changed in those ten years. He was bigger, taller, more experienced and had a lot more money than he did then. He had a business that made more money than he could dream of, and one man trying to partner with him. Emerson Cartwright worked for one massive company. They had businesses all over the world. Liam knew exactly why they wanted his company to join them. He had the pubs in Ireland on his side. He had the systems for those pubs. He had something they wanted in their restaurants in America, and it was the perfect reason to at least meet them. The deal was, if they were partnering with him, he'd have to be bi-coastal. He'd have to have a place in Charleston.

When he got to the airport to head to Charleston, he remembered that day. The day where he lost the girl. The day that she'd vanished from his life completely. One or two calls, one or two letters then she'd vanished into America somewhere. It was a lot bigger than Ireland, but he hoped that somehow he'd find her again. Even if it took forever. At least he'd remembered that promise.

The plane took off and they handed Liam his drink. "The WIFI should be up and functioning in the next 15 minutes. Can I get you anything," the attendant asked. Liam shook his head.

"Thank you, but no," Liam said as he went into his email, then google and searched Kelly's name. It was a common name. He had no idea where she was even living. She could've married, changed her name, died. He had no idea. He searched Kelly Ryan in Charleston and when a photo came up, he thought he'd seen a ghost. He zoomed in. If that photo was really her, he'd found her. If it wasn't, he'd keep looking. One way or another, before he was gone from this world, he was gonna find her again.

"What do you need me to do," Kelly asked.

"He's flying in today. If the deal goes through, he needs a place. If he wants the beach, take him to Isle of Palms. You can work with the real estate agent. Just meet with him and figure it out," her boss asked.

"What hotel are we putting him up at," Kelly asked.

"Belmond Charleston Place. Penthouse Suite. The spa is there in case he wants to use it. Full amount is paid for on our account," the president said.

"And what business is it?"

"Restaurant division. He created a software that somewhat revolutionized the system we have for the bars and restaurants. Honestly, I think it's one of the first times he's been in the USA," the President said.

"I doubt that, but okay," Kelly said.

"He lands in 45 minutes. We sent a driver to pick him up unless you want to go yourself," the President said.

"I'll go. Might as well start it off right," Kelly said as she finished the meeting and changed. She saw the name and swore it sounded familiar.

She remembered back to a boy she'd met long before. Dark hair, emerald eyes, taller and drop dead handsome. It had been so long ago. Every time she'd had a heartbreak since, she'd thought of him.

She shook her head, grabbed her purse and the driver took her out to the arrivals at the airport. His flight was landing any minute. Kelly shook her head and looked at the photo, shaking her head. It was May. If he'd never been to Charleston in the summer, he was gonna need clothes and air conditioning. Kelly smirked, grabbing the card for the driver and writing the last name. Murphy. There had to be a million of them in Ireland. In Dublin alone, it was probably a common last name.

When she heard footsteps walking towards her in the terminal, she got up and saw a man that was sexy as all get out. He was 6 foot 5, muscular, dark reddish hair, eyes that almost glowed emerald green and a scruff that was sexy. The dress shirt had been wrinkled from the flight and his jeans were perfect. "Mr. Murphy?"

He nodded. "I gather you're my welcome committee," Liam said not even looking up, staring at the photo on his phone.

"Yes. How was your flight," Kelly said not staring into his eyes.

"Good. Got me here in one piece. Where are we heading," he asked.

"Have you been to Charleston before," she asked.

"Not in a long time. Always meant to come sooner," Liam said.

"Well, unfortunately, the weather is a little overly humid today. We're in the midst of a heat wave. Do you have any bags," Kelly asked.

"One. I didn't catch your name," he said wondering and looking up. He was almost speechless.

"Sorry about that. I'm Kelly..."

"Ryan," he said finishing her sentence.

She nodded. "Have we met?"

He took a deep breath. "We can talk in the car."

She looked up at him. "Excuse me?" He got his bag and they walked out to the waiting car. Kelly slid in and he hopped in beside her.

"Really though. Did you need anything before I show you the hotel?"

"Coffee, but I'll grab it in the lobby," he said.

Kelly looked at him. The driver headed off and Kelly tried to make small talk. "So, I thought we could show you around Charleston a little. Some of the tourist stops."

"Hotel," Liam said. They went the long way to the hotel, showed him the waterfront park, the bridge, city market and King street then pulled up the main drive of the hotel. She went inside, got the key and he requested a second key.

"Right this way," Kelly said. He was too quiet. She could hear him huffing and puffing like he was about to yell at someone. "Is anything wrong?"

"We need to talk," he replied.

"I don't think we have actually..."

The door to the elevator opened and he walked down the hallway as she opened his door for him. "After you," Liam said.

She started getting a weird feeling. One she wasn't sure was good. "I'll just wait..."

"Sit," he said.

"Excuse me?"

He walked into the massive bedroom, put his bag on the luggage rack and walked into the living room. "I need to ask you something. You want to get mad, fine. You don't want to help me find a place, sure. Just answer me one question."

"What," Kelly asked.

"Have you ever been to Dublin?"

She looked at him. "Why? Does that really matter?"

"When you were 18."

Kelly looked at him. "Why?"

"Yes or no?"

SOUTHERN TEMPTATION 11

"Mr. Murphy, I appreciate that you're in a strange country..."

"On a tour bus."

She shook her head. "A lot of people go to Ireland."

"For 2 weeks on tour then another with a kid in Dublin."

She looked at him. "I think you have the wrong girl."

He made a phone call and she felt her phone buzz. "I don't."

"We really should get..."

"Kelly."

Even the way he said her name made her toes curl. There was no way it was the same kid. This was the equivalent of a damn GQ model. That kid was scrawny and lanky at best. He sang in pubs. Half the time that she'd spent with that kid was spent in a pub. There was no way possible that it was the same person. This guy was way too sexy. Way too hot.

"You may have me confused with someone else," Kelly said.

"You had your first pint and your first shot of Jameson whiskey with me." She shook her head. "And the first time you ever slept beside a guy."

She looked at him. "Excuse me?"

"And you almost got a shamrock tattoo on your neck behind your ear before I talked you out of it."

She looked at him again. "What?"

"Fine. I need to change. Give me 10 minutes," he said as he walked into the bedroom. He closed the door and Kelly sat down, breathless and in shock.

Liam went and had a cold shower, trying to calm his system down before he pounced on her in the suite. He shook his head, stepped out of the shower, wrapped a towel around his hips and pulled his dress pants and dress shirt on, put on his cologne and came back into the living room, shirt undone.

She saw the tattoo. The one with the initials LM and KR in a 4-leaf clover over his chest. "Did you bring shorts," Kelly asked.

"Yeah. Kinda guessed they may be necessary. Where are we headed," he asked.

"I can show you around a bit in town if you want. Have you eaten?"

"Kelly."

"I can get us a reservation down in the café," she said suddenly completely flustered.

"Sure," Liam said. She made the reservation and went to grab her purse.

"How far to the office," he asked.

"15-minute walk. Why," Kelly asked.

"When is the meeting?"

"Around 3. They wanted to give you some time to get settled."

"Good. We have time," he said.

"Meaning what," Kelly asked.

"Lunch. Then we can talk."

"You do realize…"

He got the door and they made their way downstairs to the café. They walked down the hall and when they made it back into the elevator, he was almost radiating sex.

"I know you think that…"

"We met when you went back to the cliffs and I snuck onto the tour bus. Before I had the money to commandeer one myself obviously."

She was almost trembling. The elevator opened and they went down to the café, got a quiet corner table and sat down. She ordered a sweet tea and sandwich and he ordered a Guinness. Even the way he said it was the same.

"And two shots of Jameson whiskey," he asked.

Kelly looked at him.

"Sinking in," he asked.

"There's no way."

"Yeah, I kinda thought the same thing on the way here. There you were. Sitting at the airport, waiting on me. If I'd known that you were here..."

"Liam."

"What," he asked.

"You must..."

"Don't say I have you mixed up with someone else Kelly. I heard your phone buzz," Liam said.

"I really need to get back to the office, but I can..."

"No."

"What do you mean no?"

"You aren't leaving again. You can show me around and we can talk. Beach first."

She shook her head. "I can't. I'll get someone else..."

"It took me 10 years Kelly. Ten. Ten years to find you again. Ten years of waiting for a call back or an email or a letter. I got nothing. You walked out in Dublin and ran home like a good little girl. You promised me."

Kelly got up and he grabbed her hand.

"Sit down."

"I need to make a call."

"No, you don't love."

She was about to leave and her phone buzzed. She looked and sat down. "Sir."

"Is he settled?"

"Yes. We're just having lunch."

"We're changing the meeting to tomorrow morning. Gives him time to rest. Are you heading to the office or are you going to show him around," the president of the company asked.

"I'll be in later this afternoon. If I don't see you, I'll see you at the meeting," Kelly said.

"Alright. If he needs anything let me know."

"I will," Kelly said as she hung up.

They finished lunch in silence and she went to show him around the rest of the hotel. "Come with me," he said.

"I thought we could start on..."

"Kelly."

She shook her head. "I'll show you Isle of Palms and Sullivan's Island. The two beaches nearby. Folly is the other..."

"Kelly."

She went to walk down the hall and he took her hand and walked her to the elevator and pressed the button to take them up to the suite.

"After 10 years, you seriously think that I wouldn't recognize you? You still wear the same perfume. The eyes are the same."

"I really don't..."

He stared a hole in her the entire way up the elevator. "Don't what," he asked.

"This is business. Just leave it at business." The elevator doors opened and he walked her down the hallway, into the suite and slid the room key in her purse. He locked the door behind him and went and grabbed the bottle from his bag.

"What," Kelly asked.

He poured two glasses of whiskey and handed one to her, walking her to the sofa. "Sit."

"I really don't..."

"It'll jog your foggy memory," he said.

"I don't understand why you're so determined to make me into the..."

"Because you are. I remember it Kelly. I relived it in my dreams. I have since we met."

"It was a long time ago."

"Not that long. Are you seriously trying to pretend that you don't remember that? You cried on the damn phone with me when I called that first time. You said you wanted to come back to Dublin and you ghosted me instead." She shook her head, grabbed her purse and went to leave. "What in the hell are you afraid of?"

"I need to go."

"Why? Because you have a life now? You have no ring. Until there's a ring on that hand, you..." She shook her head and went to walk out when he stopped her. "What?"

"I run my own division Liam. I'm in charge of the business that you have to deal with. I can't mix business..."

"Then don't. I'll turn down the damn contract. I just want you back. I wanted you back for 10 years." She shook her head and still couldn't look at him. "Look at me." She shook her head. "Kelly, look at me. The only thing that's different is that I grew up. That I worked out instead of drinking my way through the pubs. I got taller. Bigger. That's it. You're the one that went from carefree, happy and laughing to this."

Kelly took a deep breath. "I need to go."

"Are you gonna keep pretending that we don't know each other? That we didn't sleep beside each other? That I didn't kiss you?"

"It was a long time ago Liam. Leave it."

"You promised me something Kelly." She shook her head. "You promised me that it wasn't over. It isn't. It never has been and never will be."

"Yeah it is Liam. I have a boyfriend."

"Let me meet him."

She shook her head. "I have to go."

"Kelly." Her phone went off two seconds later.

"Hello," she said.

"Hey. I was gonna see what you were up to tonight. You still have that work thing?"

"Yeah. Sort of in the middle of something."

"We need to talk Kelly. I get that you're all busy with work and stuff, but you can't keep blowing me off. We can't work like this," her boyfriend Andrew said.

"Can we talk about this another time," Kelly said. When she heard a woman laughing a little too close to the phone, she shook her head.

"I'll be at the beach then. Bye," Andrew said.

Kelly hung up and Liam shook his head. "You need a man Kelly. Not a little boy out to play games with the girlies on the beach."

"Liam, you don't know..."

He leaned in. "What?"

"You don't know what I..."

Liam looked at her. "Go ahead and say it love."

"You haven't seen me in 10 years. You don't know what I want or need. This is work Liam. Leave it."

He looked down at her. "Come have your drink. We can talk then."

"I need to get back."

"Kelly." She shook her head and found a way out, making her way down the hallway. She got into the elevator, made her way downstairs and walked out the front doors, intentionally walking back to the office. She needed the air even though it was past muggy and into sticky sweat instead of a breeze.

She walked into her office and got paperwork done. When her phone buzzed at 3, she looked.

"What can I do for you," Kelly asked as she smirked and was thankful for it being her Dad on the phone.

"Well, I wanted to let you know that Mom and I are going on a vacation. She deserves one after this insane year. I'm thinking about taking her to London. What do you think," her Dad asked.

"London is beautiful. Maybe a tad muggy like it is here right now, but you two always loved it."

"We're leaving right after your birthday. How's work?"

"Good. Had a déjà vu moment today, but other than that."

"Why," her Dad asked as she heard him get comfy in his favorite chair.

"Do you remember when I went away to Dublin?"

"Of course. You saved up for three summers to go. Why," he asked.

"A friend I met there is actually in Charleston. He flew in today. The company is partnering with him."

"Great! Go and catch up. Mom and I are going up to Myrtle Beach for the weekend anyway. Go have fun."

"Thanks. Honestly, I think it's good timing. Andrew and I..."

"I never liked him anyway. He's an overgrown child," her Dad said. She talked to him for a while and when she hung up, she could smell cologne.

She slid her jacket off and looked out at the view. "Miss Ryan, Liam Murphy is here to see you," her assistant said.

She shook her head and nodded. "Whatever," she said.

"Doesn't sound good there lass," he said as he walked in and closed and locked the office door behind him.

"We don't lock doors here Liam."

"Then sit and talk."

"You do realize that this is my career right?"

"And I also know by that look on your face that you have no plans this weekend. Did the so-called boyfriend need a diaper change?"

"Liam."

"You always needed a man Kelly. A real one. Not a child pretending to be one. Why did you take off?"

"Because I have work to do," Kelly replied.

"And still, you're staring out the window at a view that you love. You could be outside in the sunshine and sweltering heat."

She shook her head and sat down at her desk. "Are you getting a place here?"

"Depends on whether you're gonna play work Kelly or sexy Dublin Kelly."

She glared at him. "I want something like my place at home."

"Which is?"

"Lots of space. Room to go for a morning lap. Water. 3 bedrooms."

"Kids?"

"If only you'd stayed. We would've by now."

"Liam."

"No. Not yet."

She shook her head and took a deep breath. "What area? Beach? Downtown? Out of downtown? Plantation home?"

"Where do you live?"

"Liam, seriously."

"Beach."

"I'll get some viewings set up." He made her nervous. Now even more than before. The cologne was even intoxicating.

"What time are you off," he asked.

"5. Why?"

"Went past Hall's something or other. I made a reservation. We're going."

"Not really happening."

He looked down at her. "Date. One date. A real one."

"While I appreciate…"

"You aren't backing out of it. We're sitting down like adults and talking," Liam said.

"Do you want to buy or rent," Kelly asked intentionally staying on business topics.

"Depends on our date night." She looked up at him. "How I love that look. Buy."

"Try to stay professional alright?"

"Where did you go after you came home from Ireland?"

"University of North Carolina. I was going to go pre-law."

"And?"

"Got this job. Worked up from nothing and got a promotion from the Media division."

"Books. Much more you."

"Liam, please. Any house style?"

"Craftsman or country. Something that feels like home instead of a sanitary room." She shook her head. "What?"

"Nothing. Price range?"

"Max 7."

She looked at him. "What?"

"Did you think I didn't work after you left?"

She shook her head. "Well, there's 5 right now that are still on the market. You can take a look with the agent…"

"You."

Faith looked up at him. "Liam, I'm an exec. I'm not a real estate agent."

"You're coming with me."

She shook her head, taking a deep breath. Just as he was about to get up and walk over to her, there was a knock at her door. She got up and answered. "Your papers you needed. Contract needs to be signed tomorrow. 3 copies. And who..."

"Thanks Reagan. I will get them to you tomorrow after the meeting," Kelly said. Her friend Reagan headed off with a smirk ear to ear.

"Friend of yours," he asked.

Kelly nodded. "She's in legal."

"It's almost 5. Come," he said.

"Liam, this is my workplace."

"Then I'll take your hand in the elevator."

She shook her head, grabbed her purse, locked up her laptop and headed out. "Off for the night," Kelly said as she said goodbye to her assistant. Liam followed, watching the dress glide against her silky legs. Her being in a huff was hot. Hell. He missed those legs.

When he'd met her, she was all dark hair and sexy eyes, but now, she was dark hair, sexy eyes, a body that had him past turned on and legs that were sexy and would be even sexier wrapped around him. Now, she was almost 5 foot 7 and tanned. She wasn't the awkward teen anymore. She was a full body woman and one that he wasn't about to let go of.

When she stepped into the elevator, he pressed the main floor and stared. "I'm not a piece of meat Liam. Stop."

"Just as sexy as they were when we were..."

"Liam, seriously."

They got to the main floor and her phone buzzed with a reminder to pick up her dress at the cleaners. "What," he asked.

"I have to make a stop."

"For what?"

"Dry cleaning." She went and got her dress and headed down to her truck.

"What time is the reservation," Kelly asked.

"7:30."

"I'll take you to…"

"You can change at the hotel."

"Liam."

"I just found you after 10 years. I'm not letting you out of my sight."

She shook her head, hopped in the truck, he slid in beside her and she headed to the hotel. "We're keeping this professional," Kelly said.

"Yes ma'am," he teased.

They got up to his suite and she walked in with him to see roses waiting. Sterling roses. She shrugged it off. "Give me a minute…"

He took the dress and her purse out of her hands and put it on the chair. "What," Kelly asked.

"Something I've been waiting to do for 10 bloody years." He leaned over and kissed her. That kiss was enough to light a fire in an ice storm. He picked her up, ever so slightly, and deepened the kiss until her heels slid to the floor.

When the kiss broke, she looked at him. "I can't," Faith said.

"What?"

"I can't do this."

She went to grab her dress and he stopped her. "What can't you do?"

"Liam, I'm not the same person you knew alright?"

He kissed her again. "Yeah you are love. You just grew up."

He set her on her feet and she shook her head. "I need to change."

"Bedroom," he replied. She shook her head, took the dress and got changed, freshening up a little. When she came back into the living room, he was sitting on the sofa, shirt off, and pouring two glasses of Jameson's.

"Liam, I kinda have to drive myself home. I can't be drinking."

He handed one to her. "Dinner isn't that far from here Kelly. We can walk."

She looked at him. "Why now?"

"Why now what? Why did I come here? I waited for you. I hoped every damn night that you'd show up. I texted. I emailed you. I sent you damn letters love. What else did you want me to do?"

"Leave it. Leave it as a stupid fling on a stupid..."

He kissed her again making her knees go weak. "It was never a fling," he said as she drank the entire glass of Jameson's and went and grabbed a bottle of water.

"Do I make you that nervous?"

"You show up after 10 years looking like that with my damn initials carved into your chest? Yeah. Yeah, you do."

"I meant what I said then."

She shook her head. Either she was gonna need a few bottles of Irish whiskey to get through the night or she was gonna need one hell of an escape plan.

"Meaning?"

He looked at her with the emerald, green eyes that had haunted her daydreams and fantasies. "I knew then that..." Her phone buzzed and he wanted more than anything to throw it into the ocean.

"Yes," Faith said.

"Did you need me to come by and do a full clean," her housekeeper asked.

"Thank you. I'd appreciate it. Tomorrow morning?"

"Alright. Have a good night Miss Kelly." Kelly hung up with her and Liam handed her another glass.

"Are you attempting to get me tipsy?"

"If it means you acting like the Kelly I know, yeah."

"Liam."

He kissed her again. "What?"

"I changed."

"I see that. All legs and sex and long hair and everything. You just got sexier Kelly. A lot sexier."

She looked at him. "You can stop trying to picture me naked."

"I've already seen you partially naked Kelly. This is just a bonus."

"We never..."

"We almost did. I saw enough love."

She shook her head. "So, you came all this way why? Because you wanted to get laid?"

"Because I had business. Honestly, I didn't even know that it was really you until I saw you at the airport. I missed you."

"Liam, I have to keep things professional at the office alright? Business. Period."

"And when you're not in the office and you wake up in my bed with me?"

She looked at him. "Yeah, I'm going home."

"No, you don't. I'm teasing love."

"No, you aren't."

"No, I'm not, but I am. Not that I would ever turn down you in my bed, but if it.."

"Liam, does that ever actually work?"

"Only once."

"Maybe don't try that again."

He smirked and took a sip of his drink. "What time are you to be in tomorrow?"

"8. I have to go home tonight."

"Where do you want me to sleep?"

"Here." He looked at her. "Don't."

"Do we have time for you to run home and get an overnight..."

"Liam." He smirked. His phone buzzed a minute later.

"Yes."

"I'm calling from Hall's Chop House. We aren't able to accommodate the 7:30 reservation. We can get you a table in about 20 minutes if that's alright instead," the hostess said.

"Fine. We'll be there in a few moments," he said as he looked at Kelly.

"What," Kelly asked.

"Come. We're going to dinner now."

"Liam, I told you..."

He kissed her, devouring her lips and nibbling them. When the kiss broke, he took her hand and walked her down the hall to the elevator then made their way to the restaurant.

When they walked in and were seated at the table, she looked at him.

"What was that?"

"Meaning what love?"

"Don't do that Liam. Just don't." He smirked and ordered them drinks. "Liam."

"What?" She looked at him and shook her head. "What did you want for dinner," he asked.

"Are you even listening to me?"

"Remembering that lass in the pub. The one who remembered how to laugh."

They ordered dinner and Liam looked over at her, looking her up and down. "I'm not falling for it Liam."

"Fallin for what?"

"You know what. I was 18 when we met. I didn't know any better," she said as she took a sip of her drink.

"Come here for a sec," Liam said.

She shook her head. "No."

"I'm not gonna bite Kelly," he said.

"Whatever," she said.

"Ten. Ten years and you never replied to an email. How did you think I was gonna act when I saw you?"

"I didn't get emails Liam. I got one letter. I left it at that. You haven't even tried in 10 years."

"I called every year. Every Christmas, every holiday. Every St. Patrick's Day I called you. You never answered."

"Liam, stop."

"Did you never even think about contacting me?"

"I had..."

He kissed her. "Had love. Had a boyfriend. One who obviously has no idea what he has."

"I had to go home Liam. I was in university for 3 years. I ate, slept and studied. Sure, I wish I could've just vanished and gone back to Ireland, but I couldn't. I started working while I was at school. I haven't stopped working."

He looked at her. "What happened then?"

"Meaning what?"

"What happened when you left and came home?"

"My gran passed. My grandfather passed two weeks after that. Sorry that I wasn't at your damn beck and call," she said as she gulped down her drink and saw the waitress with a second round.

"Come here."

"Liam."

"Come." She shook her head and he slid her to him in the booth.

"What?"

He kissed her. "I didn't know," he said.

"I know you didn't," she said sliding away from him. He moved her table setting over so they were side by side. "Liam."

He shook his head. "Stop pushing me away love. I'm not trying to upset you. I just want you around me."

"And you haven't said anything other than me and I and me."

He kissed her shoulder. "I'm sorry about your gran and granddad. I'm sorry."

"Liam, I can't do this."

"Why?"

She shook her head. "I need to..."
He kissed her. "Don't go."

Chapter 2

"Liam."

"Just stay and have dinner. We can go for a walk after," he said.

"Liam, I have..."

"Please."

She took a deep breath. "Fine. After that I have to go home."

He looked at her. "Then we go get you an overnight..."

"Liam. Stop. I'm not staying at the hotel with you."

He shook his head. "What time is the meeting?"

"10."

"Lots of time love."

Kelly got up. "Where are you going?"

She walked off and went to the bathroom. She needed air. She needed space. She took a deep breath and when she came back to the table, 4 glasses of Jameson's were sitting on the table. "What is..."

"Come sit."

"That whole thing where I said I had to drive home. Just went out the window?" He handed her a glass. "Liam."

He kissed her and they both had their whiskey. "Just lean back and relax." Dinner came and by the time they finally managed to leave, Kelly was feeling the whiskey.

"You know you could've called me and told me about them," Liam said as they started walking back to the truck.

"I know. I had a few other things going on Liam."

He walked her down to the waterfront park and she shook her head. "I need to go home. I need sleep," Kelly said. They walked out to the dock, watching the boats go by.

"I know what I need Kelly. I know what I always needed."

"Like there wasn't anyone else. I'm just..."

He kissed her, holding her face in his hands like he had the first time he ever kissed her. "You're just what?"

"I'm just a regular woman Liam."

"And one that I never ever stopped thinking about. One I never got out of my soul."

She looked at him. "One week. One. What did I do in one week..."

He took her hand and they started walking back towards the hotel. "What did I do?"

"Made me realize that I wanted a lass of my own. That if I had to swim all the way here, I would do it to be with you again."

Kelly looked at him. "One week."

"One week that changed literally everything."

"Why? How?"

"Because I had everything I ever wanted and lost it in an airport. I wanted to bust through that glass and jump onto that plane beside you."

Kelly shook her head and they made their way to the hotel. "I need to go," Kelly said. He shook his head, took her hand and walked her to the elevator. They made their way up to his suite and he walked her in.

"What," she asked.

He slid his arms around her and kissed her. She felt him pick her up and lean her onto the bed in the massive bedroom. "What are you..."

He kissed down her neck. "I needed you then, and I need you now," Liam said.

She shook her head. "Liam, I'm not..."

He kissed her again. The kiss that tasted like Jameson's. The lips that could make every muscle in her body throb. The eyes that made her fall into them. The arms that made her want them wrapped around her. She felt him slide his shirt off and lean into her arms. "Liam, I have to go." She felt his lips against her chest and knew she was screwed.

The strap slid from her shoulder and she felt his lips and his beard against her skin. "I need to go Liam."

"We have time."

She shook her head. "Liam, please."

He kissed her. "I wanted this before you left."

"Just stop."

He leaned to his back and pulled her to him. "Tell me what I have to do so I never lose you again."

Kelly looked at him. "I'm not a possession Liam."

He kissed her again with a kiss that turned her toes into knots, made her legs almost tremble and her body throb like there was no tomorrow.

"Stay," he asked.

"Hmm?"

He smirked and kissed her again. "Stay tonight. I'll get you home in the mornin." She went to answer and he kissed her, nibbling her lips. "Stay."

She shook her head. "Liam, I need…"

He wrapped his arms tight around her and slid her leg across his. "I won't…"

"Don't lie to me Liam."

"Fine. I'll do my best not to taste every single inch of you while you sleep." Her toes went into triple knots. Whether it was him, his cologne, his muscles or the Irish brogue that had her even more hot and bothered or not, saying no to that voice was the hardest thing she'd ever done. She'd be at his mercy all night and he knew it. The way she felt with his arm around her was making her overheat. "Kelly," he said as he kissed her forehead then the tip of her nose.

"Don't make me say it," Kelly said.

He leaned her to her back, sliding into her arms. She felt his body tight to her and felt her legs pull around his hips. "I've wanted you since you showed up at the cliffs that day."

"I have to go Liam. I…" He kissed her again.

"I can't let go love. It's like asking me not to breathe."

One more kiss and she was starting to overheat. "Liam, I have to…"

"Don't." She shook her head and got up. "Kelly."

She grabbed her other dress and her purse and was out the door and in the elevator before he made it to her. She got down to her truck and headed home. She had the windows open and the A/C on high the entire way there. She tried to concentrate, but she had flashes back to what they'd done in Ireland.

When she got back to her place, she locked up the truck and headed inside, dropping everything at the door. She locked up, grabbed her phone, threw it on the charger, kicked her clothes off and went into a cool shower. One way or another, she had to calm herself down.

She remembered back to those nights. They had a few pints then spent all night talking and making out. It wasn't until the last two nights she had before she left that things got hotter. The stormy night, curling up by the gas fireplace in her suite. Almost going one step too far among a pile of pillows on the floor. If he'd known that she almost hadn't left, he'd never have let her go.

She shook her head, cooling the water enough to snap her out of the daydream. She shook her head, flipped the water off, grabbed a towel and walked into the bedroom. "It's a dream Kelly. It's not happening. He's here temporarily," she said to herself. She slid her silky chemise on and opened up the sliding door, looking out at the beach. When her grandparents had left her the house, she thought she'd hit the motherload. The beach she loved and the house? She took a deep breath and tried snapping herself back into reality.

Just as she was starting to dry off, her phone buzzed. She looked at the call display and saw his name. She shook her head and ignored the call. When it rang again 2 minutes later, she took a deep breath of warm salt air and answered.

"Much better," Liam said.

"What do you want Liam?"

"Address."

She shook her head. "No."

"You're at the beach."

"Liam, no."

"Kelly."

"What?"

She could hear him. "We can talk."

She sat down on the porch swing. "I get it Liam. You want..."

"Give me the address."

"No."

"Fine. Talk."

She shook her head and walked downstairs and poured herself a glass of Jameson and sat down on her porch. "Liam, I get it. You want to go back to..."

"I don't care where we go. I just want to be with you."

"I need to get sleep. I have to be at work tomorrow."

"Grab a bag. Just come here. I'll sleep on the sofa."

Kelly shook her head. "Not tonight."

She looked out at the water. It was as calm as ever. "I wanted you to stay in Dublin. You know that right?"

"Liam."

"I almost went out and bought a ring before you left. I didn't want to lose you and I still don't."

"Liam, you changed just like I did. I'm not that same person you knew. I grew up and snapped out of it. I couldn't have stayed there even if I wanted to. I wouldn't be here right now if I had."

"I almost bought a ticket so you wouldn't be flying alone."

She took a sip of her drink and exhaled. "I missed you too. I just didn't know what else to say. The funerals sort of

SOUTHERN TEMPTATION

took over and everything else went to the back of the pile. I didn't want you in the middle of it."

"Kelly, I worked for this long so I had a reason to come and find you. I was searching for you for years. There was only once that you ever answered, and it wasn't even you."

"What?"

"A guy answered."

"When," Kelly asked.

"Two years ago. On your birthday."

"Liam."

"Same punk that dumped you over the phone?"

Kelly shook her head. "Yeah. Last time we broke up."

"What?"

"Morning of my birthday, waited 2 months then tried to get me back."

"I'll kill him."

"Liam, we aren't dating. I'm not even dating him anymore. Leave it alone."

She shook her head. "Let me come over there."

"No."

"Kelly, come on now." She shook her head. She'd always wondered why her phone had all of a sudden cleared it's call history. Now it made sense.

"Liam, I get that you want to be here, but I can't do this. I changed Liam. I can't be doing this. I have work to actually concentrate on. You're going home. There's no point."

"I'm buying a house Kelly. Buying. Not renting, not borrowing. I'm buying. I'm going back and forth between here and Dublin."

"Then find someone else. I can't."

"Kelly."

"Goodnight," she said.

"Kelly, don't hang up."

"Why?"

"Because I just found you again love. I've wanted to hear that voice for 10 years. Don't."

"Goodnight Liam," she said as she hung up. She finished her drink, locked up and went back upstairs. She curled up on her bed, put her phone on the charger and went to sleep.

He leaned onto the way too fluffy pillows and bed and shook his head. He tried to get comfortable and could smell her shampoo. "Enough is enough. Just get up and find her," he said as he got up and had a cold shower. He stepped out not long later and stared at the phone, willing it to ring. He slid boxers on and texted her:

I get it love. Things changed. For me, they didn't.
I'm not gonna be sleeping anyway. Come back over.
I won't say anything.

He put his phone on the charger and attempted to sleep. He'd need it if he had to think straight the next morning. Thinking about her was just getting him turned on. He'd had other women. A few. None of them really compared, but seeing her sexy legs, and that walk that had made him want her that first day in Dublin had him hot for her. Really hot. When his phone buzzed, he almost jumped:

Goodnight.

He shook his head, closed the curtains, set his alarm and sent her a reply:

The extra key is in your purse. Come over in the morning. I'll buy breakfast.

When there was no reply, he flipped the light off and attempted to sleep.

The next morning, Kelly got up and went for a run, got showered and dressed and saw the text about breakfast. She had a protein shake, got her things together and headed downtown.

Liam woke up at 5, did a run and a workout and went up to his suite to see breakfast waiting. When he saw two plates and two sets of cutlery he almost hoped. Almost. He went to have a quick shower and when he stepped out of the shower, he saw a text on his phone:

Breakfast. Nothing else. You need a cold shower.

He smirked, washed up and slid dress pants on as he heard a knock at the door. He walked over and opened it, seeing Kelly in a pale green dress. "Good morning," he said as she saw him shirtless, reminding her of the tattoo.

"Morning. Did you get breakfast?"

She nodded as he took her hand. She came in and he set breakfast up on the table and pulled out her chair for her. "Liam."

"Eat first. We can talk after."

"Did you sleep," Kelly asked.

He nodded. "Not exactly that well. Was thinking about this woman I know all night."

She looked at him. "Liam, professional. For once. Please?"

He took a gulp of his coffee. "What," he asked as they both finished eating.

"I can't."

"Can't what love?"

"Liam, I get it. You want what you want. I just can't..." He put his cup down and took her hand. "What?"

He kissed her with a kiss that got him turned on in a matter of seconds. He picked her up and walked into the bedroom, leaned her onto the bed and slid her heels off, pulling her legs around him. "Liam."

He looked at her. "What love," he asked as his hands slid up her thighs.

"We..."

He kissed her again. "We what?"

"I have to go into the office. We can't do this."

"We can do whatever we want love. I want..."

"Liam."

He kissed her again, devouring her lips until he couldn't hide how turned on he was. "I need you," he said.

"Liam, just..."

He kissed her again with a kiss that had her toes and her stomach in knots. "Just tell me that you want me," Liam said.

"It doesn't change..." He kissed her again and he felt her arms slide around him.

"Kelly, love, just say that you want me. Tell me what I waited 10 years to hear," he whispered as he kissed down her neck and slid the strap of her dress off her shoulder.

"I have work."

"Say yes," he said.

"Liam, please."

"Kelly, say yes. I want you so bad I can't even think. Please love."

"I have to..."

"Please." He kissed her again and he felt his way up her legs again. "Kelly."

She kissed him and he went for the lacy panties. "Liam."

He grabbed a condom from the bedside table and kicked his pants and boxers off. When his hand touched her inner thigh, she knew there was no going back. He wasn't the only one that had dreamed about that moment. "Say yes," he said as he almost growled into her ear.

"We can't..."

He kissed her. "Say it."

She nodded and in what felt like a matter of minutes, they were having sex on the bed. He was almost shaking in her arms as he leaned into her.

"Aah."

"I wanted you the minute you were on that stupid bus. Hell. I wanted you the minute I saw you in the damn airport."

"Liam."

He kissed her and kept going. He peeled her clothes off, throwing them onto the end of the bed and he just went deeper. It was hotter. Every time his body collided with hers, her body throbbed around him. His cologne intoxicated her. His kiss had her toes curled, and every inch of her craving him. When his body climaxed, he held her tight to him.

"Kelly," he said catching his breath.

"Aah," she said as her body crashed into another orgasm.

"Don't ever leave me again," he said as he leaned to his back and brought her with him.

"I can't even move," Kelly said.

"Don't leave."

"I can't move my legs. Hell. I doubt I can even walk," she said.

He kissed her, holding her face in his hands. "Promise me," he said.

"Promise what?"

"No more leaving."

She was almost trembling in his arms. "I have…"

He kissed her again and her body started overheating all over again. "I have to be at a meeting," she said. He smirked and kissed her forehead.

"It's not even 8."

"Liam, I have to get up."

He slid his arms around her again. "I'm not letting go love. You know that right?"

She nodded, tried to get up and he pulled her back to him. "What," she asked.

"Are you okay?" She nodded. "Kelly."

She got up, grabbed her panties and dress and walked into the bathroom. Her legs were still shaky, but she got a grin ear to ear. That's what she'd been missing in Dublin. That mind-blowing, sex that could cripple her that was the sexiness of Liam. She cleaned up a little and got re-dressed. When she came back into the bedroom just as dressed as she had been when she first arrived, he shook his head.

"What," Kelly asked.

"Promise me," he said.

"What?"

"You don't vanish on me again. Promise me."

"Liam, we have a meeting to get to."

"Say it."

"Fine."

"And since you don't have work tomorrow, you can stay here."

She shook her head. "Liam, I have to be at the office in a half hour."

He got up, leaned over and kissed her again and went and had a quick shower, came out and got dressed, grabbed his bag and phone, and walked with her to the elevator. He kissed the back of her neck as they waited.

"Stop."

"Can't help it."

She shook her head and they stepped on. His arm slid around her waist. "Liam."

"Either you're staying or I'm coming with you," he whispered.

She shook her head. "I have plans."

"It's a holiday weekend love. Don't think I don't know that," he whispered as she got goosebumps.

"Family weekend."

"Nice try."

They stepped off the elevator and went out to her truck, heading over to the office. When his hand slid to her thigh, she shook her head. "Liam, work. Business. Nothing else. No hands, no nothing."

"Okay," he said as he smirked.

"I mean it."

They got there and she parked. "Before you go up there all business like and everything," he said.

"What?"

He kissed her and she shook her head, brushed her lipstick off his lips and grabbed her purse and bag. They locked up the truck and went into the building. She took him upstairs to the meeting and he followed her.

"Miss Ryan. Good timing. The meeting was just about to start," her boss said.

"This is Liam Murphy. He created the software system that we were all discussing for the restaurant, pub and hotel sector," Kelly said as she poured him a coffee. The entire way through the meeting, he was attempting to stay professional, but when his hand slid on her leg, she almost got goosebumps. She brushed him off and when they went to start a video with more information, his hand slid back to her leg. She grabbed her phone to make it look like she was checking emails and saw a text from Liam:

Sexy. Very, very, sexy. We're finishing what you started this morning. Even if I have to chase you down.

She shook her head and sent a reply:

For once in your dang life, please just stay professional in the meeting. Period. Stop with the dirty thoughts Liam.

They finished the meeting around noon and she knew that the rest of the day was a wash. Everyone was leaving early for the weekend, and she had to show him houses that were practically on her back porch.

"Lunch," she asked as they walked down to her office.

"We can discuss it. When did you say the real estate person would be meeting us to look at houses?"

"Around 1:30. We have time to stop for lunch," she said.

"Or we just go back to the suite."

She shook her head. She closed her office door and he kissed her. "Liam."

"What?" She shook her head and got a text from her friend:

So, I gather you know the sexy Irish. Hot damn girl.

She sat down at her desk. "I'll order up lunch. What did you want," she asked.

"You. Side salad," he teased.

She shook her head. She messaged her assistant that she needed two sandwiches, fries and two ice waters. "Not gonna say anything now are you?"

"Liam, work."

He sat down at the table in her office, went over emails and got everything together, reading over the contract they gave him to sign. "It's actually a good contract," he said.

"The CEO and COO are well known for really fair contracts. If they like something, they kinda always run with it," Kelly said.

"Missing something though," he said.

"Which would be?"

"You coming to Dublin."

Kelly shook her head. "Not part of my job Liam."

"I want you to come back."

"I take care of the properties in the company portfolio. Not taking care of the guy who made the software."

"I want it added in."

"Liam."

"Twice a year, return to Dublin."

She shook her head. "I don't have time."

"Make time love. My folks want to meet you. They did then. When I told them I was coming to America for a while, they said if I saw you to invite you to their house for dinner."

Kelly took a deep breath. "Liam, you realize that I have a life here right? I can't just take off and go to Ireland."

He looked at her. "How much vacation time do you get every year?"

"3 and a half weeks."

"Then you have time." She shook her head. He was determined. Fact was, she wasn't sure if she even wanted to go back. At least, not with Liam. When his phone rang, he got up and sat down on the sofa.

"Kieran," he said.

"Long time no see. Wanted to let you know that the pay for the pubs went through. I checked it over for any issues.

The software is perfect. We had bets running whether you ever found that girl or not," his friend said.

"We can talk later."

"Are you kidding me? How," Kieran asked.

"Like I said, later."

"Alright. We're having a pint or two. I need to hear the story when you're back," Kieran said.

"Alright," Liam said as he hung up. He went into emails and sent him off an email:

> *I walked off the plane and saw her. The company that's buying the software. She works for them. She looks sexier than when I saw her last. Longer legs. Sexy all over. She's mine. Will be. We can talk later.*

Kelly shook her head. "You do realize I could hear you right? I could hear the call," she said.

"He asked if I saw you."

Kelly shook her head. "As I said, not a piece of property Liam."

"Didn't seem to mind this morning."

She looked at him and threw a pillow at him. "Seriously," Kelly said as she shook her head. Not two minutes later, lunch arrived. "Miss Kelly, your mail," her assistant said as she put down the lunch.

"Thank you," Kelly said as her assistant handed it to her. She went through the mail and got everything sent off to whoever needed it.

"Are you coming to eat," Liam asked. She got up and walked over to sit down with him to eat. "And what's the plan this weekend," he asked.

"Aren't you heading home?"

"Nope. Staying until the end of the week."

"What week?"

"End of June. If not longer," he said as Kelly looked at him.

"I wasn't told that."

"And I have to go back to Dublin for a few days next weekend. I have our tickets booked."

"Our? Since when am I coming?"

"Private flight Kelly."

"Still not an answer Liam," she said.

"Since this morning." She shook her head. "You got the okay by the way. I need you to help with paperwork," he said.

"I can do that from here."

"Nope," he replied as he smirked.

"You do realize that this isn't a game right?"

"I have to get the paperwork done so I can go back and forth. There's no point in you being here when you have the paperwork. I'm getting you a visa for Ireland as well."

"Why? I'm not working there Liam."

"Might be."

She shook her head. "Seriously. This isn't a relationship that I want. I'm not something you can drag wherever. This is my job. I'm staying in Charleston." Not two minutes later, her phone buzzed.

"Miss Ryan. It's Mr. Cartwright. Is Mr. Murphy there with you?"

"Yes. What can I do for you?"

"The software situation is going to involve a lot of back and forth to Dublin. Would you be willing to take care of that portion of the project?"

She glared at Liam and shook her head. "If you need me to. I do have quite a bit to do here."

"Understood. It'll be a promotion of sorts. You'd be taking care of international business instead of just business management."

"So, it's an official..."

"Yes. I sent over the update to your company email."

"Alright then. Thank you Sir."

"Most welcome and congrats," he said.

"Liam."

"Yes love."

She shook her head. "Interfering in my work now?"

"Nope. Told him I'd sign so long as you were able to work with the company in Dublin. Done," he said.

"Does anyone ever say no to you?"

"Just you love."

"Liam, workplace." He locked the office door then walked over to her. "What," she asked.

He kissed her until her knees almost buckled and sat her on the edge of the table they ate on.

"You were saying?"

She shook her head. "Unlock..."

He kissed her.

"Unlock the door," Kelly said as she walked back over to her desk. He smirked and unlocked it then brought his laptop over to her desk.

"What," she asked as he sat there with a smirk.

"Still thinking that we need to add in those Ireland trips to the contract."

She shook her head. "Liam."

"Yes love."

"Stop screwing with my job."

He smirked. When her phone buzzed to remind her that they had an appointment to look at places, she shook her head. "We're heading out. Do you think it's possible to restrain yourself while we look at the houses?"

"From what?"

"You know what," she asked.

He kissed her forehead. "Maybe. Are you gonna show me your place?"

"No."

"Do I get to know where it is?"

Kelly shook her head. He smirked, pulled her to him and kissed her. "We're having dinner tonight by the way."

"You could ask instead of telling me. You do realize that right?"

She let her assistant know that she was heading out and they left, making their way out to Isle of Palms. "Nice bridge," he said as he slid his arm around her seat.

"Liam, business."

"If I was not being professional, I would've done a lot worse love."

"Don't even bother telling me. Liam, you weren't like this when I was there. What happened that you turned into a control freak bossy person?"

"You left and vanished."

SOUTHERN TEMPTATION   49

"And that's when you went all control freak?"

"That's when I started dreaming what I was gonna do when I saw you again."

"Liam, stop."

They got to a light and he leaned over and kissed her shoulder. "Hand," he asked.

"No. I'm driving."

They got down to the first house for him to look at and he already hated it. "What don't you like," she asked.

"It seems very cold. It doesn't feel like a home. It feels like a hospital," he said.

She shook her head. "Next one," Kelly said.

After two more houses, he pointed at one he did like. "That," Kelly asked.

"It's like a home instead of a sanitary cold place."

"It's not for sale Liam."

He could see the look on her face. "Why don't we just go in and have a sweet tea," he replied.

"No," Kelly said.

"Yours?" She shook her head. "Show me yours."

She shook her head. "I said no."

"Then we go for a walk on the beach."

Kelly shook her head. "Liam, I get that you want what you want. This is the way homes are here unless you're out of downtown and away from here. Those are your options."

"Show me."

She shook her head and he got her to park. "What?"

He looked at her. "Why are you so worried about me seeing your house?"

"Because you're not coming in and you aren't staying."

He hopped out, got her door and took her keys. "What?"

"I'm driving."

"Liam, this is the USA. We're on the other side of the road."

"Get in." He pressed home on the GPS and took her to her place.

They pulled in through the gate and he smirked. "See what I mean? Lived in. Home feeling."

She shook her head. He hopped out, got her door and handed Kelly her keys. "No."

"Why?"

"No Liam."

He kissed her and slid his hand in hers. "Open the door Kelly."

"I'm taking you back to the hotel Liam. You aren't staying out here."

He smirked. "We can get dinner and just talk on the beach." She shook her head.

She opened the door, walked him into the kitchen and he pulled her to him. "What?"

He kissed her. "Kelly."

"What?"

"Why are you determined to push me away?"

"Because I say no and you turn around and do what I say not to. I say that I don't want to sleep with you, and you turn around and…"

He kissed her. "What do you want me to do?"

"Stop pushing. Stop interfering in my career. Stop making me do things I don't…"

He kissed her again. "Fine. Can we at least sit and talk?"

"Liam."

"Talk." She shook her head and went and got two glasses of Jameson's, handing one to him and walked him outside to the beach. "This place really is perfect," Liam said.

Kelly shook her head. "It was my grandparents' house. I overhauled it when I got possession."

"Are you hungry?"

"Liam."

"There's a place down the beach. We can go get dinner or get something brought here."

She shook her head and took a deep breath. "Liam, I get it. You finally got what you wanted. I can't do this."

"Why? What's wrong that you keep pushing me as far away as possible?"

"You don't want my insane life Liam. My life is that job. Period. I go in and work on the dang weekend when I can. There's no reason..."

He kissed her hand. "I get it. I've been the same way since you left Dublin. I wrote that software up after I took a course at school. I had no idea that it was such a big thing until now. I just...I thought it'd give me a reason to try again to find you."

"But why me?"

He looked at her. "You don't see it do you?"

"Meaning what Liam?"

"The lass that I fell in love with in Dublin is still sitting right here love. I never stopped caring. I fell hard," he said.

"Liam."

"You have no idea do you? I told you when you were in Dublin."

"When?"

He shook his head. "If I'd known then that you weren't coming back, I would've proposed."

"What?" She looked at him in shock and he looked at her.

"Those ten years were hell."

"You're joking right?"

"I got in trouble a billion times over. I was drinking after you vanished."

Kelly looked at him." "Liam." He finished his drink, grabbed the glasses, took her hand and walked her inside. "What are you doing?"

She closed the door and he locked it, leaning her against it. "Sofa."

"Liam."

He took her hand, walking her to the sofa and sat her on it. "I exploded when you left. When my family told me to go do something with the computer skills, I wrote up the software for a friend of mine to pay off what I owed him for my pub tab," he said.

Kelly shook her head. "Liam, this..."

He kissed her. "If I'd had you there with me, I might not have even made the software."

"Then it's good that..."

He shook his head. "Come here."

"Liam."

"Come," he asked.

"What," Kelly asked as he slid her closer to him.

"You're what I wanted then. I get it. You didn't see it. I did."

"Liam."

He pulled her into his lap and kissed her. The kiss gave her more than goosebumps. Even when she didn't want him near her, that kiss made her crave him. Hell. It was past hot. It was leg shaking, body humming hot. When she felt like she was falling, she ended up with her head on the pillows and Liam in her arms, devouring her lips like he had all those years ago. "What do you want Liam?"

"If you haven't figured it out yet, I'm not trying hard enough," he replied as he kissed her again and her body reacted.

He slid her heels off, wrapped her legs around him and undid his shirt.

"We can't keep doing this. I can't."

He kissed her. "Bedroom." She shook her head. "Either you show me..." He kissed her again, picking her up and walked up the steps, seeing the massive main bedroom. He walked in and leaned her onto the bed, leaning back into her arms again.

"Love, talk to me."

"About what," Kelly asked.

He kissed her. "Are you okay?"

"I'm a mess. I've been a mess for years."

He shook his head. "Not to me."

"Liam." He kissed her, devouring her lips and slid the strap from her shoulder. "We can't keep..."

He kissed her, a kiss that she felt to the tips of her toes and back. He kicked his dress pants off, knocking them to the floor and peeled her dress off. "Liam."

"What?"

"I don't have..."

His hands slid to her backside. "Still sexy," he said as he kissed down her neck then nibbled at her breast through the lace bra.

"Aah," she said as her breath hitched.

"So damn sexy," he said as he kissed her stomach.

"Liam."

"What?"

"We can't..."

He kissed her hip. "Can't what love?"

"I don't..."

"I have it." When she felt her lace panties slide down, she shook her head.

"Always wanted to know," Liam said.

"What?"

"How you tasted."

She felt his lips against her, nibbling and sucking until her toes were pretzels. "Mine," he said as she felt his fingers start teasing.

"Liam."

"What love," he said with a smirk that could've melted solid gold.

"I..."

He nibbled again and kept going until he saw her stomach almost trembling. "Missed me," he teased.

"We..."

He kept going until her body clenched around his fingers. "Well damn lass." He kissed back up her torso and kissed her, nibbling and sucking and teasing the tiny peaks of her breasts. "Yeah. I'm not done," he said as he kissed her again and devoured her lips.

"I can't even move."

He kissed her. "Kelly."

"Um hm." He smirked and kissed her again. When she heard him ripping something, she shook her head. "Liam."

He kissed her, kicked his boxers to the floor and leaned into her arms, wrapping her legs tight around him. He pulled her to face him and she slid on top. "All yours," he said as they had sex. It was hot, really deep, and almost too much. They kept going and going until she felt nails on her back and she could barely even move. Up and down over and over until she thought her body was about to explode.

"Kelly," he said as she could feel him throbbing in her.

"Aaah."

"Don't move," he said.

"Aah."

"Damn," he said as he leaned her onto her back.

"You alright?" She nodded trying to catch her breath as her heart raced.

"My girl," he said as he leaned into her arms and pulled her to him as he leaned onto his back.

"I can't move," she said.

"I don't want to," he teased.

"Liam."

"Don't."

He kissed her forehead and snuggled her to his side. "I can't do this," Kelly said.

"Do what? Be with me?"

"Liam."

He kissed her. "What's so wrong?"

"I can't. You're going..."

He kissed her. "If I go, you're coming with me. I'm not leaving without you," he said as he kissed her.

"You need clothes."

He smirked. "This mean that you're gonna let me come stay with you?"

"You still need to find a house."

"Sorta did. This one," he replied.

Kelly shook her head. "Liam." He kissed her and she went to get up.

"Where are you goin now love?"

"Ordering dinner."

He pulled on his boxers and dress pants and Kelly slid a sundress on. "What did you order?"

"If you're gonna be in Charleston, you need to have some seafood. The place is down the street, but it's really good."

"And what did you order?"

"Since I knew you might want it, seafood tower type thing. Some shrimp, crab, lobster and oysters," Kelly said as he smirked.

"How far away are they?"

"Maybe 5 minutes. Ten max. Why?"

He smirked and kissed her neck. "Liam."

"Oysters."

She shook her head, poured them each another Jameson's and a sweet tea.

"Are you gonna stay tonight with me?"

She shook her head. "I'm coming back..."

He kissed her. "Then I'll get a bag."

"Liam."

"And we're gonna have to make a stop."

She looked at him. "For?" He smirked. "Really?"

He nodded. "A few." She shook her head and he kissed her shoulder.

Chapter 3

Just as he was about to make another move, there was a knock at the door. She went and answered, handing the food to Liam. "Mama added in the strawberry chocolate pie," the delivery guy said as Kelly handed him cash.

"Thank you for this," Kelly said as he headed off and Liam kissed her shoulder. "What," she asked.

"Nothin love. Come sit down so you can open this thing," he said.

They ate and he had a grin ear to ear. "And," Kelly asked.

"And why do people eat anything but this," he asked.

"Right? I love seafood. Always have," she said.

"You should go to Greece then."

"Liam."

He smirked. "I'll take you."

She shook her head and cleaned up. "What do you think," she asked.

"We may need more oysters," he said.

"I doubt it," Kelly said.

"They're really good. When did you find that place," he asked.

"Been a favorite for years. They make really good pie," Kelly replied as she put the dishes into the washer and he got up coming up behind her.

"Did you want some dessert," she asked. He kissed her shoulder, then kissed up her neck, leaning his body against her. "Liam, stop."

"Getting overheated," he asked.

"Just breathe."

"We really should go unless you have a way to get them delivered." She shook her head and he kissed down her neck.

"Give me a minute to get changed." He shook his head. She smirked and went upstairs, slid into shorts and a tank, slid her shoes on and grabbed his shirt, handing it to him. "Your phone was buzzing by the way," Kelly said.

"Ah. Good timing."

"Hello," he said.

"Did you make it there alright son," his mom asked.

"Yes. You won't believe who I bumped into at the airport."

Kelly shook her head and he sat her on the counter. "You've been trying to find her for years," his mom said.

"She's right here actually. We had dinner," he said.

"But how are you? Did you have a good flight?"

"Yes mum. I slept most of it. I thought I was dreaming when I got here."

"Blue water is blue water," his mom said.

"I meant to call yesterday. Are you two alright?"

"Yes love. A package showed at the house for you."

"Good. Those are the shirts I was waiting on."

He talked to his mom, not letting Kelly out of his sight. "Can you take me off speaker," his mom asked.

"Yes mum. What's wrong," he asked.

"I know that you've liked this girl for a while, but you do realize that you can't just do this for a chance with a lass. She's grand and all, but I don't want you throwing the future away," his mom said.

"I know. I'm not. She's coming back with me for a few days. You can see for yourself."

He finished talking to his mom, hung up and she walked him out, locked up and took him back downtown to his suite. "Are we stopping at the shop," he asked.

Kelly nodded, stopping off at the market and walking inside with him. "If you want anything for the weekend, we can grab it."

He kissed her shoulder. "I'll get the ice and the ice cream and cold stuff dropped off at the house."

He grabbed a few things, grabbing fruit and stuff for breakfast. When he got to the pharmacy area, he grabbed what he needed, putting it into the cart. "Liam."

"What?"

"Really?"

He nodded and kissed her shoulder. She shook her head and they checked out, loaded up the truck and headed to the hotel.

"Three boxes?"

He nodded. "Never know love."

She shook her head and he kissed her shoulder. She got to the parking area, parked the truck and went upstairs to his suite to grab a bag of clothes for the weekend. He handed her a box. "What's this," Kelly asked.

"Just hold onto it for me."

She slid it in her purse and he smirked. "What?"

"Nothin love." He grabbed his bag and they headed back downstairs.

"Did you bring a charger?"

"I have yours."

"You still need one."

"I have it. It's fine."

"Do you have everything?"

He nodded. "Never really unpacked."

She shook her head, walked back to the elevator and headed down to the parking. "Let me drive," he asked.

Kelly shook her head. "It's the Friday of a long weekend. People drive like idiots. I'll drive us."

They both hopped in and headed off. "Kelly."

"Yes Liam."

"What is there to do around here," he asked.

"Such as?"

"Beach I get. What about a pub or a place I have to see and tell people about at home?"

"I have a bunch of favorite places," she said.

"Then you can show me?"

Kelly nodded. They made their way back through the traffic and when they pulled in, the grocer was showing with the milk, ice, ice cream, popsicles and yogurt. She took it all in and put the groceries away and Liam helped. He put his bag into the bedroom and walked downstairs, pouring two more glasses of Jameson's. He handed one to Kelly and took her hand, walking her back outside. "What," she asked.

He kissed her shoulder and they sat down on the oversized chaise together. "I missed you. A lot," he said.

"If I'm gonna be honest, I missed you too."

He smirked. "And there's my girl. My carefree, relaxed, sexy lass who stole my heart on her way to the airport," he teased.

"Liam."

"You did. You did the minute we met."

She looked at him and he kissed her. "Do you still have the box?"

"Liam." He smirked. "Not talking about the box. Just watch the sunset."

He watched and they sipped on their whiskey. "It is kind of beautiful out here," he said.

"And after 5pm, no random tourists are allowed out here unless they're staying at the resort or staying here."

"Kind of handy," he said.

"Liam."

"Don't."

"Why? Of all times, why me? Why now?"

"I didn't know that you were there. I didn't know you were coming. I didn't even know that you were still here until I saw you. I thought I was hallucinating Kelly. All I know is that I wanted to swing you around in my arms and devour your lips when I saw you. I didn't care who else was there."

She looked at him. "There are other women out there Liam."

He pulled her to him and kissed her, devouring her lips. "There is no other you love. Nowhere in the world." He kissed her again and he picked her up, pulling her into his lap. "What happened after you came home? Where'd all this doubt come from?"

"It was there Liam. I just did..."

He kissed her and devoured her lips. "Who broke you? Who broke that woman I loved?"

"Not being enough. More than once Liam."

He kissed her. "You're all I wanted. All I ever wanted. Hell. You're all I want now." He pulled her into his arms and snuggled her to him. He kissed her and smirked. "I've wanted you in my damn life since we were 18. I don't want to lose that."

"Liam."

He kissed her again. "Come inside."

"You don't want to go for a walk?" He shook his head, picked her up, handed her the glasses and walked inside, locking up behind him and walked back up to the bedroom, leaning her onto her bed.

He put the glasses on the bedside table and kissed her. "What," Kelly asked.

"Tell me what happened."

"Liam."

"Tell me love. I'm not gonna fly off the handle. Just tell me."

"Liam, I don't..."

He kissed her. "What?"

"I dated someone who wasn't exactly nice alright?"

"Did he hurt you?"

"Liam."

"Did he put his hands on you?"

"Yes."

"Who is he," Liam said about to fly off the handle.

"He's not around. I haven't seen him since I was in college."

SOUTHERN TEMPTATION

He slid his hands to her face. "Nobody hurts you. Not now, not ever."

Kelly nodded and he kissed her again. "Liam, I'm just not the same person."

He kissed her again, devouring her lips until he was pulling her shirt off. "We..."

He kissed down her neck. "Never ever happening again. It does, I kill him."

She looked at him." Liam."

"Nobody is hurting you."

She went to get up and he pulled her back to him. "Liam, don't." She got up, walked into the bathroom and got undressed, sliding into a cool shower. She needed it for no other reason than to calm her down. She would've gone swimming in the ocean if he hadn't wanted to come back inside. When she stepped out, he was sitting on the end of the bed shirtless and in nothing but boxers.

She went and grabbed her pajamas and his arms slid around her, pulling her to him. "What?"

"I'm sorry."

"If you'd been here, it wouldn't have happened anyway Liam."

She went to back away and he pulled her closer. "What?"

He kissed her. "Tell me what you want," he asked.

"About what?"

He looked at her. "You know what."

"Liam."

"Do you want a man in your life?"

"Yeah, but not if he doesn't live here."

He kissed her. "Solved. What else?"

"Liam."

"Do you want me Kelly?"

She looked at him. "You wouldn't be here if I didn't."

He shook his head. "I'm never letting you go. You know that right?"

She went to back away so she could put her satin chemise on and he pulled her to him. "What?"

He pulled her into his lap. "Liam."

"Where's the box?"

"In my bag downstairs." He kissed her and got up, walking downstairs, grabbed it from her bag along with her cell and handed both to her. "What?"

"Open the box."

"Liam."

"I brought it in case I saw you."

She looked at him. "Are you kidding me right now?"

"I wanted to give it to you when you were there 10 years ago."

She shook her head and handed it back to him, putting her chemise on and going downstairs to refill their drinks. She came back upstairs and put the drinks on the side table.

"Kelly."

"Liam, don't."

"Just open the box."

She shook her head and walked out onto her balcony. He shook his head, got up, grabbed the box and his drink and stood out there beside her. "It's not a damn diamond if that's what you think."

"Liam."

He opened it and put it in front of her. "It's my nan's claddagh ring. She left it to me. She passed 5 years ago when I was going through hell and missing you. She said if I ever saw you again, to give it to you."

"I..." He slid it on her right-hand ring finger and it fit perfectly.

"Liam."

He kissed her forehead and slid his arm around her. "That's where it was meant to be," he said.

"You're seriously doing this 24 hours after..." He kissed her and took her hand. "What?"

He put the glass down, taking hers and putting it beside his. "Come." He sat on the bed and pulled her into his lap so she was straddling him.

"What?"

"Movie."

She shook her head. He kissed her and leaned her onto the bed, curling up into her arms. "Tell me what you're worried about."

"Liam, I'm not the woman that you think I am."

He kissed her. "You're better."

She shook her head. "That's the horny man talking."

"No, it isn't love. I promise you."

"Then what..."

He kissed her again and curled up with her, making out until the kiss went too far. She had him as horny as a dang teenager. When things started heating up all over again, her phone buzzed.

"Don't," he said as he kissed down her neck. She looked and saw the caller and shook her head.

"Liam."

"Yes beautiful."

"We need to stop."

"Why?"

"I get it, but I need sleep."

He kissed her and slid his arms around her, wrapping her legs around his hips. "You'll get sleep love."

When she felt his hand slide down her hip, she shook her head. "You are insatiable."

"Around you. Always."

It took one hand. One to make her body almost tremble in his arms. "You feel so damn good," Liam said.

Her body curled as he started teasing again. He kissed down her neck. "Liam."

"Yes sexy," he said as he nibbled at her breasts and kept teasing.

"What about..."

"I have them. On the table beside you."

He kissed her stomach, then her hip. "Aah."

She felt the warmth of his breath against her and her body almost purred. She felt his finger then a second, then a third as the nibbles against her got her even hotter. "Mm," he said as she felt his tongue against her and then something even more intense.

"Mine," he said as her toes curled. "All mine." He kept going until her body exploded once, twice, three times. He kept going and when she grabbed at his hand, he intensified it all then worked his way back up, continuing to tease until they were having sex.

SOUTHERN TEMPTATION

Her body throbbing around him was hot, but she got him even hotter. The sex went from a ten to a 50 until they both collapsed onto the bed. "Damn," he said.

"I can't move."

"I don't think you're allowed to," he teased.

Kelly shook her head. "My legs are still shaking," she said.

He curled her to him and they curled up on the bed. She pulled up a blanket and he smirked. "What," she asked.

He slid the condom off and curled in close to her. "Yeah, you can't vanish on me ever again," he whispered.

"Meaning what?"

"Mine."

"Liam."

He kissed her shoulder. "Come here love."

She curled into his arms, leaning her head onto his chest. "What?"

He handed Kelly her glass and they finished their drinks. "Now all we need is a couple pints of Guinness."

She shook her head and kissed him. "Before I came to Dublin, I literally had never had any of it. I never wanted to."

"Part of the tradition. Bring the lassies to Dublin, hand them a Guinness and they never leave," he teased.

She shook her head. "Whatever you say handsome."

He kissed her. They curled up together and after talking even more, they both nodded off. When her phone went off at 2am, she woke up and grabbed it, seeing her boyfriend's name on the call display.

"What?"

"Let me in."

"No. We broke up. Go away."

"Why? Because some random hookup is there?"

"Yeah."

Kelly hung up and Liam's arms tightened around her. "What's the problem?"

"Nothing. Get some sleep."

"Kelly."

"He's here." Liam shook his head, got up, pulled his jeans and a hoodie on and walked downstairs.

When he opened the door, the guy in front of him looked up. "Can I help you," Liam said.

"Where's Kell," Andrew asked.

"In bed waiting for me. Why?"

"She changed the locks."

"You don't live here."

"Can you get her for me?"

"No."

"Dude, I get that you think…"

"You insult my fiancée, I will…"

"What?"

"You heard me. Leave." He took off and Liam locked up, coming back upstairs. He kicked his jeans off, put his hoodie on top of his jeans and slid back into bed with her. She'd already curled the other way when he snuggled her back to him. "What'd you say," Kelly asked.

"Turn over."

She did and looked at him. "Liam."

He kissed her. "He's gone."

"What did you say to him?"

"To stay away from you."

SOUTHERN TEMPTATION

She shook her head. "You said something else." He shook his head and she turned away from him.

She swore she heard something ripping when his hand slid over her hip. "Liam." He almost growled in her ear. They had sex again, but somehow it was harder and even more intense than previously. When she felt her body throb around him and he kept going, her body reacted. He kissed her neck and felt him climax. He was almost trembling behind her. "Liam."

"Yes love," he said as his body almost melted into hers.

"Are you okay?"

He nodded and kissed her shoulder. "Are you?"

"Depends."

She felt him pull away then turned her to face him. "What," she asked.

He kissed her. Not a moment later, he was asleep, with her head on his chest. She pulled the blanket up and fell asleep again in his arms.

The next morning, she woke up with his arms still around her. "Morning love."

She looked up at him. "What are you doing up so early?"

"It's almost 8."

She looked at her watch and smirked. "Are you hungry?"

When she saw the look on his face, she shook her head. "Liam."

"Wanted to make sure you were awake first."

"For what?"

He kissed her. "Nothing," he teased.

"Liam, do you remember what happened last night?"

He nodded and kissed her. "Are you gonna tell me what you said to get him to leave?" He kissed her then kissed her neck and made his way down her torso. "Liam." When he kissed her hip, she knew what he was doing. He nibbled her inner thigh and when her toes started to curl, he opted for breakfast then a second and third helping, as he taunted her body into curling to his whim. "Aah," she said as her breath hitched. "Liam," she said as things got even more intense.

"Liam, aah."

He smirked and nibbled her inner thigh and worked his way back up her torso until he kissed her lips. "Mine," he teased as they had sex again.

"Liam," she said as her body crashed around his and his collided with hers. He kissed her again. When he leaned onto his back, he pulled her to him.

"We used..."

"Yeah," he said.

"Liam."

He devoured her lips. "Good morning love."

"You do realize that we have to make it out of bed right?"

He nodded. "What did you tell him last night anyway?"

He kissed her. "Doesn't matter," he said.

"Kind of does," Kelly said.

He smirked. She shook her head, slid out of bed and slid her satin robe on. "Where are you heading love?"

"Breakfast." She went downstairs, put on coffee and made something to eat. When he came downstairs in boxers and nothing else, he slid in behind her and wrapped his arms around her.

"Are you gonna tell me?"

"No."

"Liam."

"I got rid of him. He's not coming back."

She looked at the ring again and something jumped out at her. "What does the ring mean," Kelly asked as she flipped the sausage and bacon and then the eggs.

"Friendship, love and loyalty." He almost worried she'd ask what it meant that the heart was facing inwards.

"Liam, just tell me."

"I told him you were my fiancée," he said as he kissed her neck.

She almost choked on her juice. "What?"

"Got rid of him didn't it?"

"You actually said that to him?"

He nodded and took over cooking. "You can't just..."

"That's what the ring means."

She looked at him. "So, you put a ring..."

"You wouldn't let me give you anything else."

"Liam, you need to take it back."

"No." He plated the food, handed her a plate and sat down.

"Is that why you did it," Kelly asked as she added Baileys to her coffee.

"Partially. If you're adding Baileys, you can add some in here too love."

"Partially?"

He smirked and she sat down. "Meaning what?"

"I wanted to be with you. I always have."

"Is that why you put it on my finger?"

"Part of it."

"Liam."

"Come sit and have breakfast," he said.

"Are you serious?"

"You can ask it again a few more times. You're still getting the same answer love."

She shook her head and had breakfast with him and he slid his hand in hers. "I can't believe you," Kelly said.

"Nobody knows what it means unless they're Irish Kelly. It's between us."

"Liam, you could've at least..."

He kissed her and refilled their coffees adding Jameson's to his. "So, what did you want to do today?"

Kelly shook her head. "It's not funny Liam."

"Never said it was love. I meant it."

She shook her head and had her coffee. "What," he asked.

"You do realize that telling me might have been a good plan right?"

"I did love," he said with that smirk that irritated her to no end.

"And what was that last night?"

"What was what?"

She shook her head. "Liam."

"Mine."

"Again, you don't own me. I'm not a possession."

He motioned for her to come closer. "No."

"Love, come here."

"You told him we were engaged Liam. Engaged. That's insane."

"Not when it's gonna happen anyway."

Kelly shook her head, finished her coffee and put the mug in the washer and went to walk out. "Kelly."

"Don't. Just don't." He grabbed her hand and pulled her into his lap. His hand slid to her face, and he kissed her devouring and nibbling at her lips until he managed to wrap her legs around his hips.

"Liam," she said as he kissed down her neck.

"What love?"

"Not cool." She went to get up and he pulled her back to him.

"It was the only way I could think of to get rid of him. That's all. I promise you." When she felt his hand brush against her inner thigh, she shook her head.

"Don't." She got up and walked upstairs. She pulled on her run gear and he came up behind her.

"Where are you going?"

"For a run on the beach. If you want to come, then come. No more fiancée stuff." He smirked and kissed her.

"Done," he replied as he went and slid into run shorts and his sneakers.

"Sunscreen," she said.

He smirked and she sprayed his back, arms and legs for him. "Kelly."

"What?" He motioned for her to come closer.

"And what's with the tattoo?" He kissed her, nibbling and sucking her lips until he felt her arms wrap around his neck.

"The tattoo I got the day after you left Dublin. I knew then Kelly."

"And if you'd shown up and I was married?"

"I'd feel bad for the guy getting ditched like that," he teased.

"Liam."

"I would. I know what I want. I always did," Liam said.

She shook her head, and he pulled her tight to him. "Honestly, what would you have done if I wasn't available when you showed up?"

"Made sure you knew that you were with the wrong person and ravished you until you walked away with me instead of whoever it was."

"Liam."

"I mean it. We're meant to be together and you know it love. You always have even if you don't want to admit it. My life and yours went to crap the minute you left Dublin. If I'd known it'd take me 10 years to find you and be with you again, I never would've let you leave. I would've taken you to a church somewhere and..."

"Liam."

"I'm an all-in or nothing guy Kelly. I always have been."

She kissed him. "And you're insane."

"The sexy Irish thing doesn't cover?"

She shook her head. "Not that kind of crazy. A week and you were really thinking that?"

He kissed her. "I would've surgically attached myself to you until you screamed my name if I had to."

Kelly shook her head. "Liam."

"I'm yours Kelly. Head to toe. Every inch is yours." He picked her up, untied her robe and slid it to the floor, kicking his boxers off.

"Liam, I'm..."

SOUTHERN TEMPTATION

He kissed her again, devouring, nibbling and sucking at her lips until her body curved into his arms. The kiss was intoxicating as all get out, but what he did next got her even hotter. Kissing down her neck, he carried her into the oversized shower, flipped the water on and leaned her against the cool tile wall, pinning her to it with his body.

"Liam." He kissed her and she felt his hand slide to her backside. "Stop."

"Why," he asked.

"Because we aren't..."

He kissed her again and Kelly shook her head. "Aren't you forgetting something," she teased.

He smirked and shook his head. "Not one bit," he teased.

"Liam."

He kissed her again. "Shower. We're not doing..."

He kissed her again and pinned her against the wall again.

"Liam."

He kissed her and picked her back up. "We..." He kissed her and his hand slid almost too close.

"Liam, we can't without..."

He kissed her and she slid to her feet. "You forgot." He shook his head and kissed her.

"Liam."

"Why," he asked.

She shook her head. "So, nobody taught you about the birds..."

His hand slid between her legs, taunting her. "They did lass," he said as he continued to taunt.

"And?"

He kissed her. "Liam, we..."

He kissed her, linking their fingers and pinned her hands against the shower wall. When he picked her up, he devoured her lips as she felt that full feeling again and they were having sex against the wall. It was harder, more intense, more passionate than ever.

"Aah," she said as he kissed her.

"Mine."

"Liam." Her body crumbed and crashed around him and he kissed her again, devouring her lips until she was about to collapse completely. He sat her on the shower bench and kissed her again.

"Liam."

"What love?"

"Condom," she replied.

He kissed her and slid it off. "Did you think I'd forget," he asked.

She shook her head and he smirked. "I still can't believe you said that. You realize that everyone is gonna start asking a million questions right?"

"Who?"

"Liam."

He kissed her. "We're good love. This is the way it's supposed to be," he said.

Kelly shook her head. All of it was too much. Way too much and way too soon. When he sat down beside her, Kelly shook her head and got up. She washed her hair and he kissed up her torso.

"Liam, we aren't 18 anymore. We need to get out of the house."

"Beach."

"Then you need a swimsuit." He kissed her and she finished washing up then he smirked.

"What?" He kissed her. "Liam."

"What beautiful lass of mine?"

"Don't start giving me that look again," she teased.

She stepped out of the shower, slid a towel around her and he stepped out behind her, wrapping a towel around his hips. "I get the feeling that you're mad at me," he teased as he kissed her shoulder then up her neck.

"Liam, telling people that we're engaged is kinda not cool. It's nothing to joke about." "I wasn't joking," he said kissing her neck.

"Liam."

"I knew the minute I saw you that I wasn't taking a minute for granted. I'm not. Not now, not ever."

"Liam."

"You don't think that I was thinking about it before?" Kelly shook her head and started fussing.

"Breathe."

"Liam, you've been here 48 hours and upended my life, my career..."

He kissed her. "You just wake up wound to the hilt don't you," he asked.

"I can't Liam."

"We're going out and getting your shoulders back to normal. You're all frustrated and losing your marbles. You need to relax love."

She shook her head, grabbed her bikini out of the drawer and slid it on as he slid up behind her. "I like," he said.

"Liam, you can't go on the beach naked."

He smirked and kissed her shoulder, tying the back of her bikini top for her. "I kinda love this bikini thing," he said.

"Liam." He kissed her shoulder, grabbed his swimsuit and they headed out to the beach.

She laid out the beach blanket, put her keys and phone in her waterproof case and they went out into the water. "Okay. Officially love this," he said.

"The salt water?" Liam nodded as he pulled her back towards him and into his arms. "What," Kelly said.

"Shoulders all back to normal love."

She shook her head and he kissed her as the wave hit them and he pulled her tight to him. She smirked and kissed him. "I know. Now you understand why I love being here."

"Is it better than a pint and a whiskey at the pub with a big roaring fire?"

She looked at him. "Different kind of perfect," she said.

"I want you to come home."

"Liam, this is home. The white sand, the sunshine, the seashells and the salt water. All of it is home."

He shook his head. "Tomorrow, I'll take you to a few places to see what I mean. It's a more humid, hotter version of home." He kissed her, picked her up and walked further into the water until they were up to their necks in warm saltwater.

"What," she asked.

He kissed her. "I have an idea."

"Which would be," Kelly asked as she felt his hand slide to her backside.

"Show me somewhere that reminds you of Dublin."

She smirked. "You want to go for a pint?"

He nodded. "Walk on the beach then we head back," she said. He kissed her. "Do you remember when I told you about that movie I loved?"

He nodded as he wrapped her legs around him. "They filmed part of it here."

He kissed her. "Then we go see it. Wherever you want love."

He kissed her again, devouring her lips until she felt his hand by the tie of her bikini bottoms. "Don't you dare," Kelly said.

He kissed her and smirked. "Love, we need to go."

"Why?"

"Because last night is coming back."

When she saw her ex heading straight towards them, she shook her head. She dove under the water and made it back to shore with Liam a few steps behind her. "So, you're just gonna blow me off like that," her ex asked.

"Meaning what," Kelly asked.

"Engaged? We've been together two damn years and you're engaged? You think screwing around on me is a good move," her ex, Andrew, asked.

"You want your life back, go. It's not like you were faithful," Kelly said as he grabbed her by the throat.

"How dare you, you little bitch," Andrew said as Kelly pushed him away.

Not two seconds later, she saw a fist fly and Ian flat on his back on the sand with blood coming out of his nose and lip. "You lay one finger on her again and you're gonna wish that you..."

Kelly pulled him back. "Are you alright?"

"You're not staying here." "Liam." "You aren't." He grabbed the beach towel, handed it to her and walked into the house.

"Are you alright?"

"Liam."

"Are you alright? You're bruised," Liam said."

"Liam, stop."

"He could've..." He kissed her. "We're getting out of here."

"Liam. Stop."

He shook his head. "Baby, are you alright?"

She shook her head. "I'm fine," she said as she broke away from him and walked upstairs. She went and peeled her swimsuit off, showered and came out of the bathroom. She went and slid on a pair of shorts and a tank. She shook her head and sat down on the bed. Liam came in not two seconds later, handing her a drink and wrapping his arms around her.

"Are you alright love?"

"No."

"I swear, if I see him again, I'll bury him."

"Liam, it doesn't work that way here. You can't just clock someone in the face and walk away."

He looked at her. "He was choking you."

"Liam."

"You let him do that?"

She shook her head and walked off. He looked at her and got dressed. "Come here."

"Liam, leave me alone for two dang seconds." He kissed her shoulder and she walked off and went downstairs, sitting on her deck. She needed to breathe.

He got dressed into shorts and a tee, came outside and took her hand, walking her inside. "What," Kelly asked.

"Come. We're going downtown."

"Liam."

"We're not staying here. He tried to strangle you. We're staying at the hotel tonight."

"No, I'm not Liam."

He kissed her. "What do you want me to do Kelly? Tell me what it is."

She shook her head. "Liam, he's been like this for years. We get in a fight and he does that. You telling him we were engaged only made it worse."

"And that gives that little piece of crap permission to hurt you?"

"Liam."

"No. I'd never hurt you like that. Never."

"I have crap taste in people Liam. Happy?" Kelly shook her head and went and curled up on the sofa.

Liam followed her and looked at her. "Come here," he said as he sat down with her.

"Liam."

He pulled her into his arms and laid down on the sofa with her. "I'm sorry that idiot did that alright? I'm sorry love. Are you alright?"

She shook her head and he knew. He remembered her crying before she had to go. He remembered her trembling in the safety of his arms and the feel of her tears hitting his chest. It felt like they'd burned a hole in his heart. That moment was no different. He wrapped his arms around her and let her cry it out. "I can't watch someone hurt you love. Not because of something I said."

She shook her head. "Couldn't just fade into the damn distance," Kelly said as he kissed her head and snuggled her. "Tell me what you want."

"Running off isn't gonna change anything. Besides the fact that it would take 2 hours to get back here."

He kissed her again. "Tell me what you want to do."

"Walk."

"Name the place and we'll go love."

"How did my life get this screwed up," Kelly asked.

"You left Dublin," he teased. She shook her head and laughed a little. Just enough so he knew she was still there. "Come. We'll get you one of those coffees and go for a walk." She smirked. And they got up.

"Where are we heading beautiful love of my life?"

"Coffee then walk at Pitt street bridge."

He looked at her and she smirked. "A bridge?"

She smirked. "When you see it, you'll understand. It is a pretty great sunset spot."

She kissed his cheek and he wrapped his arms around her. "Do you want to go to the hotel?"

She shook her head. "You can't even stay forever. You still have a house to find," Kelly said.

"I meant what I said about here."

"And I meant what I said about you not living here." He kissed her neck and they locked up and headed off. She got them coffees and they made their way out there.

"It's a bridge to nowhere." Kelly smirked.

"People go fishing, walk, look at the view. It is kinda pretty," Kelly said.

They walked, looked out at the view and calmed everything down. "You sure you're okay love."

She nodded. "He's not the first one Liam."

He shook his head and hugged her, pulling her into his arms. "Never again love. Never again is there ever gonna be a man putting his hands on you like that. Never. The closest you'll ever get is me kissing you from now on. Nobody hurts you. Not one hair love."

Kelly kissed him. "I love that you want that," she said knowing that he couldn't promise that. He kissed her, wrapping his arms around her and picking her up, wrapping her legs around him. He sat down on the bench with a smirk. "Liam."

"Yes beautiful."

"If I hadn't left, who knows what would've happened."

"You'd have a ring on that finger love. We'd have babies. Our lives would be different."

"And if you'd hopped on a plane with me?"

"We'd be married with babies. Don't care where."

Kelly smirked and kissed him. "Liam."

"Yes love."

"Do you like it here?"

"Better. I never did like the big city stuff. I was happy with a pub and some friends and time to take off and travel. That's all I wanted."

"Really," she teased.

"That and the lass that lived in my dreams for 10 years."

She kissed him. "You really have no idea who I am now Liam."

"One thing I do know is that you can do anything you set your mind to do. Always have. I promise you; nobody is comin near you like that again. Nobody," he said. He kissed her, devouring her lips.

"Liam."

"What beautiful?"

"I am kinda worried."

"About what?" She looked at him. "Then we stay at the hotel. No dishes, no cleaning, no nothing. Just stay."

Kelly shook her head. "I'm worried that he's gonna go to the police," she said.

He kissed her. "I'm not leaving your side."

"Liam."

He shook his head. "I'm staying with you. I don't want him near you. I'd rather ravish you all night in bed then us going out."

"We need dinner."

"Delivery. Oysters, seafood, more oysters and whatever you want," he joked.

Kelly shook her head. "You're the last one that needs oysters handsome."

He smirked and kissed her neck. "Where else do you wanna go sexy?"

She kissed him and they took time, making their way back to the main road. They wandered and shopped a bit and stopped off to get a few more things then headed back to the house through the traffic. "And what do you want to do for dinner," Liam asked.

"I came up with an idea. We kinda have to change and drop this stuff off, then we're going out."

"Where?"

"You'll see," Kelly said.

They got changed, got ready and she took him to the pub. It reminded her of when they were in Dublin together and the minute he walked in, he felt the same. A little piece of Ireland in Charleston."

"And," Kelly asked as she got them each a pint and a Jameson's.

He smirked. "All we need is fish and chips," he said.

Kelly kissed him. "Better?"

He nodded. "This is what I wanted. It's almost like a comfort," he said.

"Liam."

"Yes my love."

"We can have both. I can't run away to Dublin with you all the time. You can't be here all the time. We have to find a way so we can have a little of each."

He kissed her and nodded, snuggling her to him. "You know I have dual citizenship right?"

Kelly looked at him. "What?"

Chapter 4

"I didn't tell you?"

"Liam, how in the world did you manage to get dual citizenship?"

He kissed her. "Dad was born in Chicago. I didn't even know until I was almost 20."

Kelly shook her head and took a gulp of her Guinness. "Liam."

He kissed her. "I never knew him. When I found out, I got a dual citizenship so I could travel. I never did, but I could've."

Kelly shook her head. "What else don't I know," she joked.

He kissed her neck. "Only time I ever get..."

"Liam, we're in a restaurant."

"All because of you love. Just you. I never wanted to date anyone else."

"In 10 years, you didn't..."

He kissed her. "Oh, I did. Never worked out and never lasted past a date or two."

"In all that time?"

He nodded and nibbled her shoulder. "I knew. I had people ask who's initials were on my chest. I had to tell them."

"Liam, why did you get that tattoo?" He gulped down the pint and smirked.

"It was when you left. I needed a piece of you with me."

She shook her head and he kissed her. "And if I'd said no," Kelly asked.

He turned her face so they were eye to eye. "You tried already. Didn't work out. You missed me even if you never said it."

"We never slept together Liam."

"We might as well have love. I craved every single inch of you." He ordered them dinner and another pint and they sat and talked about old memories. The time they spent in the pubs, the hotel she stayed in, with him not leaving her side. Going and seeing places that nobody knew about. Swimming in the lake that everyone said was haunted by a spirit. "If you hadn't left, I would've married you in a heartbeat."

"Things would've been different. A lot different."

"And you wouldn't have ever thought that what happened today was normal. That wasn't. Any man that did that to a woman would get two broken arms."

"Promise me that you don't start fighting people."

He smirked. "Okay love."

"Liam."

"Better topic. What are we doing tonight?"

"This is about it. That's all I planned," Kelly said.

"Soak in that big tub."

She shook her head. "And then what?"

"I'll give you a hint," he teased as his hand slid around her waist and under the edge of her shorts.

"Not in here."

"I have plans love. Big plans," he teased as she shook her head with a smirk ear to ear. "Big plans that don't involve a movie or anything else."

He kissed her. "Exactly love."

"And, if I said that you needed to behave?"

"Not likely around the woman who could distract me from just about anything in the entire world," he said as she got goosebumps.

They had dinner, another pint and they made their way back to the house to see a package on her front steps. "What is that," she asked.

"She actually sent it overnight. Wow," Liam said.

"Sent what," Kelly asked.

"A few things I needed from home."

"Liam, what do you really wanna do about a place?"

"I don't need anything. I'll help you change what you want to change here. We can make it what you want it to be and do it together."

She shook her head. "A grand idea Liam. Problem is that you still need a house of your own."

He kissed down her neck. "You couldn't sleep without me," he teased.

"Yeah I could."

He shook his head and smirked. "Do you want to see," he asked. He brought it in and opened up the package.

On top was his mail from home, then shirts and a box. "I can't believe she sent it."

"Liam."

He kissed her and handed her the small box. "No."

He smirked, saw the swimsuits, the shorts, then a few books and another leather-bound book that he handed to Kelly.

"What," she asked.

"Alright. Come sit. I'll tell you."

He grabbed the bottle of Jameson's and she shook her head. "I don't even wanna know," she joked.

He poured them each a glass and slid her into his arms. "Now. The book is something I had before you came to Dublin and I wrote in it when we were together. That page mark is what I wrote," he said.

"And she sent it why," Kelly asked.

He handed it to her. "Read."

She opened the page and he took a sip of his drink.

I was in love with her the minute those eyes looked at me. The ones who stare at me every night, who haunt my dreams. I don't feel whole without her. I never did. I knew something was missing, but meeting this lass at the cliffs? I almost didn't go. I almost stayed home. Instead, I just spent the past 24 hours with the most amazing lass I ever met. I'm not the guy that has one girl and only one, but if I can keep her here. If I could keep her here, I'd marry her. I'd give her everything I have, everything I am. That kiss was like fire. I would've peeled that stupid sweater off of her and every ounce of clothing if she'd let me.

"Liam."

"Keep reading love."

She'd be worth giving my life away. She'd be worth leaving everything behind and sleeping in a box on the street if I had to, just so I could be with her. I can't even get my body to react to other women. I tried. I can't let her leave. I need to be there. I need to feel her in my arms. I need to be with her. I need to taste her skin, feel her body around me. I'll give up ever having a lass in my bed again if I can have her.

"Liam."

"What love," he said as he kissed down her neck.

"One day? One day and you were like this?"

"That was the night you set me on the sofa instead of letting me sleep beside you. I wanted you so badly that I literally couldn't even imagine moving. Not if it meant that I wouldn't have you."

She looked at him. "Why did she send it here?"

"Because I promised if I saw you again, I'd give it to you."

Kelly shook her head and took a gulp of the whiskey. "I don't get it."

"Open the box."

"No."

"Kelly, open the box."

She opened it and saw a diamond ring with an emerald, green halo. "What's this?"

"You know what," he said.

She shook her head and turned to face him. "You've been here 48 hours."

"And you've been gone 10 years."

"Liam, put the ring away."

"Fine, but you do know that it is yours right? It's not going on another finger whether we're together or not."

She took a deep breath. She went to get up and he stopped her. "Liam."

He turned her to face him and pulled her legs around him. "What," she asked.

"That book is yours."

"No, it isn't."

"Kelly, I got her to send it for you." She shook her head and he kissed her. He closed the ring box, marked the page of the notebook and brought them both upstairs, taking her hand and walking her up to her bedroom, then went and drew them a hot bath.

"What," Kelly asked.

"We're relaxing. No stress, just you and me," he asked.

"Liam, I get that you want..."

He kissed her, devouring her lips and slid her clothes off little by little. He peeled his shirt and shorts off, kicked his boxers off and slid into the tub with her, leaning back into the warm water and pulling her into his arms. "You actually wrote that when I was there?"

"You booted me to the sofa that first night. Literally, I didn't care as long as we were near each other."

"Liam."

He kissed her. "I told you. All I wanted was you with me. I didn't care where."

She shook her head. "It's kind of a lot," Kelly said.

"You haven't even finished reading it," he said.

"Meaning what?"

"Read it. I stopped writing after the last time that I talked to you. It's been sitting there waiting."

She shook her head. "I still think the ring is a little much."

"And I think that it was meant to be on your finger love. That's where it was always meant to be." She shook her head again and he pulled her onto his lap. The water rushed around them and almost attracted their bodies to each other.

"What do you want me to do Liam?"

"I want you to read it. If you do, you'll understand."

"Why don't you just tell me?"

He kissed her, devouring her lips. "You really want me to say it?"

She nodded and his hands slid over her backside and started taunting. "Liam."

"Can't help it love."

"Fine," Kelly said as she slid to her side of the tub. "Say it."

"The first night after we spent the day at the pub and walking around Dublin, we went back to your hotel. We got takeout meat pies and brought a bunch of Guinness back to the room and a bottle of whiskey," he said handing Kelly her glass.

"That's when you got me the shamrock keychain."

He smirked and nodded. "We sat up there and talked until I don't even remember what time. That was the first time you let me stay with you. We fell asleep on your bed, curled up together. You had your head on my chest."

She shook her head. "Liam."

He took a deep breath. "I hadn't slept like that ever. It was literally the best sleep I ever got. I woke up and realized where we were. I kissed you and it's like I woke you up like sleeping beauty."

She shook her head. "I remember waking up and you didn't have a shirt on and your hoodie was over my shoulders."

"And that day, remember, it was like time flew by so fast?" Kelly nodded. He kissed her hand. "That moment when you woke up, I knew. I was in love with you. I forgot anything and everything else. I forgot to charge my dang cell phone."

Kelly shook her head. "Liam."

"I knew that I loved you then. It changed me love. That next night, we almost..."

"Liam, I get it. Did you think I didn't feel the same way?"

He looked at her. "But you left."

"Because I had to."

He shook his head. "I didn't know," he said.

"Liam, we met and it took every ounce of my soul to get on that plane. I didn't want to leave any more than you wanted me to."

He almost started welling up. "We almost..."

"I know. I waited Liam. Deep down, part of me thought you forgot me. That you moved on."

"I went and stared at that airport. I did for weeks."

"If you knew what..." He pulled her to him. Holding her in his arms was all that he needed.

"Every time we were that close, that..."

"Liam."

"We never did. I wanted more than anything to do it, but I couldn't."

"We almost did that last night before I left."

He nodded as she slid into his arms and leaned her head on his shoulder. "I would've given anything in the world for you to stay. Anything."

She kissed him. "That's why I went nuts when you actually did. I regretted not saying it. I regretted us not sleeping together. I regretted not finding a way so you never had to leave."

"And what would've happened if I'd stayed?"

He looked at her. "You sure you wanna know?"

"Thought it all out didn't you?"

"In detail."

Kelly smirked. "The water's getting cold. Let's hop out."

He kissed her. "Bed," he said.

Kelly kissed him. "Come on handsome."

She stepped out, wrapping a towel around her and handing him the other one. He pulled on pajama pants and she slid a silky chemise on and they curled up in bed. He couldn't help the grin. "What," Kelly asked.

"Like a bedtime story," he teased.

"Finish what you were saying," she teased.

"I remember that last night. I had it planned. I would give you my gran's Claddagh ring until I found a way to get a real ring. We'd stay at the cottage that I went to in the summer with my parents."

Kelly shook her head. "Logic," Kelly teased.

"I had a job. I worked at the pub. My boss was the one that gave me the time off when he met you."

She looked at him. "Jimmy?"

He nodded. "I used to clean up and help with serving food," he replied. She shook her head and kissed him. "We'd be alright. It would never be glamorous or anything, but we'd have each other."

He kissed her forehead. "And then what," she asked.

"Babies. Old and gray having pints by the fire."

Kelly smirked. "I like the idea."

He kissed her. "If I could've found a way so we could've stayed together, I would've given anything."

"I fell asleep on the plane and it felt like I was still there."

He looked at her. "Seriously," he asked.

Kelly nodded. When I woke up and realized I was back in the USA, I was almost in tears."

He kissed her, devouring her lips. "I get that life went to crap when we ended up apart. So did mine. I just don't want us apart again. Never."

She shook her head and he kissed her. The moment overtook him and they were making out like they always had when they were in Dublin.

"Kelly."

"What," she asked as he kissed her neck.

"Promise me we never have to be apart again."

Before she could say a word, she felt his hand grab her backside and pull her leg around him. She grabbed the headboard and he kissed her. His hand slid down her leg and he leaned her onto her back. Before she could say a word, he was ripping into a condom.

"Liam."

"I need you," he said as her body curved tight to him as he devoured her lips.

His kisses trailed down her neck, pulling off the silky lingerie and knocked it to the floor, kicking off his pajama pants. "Liam."

"Yes love," he said as he nibbled and kissed each breast and making the goosebumps reappear.

"I..."

When he nibbled at her hip, Kelly's toes curled. "You what love," he asked as his fingers started teasing her and he kissed back up her torso.

"Are you sure that you..."

He kissed her. He didn't want to hear her doubting herself or them. "Aah," she said as he muffled her moans with his kiss.

"Kelly," he said.

"Mm," she replied.

"Say yes."

"To what," she asked as she looked at him and he kissed her neck.

"Tell me that we're never gonna be apart again."

She shook her head and he kissed back down her torso then started teasing her body into overheating.

"Liam."

"Yes sexy."

"Come here." She felt his warm breath against her then his tongue, then his teeth nibbling and licking her into crashing through another orgasm. She grabbed his hand and he kissed his way back up and before a word could be said, they were having sex. He went so deep, she thought he was taking every inch of her and turning her inside out. Her body throbbed around him as he kept going harder, deeper and when her knees were under his arms, he kissed her.

"Liam."

He kissed her again with a kiss that made her forget time, space and the existence of anything beyond the walls of the bedroom. "I love you Kelly," he said as his body reached its climax.

"I'm yours," Kelly replied as her body almost hugged him from the inside out, tightening around him as her body reached orgasm again.

"Did you mean that," he asked when they caught their breaths and she curled into his arms.

"Mean what?"

"You know what," he said as he kissed her again. She smirked and kissed him as he curled her to him.

"I know that the past was insane. No matter what way things went, what happened, happened. We can't change it even though we want to," she said.

He kissed her. "And you also know that we have a chance. Make up for what we missed all this time."

She kissed him. She needed reality. She felt like they were in a bubble. That the outside world stopped existing when they were at the pub, all the way back to the house and from that moment on. Something was different. He kissed her, devouring her lips again.

"Tell me that you want us," Liam asked.

Kelly kissed him. "Liam, you have a home in Dublin."

"And so do you love. One where guys don't put hands on you. One where the closest you get to that is me holding you in my arms."

"Liam, I can't leave."

"Then I'll stay here with you."

Her mind was racing. It's like she couldn't think straight around him. Like her brain was in a fantasy world. "You're not giving up your life to be here."

"If it means us, I'll do whatever you want Kelly. Anything." He kissed her and held on, leaning into her arms again. "Say it," he asked.

She shook her head and he kissed her again. "I need to get up," Kelly said.

"Please love. Please just say it."

She got up and grabbed her robe, walking out onto the balcony and sat down on the chair.

She needed to breathe. The minute she was around him it's like she was falling down a bottomless rabbit hole into fantasy land. There was no way that he was gonna give up his life in Dublin to be there with her. A weekend was just a weekend whether it was good or not. She shook her head and a few minutes later, Liam's hand slid in hers.

"What's wrong," he asked.

"Liam, you do realize that it's been a few days. We're still in freaking fantasy land right now."

"Meaning what?"

"You handed me a ring Liam." He took a deep breath and sat down beside her as they looked out at the crystal-clear water. The sun was almost set and the colors of pink and yellow and purple sat on the horizon. The sun was a hot red and it was better than a postcard. It was just as intoxicating.

"I want our forever Kelly. I wanted our forever a long time ago. I carried that ring all over Ireland. All over everywhere. When I was coming here, I thought there was no reason to. That there was no chance you'd be there. That I wouldn't find you. When I saw you..."

"Liam."

"When I saw you I really thought that you were a damn mirage. When I realized it was you I asked her to send it. That I wasn't losing another chance."

"I can't marry you when we haven't seen..."

He kissed her. "It doesn't matter how long. You know and I know that you love me. You know I love you."

"Liam, one week ten years ago doesn't make a marriage."

"Kelly." She looked at him. "Stop worrying what could happen. Stop being scared that it won't work."

"People date for years before they get married and even they end up divorced."

He kissed her. "I'm not letting go Kelly. Never. I want you to come to Dublin with me. I want us to be together."

"Then wait on the ring for a while."

He looked at her. "Keep the other one on."

She shook her head. "Fine. Just please..."

He kissed her. "I'm yours love. I have been since the minute we met."

"I know."

"You're my love. You always will be."

She nodded, trying to get herself out of the clouds that she'd been floating in. "Come inside," he said. She nodded.

"Come for a walk?" He nodded and kissed her. They went inside and Kelly slid into a sundress. He pulled on a pair of jeans and they grabbed the keys and their phones and opted to walk, locking up behind them.

They walked along the pristine warm sand, letting it run through their toes. "It is kind of beautiful out here," Liam said.

"This is what I loved. It's peaceful and serene. It's like being outside when we were at the cliffs. When the tourists aren't around, and the public aren't making a mess, it's relaxing. That's why I loved being here."

"Kelly."

"What?"

"I get it. I love it when it's nice and quiet like this," he said as they walked past couples on porch swings, couples playing in the water, a few couples having wine on their decks.

"There's something about being here. There are people down here who have it all Liam. I mean that one with the sign by it, that one was my favorite house."

"You want one then tell me and I'll get it," he said.

"Liam."

"You don't know what was in that contract do you?"

She looked at him. "Meaning what," Kelly asked.

He kissed her. "More than enough to buy a couple of them to be honest."

"Liam."

"8 figures."

She shook her head. "It doesn't matter. I don't have anyone..."

He kissed her. "You have me. You always will love. I'm not leaving. Not without you ever again."

She shook her head and they walked back towards her place. "You never have to be lonely here Kelly. I want to be with you. If you don't like the house, we fix it up. You want another house somewhere else; we get it. Just tell me."

Kelly kissed him. "I love that you want to do it. I just don't even know what I want anymore," Kelly said.

He shook his head. "Do you want to come to Dublin with me?"

"You just got here."

"And I have to go back at some point. Do you want to come?"

"Am I allowed to think about it?" He nodded and kissed her.

Liam wrapped his arms around her and when they got to the house, he picked her up. "What are you doing?"

He kissed her. "Taking my girl to the sofa."

He unlocked the door, walked in and leaned her onto the sofa, locking the door behind them.

"And now what," Kelly teased.

He kissed her. "Well, I thought I'd start with making your toes curl, then making you..." He kissed her again with a smirk ear to ear. Just as he leaned into her arms, her phone buzzed. He handed it to her and slid onto the sofa behind her.

"Hello," Kelly said.

"And you really think that him punching me was gonna..."

"What do you want?"

"Outside. Now." Kelly hung up.

"What," he asked seeing her all of a sudden completely tense up.

"He's here."

"Who?"

She shook her head. "You know who. A black eye isn't working to make him go away."

"I'll handle..."

"Liam, it's my problem."

Kelly got up and he followed. She went to walk outside and Liam grabbed her hand. "What do you want," Kelly asked staring her ex in the face.

"Mine. Every inch is mine," he said.

"Again, not a possession. You wanted to be single. I heard her voice. Go and be with her and just leave me alone," Kelly said.

"I want my stuff," her ex said.

"You don't have anything here and you know it. I handed it all to you last weekend when I saw you with her. Just go away." When he went to grab her throat, Liam's arm came out of nowhere, pushing him away from Kelly.

"Did nobody ever teach you that putting your hands on a woman was a coward move you little piece of crap?"

"Whatever dude. You want my sloppy seconds, go ahead. She's better when she's drunk. You can do whatever you want," Sam said as Kelly shook her head.

"And you're better gone," Kelly replied.

"What was that bitch," Sam said as Liam picked him up by the throat.

"You disrespect her, you deal with me and trust me little boy, you don't want to piss me off," he said as he walked out and pushed him into his jeep.

"You'll come to your senses. She isn't worth the condom," Sam said as Liam almost knocked him out.

"Leave and don't come back. Next time, I'm not playing nice with you," Liam said.

"Right. She'll call me when she wants me," he said.

"No she won't," Liam said as Andrew took off.

He walked back over to the front door and saw the door closed. He came inside, locked up and heard Kelly being sick. He grabbed a face cloth, soaked it in cool water and held it to the back of her head. "Don't," Kelly said.

"Don't push me away."

She shook her head and curled into the fetal position. He handed the cool towel to her and sat down beside her, curling his arm around her. "Baby."

She shook her head. "What did you say to him, so he'd leave?"

"That next time he doesn't get Mr. Nice guy."

"Liam."

He picked her up. "What," he asked.

He leaned her onto the bed, curled up beside her and curled her into his arms. "Liam."

He shook his head. "Just breathe," he said.

"What else did he say," Kelly asked.

"Nothing that I'd ever take seriously."

She shook her head. "Liam."

"I want to pulverize him. You know that right?"

Kelly nodded and ran for the bathroom again. "Kelly, what's wrong," he asked.

She shook her head and slid the sundress off, stepping into the shower and turning on the cooler water. She needed to eliminate the feeling. When she stepped out, Liam wrapped a towel around her and picked her up, carrying her back to bed. "Talk to me," he said.

"I don't even understand why he's here," Kelly said.

"Jealous."

She shook her head. "He didn't want me when he had me. Now that he doesn't, he's determined to get me back?"

Liam nodded. "Also, the man is a complete moron. He's a disgusting human being. You don't need that," Liam said.

"I never did. I made the mistake, and I can't move on when he won't go away."

"Then come with me."

"Where? Run away to Dublin and come home to my house burned to the ground?"

He looked at her. "Is that really what you're worried about?"

Kelly nodded. "Partially."

He kissed her. "Fine. Grab an overnight bag."

"What?"

"Grab an overnight bag. You're staying at the hotel with me."

"Liam."

"You're coming."

He grabbed his bag and put it on the bed. "What would the point be?"

"You not shaking and actually relaxing without anyone showing up uninvited."

She shook her head. "In other words, hide away from the world."

"For a night. We can come back over here tomorrow love. One night."

She shook her head, grabbed a change of clothes and bathing suit, and put it into her bag with her toiletries. "And here I thought you'd fight me on it," he teased. Kelly kissed him and slid the notebook in her bag.

They grabbed the whiskey and headed back to his hotel. "You alright," he asked.

"No."

They parked and locked up the truck and headed inside and up to his suite hand in hand. "You're too quiet love."

"You know, the minute you showed..."

He kissed her. "Felt like everything just clicked," he asked.

"More like my life flew out the window."

"Kelly."

They walked into the suite and saw a fruit tray waiting on them. "What did you do?"

"Snacks."

She shook her head and he put the bags in the bedroom, seeing the turndown service was done. "Get my mind off it," she asked.

He picked her up, carried her to the bed and leaned her onto it. "Don't have to ask me twice," he teased.

They curled up on the bed together and he slid into her arms, wrapping her legs around him. One kiss was all it ever took with him, but he wasn't about to push anything. Not after all of that. They took their time, giving him time to taunt and tease until her toes were in knots. She slid his shirt off and he leaned into her arms, wrapping his arms tight around her.

"Tell me what you need," he asked.

She kissed him and he peeled her shirt off, then went for her shorts. "Kelly." She looked at him. "You sure you're okay?"

She kissed him and he smirked. She was a woman of few words at that moment. She didn't want to talk about it, or her mistakes or even the idiot that had shown at the house. At that moment, she only wanted them alone in a room in the sky. No worries, no outside noise, nothing getting in the way of them spending a night alone. He peeled the rest of her clothes off and kissed down her neck, then worked his way down her torso.

She needed to forget the day. Forget the bad half anyway. The feel of his lips against her skin was like him wiping away all the scared feelings and the irritation. When he slid to the apex of her thighs and teased until her toes curled again, she thought that just maybe he could rid her of her past. Her mistakes. She was supposed to have the passion she had now. The love. The undying passion. The more he teased and devoured her, the more she wanted to just close her eyes and forget anything between when she left Dublin and when he showed up. She felt the nibbles, the kisses, the soothing of his lips and tongue against her. When she felt the kisses work their way back up her torso, he was shirtless, and all she could even see was the tattoo. The one that had their initials. She kissed him and they had sex. This time, more passionate, more seduction than powerful. Her body was almost humming.

"I love you," he said as she held onto him with her legs and her lips.

Her arms wrapped around his neck and he couldn't and wouldn't let go. "Aah," Kelly said as he went deeper and her body throbbed around him.

"Kelly," he said as his body was calming down from the intensity.

"Yes."

"I love you." She kissed him and he devoured her lips until her body curled to him and he leaned over.

"Are you okay," he asked. Kelly nodded and kissed him, not letting go of the connection. He pulled the blanket over them and held her tight to him.

"You sure you're okay?"

Kelly nodded, tracing the outline of the tattoo with her finger. "Why," she asked.

"Why what love?"

"Why did you do it?"

"Because I knew who my woman was. I knew who I was meant to be with love. I knew then and I know now."

Kelly looked at him. "But why a tattoo?"

"Because you had my heart then and you still do love. Always." She looked at him and kissed him. "Are you okay," he asked.

"I never should've left."

The minute she said the words, he wanted to get her on a plane and take her back to Dublin. If she would've come willingly, he would've taken her in a heartbeat. "Kelly." She looked up at him. "Do you mean it," he asked.

"Mean what," she asked as she tried to forget the nastiness of the day.

"That you shouldn't have left."

"I love my career now, and I loved being at school, but the relationship stuff. I was a lot better off on that end if I'd stayed with you."

Liam looked at her. "Come here."

She slid her arm around him. "What," she asked.

"We're here now love. I'm not leaving you."

"Good," Kelly said as they curled up together and they nodded off. When she woke up at 2am, she shook her head. His arm was wrapped around her waist, giving her just enough room to grab the notebook without waking him. She opened it up and went back to the page she'd stopped reading:

> *There is nobody else. There never will be again. She's in another room and I'm sitting here miserable, craving her. I could do something stupid. I could walk in there and wake her from her sleep, kissing her like I want to right now, but I know I can't. I can't imagine life without her. I can see the hole I'm about to throw myself into body and soul. I need her like I need air and water and food. That lass in that bed is the girl I dreamt of. I don't even know what took me to the cliffs that day. I could've gone*

anywhere else. I could've gone to an old church. I could've just stayed home like I'd planned. Instead, I followed my head and fell down a rabbit hole. She is what I want. If I have to swim to America I would.

She took a deep breath and saw another page marker:

It's been 5 years today. The day I walked her to the airport and watched her plane vanish into the horizon. The day that my future went into the trash. I owe them too much at the pub to keep drinking like this. To keep going back and sitting in the same booth that we sat in. I made up software that probably won't work anyway. I just need to get there. I need to get a ticket then I'll walk until I find her again. I tried to get past it every damn night I ended up in a drunk haze with a random tourist that I knew wasn't her. Thankfully, Jimmy stopped me from doing it again. I need to get better. Be better for her. For the woman who's in my arms in my dreams every night. I can still smell the shampoo from her hair. I still feel her in my arms when I'm sleeping. My boys tonight said they were concerned for my health. I need her. I need one night with her. One. I need to be in her arms. In her bed. I need to feel her skin against mine. I need to feel her kiss on my lips. I miss those kisses. Hell. I miss her. There's no doubt that she probably found someone and vanished into abyss, but if I do find her I'm not letting go. I'll find a way. I just want my soul mate. I want the feeling again. The one I know isn't possible without her. I need a reason to keep trying. Somehow, I'll find a way even if I have to swim.

Kelly felt him pulling her tighter into his arms and put the notebook down. When she felt kisses against her neck, she smirked. "Good reading," he teased.

"Liam."

"Yes love."

"Thank you."

"For what," he asked nibbling her earlobe.

"Being here."

His arm tightened around her, pulling her tight against him. "I love you. I always have."

"How long did you have this," Kelly asked.

"The notebook?"

She nodded. "11 years. A year before you came and up until I left to come here," he replied. He nuzzled her neck. "Can't sleep?"

"I figured if I couldn't, I could read."

Liam kissed her shoulder. "Close your eyes love. You need sleep." Kelly nodded and he snuggled her, pulling up the blanket.

She fell back asleep and all she could see was him making every excuse for her not to leave Dublin, like it was replaying in her mind. When she woke up a few hours later. She had her head on his chest and he was sipping coffee.

"What are you doing up," Kelly asked.

"Sleep love. You were tossing and turning all night."

She shook her head. "What time is it?"

"Almost 7. We have time."

"Liam."

"I ordered breakfast. It's all warm until we're ready to eat."

She looked at him. "What time did you wake up?"

"5:30. I was attempting to behave so I got coffee," he teased as he handed her an iced version with Bailey's added in.

"Liam."

"You had a rough night. You feelin any better?"

Kelly nodded. "Maybe you were right. That I needed to get out of the house for a while."

He kissed her. "I don't know how you put up with that. I really don't." Kelly shook her head and went to get up. "Kelly."

She shook her head, grabbed her hoodie from her bag and went and grabbed breakfast. She brought his in for him, handing him a plate and sat down at the table in the bedroom.

"Kelly."

"Yes."

He came and sat down beside her. "What's wrong?"

"Just thinking too much. Overthinking. This isn't allowed."

"What about it isn't?"

"I can't be with a client or a partner of the company."

"Kelly."

"I'm gonna end up in trouble."

He shook his head. "Then message your boss. Tell him."

She looked at Liam. "You sure?"

"Sure as I want that ring on your finger." She shook her head and sent off an email:

> *Hope you're having a great holiday weekend. I wanted to know if you happened to have paperwork to declare a relationship. Liam and I knew each other as kids and have started a relationship. I wanted to ensure that I'm not breaking any rules.*

She sent it off and within 10 minutes, got a reply:

> *I had a feeling you two knew each other. He'd spoken to me about a girl he once knew that lived in Charleston. Glad to hear you two rekindled. No paperwork needed. He's not an employee but thank you for letting me know – Mr. Cartwright.*

Liam saw it and smirked. "You talked to him about me," Kelly asked.

"I told him that a lass I once dated lived in South Carolina somewhere and he laughed."

Kelly shook her head. "Great," she said as she finished the last of her Eggs Benedict.

"Kelly."

"Why do I not get all the information ever," she teased.

He kissed her. "I didn't even know that I'd see you."

"Well, at least I'm not gonna get in trouble." He smirked.

Chapter 5

"Kelly."

"So, now I get set up by my boss and you."

"I didn't know it was you and either did your boss."

She shook her head. "What did you read last night?"

She shook her head. "Just random..."

He looked at her. "I know what page you were on."

Kelly shook her head. "How many," she asked.

"I honestly don't know. Half the time I was drunk and calling them by your name. Maybe 3. I don't even remember."

She looked at him. "Liam."

"The only time I ever saw one of them, they told me I called them Kelly. When I stopped drinking and burying myself in pub bills, I stopped everything. I wasn't around anyone other than my friends." Kelly looked at him.

"What," he asked.

She shook her head. "And when you stopped drinking?"

"I just didn't. No craving to be with someone else. I think I only met one other person and it never left the pub. I ended up talking about you."

She figured it was him just bring overly dramatic and he knew it. "Kelly."

"And then there was me going through more than one crap relationship. Having to call police more than once, having my friend have to fight someone off me."

He shook his head and took her hand in his. "Sofa," he replied.

"Liam." He walked her over to the sofa and sat down with her.

"I love you. I need you to tell me."

She shook her head. "No."

"Kelly."

"I don't want to rehash it Liam."

"Worst moment."

She took a deep breath. "The first one tried to strangle me when I wouldn't sleep with him."

"What," he asked as he looked in horror.

"The second grabbed me by the throat when I tried to walk away."

"Kelly."

She shook her head. "I don't wanna talk about it Liam."

He kissed her. "It's not happening again. Not to you. Never ever again."

"One of the two you already met. The other is in a jail cell."

"For what?"

"Attempted murder."

Liam couldn't believe what he was hearing. It's no wonder she'd had such a hard life. He pulled her to him and hugged her. "Liam."

He kissed her, holding her face in his hands. "Not happening again. That guy shows again, I'm calling the police."

"The one that you told that we were engaged? Liam, it's called jealousy."

He kissed her again. "Never ever again. Does the house have a security alarm?"

She nodded. "Did we turn it on?"

Kelly nodded. "I can turn it on from my phone."

"Good."

"Why? I'm going back today."

He shook his head. "What?"

"We're staying here tonight."

She looked at Liam. "It's my house Liam."

"Then we go for the day and come back here."

Kelly smirked and shook her head. "Not likely. There's fireworks tonight I think."

He kissed her. "Kelly."

She shook her head and took a deep breath. "We're going back. I can let the detective know what happened," Kelly said.

"What detective?"

"The one that dealt with him last time," she replied as she went to get up.

"Come here."

"I'm gonna go and shower."

He pulled her into his lap. "What," she asked.

"You need to get sleep love. You slept better here."

"I sleep better when it's quiet. I honestly sleep better with the waves nearby."

He shook his head and kissed her with a kiss that went from simple to deep, to Liam getting turned on. He undid the belt of her robe and she shook her head. "Not here," Kelly said. He kissed her again and his hand slid down her side then to the warmest part of her. "Liam." He kissed her and kept taunting until she forgot about where they were. When he picked her up and carried her back to the bed, she shook her head.

"What," Kelly asked as he leaned her onto the bed.

"Mine. Every inch of that heart, that mind, that soul is mine," he said.

She kissed him and pulled at his boxers. He kissed down her torso and let his lips and tongue take over the teasing that his fingers had started. "Liam."

"Yes love," he said as he continued teasing every inch of her until her body was too sensitive. He smirked and she pulled him to her. "What," he asked as he moved up her torso, sliding into her arms. She slid her hands to his face and kissed him. Now, it was passion. Love. More than just making love. He devoured her lips and she pulled him tighter so they were having sex.

"Kelly." She kissed him again and he shook his head, feeling everything. He tried to stop, but his body had other plans. They kept going and when his body found its release, he shook his head and kissed her again. "Kelly."

"What?"

"We um." She shook her head and kissed him again.

"Really," she asked as she broke the kiss. "What?"

"We didn't..."

"Liam."

"I tried to grab..."

"I don't care."

He looked at her. "Kelly."

"I don't care. I don't care if..."

He kissed her. "What are you saying," he asked.

"One time isn't..."

He devoured her lips as if those words just got him turned on all over again. He hadn't even moved. "Kelly."

"Yes." He looked at her, staring into her eyes and falling deep. He didn't care about the outside world anymore. He was buried deep into the woman he'd loved for what felt like a billion lifetimes. He kissed her again and she curled to him like she was trying to meld to him. When he let her up for air, he kissed down her neck.

"Kelly."

"What?"

"Are you sure?"

She kissed him. She nodded and he brushed a stray hair from her face.

"I'm not letting go. You know that right," he asked as his body got even more turned on. She nodded and kissed him. He had no idea what she'd read that changed everything. What she'd realized. All he knew was that he had her body, soul, heart and mind and he was never losing her again.

They had sex again with the passion overflowing between them. It was soft, passionate, slow and so intense that her body throbbed right to her core with every thrust. He kissed her again and kept going, until she found her release more than once. When he finally collapsed into her arms, he was past sated. He was past exhausted but he didn't care. He had her. All of her. Every ounce of her wrapped around him like a wool blanket from home. He kissed her again and he leaned to his back, bringing her with him as he pulled the blankets up. "You sure you're alright?" Kelly kissed him. His body calmed and he felt warmth against him. Liquid. Tears. He wrapped his arms around her and felt her crying.

"What's wrong," Liam asked.

"I wish you'd have flown home with me."

He took a deep breath, kissed her forehead and almost cradled her to him. "So do I love. So do I."

He brushed her tears away, kissed that spot between her eyebrows and held her. "Baby," he said.

"Don't leave alright?"

He kissed her forehead. "I never will unless I'm bringing you with me."

She held on tighter to him. "Do you want to go back to your house," he asked. She kissed him. "Kelly." She nodded. "We're good love. I'm here. Nobody is gonna hurt you. They try, they're gone."

He kissed her and Kelly snuggled in tighter to him. "Liam."

"Yes love."

"What if we just disappeared somewhere?"

He smirked. "You mean since you have work on Tuesday. I think your boss might be a little mad," he teased.

"I meant today and tomorrow."

"Name it love."

She smirked. "Beach or a little piece of home," she asked.

"Home. Always."

She kissed him. "Then we need to get dressed. We have a 2-hour drive ahead." He kissed her and they tried to get up. She slid her bikini on, sliding her shirt over it.

"Kelly."

"What," she asked as he came up behind her.

"I'm thinking that this bikini may be too much," he teased.

"Why?"

"Are you letting me drive?"

She shook her head. "No. Why?"

"Yeah. You need a hoodie." She smirked and kissed him as she turned to face him and the shirt slid back off.

"Bikini too much for you?" He nodded as his hands slid to her back and he teased with an oops when the back came undone.

He kissed her neck and then nibbled and kissed each breast getting turned on again. "At this rate we're never gonna make it," Kelly said.

"That a bad thing," he teased with a smirk that was way too sexy.

"Liam."

He nibbled. "Yes love."

"You need to get dressed."

He kissed her again, picked her up, sliding her shorts off, undid her bikini bottoms and walked her into the shower with him. "What," Kelly teased.

"You sure you're okay with that not using anything thing?"

She kissed him. "We'll be fine," she said. He flipped the water on and slid her under the water.

"What did you read last night?"

She shook her head. "Doesn't matter."

He kissed her, devouring her lips and washed her hair for her. "Yeah it does love."

She shook her head. "Was it the page that was marked with the leather?"

She rinsed her shampoo out, slid the conditioner in and he saw the look. "It was. It was when I stopped trying to drown the..."

She kissed him. He shook his head, kissed her and washed up. "Liam."

"Yes beautiful lass of mine."

"I love you too," she said as she rinsed the conditioner out.

"Hold on. Wait a minute. Did you just say what I think you did," he asked.

Kelly kissed him and went to step out when he pulled her back into his arms. "Say it again."

She shook her head. "Kelly, please love."

"I love you too," she replied as she kissed him and stepped out of the shower, sliding a towel around her and drying her hair just enough with the other. He stepped out a few minutes later and slid his arms around her.

"What," Kelly asked.

He turned her to face him and sat her on the countertop. "You said those words and just hop out of the shower? Really love?"

She kissed him and went to slide her hair into a loose ponytail. "What?"

He shook his head with a smirk ear to ear. "You have no idea how long..."

She kissed him. "I know."

He wrapped his arms around her giving her a full-body bear hug.

"Liam."

He kissed her, devouring and deepening the kiss until she had goosebumps and her body was throbbing all over again. "Do you mean it?"

She nodded and he untied her towel. "Liam."

He kissed her again, nibbling at her lips until they went from red to pink to red again. He pulled her legs around him and he leaned against her, pinning her hands against the mirror. He slid inside her and from that point on, he couldn't care less about them leaving that room, let alone that spot. Her legs slid tight to his sides as her body throbbed around him almost continually. When his body gave in and he climaxed, he kissed her.

"Kelly."

"Yes handsome."

He smirked and kissed her again. "Marry me."

She kissed him and shook her head. "Still too soon handsome."

"Then we wait to do everything else. Just say yes."

She kissed him. "We can talk about it when we're driving."

He smirked. "Fine," he teased as her legs were almost shaking.

One more kiss and he managed to clean up, get dressed and saw her sliding her bikini and shorts back on. He shook his head with a grin ear to ear. "What," she asked.

"My sexy lass. All mine," he teased.

Kelly shook her head, pulled her shirt overtop and slid her shoes on. "Where are we heading?" "Savannah Georgia." "And we're going there why?" "You'll see."

They got their things and went to head down when he stopped her. "What," Kelly asked.

"Do you want to come back here tonight? I can grab the bags."

"We'll come on our way back and figure it out."

He nodded and kissed her. "Coffee," he asked.

"Probably a good idea without the Bailey's in it," Kelly teased as they hopped into the truck, got coffee and headed off towards Savannah.

She took him to a few stores that reminded him of home, stopped for lunch at an Irish pub then she took him to the Cathedral. "Kelly."

"Yes."

"Where are we?"

"Church. Why?"

He shook his head. "If you come, you have to see it," she said as they came inside. He was in awe and they took a seat.

The things running through his mind would've got Kelly mad beyond belief, but he smirked. "What," she asked.

"Pretty place for a wedding."

She shook her head. "Liam."

"Just saying beautiful."

Kelly kissed him and they walked around then made their way back out. "I meant it," Liam said.

"I know. There's another one in Charleston."

"You wouldn't even think about..."

"Liam."

"What love?"

"I want to meet your mom first."

He kissed her. "Good. She's looking forward to seeing you too. I messaged her this morning before you woke up."

"And what else did you say to her with me asleep beside you?"

"I told her about what happened. That I wanted to bring you back to Dublin. Her exact words were, "If this is the same lass that you were with all those years ago, I need to meet my soon to be daughter in law."

She shook her head. "Liam."

"She put the ring in the box love. She told me to show you the notebook and let you read it so you knew the good, bad and horrid."

She shook her head. "Does she have an iPhone?"

Liam nodded with a smirk. "Did you do anything else this morning?"

"Yes." He showed her the photo he took with them curled up together.

"My peaceful angel all calm and relaxed. Sleeping like a baby in my arms."

Kelly shook her head. "No more pictures when I'm asleep."

He smirked. "I can't promise that. Not now," he teased.

"Meaning?"

"Not when that photo is of my..."

"Liam."

"You will be. When you give in that is."

"Can we stop talking about it and just go enjoy our day?"

He kissed her. "Alright," he said as he kissed her and they paid their tab at the pub and headed downtown, then over to Forsyth park.

"This is where they have the fountain green," Liam said.

"One of them. It actually starts at a different park."

She kissed him. "Kelly."

"What?"

"Are you feeling better?"

"You mean since last night or since this morning," she teased.

He kissed her. "Last night."

She nodded and he kissed her.

"I can take a photo of you if you'd like," a tourist said as Liam snuggled Kelly.

Liam nodded and the photographer snapped a photo of Liam kissing her in front of the fountain. They gave Liam back his phone and Kelly shook her head. "Now what beautiful?"

"Beach or trees," she asked.

"Trees," he replied. They stopped and got a few treats and they headed off, doing a tour of a few places, going to Wormsloe state historic site, then going to Skidaway park and walking along the pathways.

"See, this feels more like home," Liam said.

They looked out at the marshes, the birds, the views and made their way to the lighthouse. "And," she asked.

He leaned over and kissed her, picking her up and wrapping her legs around him. "I love you," he said.

"And I love you back. What's wrong," Kelly asked.

"Am I allowed to say that you in that bikini is very distracting?"

"What if we went to the beach?"

He kissed her. "You may never make it out of the water." Kelly smirked and they headed off, making their way to the truck. "Where are we really going," he asked.

"The beach," Kelly teased taking the back route to Tybee Island.

"Where is everyone," Liam asked as she parked away from the crowds and walked out into the pristine white sand with him.

"Down closer to the pavilion. I kinda like it away from everyone," Kelly said.

He smirked. "What?"

He slid her shirt off, undid her shorts and put the beach towel down that he'd brought from the truck, hiding their things inside it.

"Liam." He peeled his shirt off, kicked off his shoes and picked her up, running into the waves. They dove into the waves and he walked her out far enough that he was up to his neck in the warm salt water. He pulled her to him and they played around, splashing around in the waves.

"And," Kelly asked.

He kissed her. "Reminds me of your house. I like that we aren't bumping into your ex-mistake though. It's a little more relaxing for my girl."

She kissed him. "All face the same way," Kelly said.

"Which," he teased as he kissed her.

"Ireland's that way," she said as she pointed.

"Do you want to start swimming now? Might make it in time for Christmas," he teased.

Kelly kissed him. "I remember getting back to the house when I flew home and would stare out that direction at night hoping you could see me."

He smirked. "And I stared at that airport, wishing that you'd come running out and back into my arms."

"I almost wish you'd just jumped on the plane beside me. I mean, how insane..."

He kissed her. "If I'd had my passport, I would've in a heartbeat."

Kelly kissed him and his hands slid past the ties of her bikini bottoms to her backside. "Kelly."

She shook her head. "Not out here."

He smirked. "Not what," he asked as she felt his hand slide under the middle of her bikini bottoms.

"Liam," she said as he felt her legs twitch with every flick of his finger.

"Yes love," he said as one finger then two slid inside her.

"I know what you're..."

He kissed her again. "And," he asked.

Kelly shook her head and he got a grin ear to ear. "I missed that," he said. "Missed what?"

"Being carefree for once. Taunting my fiancée," he teased.

"We haven't..."

He kissed her. "You know what I mean," he said as her body tightened around his fingers.

"Stop," she said.

"Why?"

"Because you need...." He kept going and she almost moaned into his mouth.

"Never," he replied as he kissed her.

"Stop. I can't even..."

He kissed her and he smirked, sliding his fingers away from her. "Seriously. Had to do it," Kelly teased.

"I warned you about this bikini," he teased.

She shook her head and slid into the water, swimming back towards the shore as he followed. "I can't..." He kissed her, picking her up and wrapping her legs around his hips. "What," he teased.

"You are so bad," Kelly said. He nodded with a wink and handed Kelly her stuff and his from the sand, grabbed the beach towel and walked her to the truck.

"Liam." He kissed her again, sitting her on the tailgate and leaning into her arms.

"What love?"

"You don't want to stay?"

He smirked. "If we stay any longer, we're gonna get in trouble."

"For what?" He smirked and she shook her head. "You do realize that we are getting slightly carried away right?"

"And I love it. I really missed you. A lot."

"I kinda guessed this morning," she joked as he kissed her.

"Do you want to head back," he asked.

Kelly kissed him. "It's up to you my love," Kelly replied.

He smirked and kissed her. "Say it again."

"What?"

"You know what."

She smirked. "Liam."

He looked at her, silently begging. "When I called you my love," she asked as he snuggled her.

Everything that had happened that day was what he'd dreamed it to be. He almost thought he needed to pinch himself and make sure he was awake. He'd spent 10 years dreaming of moments like that. Making out in the waves, making out and having sex for breakfast. All of it. Being with her, alone was all he could've dreamt of, but her telling him that she loved him and being with him was almost too much emotion. He'd wanted it for most of his adult life. He'd wanted her for what felt like his entire life. Now, he had her. Every inch of her sexy body. Every single cell of her being was his. He loved her on another level. One that was spiritual. He loved her soul. He loved her mind. He loved her imperfections and her flaws. He didn't care what the package was that it came in. He just never ever wanted to lose her or lose that feeling.

"You went all quiet," Kelly said as he held her in his arms.

"Just realizing something," he said.

"What's wrong?"

"I remember when I first started trying to find you. I used to wish for days like today. Alone, happy and with you in my arms. That's all I wanted. The money was a bonus. I could get whatever I needed to. What I knew was that money wouldn't bring you back to me. I needed to see you myself. I needed to find you myself. I needed to wrap my arms around you to make sure you were real," he said.

SOUTHERN TEMPTATION 133

She kissed him. "And now what," Kelly asked.

"I can't let go."

"Good."

He kissed her and she shook her head with a grin ear to ear. "What," he asked.

"Let's head back so we can get home."

He nodded and kissed her, devouring her lips. "Just don't be surprised when we get back to the hotel."

"And why is that handsome?"

He winked and kissed her. "Because neither of us are getting any sleep tonight," he whispered.

Kelly shook her head, kissed him and they slid out of the back of the truck, got re-dressed and headed around to her side, sliding in and sliding her sandals back on. Liam hopped in beside her and they headed back across the bridge and headed home. "Kelly," he said.

"Yes handsome."

"Where did you want to go tonight? Hotel or your place?"

"Kinda up to you."

"Good. Then I can order room service so we can relax."

She shook her head. "You sure you want to be at the hotel?"

"You mean would I rather christen every inch of that house with you, yeah," he teased.

Kelly shook her head. "We are gonna need sleep at some point," Kelly said.

"House. We'll get dinner delivered so we can curl up and not see anyone for a few days," he teased.

"You seriously have one heck of a dirty mind don't you," Kelly asked.

"When it comes to you, yes. Always."

Kelly smirked and they drove through the backroads, heading back past the waterways and houses. "Odd question, but why didn't you live out here instead of by the beach," Liam asked.

"These houses are completely out of the price range or were anyway."

He saw the houses with the long docks out to the river and smirked. "If you want one, we can get one out here," he said.

"I don't need one..."

He kissed her at the light. "Honestly, I love being at the beach. If I had money like my boss, I'd probably have both," Kelly teased.

"And if I said that we did?"

"We?"

He looked at her. "We."

Kelly shook her head. "I'd say that it's your money not mine."

He linked fingers with her, kissing her hand. "And I would say that it's ours."

"Why?"

"You were my inspiration. I kept trying to figure out how to make things easier. That system was created as payment for something. Something that happened because I couldn't forget you. It went from one pub to 20 to hotels and restaurants all over the UK. Pubs all over Europe. That's why he wanted to partner with me to bring it here," Liam said.

"Still your money handsome."

He shook his head. "And another reason why I love you," he teased.

"Liam."

"When that ring goes on that finger of yours, it's officially ours instead of mine."

Kelly shook her head. "Then you should probably meet my folks."

He smirked. "Name the day."

"Monday."

"Oh. You mean for real," he asked.

Kelly nodded. "They're coming down to the house to have dinner for the holiday."

He smirked. "Did we get enough food," he asked.

Kelly nodded. "Grill is clean and ready. We're doing most of it outside anyway."

"Then I need flowers."

"What for," Kelly asked as they headed down the main road to get to her place.

"Your mum."

She smirked. The truck stopped at the light and he turned her face and kissed her. "You don't have to."

"Kind of do since I'm marrying her daughter."

Kelly smirked. "Then we'll stop and get them tomorrow," Kelly said.

When they managed to get back to the house, they took their things in and their bags, put their stuff into the bedroom and Kelly ordered the seafood for the family get-together and their dinner all at once. "What did you order?"

"Since you loved them, oysters. Plus, I got the seafood for Monday and the crab pasta for us."

Kelly smirked and went to set the table, getting two glasses out. When he poured them each a drink, she smirked. "What else do we need?"

"Nothin," Kelly teased. He kissed her, picking her up and leaning her onto the sofa in the living room. "And what would you like handsome?"

"For starters, this bikini off."

She kissed him and untied the bikini top. "Before I do what I know I'm going to, how much was dinner?"

"I got it."

"Kelly."

"I ordered Monday's seafood for dinner."

"Answer," he asked.

"$140."

He kissed her. "I don't want you paying..."

She kissed him. "It's fine."

He shook his head. "No. From now on, I'm buying dinner and whatever else we need."

"Liam."

"Please."

She nodded and he kissed her, devouring her lips and pulling the bikini off. "We should maybe go upstairs," Kelly said.

He smirked. "Good point," he teased as he carried her up the steps and into her bedroom, leaning her onto the bed.

"Liam."

"Yes sexy."

"You sure about me meeting your mom," she asked.

"You're gonna ask that all naked in my arms?"

"Well?"

He smirked. "I'm positive. I know that you can't get rid of me love. You're stuck with me for life."

Just as he was about to kick his swim shorts off, there was a knock at the door.

He shook his head. "I'll get my sundress," Kelly teased.

He kissed her, walked downstairs and got the food, putting the stuff for Monday into the fridge and plating their food for dinner. She came downstairs a few minutes later in her satin robe with only a belt holding it together. He shook his head.

"What," Kelly asked.

"Dinner and dessert. Nice," he teased as he kissed her and handed her a drink.

"At the rate you're going, I may not even be able to walk on Monday," Kelly teased.

"We can't have that," he teased.

Kelly kissed him and they sat down to eat. "You sure you don't want one," he asked offering Kelly an oyster.

"All yours handsome. I'm good with my pasta." He smirked. "What?"

"Nothin."

She saw him looking her up and down like a tiger eyeing their prey. "Liam, stop."

"Stop what," he teased.

"I know what you're doing."

"You're the one that came down here all naked like."

Kelly shook her head. "No more oysters for you," she teased.

They finished their dinner and when she got up to clean up, he slid up behind her. "Liam."

"Yes love."

"I wash, you dry," she said.

"You have a dishwasher." She shook her head and he put all the dishes into the washer, poured them a refill of their drinks and sat her on the counter.

"What?"

"I have an idea," he said.

"Oh boy," Kelly replied as she teased.

"May need more clothes," he joked.

"Meaning what?"

He kissed her, walked her upstairs and curled up with her. "What are you doing?"

He pressed buttons on his phone and within a few moments, a woman was on his phone screen.

"Liam. My baby boy. How are you," his mom said.

"I'm good. I thought I'd check in and see how you were since I left."

"I'm good. How is the trip," his mom asked.

"Yes she read it Mum. She won't tell me what part, but she read it."

"Good."

"Mum, remember when you said you wanted to meet her," he asked.

"Liam."

"Yes," he asked.

"You two need quiet time together."

"Mum, this is Kelly. Kelly, this is my Mum," he said as he turned the phone so she could see Kelly.

"Oh my. Hi Kelly," his mom said.

"Hi. Nice to sort of meet you," Kelly said.

"Oh Liam. I'm so glad you two finally got back together."

"Well, she's wearing Nana's Claddagh ring."

"Does this mean that you gave her the other item?"

"I tried Mum. She said it was too soon."

"Well, I must say that she's right. You two have a lot of catching up to do," his mom said.

"I know. I just wanted you to meet her since you didn't get to all those years ago."

"You've both grown up Liam. There's a lot you both have to learn."

"I did mention that to him. He's just happy to be here beside me," Kelly replied.

"Listen to the lass Liam. When are you heading back," his mom asked.

"As soon as I can talk Kelly into coming. Probably in the next few weeks," Liam said as Kelly smirked.

"You two go and relax. It was nice to finally put a face to the name Kelly. I can't wait to meet you in person," his mom said.

"You too," Kelly said as Liam kissed Kelly's forehead.

"Mum."

"Yes love," his mom replied.

"Love you."

"Love you too. Talk to you soon love." He hung up with his mom and Kelly smirked.

"What," he asked.

"You have her eyes."

He kissed her. "She loves you."

"Liam."

"I know that look."

"When we get there, we will meet for real."

He kissed her again. "And we can go see all the places we loved. They're all still there," he said.

"Liam."

He kissed her forehead. "What," he asked.

"What would you think about moving here?"

He looked at her. "I could. We can both go between the two places."

Kelly nodded. "As long as I have you, I'm fine with it. I'm not going anywhere without you."

"Even if I have to stay?"

He looked at her. "I went 10 years without feeling you in my arms. I'm not going another day. If you can't come, I wait until you can."

She shook her head and he pulled her to him. "What are you worried about love?"

"I have work. I may run that section of it, but if I can't…"

He kissed her. "Worry about it when it comes to it."

Kelly nodded and he slid her to her back and leaned into her arms. "What," Kelly asked.

"Movie?"

She nodded. "Pick one," she said as she grabbed the remote and handed it to him.

"Kelly."

"What?"

He flipped on a movie to keep them in a good mood. "What did you choose?"

When she looked at the screen and saw Leap Year, she smirked. "Of course you did," she joked as she saw Leap Year. He cuddled her to him and kissed her forehead. She pulled up the blankets and they curled up in bed together, having their drinks and watching a movie that reminded him of home.

By the time the movie was done, he was missing home. "You okay," Kelly asked.

He nodded and kissed her. "Was thinking about home."

"It's okay to be homesick Liam."

"It's not even that. Why aren't you out with your girlies? Why are you not getting a million and one phone calls to hang out with your friends?"

"A lot of them are with their families. I got a few emails from a few friends asking why I haven't been on social media."

"I have an idea," he said.

"Liam."

He grabbed her laptop, handing it to her and flipping it on. "What?"

"Go on your social media."

She went on and he went on his, finding her profile and adding her as a friend. She shook her head. "Did you really want to be on my Facebook that badly?"

He kissed her, uploaded the photo of them together to his social media and edited. "What?"

"You'll see in a minute love."

Within a few seconds, her social media asked her to confirm that they were dating. "Liam."

"Just say yes."

"As long as you don't change it to engaged." He kissed her and pressed confirm on her laptop.

He loaded the photo of them as his profile photo and tagged her in it. "Liam."

He smirked. "Much better," he teased as he started seeing comments pop up. Kelly shook her head and saw comments from friends, guys that she knew had to be his friends and then one comment that was completely out of place:

So now you're cheating on me.

It wasn't her friend, and from the look on his face, she knew it was someone he knew. "Liam."

"Kelly, don't..."

She shook her head. "Who is Ellory Chambers," Kelly asked.

"A girl I had maybe 2 dates with. It was before I planned to come here."

She shook her head and went to get up. He stopped her. He sent a message to her:

You remember me telling you about her. How she was why I couldn't be in a relationship. Why are you seriously going to start a problem? Delete the comment.

Kelly got up. "Where are you going?"
"Pajamas. Get ready for bed."
"Kelly." She shook her head and within a few minutes, his phone rang.
"What do you want," Liam asked.

"You don't have to make up a story Liam," Ellory said.

"She's wearing my nan's Claddagh ring. That enough?"

"Liam."

"Why are you seriously starting a problem?"

"Because I thought we were gonna at least try," Ellory said.

"And I told you that if I ever found her again, I was staying with her. I am. She's right here," he said.

"Whatever," Ellory said.

"Kelly," he said.

"No," Kelly replied.

"I don't blame her. Dating a guy who cheats on everyone."

He got up and walked into the bathroom to see Kelly peeved. "Baby, just say hi to her," Liam said.

"Why? What's the point Liam," Kelly said.

"She has a point," Ellory said.

"Apologize. I broke up with you before I left and you know it. I said there was no point in a date. That nothing was gonna come of it."

"And I know that you wanted me."

"Fine. This is the way you want it, fine," he said as he hung up, blocked her account and deleted the message and the comment.

When he saw Kelly walk past him, he grabbed her hand. "Where are you going," Liam asked.

"Outside." She walked down the steps, grabbed her phone and went outside to the deck. She watched the water, the one thing that had always calmed her. She had the last of her drink and saw the comments that her friends posted congratulating her or saying they couldn't wait to meet him. She shook her head. Even his friends said congrats and cheers on the hot woman. The fact was, making that move was a lot bigger than he thought. It opened it up to everyone commenting on their relationship, the photo and everything else. When she got a text a little while later, she looked and saw her ex's name on the screen:

> *Social media official? Could've sworn I saw a girl post about him cheating. Mr. Perfect isn't so perfect. Go figure. Come over.*

Kelly shook her head and sent a reply:

> *An old ex with a grudge just like you. Sorry. I'll pass on the whole strangle me until I do what you want thing. I'd rather swim in lava. FYI, you may want to heed his warning. He meant it.*

When she got a text a few minutes later from Liam, she wanted to ignore it:

> *I know you're mad. Giving you space. You gonna come back inside? I'm sorry she's starting crap. Please love just come inside.*

She finished her drink and her phone rang. "Hi Faith," she said.

"Hey yourself. Is that who I think it is? Is that the guy that you told me about when you were a kid," Faith Sams said as Kelly shook her head.

"Yes. The same guy that was in that meeting with us on Thursday."

"Girl, if I wasn't married to Ridge, I'd so be your competition. How are you two doing?"

"Good. Having a barbecue with the folks Monday."

"You know, if you wanna take off and go to Dublin, tell me. You can take time if you want. You haven't taken any vacation time in 5 years."

"I know. I just didn't want to put anyone out."

"Dad would give you the plane if that's what you want. Just go. I'm glad to see you with a smile like that. We'll talk Tuesday."

"Alright Faith. See you on Tuesday. Have a good holiday," Kelly said as she hung up.

Chapter 6

"Faith as in Faith Sams? Mr. Cartwright's daughter," Liam asked.

"What do you want Liam?"

"Is it?"

"Yes. I knew Faith in high school."

Liam shook his head and slid his arm around her waist. "And what did Miss Sams want," he asked.

"Nothing."

"So, you're mad at me."

"Liam, go back inside."

"Can't do that love."

"What'd your girlfriend have..."

He turned her to face him and kissed her. "Not my girlfriend. Literally, two dates that both tanked. She's eliminated."

Kelly nodded and turned back around to look out at the water. "Kelly."

"Ex texted by the way."

"And?"

"Hopefully he's going away."

He slid his arm around her waist. "Kelly, come inside."

She shook her head. "Just go..."

He picked her up and carried her inside, closing and locking the sliding door behind him. "Liam."

"What?"

"Can you not just leave me..."

He kissed her, leaned her onto the bed and leaned into her arms. "No, I can't," he replied.

"Did you sleep with her?"

He shook his head. "I wasn't attracted to her like that. I even told her that."

Kelly shook her head and tried to get up. "You don't believe me," Liam asked.

"To be honest, no."

"I can count on one hand how many women I slept with in 10 years Kelly. One."

"And the ones when you weren't sober?"

"Kelly."

"Can I get up please?"

He shook his head. "You don't believe me at all." She managed to get up and walked out to the balcony, sitting back down. She saw more comments from people he knew then more from people she knew from work. When she got a message from her mom, she shook her head and within seconds her phone rang.

"Hi Mom," Kelly said.

"Is this the same Liam from when you were in Dublin?"

"Yeah. You can meet him on Monday."

"Kelly."

"What?"

"You sure you're okay?"

"I'm fine."

"Then why am I concerned?"

"It's fine. He showed and I didn't even put two and two together. He did in a heartbeat. We've kinda been hanging out ever since."

Her Dad got on the phone and Liam came outside, sliding onto the chair with her. "He's right here Dad," Kelly said.

"Liam," her Dad said as she put the phone on speaker.

"Good evening," Liam said.

"About time you made it here. We were going to go fishing Monday before dinner if you wanted to come. Kelly's brother and I had it planned. Would you like to join us," her Dad asked.

"Sure," he replied as Kelly shook her head.

"Alright. We'll see you Monday. Baby, mom's bringing the corn and the salad."

"Thank you," Kelly said.

"Welcome. See you both on Monday," her Dad said.

"You still mad," Liam asked.

Kelly got up and he pulled her back into his lap. "Talk Kelly."

"What's the point?"

She got up and walked inside, went downstairs and finished her drink then came back up with a sweet tea. "Kelly, come on."

She shook her head and laid down in bed. She pulled up the blankets and put her phone on the charger. He slid his on beside hers and kissed her cheek. "Talk," Liam said.

"No point Liam." She got comfortable and he sat down beside her.

"Whatever you want to say, just say it love. We're not going to bed mad."

"Liam, I get you had a life before we met and while we were apart. Just be flipping honest."

He pulled her so she was sitting up. "In the haze, maybe 7. Outside of it, less than 5."

"Were you dating her before you left?"

"I broke up with her when your boss started negotiations."

"And you..."

"No."

"Were you checked for..."

"Kelly."

"Were you?"

He nodded. "Completely healthy."

"I get..."

He kissed her. "I love you. What happened before we met or while we were apart doesn't matter anymore. We're together. Neither of us have ties to anyone. Anyone that isn't happy for us can go away. Are you alright love?"

She shook her head. "Just rubbed me the wrong way."

"Are we alright?"

Kelly nodded. "Just don't want..." He kissed her. "I don't want to talk about it anymore," Kelly said.

He nodded and got changed for bed, sliding under the blankets with her. When he saw his notebook on the bedside table, he smirked and snuggled her to him. "Liam."

"Yes love."

"Promise me there isn't anyone else?"

"Other than my mum and my sister, nobody."

"Sister?"

"Katherine. She's living in Belfast with her husband and her 3 kids. Taunted me when I left that if I didn't find you, I'd have to stop looking."

Kelly shook her head. A minute later, as if she knew, his phone rang. He saw the call display and answered, flipping the light on. "And how's my sister," Liam asked as he answered on FaceTime.

"Good. Where are you," she asked.

"With Kelly. What are you up to?"

"Put the kids down. Where is she?"

"Right here. What's up," he asked.

"You're hiding this one away? Really Liam. There's no way that you found that fantasy..."

"Hi," Kelly said in the background.

"Miss Kelly, come over here so I can see you," his sister asked. She slid over beside him and Liam's arm wrapped around her.

"Kelly, my sister Katie. Katie, my Kelly," he replied.

Kelly waved. "My goodness. I truly thought that you were making her up all that time. Wow. Well, hello Kelly. Ignore my brother being a bum. When is he dragging you to Dublin," she asked.

"Probably in a few weeks. Have to get time off," Kelly said.

"Understood. When you have a date, let me know. I'll bring the kids," Katie said.

"I'll let you know. Kids good," Liam asked.

"I'll call you," Katie said as they hung up on FaceTime.

"Go talk to your sister. I'm gonna try and get some rest."

"Kelly, it's not even 10."

"Still tired. Someone tired me out all day." He kissed her and sat down in the chair by the bed and called his sister.

"I can't believe you actually found her," Katie said.

"Honestly, either can I," Liam said.

"I saw Nana's claddagh. You're really doing it?"

"If she'd stop telling me it's too soon."

"Liam, don't go losing your mind alright? I know she's beautiful and very much the amazing woman you told me about, but you two are from different worlds. You sure that she's okay settling down with you?"

"She's the only woman I ever loved short of you and mom and Nan. I never forgot her," he said.

"Liam, are you sure?"

"I'm sure. When we get to Dublin, you'll understand."

"Alright then. Your brother-in-law wants to say hi," she said.

"And how is Finn?"

"Good. Nice going by the way brother. Pretty lass," Finn said.

"Thank you. I can't wait for you two to meet her. How are my nieces," he asked.

"Hellions. Both determined to fight over everything. All the normal stuff," he teased.

"Give them a hug for me."

"I will. I know you said you were gonna do it, but wow. You found the lass we all thought was a hallucination," he joked.

"She's pretty amazing. I can't wait for you to meet her. I'll let you know when we're heading back."

"Alright brother. Go be with the lass."

"I will. Give my sister a hug."

"I will." He hung up with him a little while later and slid back into the bed with Kelly.

His arms slid around her waist and snuggled her to him. "How was your call," she asked.

"Good. My sister's looking forward to meeting you. So is my brother-in-law."

Kelly nodded and he kissed her shoulder. "You alright love?"

"Just need sleep."

He kissed her neck. "Then we sleep. Come," he said as he pulled her into his arms and she fell asleep with her head on his chest. When she woke up at 4am, she shook her head feeling his body against hers. She read a little more in the notebook, hoping it would calm her down from worrying:

> *I know it's insane to say it, but she's in my soul. I can't sleep, which is pretty much normal for me. Instead, I keep all those feelings bottled like an old whiskey bottle. I can't keep holding on and hoping that she'd find her way back here. I got motion detectors so I can hear her if she shows. I know that she's probably off somewhere with someone else, but I need her. I don't even know what life is like in her world. All I know is that I want her back in mine. I can't look at other women. I can't think. She was the one that I've loved since I was a kid. I'm not a kid anymore, but I can't stop the feelings. I don't know what to even think. I dream of being at her side,*

married, babies and spending every second together. That's what I wanted. That's what I still want.

Kelly took a deep breath and opted to flip back to what was happening when they were together, marking the other page:

She's laying in bed, right beside me and it's taking all the power I have not to kiss her. Not to peel that stupid hoodie off her. Just feeling her beside me makes me feel like we're two puzzle pieces that just clicked into place. This is the woman I asked for with that first heartbreak. This, in my arms, is the lass that I dreamt of, that I willed into being here. There had to be something that brought her here. I don't know what to do. I want to be with her and never let her go. I want us to be together in every way. How is it that in 72 hours, I'm in bed beside the woman I love and I actually love her? That I can't dream of a moment without her. I want to hold on and never let go. I know it's not realistic. I know my mum would have me checked into hospital for saying it, but I want her body to meld to mine. I want to experience the world with her so long as we're together. I want to feel every inch of her. I know it's stupid. I know that after 72 hours it would scare her away, but it's like a need. A craving.

She marked the page and put the notebook down, nodding off. When Liam saw her put it down, he kissed her shoulder and went back to sleep. When he woke up the next morning, Kelly wasn't in bed. He shook his head, freshened up and made the bed, seeing the note:

Went for a run. I'll be back in an hour.

He shook his head, pulled his pajama pants on and came downstairs to see coffee made with a note:

For you.

He smirked, got his coffee and walked outside. Just as he came outside, he saw her running down the beach. He watched and saw her coming closer, running up the steps. "Hey beautiful," he said.

Kelly kissed him. "You just wake up?"

Liam nodded. "How long have you been gone," he asked.

"An hour. I needed to go for a run," she said.

"Kelly."

"After last night, I needed it. Hungry," Kelly asked as she went to walk past him.

He slid his arm around her waist and pulled her to him, devouring her lips. He picked her up, walked upstairs and into the bedroom and leaned her back onto the bed. "Good morning," he replied as he peeled her shorts, shirt, bra and panties off along with her socks and shoes. He kicked his pajama pants off and leaned into her arms. He kissed her again and pulled her legs around him.

"Missed me," Kelly asked.

He nodded and kissed her again, deepening the kiss until they both had goosebumps. Her arms slid around his neck and there were barely two words said. He needed her. He wanted her so badly that he could almost taste her lips before she even came back.

"Liam."

He looked at her. "We need..."

"But yesterday you..." She reached for it and handed him the condom. He kissed her and went back to devouring her lips as he kissed down her body. Complaining would've only destroyed the mood.

"Kelly," he said as she felt his hands against her, teasing and nibbling at her until her toes started curling.

"What?"

"Are we okay," he asked as he nibbled.

"Aah. Um. Yeah," she said as her body heated and he could feel her body start to warm. He licked and her legs started twitching. He kept going until she was reaching for him.

"You sure you want this," he asked.

"Liam." He slid the condom on and kept teasing. His fingers continued to tease until he made it back up to her face and kissed her. One kiss that deepened until they were having sex was all it ever took. Now was no different, except that something was different. Wrong even. It was more intense than ever, but still full of passion. When her body throbbed around him that third time, his body started finding it's release until it got that much hotter. She slid on top and he pulled her against him, giving her what she wanted. When she found her release along with him, they both collapsed onto the bed and he kissed her.

"What," Kelly asked seeing the look on his face.

"You still mad?"

She shook her head. "Liam."

"Just wanted to make sure. That's all."

Kelly got up and he reached for her. "Kelly."

"What?"

"Come here for a minute." She turned to face him. "Talk to me."

"Liam."

"Come." She took a deep breath and laid back down with him as he pulled the blanket over them. "Are you upset with me?"

"Liam, I'm not gonna pretend that her comment didn't irritate me. It did. It's what happened after that."

"Which was what love?"

"My ex messaging me and starting problems. I just..."

He kissed her. "If we're really trying the relationship and being together stuff, what's the problem?"

He kissed her. "I just didn't want to have people commenting on our relationship. That's all."

"Are you mad at me?"

She shook her head. "Liam, leave it."

"Kelly." She shook her head again and got up. She went and walked into the bathroom, sliding into the shower and turning the warm water on.

She took a deep breath and washed her hair, rinsed it and slid the conditioner in when she felt arms slide around her waist. "Kelly, I get it, but you realize that you can't just go all silent on me."

"Liam, I know why you wanted to. I get it. Seeing that just..."

He kissed her, pulling her face to his, cradling the back of her neck in his hands. "She's long-gone love. Long gone. The only woman I crave, the only woman I want more than anything is right here in my arms. The only woman who turns me on with one kiss is you." He picked her up, wrapping her legs around his hips.

"Liam."

He kissed her, devouring her lips as he nibbled and held on with every ounce of energy that he had. "What," he asked as he kissed down her neck and leaned her against the wall of the shower. When he kissed down to her breasts, she shook her head and with one nibble, she was at his mercy all over again. He kissed back up and kissed her lips again. "Tell me what you want," he asked.

"You know."

He kissed her and they had insane sex in that shower. When her legs started shaking, it just got more intense. He sat down on the bench and made her straddle him and keep going. "Liam."

"Yes love," he said as he knew he couldn't hold back much longer. He nibbled her breasts again and he felt her body throbbing around him and climaxing. When he followed, Kelly looked at him and he pulled her tight to him. "Crap," Kelly said.

He kissed her again. "What?"

"Just intentionally hoping aren't you," Kelly asked.

"All I'm saying is that if we didn't yesterday..."

Kelly shook her head. "Liam."

He kissed her again. "Tell me what you want love."

"Tell me that woman isn't gonna start an issue if I come to Dublin with you."

"Since you'll have my ring on your hand, it won't be a problem."

"And who says..."

He kissed her, devouring her lips. "You will love."

Kelly shook her head and got up, rinsing the conditioner out. "We alright," he asked. Kelly nodded. "And how much reading did you get in," he teased as he slid under the shower head.

"Liam."

"That's why I gave it to you."

"A page or two."

"And?"

She shook her head. "If I knew you were so sentimental..."

He kissed her. "When we get to my place, I'll show you just how sentimental."

"Liam."

He smirked. "Baby, you have no idea," he said as he kissed her. She shook her head and washed his back for him. "Thank you love," he said.

She smirked and kissed his back, sliding her arms around him. "What," she asked.

"Missed a spot," he teased as he slid her hands to the very turned-on area that was back to being at full attention.

"Liam."

"You started it," he teased. She shook her head and he turned to face her. Before she could even make a move, he picked her up, wrapping her legs around him.

"What are you up to." Kelly asked.

"That's what you do every time I feel you near me. That's why I wanted you so badly when we were at the hotel that first day. Why I didn't leave your side. Why I asked them to let you show me houses. Why I wanted to kiss you the second I got off the plane. This is what you do."

Kelly shook her head and he kissed her. "Liam."

He kissed her again and they were having sex against the wall of the shower all over again. This time, they were hotter. He flipped the water off and carried her to the bathroom counter as he pulled her legs up higher so he could go even deeper. Her entire body trembled in his arms. She barely even managed to come up for air between kisses. He kept going until her body was throbbing and his couldn't stop. Neither of them spoke. Neither of them said anything other than her moaning his name into his mouth as they kissed. When her body crumbled around him and he shook his head, they both knew their bodies were completely spent. He kissed her again and her arms slid around him.

"All the messages in the world can come. I'm not going anywhere. I promise you," he said.

"Liam, I can't even move."

He smirked and kissed her. "Good. No more fighting either."

"We weren't fighting."

"We were love. I get why."

Kelly smirked. "Just promise me that there isn't a kid running around with those eyes," Kelly said.

"Other than my niece, none that I know of," he teased.

"She'll just be a heartbreaker then."

He kissed her again. "Just imagine how amazing our kids will be," he teased.

"Will? I didn't realize you were pregnant."

He smirked and kissed her. "Working on it today."

"Nice," Kelly joked as she went to slide off the counter.

"Where are you goin," he asked.

"Breakfast." He kissed her again and she went and attempted to get dressed, with shaky legs and all. She grabbed her phone and headed downstairs, tying her bikini top and sliding her skirt over the bottoms. She walked downstairs, put on breakfast and felt her phone ring. She looked at her phone and saw a message from her mom:

Do you need me to grab anything extra for tomorrow? I heard he was gonna be there. By the way, very handsome. I can bring extra of whatever.

Kelly replied a moment later:

Extra cobbler. Beyond that, just you guys. See you tomorrow

She flipped the bacon and the eggs and poured herself a mug of coffee. Just as she was plating the food, Liam came downstairs. He smelled good even shirtless. When she felt his kisses on her neck, she smirked.

"Hungry," Kelly asked.

"Definitely," he replied. Liam kissed her shoulder then he kissed up the back of her neck.

"Liam." He smirked, took the plates and they sat down and relaxed.

"What did you want to do today," he asked.

"Other than recuperating from this morning," Kelly teased.

He nodded and kissed her. "Other than that."

"Swim. Hang out on the beach or the deck. Walk. Kinda up to you handsome."

"Walk, swim, lunch then we go do something."

"Okay. We can go out for lunch."

He nodded. "Just make sure you put on sunscreen," Kelly teased.

He kissed her and they finished up breakfast, cleaned up and made a lunch reservation. She grabbed her sunscreen and sprayed it on herself and Liam and they walked outside.

The beach was already filling up and Kelly smirked. "Swim," he asked.

She nodded and he undid the skirt and picked her up. "Towel," Kelly said.

"Put one on the chair," he teased as he ran for the water and they dove in. The water almost felt too good after the morning they'd had. They played around in the water, splashing each other and then swam out further.

"And," Kelly asked. He pulled her to him as he stood on the bottom. "What?"

He kissed her. "When you said a few weeks last night, did you mean it?"

She looked at him. "Liam."

"Did you?"

"If I can take the time off."

He smirked and kissed her. "I've been counting down to that day for 10 years."

"Oh, I know you have. Then you get me back in your lair," Kelly teased.

He got a grin ear to ear. "Wherever else you wanna go, we'll go. We can even go to the pub if you want."

Kelly smirked. "The one where I had my first Guinness?" He nodded and kissed her. "Okay," she said.

"And we can go back to the cliffs."

Kelly kissed him. "Of course," she joked.

He kissed her again. "Kelly."

She smirked. "Liam."

"Marry me."

"You really have no patience do you?"

"Just say yes already."

"Ask my Dad tomorrow. Go from there," Kelly said.

He nodded. "Secretly though, you'd say yes right," he asked.

"When it's the right time, yes."

He kissed her. "Good," he said as he smirked.

"What?" He shook his head and kissed her then they swam back in, opting to hang out on her deck instead of on the beach with the tourists.

He walked her up to the deck and they sat down together. He handed her the towel and she shook her head. "Liam."

"What sexy fiancée?"

"Not funny. You willing to come to lunch with me?"

He smirked. "Yep," he teased as he kissed her. She put her sunscreen back on, putting some on him and they curled up together for a bit, drying off and enjoying the day. She went and got both of them a sweet tea and headed in around lunch to get changed. "You could just leave it on," he teased.

Kelly smirked. "Alright handsome," she teased. He kissed her again. She slid a sundress over the bikini and he pulled on a shirt and his sneakers. They headed off a few minutes later, making their way over to the restaurant in Shem Creek.

They sat down at their table and Kelly smirked. "What do you think," she asked.

"This is a little more what I thought you'd have here."

"Well, they aren't fishing boats like shrimp boats, but I'm sure people fish for beers in a cooler on them," Kelly teased.

"And they're too big. At least have a boat you'll use." Kelly smirked. They had lunch and he intentionally paid before she could get to it.

"Now what," he asked as they finished their sweet teas.

"Now, we walk," Kelly teased.

They made their way down the boardwalk hand in hand. He kissed her when they got to the first coverage area. "What," she asked.

He smirked. "Sexy bikini. I like," he teased.

"Liam, stop," she teased as she laughed.

He kissed her, picking her up and wrapping his arms around her. "What are you all happy about?"

"What you said earlier."

"Liam."

"About you saying yes if I did propose."

"It's burning a hole in your pocket."

"Kind of. I know you were reading the notebook."

"Liam."

"Does it make you feel better knowing it all?" Kelly kissed him and he sat down with her in his lap.

"Gives me a way to get to know you more."

He kissed her. "Good answer," he smirked as he snuggled her.

"Liam." He kissed her. They walked to the end of the path and he was in awe of the view.

"It is pretty amazing."

"Now you know why I love it."

He kissed her forehead and hugged her to him. "Woman of mine. I think we need to get out and go somewhere else. Where do you want to go. Name it," Liam asked.

She smirked. "We can go shopping, or we can go to another park. Up to you."

"That big giant tree."

She kissed him. "Alright. While we're there, we can go to the tea garden."

"Done," he teased.

They drove over to the Angel Oak and his jaw hit the floor. "It's huge," Liam said.

"Looks much better in person."

She shook her head and they went in and looked. "Kelly."

"Yes handsome."

"What are you doing next weekend?"

"Liam."

"What?"

"What are you thinkin," she asked.

"Taking my fiancée somewhere."

"Which would be," Kelly asked.

"We need plane tickets."

"Liam."

"I messaged your boss."

She looked at him. "What part of stop interfering didn't you get," she teased.

"The part where he asked when we were going."

"What?"

"He said for us to go. We're flying on the jet. You can still get work done from there."

"Liam."

"What love?"

"Did you seriously talk to him this morning?"

"You don't check your emails love. He sent one to you about going." She pulled her phone out and saw the email:

> *We are considering opening up an office in Dublin. I'm sending you two over there for a week. Liam said that he wanted to take you back to where you two met. I love the story. Go. All expenses covered. I'll get my security to keep an eye on your house. Go spend some time and recharge. You haven't had a vacation ever. Go.*

Kelly shook her head. "And you didn't tell me this when we were talking this morning why?"

He kissed her. "Because you were in a good mood. I didn't want to mess with it."

Kelly shook her head. "Fine, but I need to talk to Faith before I leave. Don't plan anything until I talk to her."

SOUTHERN TEMPTATION   167

He nodded and kissed her, sitting down and pulling her into his lap. "Alright love. Promise me one thing," he asked.

"Which would be?"

"Lots of lingerie," he teased.

Kelly shook her head. "And you can bring those little things from the box."

"The ones that we didn't..."

She nodded. They relaxed and watched the tree, the limbs strong with leaves blowing in the breeze. "That big and nobody managed to chop it down," he asked.

"Do you know how live oaks survive?"

He nodded. "It's survived hurricanes. Nobody's touching her." He kissed her shoulder.

They managed to get up not long later and then they headed to the tea garden. "We should get something to bring for your mom and your sister," Kelly said.

He smirked. "Kinda already have what I want," he teased.

"Liam." "We can bring her some American tea and we can bring the kids some treats." Kelly nodded.

They got a few things then sat on the porch with a sweet tea each. "There's only one other place we need to go," Kelly said.

"Where?"

"The cookie place."

He smirked and they went to the Olde Colony bakery and went and got some more stuff to take to his family.

When they got back to Faith's, flowers were on the doorstep. "Liam."

He smirked and she saw the roses and peonies. "Liam, they're beautiful," Faith said as he kissed her and they headed inside.

She put them in water and kissed him. "Thank you."

"Welcome beautiful almost fiancée," he teased.

Kelly shook her head, put them on the table and he made a call. Within a half hour, food showed up for them for dinner. "And what's all this," Kelly asked.

"Relaxing dinner. I got an extra in case we need it tomorrow," he said as he showed her the larger bottle of Jameson's. Kelly kissed him.

"Good idea," she joked.

"And I'm grilling the lobster and steak," he said.

"Treating me tonight?"

"After last night, yes." He kissed her, picking her up and sitting her on the counter.

"And what else did you have planned," Kelly teased.

"Dessert."

She shook her head with a smirk. "Ice cream?"

"That too."

Kelly shook her head and her phone rang. He kissed her, devouring her lips then handed Kelly her phone and started kissing down her torso. "Hello."

"So, who's the guy," her friend Caroline asked.

"Can I call you back?"

"Fine," her friend said as she hung up about the time that he'd undone her bikini bottoms and started taunting her.

"Liam."

He licked. "Yes love," he said as he kept going.

"You can't do that when I'm...ahhh."

"When you're what," he asked as he nibbled.

"On the phone."

"Good thing you aren't then," he teased as he intensified it even more and had two fingers taunting her.

"Liam."

He kissed and licked her body into more than one climax. He nibbled again and her legs almost started shaking. "Yes fiancée."

Her hands slid to his shoulders. "Come here." He shook his head and then intensified it more. "Oh my aaah."

"Now, you were saying love," he teased as he kissed her. She slid her arms around his neck and with her free hand, went for the drawstring of his swim shorts.

"Nope," he teased.

"Liam, please."

He picked her up, kissing her again and locked the door, walking up to the main bedroom and leaned her onto the bed undoing the rest of her dress.

"Liam."

"You're the one walkin around all day with that sundress on half-naked underneath." She pulled him to her and pulled his shorts off as he leaned into her arms.

"Tell me what you want love."

"You." He kissed her and before the words even resonated through the room, he was inside her. He was hers all over again. Every ounce of his soul was melding with hers. The puzzle pieces clicked back together. They kept going, riding the wave of each orgasm as he slid deeper into her.

"Don't ever leave me," he said. She shook her head and he reached his climax, crashing into her as she followed, holding on for dear life. He kissed her and when her arms tangled around him, he smirked.

"What," Kelly asked.

"You sticking to the promise?"

"I won't. Not unless it's in an emergency."

He smirked. "An emergency being what," he teased.

"Liam."

"Just don't leave me in Dublin."

Kelly smirked. "You know where I'll be."

He kissed her, leaning in for a kiss again when his phone buzzed. He shook his head and kissed the tip of her nose as he slid to his back and she curled up beside him. He grabbed his cell and answered.

"Hello," Liam said.

"Are you seriously going to propose," his friend asked.

"I'll be home in a few weeks Kieran. We can talk about it." "The lass is there right now, isn't she?"

"I'm in Charleston South Carolina Kieran."

"Not the same one from when you were a kid."

"Kieran."

"Fine. Call me back."

Liam shook his head and hung up. "You do know you could've just talked to him right?"

He nodded. "Part of me almost worried what you'd do if I did that."

Kelly smirked. "I can do what you started when I answered my phone."

"Interesting," he teased.

"You think I wouldn't?"

"I would never go there. Not even a thought."

Kelly kissed him. "No."

"Go call him back and find out."

He shook his head. "We're cleaning up and eating dinner love. Before I have you for breakfast, lunch, dinner and dessert and then for a midnight snack," he teased.

"Promises, promises," Kelly joked.

He kissed her and shook his head. "You have no idea what I have planned fiancée."

"Oh, I know handsome."

He got up, went and cleaned up and pulled on his jeans and boxers. "Liam," Kelly said.

"Yes beautiful."

"Where are we gonna go when we get to Dublin?"

"My place. I have a house out there. Lots of room for us. Room for my family to come." He leaned over and kissed her, then went downstairs to make dinner while she cleaned up and slid clothes on.

He walked downstairs and called Kieran. "You're there with her? Why didn't you tell me that you found the girl Liam?"

"Hi to you too Kieran. I didn't know until I got here. She's amazing," Liam said.

"Still head over heels?"

"More."

"You didn't. Tell me you didn't."

"She's wearing the Claddagh."

"I saw the photo. I mean wow. When are you two coming back to Dublin?"

"When she gets her work stuff organized. Maybe a week or two."

"This mean we're having an engagement party?"

"Kieran, when that time comes you'll know alright?"

"Then we at least get to see her for ourselves?"

"Yes," Liam said.

"Are you grilling?"

"She lives on the beach Kieran. Yeah I'm grilling dinner."

"I can't believe you. First, sitting like a puddle in the pub and now grilling on the beach."

"She's amazing Kieran," he said as Kelly came downstairs and sat in the kitchen, hearing him on the phone.

"Just promise me that you two don't run off together into the sunset without a phone call," Kieran asked.

"I won't. I love her. Beyond that, the world can swallow me up," Liam said.

"Well, post more pictures of it and of the lass so we can see it all. Bring me something."

"Will do Kieran. Go say hi to the boys."

"I will." He hung up with his friend and Kelly handed Liam a glass of Jameson's.

"Talkin about me again," Kelly teased.

"One of my best mates from school. He's the one that called me the day we met and asked me where I was."

"And," Kelly asked.

"Excited to actually meet you since he didn't when we were in Dublin together."

"Where's your place now?"

"I have one in Belfast and one in Dublin."

"Liam."

"The one in Dublin is where I usually stay because it's close to family. The one in Belfast is where I was when I missed you too much. Smaller, but still comfy."

Kelly shook her head. "And?"

"We're flying into Belfast."

Kelly smirked. "And why is that?"

"Because I need 48 hours alone with you in Belfast."

"Why?"

He kissed her, picking her up and sitting her on the ledge and wrapped her legs around him. "Liam."

He devoured her lips. "Because I want us alone where we can be as loud as we want with nobody complaining."

"And we have..." He kissed her and nodded.

Kelly shook her head; he finished making the seafood and Kelly shook her head. "Ready," she asked.

He kissed her and she brought the food outside so they could relax. "And," he asked.

"Belfast? Sure, I guess. You know that I can't just stay there for a month or two right?"

He kissed her. "Yeah I do. I say we stay for a week or two then we come back here and figure everything else out."

"Everything else meaning," Kelly asked.

He smirked. "That ring finally going where it's supposed to."

She took a deep breath. "Liam."

"Yes love."

"I think you need to relax on that."

"Nope," he teased as they finished their dinner.

"What would you think about doing it in Ireland?"

"Doing what?" He smirked. "Liam, seriously. 3 or 4 days."

He kissed her, took her hand and pulled her into his lap. "Three or 4 days, and ten years."

"Ten years of not seeing each other or talking..."

"Not because of me love."

"Liam."

He kissed her. "We talk about it when we get there. We have time after the thing tomorrow."

"Liam."

He smirked. "I need to talk to your Dad," he said.

Kelly shook her head. "Whatever you say handsome." She kissed him and took the dishes inside as he followed behind her.

"What," she asked.

"I wash, you dry," he teased.

"No dishwasher tonight," Kelly teased.

"Good point."

He put the dishes in the washer, closed the door and poured them each another drink.

"Liam." He kissed her, sat her on the counter and wrapped her legs around him as his hands slid up her legs. "What are you up to," Kelly asked. He slid the bikini bottoms off.

"I could give you a hint," he teased.

"Meaning?" Liam smirked. "Liam."

"Dessert." She shook her head and he picked her up, walking up the steps to the bedroom.

"You are so bad."

"And," he asked.

"I thought we were going for a walk."

"I have other plans fiancée."

"You mean since we're not..."

He kissed her. "Soon," he teased.

She shook her head and he undid the dress. "Liam."

He leaned her onto the bed and leaned into her arms. "Yes sexy."

She shook her head. "You realize we could watch..." He kissed her, devouring her lips until her arms were wrapped around him.

Chapter 7

"Liam," Kelly said as he kissed down the front of her neck.

"What?"

"What are you up to really?"

"Wanting my woman every second. Never stopped," he teased.

He slid the dress off and peeled her bikini top off. "You are so bad," Kelly said.

"All your fault sexy," he teased as she undid his jeans.

"What are you up to," he asked.

"Nothin," Kelly teased as he felt her hand wrapped around him.

"Kelly."

"You want to start then so can I handsome."

He shook his head. "You're starting that?"

"Yep," Kelly teased as he grabbed her hand and slid them both above her head instead of on him. "Liam."

He kissed her. "Ruin all my fun," he teased as her legs slid around him and pulled him to her.

"Nope. Just started it."

He shook his head and kissed her, kicking his jeans and boxers off and pulled her to him. "Tell me what you want," he asked.

"You. Plain and simple. Just you."

"I'm all yours love. Until you get so sick of me that I have to talk you into..."

"You really think that will happen?"

He shook his head and leaned in, kissing her again. "Good answer."

He kissed her and then down her neck, down her chest, nibbling at her breasts until her stomach started trembling. He kissed down her stomach, kissed her hip.

"Liam."

All he had to do was look up at her with those eyes. The ones that she could fall into without even thinking. When he got to her inner thigh, then the warmest core of her, he was taunting and willing her body into his. He kept going, probing with his fingers, taunting and licking and sucking at her with his lips then when she finally reached for him, he slid into her arms and devoured her lips again, then made love to her.

"Why do I get the feeling like there's something you aren't telling me," Kelly asked as she leaned her head on his chest.

"If I'd known that you were here, and that we'd be in bed together, I might've brought a few things."

"Meaning what?"

"You'll see when we get there," he teased as he looked her up and down like she was his prey.

"Liam."

"I have a few things that could make you explode."

"I bet," she teased. She went to get up and he pulled her back to him.

"What?"

SOUTHERN TEMPTATION

"Nothing," Kelly said. She got up and walked into the bathroom, taking a deep breath. She wasn't gonna be enough, or at least that's how she felt. It wouldn't be enough. It never really was. The panic attack started to set in."

She slid her sundress back on and went to step out of the bathroom when she saw him. "Talk."

She shook her head. "I'm fine."

"No, you aren't."

She nodded, trying to put on the fake smile. "We went from okay and happy and sated to you with that look. What's wrong," he asked.

"Nothing. Did you want your drink," she asked.

"Kelly."

She kissed him and went downstairs to get a drink. She walked outside, took a gulp of her drink and flipped on the small fire pit she had on her deck. She leaned back on the chaise and felt a blanket slide around her shoulders.

"Move over a little," Liam said as he slid onto the chaise beside her in his jeans. He wrapped his arms around her and curled her to him. "You gonna tell me what's wrong," he asked as he took a sip of his drink.

Kelly took a deep breath. "Nothing's…"

"Kelly, I know better. You're like a clam shell that just snapped shut. Talk to me."

She shook her head. "I'm fine."

"Talk love. You can't just shut down. Tell me what I did." She went to shake her head and he slid a finger to her chin and made her look at him.

"I know you. Tell me what I said."

"I'm not enough."

"I never said that."

Kelly shook her head. "Baby. Please don't even think that." She took a deep breath and he slid her into his lap. "Don't ever even think that."

"Liam."

He kissed her, devouring her lips and snuggling her to him. "You're the only thing I want. You know that."

"Explode?"

"Things that will make things even..."

"Exactly."

Kelly went to get up and he wouldn't let her. "Liam, let go."

She got up, flipped the fire pit off and went to walk back inside. "Come here."

"No." She grabbed her drink and walked back inside. He shook his head. "What in the hell did I just do," he said to himself. He kicked himself then walked back inside, seeing her throwing in laundry.

"Kelly." She shook her head and he closed the washer door and sat her on the top.

"I'm not. It's fine," she said.

"Love, don't you dare start saying that. You're more than enough. You always have been," he said.

"All four days."

He shook his head and picked her up. "What are you doing?"

"We're sitting and having a conversation."

He sat her on the sofa and leaned into her arms. "Talk," he said.

"About what?"

"Did you seriously think that you aren't enough?"

"Never have been. Why start..."

"How can you even say that," Liam asked.

"I'm not."

He shook his head. "Kelly."

"I get it Liam. I've been cheated on..."

He looked at her. "You think I'd do that?"

She went to try and get up. The conversation was starting to make her feel awkward. "Did you actually think that after waiting 10 years, that I'd actually do that?"

"Yeah," Kelly said.

He kissed her. He leaned his forehead against hers. "I want you Kelly. Just you. Only you. You worry that you aren't enough. You are a hell of a lot more than I could've ever asked for. The only women I was ever with were good for nothing more than a blow in a corner. You're what I wanted. I'm not changing my mind on that love."

"You will," Kelly said.

"Because you don't think you're enough?"

"Liam."

"Answer me."

"Because I never was before." He looked at her and could feel the pain in her heart. He could feel the scars from the broken hearts. The pain she'd gone through before. She wasn't going through that again. Not on his watch.

"Look at me love."

She looked at him. "You are all I ever wanted. You're what I wanted then, and you're what I've wanted my entire life. You're what I'm always going to want. I don't care whether we have sex or not. Whether we are even in the same room. I want you in my arms. I want you in my life Kelly. Forever."

"Liam, just..."

He kissed her. One kiss. One overwhelming, intoxicating, passion filled kiss was all it took. "Like it or not love, you have me for life. I'm not leaving your side."

"And what..."

He kissed her. "It'll never come love. I choose you. Always have, always will."

"What happens when there is someone else?"

"Like what? Our baby?"

She shook her head. "Liam."

He kissed her. "There isn't."

He got up, locked the doors and handed her the glasses. "What," she asked.

He picked her up and carried her back upstairs, grabbing the bottle of Jameson's on the way. "What are you doing?"

"Fixing this thing you have about not being enough." He sat her on the bed, putting the bottle and glasses on the side table and curled back up with her. "Tell me why you're all worried really," he asked.

"Because I never have been."

He kissed her. "Well, I hate to break it to you love, but you are more that I could ever want. You are all I crave. You're all I want and need. Like it or not, you aren't getting rid of me." Kelly didn't even react. Whatever it was, shut her down completely.

The next morning, Liam woke up to an empty bed yet again. There was a note on the pillow, but it was irritating:

Went for a run. Back in an hour. Love you – K

He shook his head, pulled his jeans on and walked downstairs to see her sitting on the steps of her deck with a coffee. He went and poured himself a mug and walked outside, sitting down behind her. "How was your run," he asked.

"Good. How did you sleep?"

"You mean considering you took off for the second day in a row?"

She turned to face him. "Liam."

He grabbed her hand and walked her inside, locking the door behind them and sitting her on the kitchen counter.

"What's wrong," she asked.

"Stay in bed with me."

"I couldn't..."

"Then read. I know that's what you were doing. What's really wrong?"

"Liam."

"I'm waiting love."

She shook her head. "Kelly, please."

"Just brought up bad memories."

He kissed her. "Then start remembering something. I'm right here. I'm not leaving, I'm not cheating. Don't get up and run off."

Kelly took a deep breath. "I go for a run every morning Liam. I have for 10 years."

"I'm right here. Just stay with me."

"I need..."

"You don't need to run away from all of it. I'm right here. You need me, roll over. You need someone to wrap their arms around you, tell me." She nodded. "Kelly."

"Fine."

"What in the world did these fools do to you that got you like this?"

"You don't wanna know Liam."

"Tell me love."

One look in her eyes and he saw it. The words her ex had said when he threw him in his jeep rang through his mind. She'd been used. That much he knew. She'd been cheated on, lied to and hurt. He had no idea what the details were, and there was no chance that she'd ever tell him. The cut was still too deep on that.

"I was told so many things Liam. One guy I dated said he needed to cheat because I was horrible in..."

He kissed her. "You aren't."

"Liam."

"You aren't," he said starting to get irritated.

"One said he was only in it for the money."

"Love, I have more than you do. That I do know."

"And how is that?"

"American dollars?"

She nodded. "8 figures just last year."

She looked at him. "I live a simple life love. Always have. I had money when we met even though I didn't know it."

She shook her head and he kissed her forehead. "I just haven't had good guys to date Liam. I don't know why or how. I just haven't."

"You don't have to look anymore. You have the one."

"And if I wanna trade him in?"

"No return policy. After the first kiss, you are stuck with me for life."

He'd never really thought about how the words hurt people. Hell, he'd never hurt anyone like that before. He'd never lied about how he felt in a relationship. If they hadn't been a good match, he'd said they weren't flat out. There was no intentional attack or degradation. He'd been honest. When he met Kelly, his entire life was up in the air and he couldn't have cared less. He lived for the taste of her kiss, the taste of her skin when he kissed down her neck. The smell of her freshly shampooed hair when she stepped out of the shower. That's all he'd wanted. The minute she left, his life crashed to the floor and he was left to pick up the scattered pieces. They'd lived such different lives. Not just because he was a man and she was a woman, but because he'd been in love the minute she looked in his eyes.

"Liam." He kissed her. One kiss that silenced the noise in her head, that quieted the worry, that made her stop thinking about the past.

"We kinda need to get up."

"Why?"

"Because they're coming at noon. Kinda have to get up and showered..."

He kissed her and slid into her arms, wrapping her legs around him. "What," he asked.

"We have..."

He kissed her again. "It's 7am love. We have 4 hours."

He slid her workout gear off, piece by piece, threw them into her laundry basket, then kissed down her torso.

"Liam."

His hands started the teasing. "Yes love."

"Damn."

"That's what I thought you were gonna say," he teased as he started his taunting and teasing of her now throbbing center. To him, she tasted too good. She felt too good. If she were a drug, he would've been an addict for life. He slid her legs over his shoulders and went deeper with his fingers.

"Liam."

"Yes sexy fiancée."

"Oh my god."

He kept going until he could feel her body climaxing again.

"Mine," he teased as his jeans started feeling like they were 3 sizes too small. He was so turned on that the button of the jeans was barely holding closed. He undid his jeans and found even a small amount of pressure relieved.

"Liam." One nibble and her toes were curling. He kissed back up her torso, holding her legs where they were then sliding so deep into her that he swore he could feel her heartbeat as he thrusted. He muffled her moans with his kiss until her body started tightening around him.

"Kelly."

"Aah." He kept going and when he felt her release, his body couldn't hold back.

"Crap," Kelly said.

"All mine," he teased as he leaned into her arms.

"If you keep doin that, you know what's gonna happen."

He kissed her. "So, we try again after dinner," he teased.

"Funny," Kelly joked.

He kissed her and slid to his back, cradling her to his chest. "You feeling any better," he asked as he kissed her forehead.

"Just feels different. Like a box was closed," Kelly said.

"Good. Can we incinerate the bad mood box?"

Kelly smirked and kissed him. "I think you just did handsome."

"Good. If I had known that..."

"Liam."

He nodded. "I don't want you thinking like that again. Promise me."

"Liam."

"No. You are more than I ever dreamed. Always have been. I don't want anyone or anything else. I promise..."

Kelly kissed him. "Liam, stop."

He kissed her, cradling her face in his hands. "Say yes."

"About what," she asked.

He looked at her. "We did talk about this didn't we," Kelly asked.

He kissed her again, leaning her onto her back. "Still want my woman."

Kelly shook her head and he kissed her, sliding his hands up her legs and wrapping them around his hips. "Liam."

He kissed her again and she felt his fingers start teasing again. "We have..."

He devoured her lips as the teasing got more and more intense. "Liam."

"Wife to be."

"Funny." He kept going then ramped up the teasing as his fingers probed and taunted her body into throbbing all over again.

"Liam."

"Haven't even started," he teased as he slid down her torso and she felt his lips and tongue and teeth against her. Nibbling, sucking, probing. All of it intensified when it got deeper. He was turned on. She knew he was and when she tried to move, one nibble would settle her back in place until her knees were on his shoulders.

"Liam."

"Yes love."

"Come here."

She saw the look on his face. "Not done yet."

"Crap," Kelly said breathless and amping towards an orgasm.

"Mm," he said as Kelly shook her head.

"All mine," he teased.

He kept going pushing past her first orgasm until she was starting to get even more hot and bothered. "Liam, come here."

"Mm."

He nibbled and kissed his way up her torso and Kelly kissed him, pulling her to him as she felt the fullness of him inside her. "Mine," Kelly teased.

He nodded and devoured her lips. "For life."

"Liam." He kissed her again and went from slow and agonizing to harder, faster until her body crashed around him more than once. When he collapsed into her arms, she tightened her legs around him, not letting him move.

"Did I ever tell you how much I love these sexy legs?"
"Nope."
"I love every inch of them," he said.
"And?"
He kissed her again. "And this," he asked as his hands slid to her backside.
"Really," Kelly teased.
He kissed her, and her phone buzzed. "Don't you even think about it," he teased.
"They're..." He kissed her and grabbed the phone then handed it to her.
"Bad timing mom," he teased as he nibbled at her breasts.
"Hi Mom. What's up," Kelly asked.
"We'll be down there at 3 if we can get through the traffic jam. Is that okay," she asked.
"Yes. I'll make the sangria."
"Alright baby girl. We'll see you at 3. Tell Liam we say hi."
"I will mom. Love you guys," Kelly said as she shook her head and he smirked. She hung up with her and Liam nibbled again.
"You are so bad," Kelly said.
"What time are they coming?"
"Three."
"And it's 10. Good," he teased as he kept going.
"Liam."
"Taste too good," he teased.
"You don't quit, we're never gonna make it out of bed."
"And that's bad why?"
Kelly shook her head and he kissed back up her neck. "Shower."

He shook his head. "Nope. I refuse to get out of bed until your toes are in pretzel twists."

Kelly shook her head and he kissed her. "Liam."

"Fine. I get to ask you something first though."

"Which is sexy handsome man of mine?" He kissed her.

"Would you stay in Dublin if I didn't come back here for a while?"

"Depends on how long a while is."

"Month."

Kelly looked at him. "Trying to hide me away from the world?"

"If I wanted to do that, we'd stay in Belfast."

Kelly shook her head. "Liam."

"Yes beautiful."

"Where are we staying?"

"I'm not telling them we landed back in Ireland for a few days so we can be alone. What do you think?"

"How alone?" He smirked and kissed her.

"You'll see when we get there." Kelly kissed him and they got up and went to attempt to shower without ending up back in bed.

She flipped the water on, sliding in as she let the water soak into her hair. She slid the shampoo in and felt him kissing her breasts and nibbling all over again. "I swear you need to at least try and behave," Kelly teased as she rinsed the shampoo out and washed his hair for him. She slid the conditioner in, turned him to rinse his hair and he picked her up.

"What," she teased.

He pinned her against the wall of the shower. "Liam."

"You didn't say yes."

"If I'm with you, and don't get in trouble taking time off, yes." He kissed her again as if the word yes just got him turned on all over again. "Liam."

"I love you."

"And I love you. What's going on in that sexy brain of yours," Kelly asked.

"You meeting my Mum and my friends. You with that ring on your finger."

She smirked. "And you really think my Dad will..." He kissed her.

"I know so," he replied. He shook his head.

"What?"

"You have no idea the things I have planned," he teased.

"Such as handsome?"

"Alone. Just you and me, completely and utterly alone. Even the cell signal sucks out there. I had to get a booster so I could use the internet."

"And that's what you want?"

He nodded. "It's my favorite place. When you see it, you'll understand."

"We need to get things ready downstairs," Kelly said.

"You telling me that I have to share you?"

Kelly nodded and she felt the fullness. It felt too good. It had since the first time they were together. They had sex in the shower. Hot sex that had her legs shaking and his hands and fingers entering places they hadn't. "Liam," she said as he kept going until her body and her insides were shaking. "Aah," he said as his body almost quivered in her arms.

When they finally managed to get out of the shower, her legs were almost too shaky to stand. "Liam."

"Yes gorgeous."

"What did you do," she teased.

"Liked it," he joked.

"Never had that feeling like my entire body was about to explode."

"Good."

Kelly shook her head. "Warn me next time."

He kissed her. "Okay. Mad?"

Kelly smirked. "No."

"Good. Body, mind and soul and even that heart of yours is all mine love. I'm yours. Head to toe. Nobody else. Ever."

"Really," she asked.

He smirked. "You start something when they're here, I'm following through sexy."

She kissed him. "Good."

He cuddled her tight to him as they got washed up and ready for him to meet her folks. He slid his jeans and a t-shirt on and walked downstairs to hear a knock at the door. When he answered, the two flower bouquets had shown. He brought them inside and saw Kelly come downstairs in red shirt and jean shorts.

"Well dang," Liam said.

"What?"

"Yeah, you are gonna be one heck of a temptation for me today," he teased as he handed her the flowers.

"What's this?"

"For the sexiest lady I know."

He kissed her and they went and put the flowers in water. "Liam."

"Yes sexy," he said.

"Can you grab the sangria wine from that top shelf," she asked.

"So, you keep me around because I can reach the top shelf?"

"Partially. A long list of reasons."

"Good," he teased as he handed it to her and Kelly started chopping up peaches. "What are you making love?"

"Sangria."

She put all the fruit in, the juice, the wine then the soda. "Now what," he asked.

"Fridge." He smirked and put it into the fridge for her and slid his arms around her waist.

"What," she asked.

"All of this to impress your folks?"

"I make the sangria because nobody does it like I do. I have the salads, but I have to put a few more..."

He kissed her. "Let me help."

"We need to go get ice." He smirked and kissed her.

"Walk?"

"We could," Kelly said. She grabbed her purse, locked up and they walked down the beach and grabbed the ice. He teased her with ice cold hands all the way back to the house and when they got the ice into the freezer, she went to do something and felt cold hands sliding down the front of her shorts.

"Liam," she said as she laughed and both of them were cracking up laughing on the sofa.

"You are seriously..."

"Ice. That'll be tonight," he teased.

Kelly shook her head. "I swear, you do that I'm dumping ice on you."

He kissed her. "You have to get to it first love," he teased.

She shook her head. "Liam." He kissed her and they were snuggling up together on the sofa.

"Who's coming today," he asked.

"My parents and my brother. I don't think he's bringing the kids and the wife, but you never know," Kelly said.

"So, two guys to impress."

She kissed him. "You don't have to impress anyone."

"Kinda do."

"Liam."

He kissed her. "It's a guy thing. I do. They're the important guys you have around."

"I have to impress your folks and your sister and the kids and your brother-in-law."

"Kinda already did love. My mom called me when you were on your run and left a voicemail."

Kelly looked at him and he pressed play on it. "Liam, she's beautiful and amazing. I can see that love. I can't wait to meet her. Baby, if this is the one, you don't have to wait on me. I can already see it in her eyes. Give me a call later my sweet son. I love you."

Kelly looked at him. "Really," Kelly asked.

"You have nobody to impress."

"Your sister, her husband and the kids."

"You're good love. My friends will be interesting. Just be prepared. They all need filters on their mouths. I told them no Gaelic around you."

"Code words."

He kissed her. "I made them promise. Beyond that, we're good love. I just don't wanna wait that long."

"For what?" He smirked. Kelly shook her head and kissed him. "I love you too."

He kissed her and was about to devour her lips all over again when there was a knock at the door. She looked at her phone and it was just about the time he figured her brother would show. She went to answer with Liam right behind her.

"Yes we're freaking early. Blame it on her," her brother Colin said as she smirked.

He handed her the other salads, put them on the kitchen table and the kids ran inside. Liam gave his sister a hug and his with Hailey came in. "Hailey, big bro, this is Liam. Liam, my brother Colin and his wife Hailey. Those two crazies are Ella and Carter."

"Hi guys," Liam said as they both came over and shook Liam's hand then ran outside.

"Mom, can we go on the sand," Ella asked.

"Bathing suits first then beach," she said as they ran upstairs to the guest room and got changed, then came barreling downstairs and ran out to the beach. Hailey went outside with the kids and Colin gave Kelly another hug hinting that he kinda liked Liam.

"Let me get you a beer," Liam said.

"Thank you," Colin said as he got the beer and walked outside with Liam, giving Kelly 5 minutes to herself. She poured two glasses of sangria, handing one to Hailey and they hung out.

"So, who's the guy," Hailey asked.

"I met him when I was 18 on vacation. He started a business and ended up with a meeting with my boss. They asked me to pick him up at the airport and we've kinda been stuck at the hip since," Kelly said.

"I haven't seen this side of you girl. You never let guys around your folks or us for that matter. What's the deal," Hailey asked.

"I know him. I also know that he gave me this," Kelly said showing her the ring.

"He's Irish?"

Kelly nodded. "I met…"

"He knows what that ring means Kelly. That's kinda huge. When are you two getting…"

"Not yet. He wants to talk to Colin and my Dad."

"Well, he already won Colin over and both the kids," Hailey joked as the kids came over with shells they found.

"Come here for a minute. What do you two think of Liam," she asked the kids.

"Funny beard and really nice," the kids said.

"Let's hope he keeps the shirt on," Kelly said.

"Why," Hailey asked.

"He got a tattoo when I came back here when Nan died. Our initials were in it," Kelly said.

Hailey gave her a hug. "You do realize that the Claddagh means a heck of a lot more than a ring right?"

"It was a family…"

"Damn."

"What," Kelly asked.

"Congrats," she whispered as the boys came over to where they were. Liam leaned over and kissed Kelly.

"What are you two doin out here," Liam asked.

"Talking. The kids are having fun. You going in," Kelly asked her brother.

"Definitely. You coming," Colin asked as Hailey got up and went inside. They got changed and were coming back outside when they saw Kelly and Liam.

"Well," Hailey asked.

"He's a cool guy. What's the deal," Colin asked.

"Remember when I told you about that family ring?"

He nodded and looked, seeing a ring on her finger. "Seriously? Wow," Colin said.

"Not a word."

Colin smirked and they headed out to the water. Liam and Kelly went back in, grabbing towels and Liam slid up behind Kelly.

"Sexy."

"Yes handsome."

"Your sis in law is Irish isn't she?"

Kelly nodded. "Well, cat's kinda out of the bag."

"I know. She probably just spilled the beans to my brother."

"We should go out to the water. Go jump in."

"No trying to take the bikini off."

"Such a party pooper," Liam teased. They went upstairs, changed into swimsuits and grabbed the beach towels then grabbed their phones, putting them into the lock box on the deck and headed out to the water. They were all playing around and splashing when Kelly swore she saw her ex. Liam slid his hand in hers and kissed her, walking her back to the deck. They sat up there and dried off, not even acknowledging him. When Liam saw him about to come up the deck, he kissed her.

"Come," he said. He pulled Kelly into his lap, devouring her lips and Andrew passed the deck, not saying a word.

When he was out of ear shot, Liam shook his head. "He's a tad bit of a psycho," Liam said.

Kelly nodded. "I think we're better off staying up here," Kelly said.

"Love, I get it, but he can't keep ruining moments for you. If you need to call the police, then call. He's practically stalking."

"Not today. He's not ruining the day."

Liam nodded and kissed her as she sat down on the chair with him and dried off a little. When the kids brought her two more seashells and handed one to Liam. "Thank you," Liam said.

"You're welcome," her niece said.

She jumped into Kelly's lap. "Auntie Kelly. Can I have a pocksicle," her niece said.

"Come on. One popsicle. You get half and your brother gets half," Kelly said handing her the popsicle she'd broken in half. She ran out and gave her brother the other half and heard a, "Thank you auntie."

She waved to her nephew and Liam's arm slid around her. "What," Kelly asked.

"Best auntie ever." She smirked and they relaxed until she heard her mom and Dad coming around. Liam kissed her and got up to help her Dad.

They carried everything back and took the heavy stuff inside. "Hey," Kelly said giving her Dad a hug then coming down and hugging her Mom.

"Mom and Dad, this is Liam. Liam, my parents," Kelly said.

"Nice to meet you both," Liam said. When her Mom gave him a hug, she smirked. He went inside and got her parents each a drink and Kelly pulled her shorts on. She came in behind him and got the pot together for the seafood to do a low country boil.

"We grilling the lobster," her Dad asked.

"Liam wanted to," Kelly teased.

"Then we can talk grilling. Come on out here," her Dad said. Her mom saw her putting the salads onto the table and tossing the green salad.

"So, that's him," her mom asked.

Kelly nodded. "He's a sweetheart mom."

"Oh, I know. He's already talking barbecue with your Dad. Your brother messaged me and told me there was a hot guy hanging with his sister. I take it that means he likes him."

"Well, that's good," Kelly said.

"And he told me about the ring."

Kelly shook her head. "Mom."

"You even look different around him. You got your confidence back. It's like he's your security blanket," her mom said.

"Sort of. We do that for each other," Kelly said.

"If he's the one you like, don't let go. Just make sure you get to know him," her mom said.

"I've known him since I was 18 and in Ireland mom."

She smirked. "I almost hoped," she teased.

"He invited me to come with him to Belfast then to Dublin."

"Kelly, be careful. That's all I'm gonna say." Kelly nodded and gave her mom a hug then headed outside to hang with the guys. Kelly kissed Liam and he slid his arm around her.

"The man knows how to grill," her Dad teased.

"Oh, I know. He made really good steaks the other night," Kelly teased as Liam kissed her forehead.

"Come with me for a minute," her Dad said as he walked her out to the beach.

"What's wrong," Kelly asked.

"That's the guy isn't it?"

"What guy," Kelly asked.

"The one you cried over when you came home from Ireland."

Kelly nodded. "He called so many times."

"Dad."

"If he proposed to you, how would you feel," her Dad asked.

"Depends. Did you give him your blessing?"

"So long as that's what you want."

Kelly nodded. "Dad, remember when you said to put my feelings on paper and it'd make me feel better?"

Her Dad nodded. "He did. He handed me the notebook."

Her Dad hugged her. "If he's the one, don't let go of him. He loves you more than you even know. I gave him my blessing. Just let me know when he does. I also have a small present for you."

"What?"

"Remember when you said you wanted to redo the steps and repaint?"

Kelly nodded. "When you go, I'm getting it done and putting in a high-end security system. He told me about the situation with the old boyfriend." Kelly took a deep breath. "You need to start keeping a gun in the house. Anyone comes near you like that again you call the police." Kelly nodded and gave her Dad a hug. "Baby girl, if it's that bad, you need to tell me. Tell someone. Please."

Kelly nodded and her niece and nephew ran over and tackled their grandpa. Colin and Hailey came in with the kids and they all sat up on the deck, drying off and enjoying the sunshine while they all caught up. Liam was either holding Kelly's hand or had his arm wrapped around her all afternoon. He helped her put the steampot on, he went and put the lobster on the grill and her Dad got up to help.

"Now I like this. The boys doing all the cooking," her mom joked as Kelly went inside to get them each refills. She handed them to her mom and came outside, handing Liam a Guinness.

"Dad, did you want a refill?"

"Do you have that famous sweet tea?"

She smirked and went in and grabbed one and handed it to her Dad. The kids were building sandcastles and Kelly brought them out a drink.

"Thank you auntie," Ella said.

"You're welcome. Nice castle by the way." They both smirked and she went to come up the steps when Liam took her hand and walked her inside.

"What's wrong," Kelly asked.

He picked her up and sat her on the counter. "You had Guinness in your fridge."

She almost laughed. "Part of the grocery delivery."

He shook his head and kissed her. "Yeah. Ice. Definitely ice. Payback."

"Yeah, yeah. You say that now," Kelly joked as he kissed her.

"Thank you."

"You're welcome handsome."

"What were you and Dad talking about?"

"You." He smirked. She kissed him, slid off the counter and walked outside with him.

"You're making me hungry," her brother said.

"Good thing, because it's done," her Dad said. Kelly got the food, and drained off the water, covered it all in seasoning and dumped it onto the table for everyone to nibble at as the kids ran up and cleaned up then were up to their elbows in old bay in minutes.

Liam plated the lobster and the adults went in and grabbed salads then sat down as a family and had dinner. "This is way too good," Liam said.

"It's a summer thing. The usual. Normally, not this much food, but it's a tradition."

"I like it," Liam said as he fed Kelly a piece of crab leg. They hung out until all the food was gone. The salads were amazing, the seafood was to die for and the kids curled up on the beach on their beach blankets to watch fireworks. Kelly brought them each a popsicle for dessert and her mom brought out the plates of cobbler for dessert for the adults.

"And what is this delicious smelling thing," Liam asked as he snuggled Kelly to him.

"Peach cobbler. One of Kelly's favorites. Homemade peach ice cream on top," her mom said.

"This is so freaking good," Liam said as he took his first taste of it.

"Now you know why it's my favorite," Kelly said.

They all had their dessert and Liam took the dishes in and cleaned up with Kelly behind him.

"And," Kelly asked.

"You need the recipe."

"I have it."

"Good."

He kissed her. "I think your Dad likes me."

"Good thing."

He kissed her. Kelly finished with the dishes and her niece came inside. "What's up pumpkin head," Kelly asked as she picked her up.

"Uncle Liam needs to come see fireworks," Ellie said.

"Alright. You come show me where the best spot is," Liam said.

She reached for him and after a kiss to Kelly, he walked her outside and sat down on the steps with the kids.

When Hailey came inside, Kelly had a smirk. "She called..."

"Yeah I heard. She now has a crush on Uncle Liam."

"When did she start calling him that," Kelly asked.

"Before dinner. She asked if she could call him that. I think the kids officially like him and so does your brother. If he's the one Kelly."

When she nodded, Hailey hugged her. "Just call me and tell me how he did it."

Kelly nodded with a smirk and they all headed outside. Kelly got a refill of her sangria and slid a sweater over her shoulders as they all came and sat down together on the steps.

"Kelly," Faith said as she walked down the beach.

"Hey. Happy Memorial Day," Kelly said.

Faith came over. "I have to. You know it's my tradition," Faith teased as Kelly handed Faith her phone and she got a photo of them all together on the steps. Faith handed the phone to Kelly, gave everyone a hug, including Liam and headed off with Ridge to walk down the beach.

Kelly sent the photo to everyone and when she sent it to Liam, she added a note:

You have a room and staircase full of people that love you. One I'm keeping my eye on. She has a little crush on Uncle Liam.

When she felt Liam's arm around her, she smirked. Her niece was in his lap. When the fireworks started, Kelly smirked as they all looked up. Kelly nudged him and he kissed her. "Still in trouble," Liam whispered. Kelly smirked and when the fireworks were done, they all finished their drinks, cleaned up and came inside.

"I'll toss the shells at the house. Thank you for all of this," her Dad said as Kelly walked them out. Her mom pulled Liam aside.

"Liam," her mom said.

"Yes."

"I know that you wanted our blessing. Seeing her happy like that, you got it. Just make sure you come and visit alright?"

Liam nodded, giving her mom a hug. They all headed off, leaving Kelly and Liam alone again. Kelly cleaned up everything else from outside, put the towels in the washer and Liam did the dishes. When she came in, everything was in the dishwasher and it was on. He sat her on the counter and Kelly smirked. "What?"

"You bought me Guinness."

"Everyone else..."

He kissed her. "I know. Your mom gave me her blessing," he said.

"Good."

"And I think you're right. Your niece hugged me."

Kelly smirked. "I know. Hailey told me she likes Uncle Liam."

"You good with her saying that?"

"You mean since I can't really get rid of you now," Kelly joked.

He kissed her and wrapped her legs around his hips. "You never could beautiful."

"I could've tried," she teased.

He locked the back door, went and locked the front door and came back over to her. "What," Kelly asked as he slid her shorts off.

"Liam." He picked her up and walked upstairs, leaning her onto the bed in her bedroom.

"What are you up to," Kelly asked.

"Stay there."

"Liam." He kissed her, walked downstairs, got two glasses of Jameson's and a glass of ice and walked upstairs. He set them down on the bedside table.

"And what are you doing with that handsome?"

"First off, I need to undo this," he said untying her bikini. When she felt kisses against her stomach, she shook her head.

"Liam."

"Yes love," he said as she felt his breath against her.

"What are you up to?"

"Seducing my woman," he teased.

Chapter 8

When the lights went out, he grabbed the glass of ice. "Liam." He kissed her hip and she felt something very cold. When she felt the ice against her, she shook her head. "Liam, what are you doin," Kelly asked.

"Payback."

She felt his fingers and her back arched as he nibbled and licked her body into almost overheating. "Liam." She felt him taunt her even more as her body was almost humming. He kissed up her torso as the taunting got worse and deeper.

"Yes sexy," he said.

Kelly kissed him and he devoured her lips. "Mm," Kelly said as he kissed her neck.

"Oh really," he teased. He kissed her again and she moaned into his mouth.

"Liam."

"All mine," he teased as she tried to stop his taunting.

"Nope."

"Liam."

He kissed her again and it got even more intense.

"Aah," she said as her toes curled.

"Keep taunting me, you get this," he joked.

"Aah," she said again as he felt her body throbbing around his fingers. She reached for the drawstring of his shorts and pulled at it, pulling him to her as he moved towards her.

"Something you want," he teased. She nodded and he felt her hand on him, getting him as turned on as she was. "Kelly."

"What," she asked. He grabbed her hand and stopped her. "You started it," she teased. He shook his head, undid the bikini top with his free hand and slid into her arms as he pulled her onto his lap so they were face to face and he could taunt her even more.

Now, it was more intense. Deeper. Hotter. He could continue to taunt and she was in control. "Kelly."

"Yes handsome."

"Don't..." She kissed him and kept going until his nails were digging into her backside.

"Shit," he said. Kelly kissed him and her body tightened around him.

"Don't move."

When she did, his eyes almost rolled into the back of his head. "Damn," he said.

"Now, what were you saying?"

He shook his head and kissed her. "You need to behave fiancée."

"Liam."

"You feel too good. Way too good. I don't want you moving one inch," he said.

"So, if I..."

He pulled her tight to him. "My turn," he teased.

"You mean if I did this," Kelly said as she did an exercise that she knew would make him squirm.

"Shit. Kelly."

"What?"

"You keep doing that and you aren't sleeping at all tonight. You may not walk all week," he whispered.

"Oh really," Kelly said. He nodded and kissed her again, leaning her back onto the bed.

"Damn woman," he said.

"What?"

"I don't think that's happened ever."

"What?"

"I could barely even think."

Kelly kissed him. "Good."

He shook his head and he slid out of her arms. "Aah," she said.

"Good. You deserve it," he teased. Kelly shook her head and he pulled her to him.

"What," Kelly asked.

"If I told you that I wanted us to do it in Belfast, what would you say?"

"Do what?"

He shook his head. "You know what love."

"Maybe."

"Very good answer." He kissed her again and he snuggled her to him.

When she felt his fingers start taunting her legs into trembling again, she stopped him. "What," he asked.

"You aren't gonna make it through that," Kelly teased.

"True," he teased. He pulled up the blanket and fell asleep with her in his arms not long later. Kelly smirked, finally getting over the bad feelings from the day before. His arm tightened around her and she was happy. In no way tired at all, but happy. She grabbed the notebook and he held on a little closer. She went back to the older entries. To when they'd spent that one week inseparable:

> *For the first time in my stupid life, I'm falling for a girl. I'm falling for the damn girl from the USA. The girl that I know won't be here next week. Why her? I kissed her today and it's like my entire body started tingling. I fell asleep with my arms around her and I was so turned on that I swore it would wake her up. I would've done something. It's only the first night that she let me sleep in here with her. I want to taste her. Feel her body connected to mine. Feel how good it feels being with the girl I'm in love with. I've messed around in my life, but never with someone where I felt like this. I want to bury myself inside her and lock myself in place. Attach us together for life. My mum would kill me if I handed her the Claddagh ring. Not after a week, but this is my soul mate. My "anam cara". The one that I'm supposed to be connected with. I can't lose her. I also can't talk her into sleeping with me. I can't talk her into letting me do what I want to. I can't. All I know is that this woman in my arms is all I ever wanted. She's all I'll ever want. Her hugs make me want her. Her body is a drug that I want more and more of. I'm gonna marry her. I'm gonna find a ring or a leaf that I can make into a ring and say it before she leaves. I have to. This is my woman. I want to*

memorize every inch. Every curve. Every single cell. I'd do whatever I have to. I want to taste her skin. I want to taste her. Hell. This is getting me even more turned on.

When she felt kisses on her shoulder, she marked the page and put the book down. "How's your reading?"

"And are you sure you wrote all of that before you came here?"

He kissed her neck and she felt him nod. "I thought you were sleeping?"

"I love you."

"Love you more handsome." When she felt his hand slide between her legs, she knew he was wide awake. "What you doin handsome?"

"Taunting you."

"And?" When he took her hand and slid it around his length, she shook her head. "You do know that you need sleep right?"

He smirked and she held on a little tighter and started taunting him. "Kelly."

"What handsome?"

"No more taunting."

"So, if I did this," she said as her backside rubbed against him.

"Then you'll need this," he said handing her the glass of Jameson's.

"And why is that," Kelly teased as his arm pulled her tight against him. He kissed her back, trailing the kisses from her shoulder, down her spine then he smirked and slid her to her stomach. "Liam, what are you up to?"

When she felt his lips against her, then his tongue, her heart started racing. "Drink," he teased as she felt his hands, then his lips kissing her backside. She finished her drink and he smirked as she put the glass on the bedside table. "Liam."

"Mm." He pulled her back and she smirked. When the teasing intensified, he smirked and Kelly's legs were starting to tremble.

"What are you up to," Kelly asked.

"Taking advantage of my fiancée," he teased.

"Meaning what," she joked.

When she felt him against her, it was almost comforting, but not knowing what he was up to was making her nervous. "My girl," Liam said.

"What," Kelly asked. They started having sex again but with him almost overpowering her on the bed. Intense was an understatement. Filling her to the hilt almost felt too good. They kept going and going until her body was reaching that climax that he craved then felt that fullness in other ways. "Liam," Kelly said.

"Too much," he asked. Kelly shook her head. He kissed her back and the feel of his scruff against her back was even too much. They kept going until her body couldn't take anymore and he collapsed onto her back. They curled up together and he smirked. She felt his chest against her back, knowing that their hearts were side by side. "You alright," Liam asked.

"That's what you were wondering," Kelly teased. He nodded, rubbing the scruff on his face against her shoulder and kissing it.

"Love."

"I'm good," she replied as he smirked.

"Good. Not mad?"

Kelly shook her head, and he kissed her with a snap noise. "And what was..."

He kissed her, got up and cleaned up a little then slid back into bed with her, snuggling her back into his arms.

"Liam."

"Yes beautiful."

"Thank you for today."

"For what? Seducing my fiancée until her entire body is spent a few times."

"For everything with my family. For distracting me. For this morning. For tonight. For all of it."

"It's called being a good boyfriend love. Besides. I like your folks and your brother and sis in law and the kids. They're good people." Kelly kissed him, then kissed his tattoo. "What," he asked.

"If I'd known then that we'd be here right now, in this bed, in my house."

"What?"

"If I'd stayed and never left." He kissed her again, devouring her lips until her hand slid to the side of his face.

"Not that I don't love being here, but if I'd had all of this and been with you too, I think I would've been just as happy as I am right now. We'd probably be..."

"Married with little kids like your niece and nephew running around?" Kelly nodded.

"We could have all of that love. If that's what you want, tell me."

She looked up at him. "Liam."

"Tell me. You want to move to Dublin; we can buy a house or renovate mine. You want to move to Belfast; we can renovate my place or buy something else. Whatever you want to do. You want to commute back and forth every other week or every other month, we do it. My business is fine. Now that your boss and I are partners in it, it means more time with you. I just want you love. I want to go home and see my folks and introduce you. I want them to spend time with you. Beyond that, I just want us."

Kelly snuggled in closer to him. "You kinda already have me Liam."

"Kinda?"

She kissed him. "Been yours since that first kiss when we were 18."

He shook his head and hugged her tight to him. "And if I said that was the one and only thing I dreamt of hearing since we met?"

She kissed him. "Get used to it," she replied as he held her close. He shook his head and they both nodded off. Feeling her head on his chest was the feeling he'd wanted. Being with her heart, body and soul was happening.

She knew every innermost thought. Every feeling he had. Every good and bad moment was in that notebook. He knew what she was reading. He knew what section because he'd marked the pages himself. She'd read about the day he knew he was in love with her. That's what had calmed her those nights that she was worried. Now, it's like a weight had been lifted. They were floating in their love cloud all over again. Happy. Calm.

Kelly woke up the next morning to arms wrapped around her and him kissing her shoulder. "Morning sexy," Liam said.

"Morning. How long have you been up," Kelly asked as he smirked.

"Long enough to see my sexy woman sleeping like an angel. Not on a run."

She turned to face him and he devoured her lips. "What's with the grin ear to ear?"

"Nice to wake up to you and not a note."

She smirked and he snuggled her to him. "Liam."

"What," he asked as he snuggled her.

"You could come with me," she teased.

"About time," he whispered. "But you have work." She looked for the clock. "It's 6:30. You're good love." She kissed him and got up. "Where are you going?"

"To get showered and changed so I can get into the office."

"Kelly."

"We."

He smirked. "Then we're conserving water," he teased as he flipped the shower on and saw her slide in. He slid her under the water and washed her hair for her, then picked her up. "What are you up to," Kelly asked.

He leaned her against the wall of the shower and kissed her, wrapping her legs tight around him. "Really," she teased.

"Would've been better if you hadn't jumped out of bed."

She kissed him and he smirked. He slid her to her feet, coming up with a much better plan, ran the conditioner through her hair and washed up. When he rinsed out his shampoo and felt her hand on him, he shook his head and got a smirk ear to ear.

"Kelly, you start that you do know that you're finishing it," he teased.

"Oh, I know," she teased.

He shook his head, rinsed her conditioner out and picked her up, sitting her on the bathroom counter. "What," she teased as she started laughing.

"Dry off."

"Liam."

"You have no idea what I'm..." She kissed him and he picked her up, walking her into the bedroom and leaning her onto the bed.

"What," Kelly asked.

"How long does it take to get to the office?"

"Half hour max. Why," Kelly asked.

He smirked. "Not promising anything, but you might end up being late."

She kissed him and felt his fingers start teasing. "Liam."

"Yes sexy fiancée." He kissed her and the taunting started getting worse. "You started it by the way," he teased.

"Oh I know," she joked as she all of a sudden felt that full feeling all over again, he went deeper, making her body throb around him. The more he thrusted into her, the more intense everything was. She kissed him and it wasn't passion. It was carnal need. A want. An addiction. He barely let that kiss break as they had sex. When he held on that much tighter, it was the best feeling in the planet to her.

"Kelly."

"What," she asked catching her breath. He kissed her and her nails were digging into his shoulders. Her body crashed around him over and over again, and when she knew that he was almost at that point, she slid him to his back.

"What," he asked. She kept going, making it even more intense for him as his nails dug into her backside. "Kelly."

"Yes sexy fiancée," she teased as his body exploded into her and he pinned her back onto the bed.

"Don't move."

"Liam." He devoured her lips, holding her tight as their hearts raced in time. "What's wrong," Kelly asked. He kissed her again with a kiss that gave her head to toe goosebumps and made her forget all sense of time.

"Promise me something," he said as he kissed down her neck.

"What?"

"You're mine forever," he said.

"Already have been, and always..."

He kissed her again. "I mean it."

"What would change Liam? Where are you going that you're gonna have to ever wonder?"

"If we don't..."

"Liam."

"If we don't work, nobody else does that."

Kelly smirked. "Never happened before. You're not going anywhere and either am I Liam. I'm not going anywhere without you."

He kissed her. "Promise me."

Kelly nodded, not knowing what that fear was behind his words. When her phone buzzed a minute later, she grabbed it. "Well, at least that's something. The morning meeting was pushed...."

He kissed her. "Wear it."

"Wear what?"

He smirked. Kelly shook her head. "After we get back from Dublin."

"How late are you working?"

"Maybe 3 or 4. Why?" He smirked. "Liam."

"Dinner. At the hotel. Grab some clothes for tomorrow and your stuff for overnight."

"Behave," Kelly teased.

Liam kissed her. "Never ever plan to. Not around you sexy fiancée."

She kissed him and when he managed to get up, Kelly smirked. She put her stuff into an overnight bag, sliding the journal in with it. He kissed her and got cleaned up and got changed while she got ready. The fact that he looked sexy as all get out in a dress shirt and dress pants was too much of a distraction.

"Liam."

"Yes sexy fiancée," he teased as he put on his cologne. She shook her head and slid on a sundress. She grabbed her blazer just in case, finished doing her hair and he kissed her neck. "Breakfast," he asked.

"Are you cooking?" He nodded and kissed her again then went downstairs to make breakfast. When she came downstairs barefoot with her blazer and phone in her hand, he smirked.

"My sexy lass. Open," he said.

He fed her the first part of the breakfast and Faith had a grin. "Lobster omelets?" He nodded and kissed her. "Yum. Thank you handsome." He kissed her and got a smirk ear to ear. "What?"

"See, at home, I'd put this over toast."

"We can if you want to," Kelly said. He shook his head and she saw the fresh peaches made to look like hearts.

She slid her arms around him and he plated their omelets, kissed her and they sat down to eat. "When do you want to fly back," Liam asked.

"I have to talk to Faith about it, but maybe a week or two. Why?"

"The guys messaged me and asked. Mom said she wanted to get some family together for when you come." Kelly smirked.

"I bet," Kelly said.

He kissed her. "Just promise me that you don't change your mind and vanish again."

"Are you that worried," Kelly asked as she cleaned up the dishes.

"To be honest, yeah."

She shook her head and he kissed her neck as he put his dishes in the washer. "What are they gonna say that I don't know," Kelly asked.

"All the stupid crap I did when I was losing it over you coming home."

She shook her head. "Liam, I don't scare that easily." He kissed her and she slid her heels on. "You ready?"

"Give me the keys."

"For what?"

"I'm driving in." She smirked and they headed off, locking up behind them. He slid his cell in his pocket, she put hers into her laptop bag, they grabbed their stuff and overnight bags and went down to the office.

He pulled in, they locked up the truck, and headed up to the office. Luckily, she made it in before a lot of the staff were there. "Why do you come in so early," Liam asked as he closed her office door.

"I get more done without everyone around. Why do you ask handsome?"

"Because there's something else I wanted to do this morning."

"I thought we did," Kelly teased as he kissed her. He sat her on the edge of her desk and slid her heels off. "What you up to," Kelly asked.

He leaned towards her and kissed her. "I love you," he said.

"And I love you back."

"Good. That thing we were talking about."

"When we go back to Ireland."

He nodded. "My friends literally have no filter. Most of what they're gonna say is a bunch of crap. You know that right?"

Kelly kissed him. "Not gonna change anything."

"You sure I can't talk you into letting me propose before we go?"

Kelly kissed him. "It's up to you when and if you decide to. All I'm saying is that I need more than a weekend."

He kissed her. "Okay," Liam said. He kissed her again and she smirked as her assistant knocked.

"Hey Allie," Kelly said as she came in. "You remember Liam."

"Mr. Murphy," her assistant said. "Here's your papers from Friday afternoon, the paperwork you need for the meeting and your messages. Can I get either of you a latte," her assistant asked.

"Remember the Irish cream one that you got me?"

"Yes ma'am."

"Two iced."

"Will do. Nice to see you back Mr. Murphy." He smirked and Kelly kissed him.

"Now, go get some actual work done handsome."

"Back at ya fiancée," Liam teased.

Both of them spent most of the morning getting caught up on paperwork until she got called into her meeting. "Do you need anything," Kelly asked.

He kissed her. "Yeah, but she's going into a meeting. You okay if I use your office?" She nodded, kissed him and went to her meeting, phone and laptop in hand.

Liam called his buddy Kieran. "I still can't believe you went all the way there for a girl you knew a week," Kieran said.

"You know what a dang mess I was when she left and we lost touch."

"And you went all the way to the USA? Seriously?"

"I came for work. I didn't even know it was her until I saw her at the airport."

"So, did you tell her?"

"Tell her what Kieran? That I was messing around and calling women by her name? That I drank myself into a dang coma practically when I thought something had happened to her?"

"That you almost ended up with a kid. That you had to be ripped off of someone when they started making comments about her."

"Kieran, please just don't. She doesn't need to hear any of it. I'm marrying this woman if she'll have me. I'm gonna be back in a few weeks. I just need everyone shutting up about messing around. About the insanity when I thought she was gone."

"You're still going through it. The difference is that she's beside you."

"Kieran."

"Fine. I'll tell the guys to keep their filters on about all of it, but you know that she's gonna know."

"I don't want that almost a Dad thing coming out Kieran. Not a damn word."

"Alright. When are you coming back?"

"Two weeks I think. I'll let you know, but I meant it. Not a word."

"Alright. Go be the showoff."

"Liam, no Gaelic."

"That I can't prevent."

Liam shook his head. "We can talk when I'm back."

"Where's the woman?"

"Meeting."

"Fine. I'll talk to you later." They hung up and Liam breathed a sigh of relief. That was the last thing he needed. Literally, the last.

Kelly got into the meeting and it was her and Faith for the first little bit. "You two are too cute," Faith said.

"About that. He wanted to take me to Ireland for a few weeks. Are you okay if I go? I mean, I can get logged into work when you…"

"Girl, you haven't taken any vacation time in years. We owe you two months. More if you count this year. Go. Dad offered the jet. Go with him. Log in whenever and check emails when you can. Something important comes up, I know how to reach you. You need to."

"He kinda…"

"Hold on. Is that one of those Irish rings?" Kelly nodded. "He proposed."

"Not exactly."

"Kelly, you haven't been there since you were a kid. Go."

Kelly nodded. "We're thinking in a week or two."

"Whenever you want to."

"I'm waiting. I have a ton of work to actually do."

"I gather he didn't get a house?"

"He was at my place all weekend," Kelly said as everyone else started coming in.

"Then go," Faith teased. Kelly nodded and they got down to business. Kelly sent an email to Liam:

To: Liam Murphy

From: That girl you knew at 18

Faith said she owes me vacation time. Two weeks. Max. I told her we were gonna go in a week or two. That work? - K

Liam was reading through emails when it popped up:

To: The sexy woman I know

From: That guy who warms your bed

Two weeks sounds good. PS you aren't gonna want to go home. Are we allowed to extend that for an extra week? You may not be out of bed yet. – Your favorite Irish fiancée.

Kelly smirked and Faith nudged her. They got the meeting done and Kelly smirked:

To: That sexy woman I love
From: Your very turned on fiancée
Hurry back love. I have a surprise for you. – L

Kelly got up and Faith smirked. "You two are so damn cute," Faith said.

"I'll keep you posted on times. I kinda don't want to stay too long," Kelly said.

"You'll change your mind when you get there. You can work from there if you want a day or two a week. Just keep up on the emails." Kelly nodded and went down to her office.

When she came into her office, he was sitting in her desk chair.

"Hey handsome," Kelly said.

"Lock the door."

She shook her head and smirked, putting her laptop and phone down. "And what did you want..." He got up, kissed her and sat her on the sofa.

"What are you up to," Kelly asked.

He kissed her again and snuggled her to him. "So, I was thinking."

"Oh no," she teased.

"What would you think about us going out to a nice restaurant for dinner."

"Where?"

"Peninsula something."

"Peninsula Grill?" He nodded. "You sure?"

"Kinda made a reservation."

Kelly kissed him. "Sounds good handsome."

"Good. I got us a booth at the back."

"Why?" He smirked. "Liam."

"And there's something coming here."

"Did you seriously online shop while I was in the meeting?"

He smirked. "While going through emails, yes."

"And sending me dirty emails."

He kissed her and slid her onto his lap. "You like those emails," he teased.

Kelly kissed him. "So bad."

He kissed her. "Nope. This would be bad," he teased as his hands slid up her legs and his hand slid under her lace panties.

"I swear, what are you doin," Kelly asked.

"Seducing my fiancée." Kelly shook her head and he kissed her as two fingers slid inside her.

"Liam."

"Shh." When she heard the zipper of his dress pants, she shook her head.

"Dirty mind," she said.

"Good thing you wore a dress," he whispered as he pulled her on top of him so they were having sex on her sofa.

"Liam," Kelly said as he kept going, teasing as he pounded into her. "What are you doing," Kelly asked as he nibbled her lips as they had sex.

"Making you want me as badly as I want you every damn second of the day."

Her body started throbbing and he kept taunting as she climaxed and he didn't stop. When he held onto her, pulling her to him, she knew that he was again at her mercy.

"Liam."

"Yes sexy."

"What are we gonna do in that corner table," she whispered as her body throbbed around him and he almost held his breath and dug his nails into her backside.

"These are staying off. Good enough answer?"

Kelly smirked and kissed him. "Depends. What are you wearing?"

He smirked. "We could just leave dinner for another night," he teased as she kissed him.

Kelly smirked. "Nope. You're behaving through dinner," she said.

"Until you see what I got."

Kelly kissed him. "What time are we allowed to get out of here?"

"3. I have another meeting."

"By the way, Kieran is looking forward to meeting you."

"And what is he going to keep quiet for you?"

"Some childhood ridiculousness. Nothing out of the norm. How I flipped out after you left."

She shook her head and slid off his lap. "Liam."

"I know."

Kelly went and sat down at her desk, readjusting her panties. "No more of that at work," Kelly joked.

He got up, kissed her and sat down at the table. "So, do you want to stay in Belfast first or in Dublin," he asked.

"Why don't we go see your mom first."

"Dublin it is."

"What are you planning?"

"Reliving a few good memories. Taking you to a few places that we went to when you were there."

Kelly smirked. "Liam, don't you have actual work to do?"

"Waiting on an email from the webmaster. They're working on linking the software so that it works for where your boss wanted it. We had all the stuff together before I left. It's just putting it all together and making sure nobody can hack it."

"And?"

"Planning on what to do when I get you on that plane."

"Liam."

"What," he teased.

"Emails." He smirked and slid his chair over to her and kissed her.

She got some work done and saw an email come in from him:

> *To: The sexy lady over there*
>
> *From: The guy you love*
>
> *Changing dinner to tomorrow night. Have a better idea for tonight. Crab shack by the water. Sundress.*

Kelly shook her head and replied:

> *To: the guy with the dirty mind*
>
> *From: The woman you're all hot for*
>
> *I left it at the house. We could go for dinner out there. PS I know what you're up to handsome. We really should check you out of the hotel – That sexy lady*

He smirked:

> *To: My dream lass*
>
> *From: That Irish guy you like*

I can go get it while you're at your meeting and meet you downstairs. We can check out in the morning. FYI I love you.

Kelly shook her head:

To: My Irish crazy fiancée

From: Your woman

And now you're dressing me? If you really want to. Just remember the truck has GPS. Press go home and it'll give you directions. By the way, bring the panties. I'm wearing them like it or not.

He got a grin ear to ear:

To: My woman.
From: Your man
You won't need them for long. Had an idea. You up for a surprise?

"What kind of surprise," Kelly asked.

When he got up and came over and whispered his answer, Kelly shook her head. "Don't you even go there," Kelly said.

He slid a small bottle in her hand. "Liam."

She saw the warming substance and shook her head. "Do you ever not have..."

He kissed her. "Around you, no."

"And where did that come from?"

"My bag that I brought with us."

"And what other things did you hide in there?"

"Something we'll need tonight and probably run out of by next weekend."

Kelly shook her head. "Liam." He kissed her. Kelly shook her head. "Behave while we're here." He nodded and sent her an email:

To: My fiancée

From: Your soon to be you know what

We'll go to the house and you can change then we'll do dinner at the crab shack place. We can go back to the hotel tonight. PS I love you.

Kelly smirked and got up. "What," Liam asked. She kissed him and went and unlocked the door. Not 10 minutes later, her assistant knocked.

"What's up," Kelly asked.

"The meeting was cancelled. The board changed it to tomorrow. They're just announcing that you got a promotion."

"What," Kelly asked. She gave Kelly the memo:

Announcing the new Vice President of Travel and media. Kelly Ryan received a promotion today to the new sector of the business working hand in hand with our President Faith Sams. Congratulations Kelly.

She looked at Liam. "What?"

"I got a promotion."

He looked and saw the email. "That's amazing," Liam said.

"And completely out of the dang blue. Nobody said a word in that meeting this morning."

"Babe."

"Liam, this is huge," Kelly said. She saw another email come in from Faith's Dad:

> *Congratulations. I heard about the trip. Go and enjoy yourself. You got a bit of a bonus too. Proud of you. Liam's a great guy. All I ask is that when you come back, you let me know. That meeting tomorrow is just a formality. I have a bunch of paperwork for you to sign. I'll get your assistant to bring it in.*

"It's actually freaking happening," Kelly said. Her assistant knocked and showed her that the update to her position was already going on her door.

"Congrats. Here's all the paperwork you needed to sign. Just let me know when y'all are ready to head out. I'll get everything else together," her assistant said.

"Lunch," Kelly asked.

"Lobster rolls on their way up," she teased. Kelly smirked. "Thank you."

"Most welcome and congrats!" Her assistant headed out and Liam got up and kissed Kelly.

"This is good right," Liam asked.

Kelly smirked. "I guess it is I think."

He kissed her again and wrapped his arms around her. "This is kinda huge. You have to admit it," Liam teased.

"This also means more work and me having to be in the office..."

He kissed her. "It's fine. I'm probably gonna have to be here more too love. It's all good."

The only thing running through her mind was that if things blew up in her face, he was gonna be a number of offices away. She'd have to face him every minute of every single day.

"Baby," he said. She shook her head. "What's wrong?"

"Nothing Liam. Just thinking."

"Then stop thinking. Just be happy. We have each other. We can do whatever you want to. You want to stay in the same office, you can. You want to go home, you can. You can do what you want to. All I wanted was for you to come to Ireland with me and now you are."

"With you worrying about what your friends are gonna say."

He looked at her and kissed her. "I love you. I'm proud of you love. I always will be."

"Liam, what if..."

He kissed her. "No stressing."

Not long later, her assistant came in with lunch for them and sodas from her favorite soda place. "Thank you," Kelly said.

"Most welcome Miss VP." Her assistant headed out, leaving them alone in her office. Liam slid her heels off and pulled her chair to his.

"What," Kelly asked.

SOUTHERN TEMPTATION

He kissed her, devouring her lips and slid her into his lap. "What would you like handsome?"

He kissed her again and smirked. "Whatever you want will happen. You know that right?"

"Meaning what Liam?"

"Meaning you want to work from Ireland, you can. You want to work from here, you can. You want us to run off into the forest in Ireland and live in a hut, we may need money, but we can. You tell me and I'll make it happen."

"And if I said I wanted to clone myself so I could be in two places at once?"

He smirked. "Not sure that I can pull it off, but I can always try love. I want that smile back that you had yesterday."

She kissed him and he pulled her tighter to him. "What," she asked.

"Attempting to behave."

She smirked and shook her head. "Then I need to sit back in my own chair."

"Nope."

She felt his hand slide up her leg. "Liam."

"What?"

"Not in here."

He kissed her. "Not happening in here Liam."

"Such a party pooper," he teased.

"You have all night tonight handsome. We're getting work done then heading out early. That's the deal," she teased.

He motioned for her to come closer. Kelly leaned into his arms. "What," she asked.

"I love you."

She kissed him, and he snuggled her to him. "I love you back," Kelly said.

"We're good. Celebrating tonight. What's the other meeting?"

"That will be a short one I think. It's just helping out with one of Faith's projects. We'll be out of here by..."

He kissed her again. "You wear dresses in here, be prepared," he joked.

"Liam."

"Yes fiancée."

"Behave." He shook his head, kissed her and they got back to having lunch.

"Why is yours bigger than mine," he teased.

"Mine has salad instead of bread," Kelly said as she handed him the half of a lobster roll that came with hers.

He smirked and kissed her again and they finished lunch. Around 1, her assistant knocked. "What's up," Kelly asked.

"Faith said she didn't need you at the meeting after all. You have the rest of the afternoon free," her assistant said.

"I'm gonna take Liam to the hotel and get him checked out then. If you need me, call. I'll be at the house."

"Alright," her assistant said with a smirk. She got her paperwork together, signed off on the contract then noticed something not normal:

If you decide to work from Ireland, must be on minimum 10 hours per week and available for meetings. Full access to company plane and only permitted to stay in company handled hotels.

Chapter 9

She shook her head. "How in the flipping world," Kelly asked.

"What else is in there that has you worried?" Kelly went through the rest of the contract, line by line and saw what her yearly salary would be, her vacation time, her yearly bonus and the other details and was stunned. When she got to the last page, there was a note from the CEO:

> *Yes I got them to add it in. You've worked your tail off for us (very much appreciated) and you deserve all of it. If you go, just keep in touch with us while you're there. Him signing on with us brought in 9 figures to the business. You're the best non-family addition to our team. Congrats!*

Kelly almost got choked up and he shook his head. "Woman, smile."

She shook her head, signed the paperwork, scanned a copy for herself, signed the second copy for legal and handed them off to her assistant. "We're heading out. If you need anything, let me know?"

Her assistant nodded and Kelly and Liam headed out with their laptops, phones and bags. "Where to fiancée," Liam asked as they got in the truck.

"We're getting you checked out of the hotel then..."

"Or we just stay tonight."

"Liam."

He smirked. "Really?"

"One night of you not vanishing for a run, one more night of curling up in bed together. I'm getting the dress for tomorrow dropped off at the hotel tonight anyway."

"I thought you wanted to go to the crab shack tonight."

He kissed her at the light. "I need a shorter skirt on you," he teased. Kelly shook her head.

They parked, got up to his suite and he saw a suit bag on the bed, a box with heels and a lingerie bag. "Liam." "What?"

"What's all of this?"

"For my fiancée."

"Do I know her?"

He slid his arms around her and slid the blazer off. "Liam."

"This way, you don't have to worry about anything. It's all here. It's to make you feel good."

Kelly turned and looked at him. "You sure you..."

He kissed her. "What," he asked.

"You sure you wanna go to the crab shack?"

He shook his head. "Not after the news today. We're celebrating."

"Liam."

He kissed her again and snuggled her to him. "What?"

"Did you talk to him about this?"

He shook his head. "Kelly."

"Did you?"

"All I said was that I was looking forward to working on the software with him. Honestly, Faith told him that we were hanging out together on the weekend. He asked how we knew each other and I told him. Nothing bad, but I told him we hung out together when we were teenagers when you were away on vacation. That's it."

She shook her head. "And?"

"That when I saw you at the airport I swore you were a hallucination. That we were just hanging and catching up."

"Nothing else?"

"Nothing love. I promise."

She shook her head. "There's no way that he..."

He kissed her. "Go get changed."

"It's not even..."

He kissed her. "Then just the stuff in the lingerie box."

Kelly shook her head. "Liam."

He kissed her again and smirked. "What?"

"It's a hotel babe."

She shook her head and he leaned her onto the sofa, leaning into her arms and undid his dress shirt. "We're supposed..."

He kissed her again. "Dress off."

She shook her head and he nodded. "Liam." She felt his hand slide up her leg and pulled the lacy panties off.

"Liam."

"Fiancée."

She slid his shirt off and threw the panties on top. "Mine." She kissed him and he inched the skirt of her dress up. He kicked his dress pants off and went for his boxers when his phone went off. "Don't care," he said.

"Liam."

He kissed her and grabbed the phone from his pants. "Crap," he said.

"What?"

"Work stuff. Give me two minutes." Kelly smirked and he sat up.

"What's wrong," Liam asked.

"Well, we have it 90% done. There's a glitch. I need you here to fix it."

"What's the glitch," Liam asked as Kelly kissed his forehead and got up. She walked into the bedroom and opened the boxes then the suit bag. The dress was fantastic. Lacy but not see-through. Satin. The lingerie was almost too hot. The sheer lace corset with the almost nothing panties were definitely hot. When she opened the heels, she smirked. All of it was like having the ultimate wardrove. Nothing she'd ever have bought herself, but it was sexy. She heard a jingling then heard clicking. He was on his laptop. She knew she had time.

She tried the corset on and took a photo of just one edge of it on her against her skin. She slid it back into the box and grabbed her bag, opting to shower before they went out. She saw the robe and smirked. She had a shower alone for the first time in days, then stepped out, dried off and combed through her hair. She wrapped herself into the robe and walked into the living room, seeing him working away on something on his laptop. "I got it. I found where it was screwy. Okay. Try it now," Liam said as she noticed he was in his dress pants and still shirtless.

When she heard him close his laptop, she sent him a photo message and curled up on the sofa in the bedroom, going through work emails. When he came into the bedroom, he looked over at her, seeing everything still in boxes and bags. "So, now you're taunting me on a work call," he joked.

"You started it," she teased.

"Come here," he asked.

"Nope. I have to finish the email. Give me 10 minutes." He shook his head.

"What?" He heard the swoosh of an email being sent, slid her phone from her hand and pulled her to her feet.

"What," Kelly teased. He pulled her into his arms and kissed her, holding her face in his hands. "And what do you want," Kelly teased.

"I'll give you a hint," he teased as he untied her robe.

"What did your friend want," Kelly asked.

He kissed her, completely ignoring the question. He deepened the kiss until she was on her tiptoes and had goosebumps. He leaned down and picked her up, wrapping her legs around him. His hands cupped her backside and had her tight to him. "Had to go get all sexy without me."

He leaned her against the wall and she smirked. "Was gonna do something else while you were..." He kissed her. "If you had..."

Faith smirked. "What?"

He shook his head and she undid his dress pants.

"What Liam," she said sliding her hand against him. He smirked, kissed her again and kicked his boxers off and filled her to the hilt all over again.

One kiss and she was at his mercy. She didn't care for a second. They had sex against the wall then onto the bed.

"Liam," Kelly said as her body throbbed around him and she felt his lips and tongue and teeth against her breasts.

"Mine," he said.

"Aah," she said as he kept going until she was almost trembling in his arms. When his body gave up, he exploded into her and kissed her with a kiss that gave her goosebumps on top of the goosebumps she already had.

"Aah."

"Kelly," he said as he tried catching his breath.

"Yes fiancée," she teased.

"I love you baby."

"I love you back handsome."

"And that lingerie is officially my kryptonite."

"Haven't even worn it yet," she teased.

He shook his head. "Woman."

She smirked. "What?"

"You are so bad," he said as he kissed her again.

"You did start it handsome."

"My woman."

"Liam."

"It's a really good thing we aren't on a commercial flight."

"And why's that?"

"Because we'd never be in our seats. We'd spend the entire…"

"Liam." He kissed her again and slid to his back, pulling her with him. "I still can't believe that you actually got the tattoo."

"I made a decision a long time ago. I only get them when it's something I never want to forget."

"And what about that one," Kelly asked seeing the other that looked like a knife in his ribs.

"How I felt when you left."

"So, they're..."

He nodded. "It has the same knots..."

"Trinity and love knots."

"Liam."

He kissed her. "You just noticed?"

She shook her head. "I just thought to ask."

He kissed her. "You never thought to..."

She shook her head and he kissed her. "It's kinda a thing with me. I never found a reason for any others." Kelly slid her arms around him and they curled up together on the bed.

"And how did your call actually go," Kelly asked.

"Fixed what he couldn't fix on his own. It's almost ready."

"Good," Kelly replied.

"And then my fiancée decided to tease me."

Kelly smirked. Just as she was about to say something else, his phone rang. Kelly kissed him and got up, handing Liam his phone. She went to leave the room and he grabbed her hand. "Declan," Liam said.

Kelly kissed Liam's forehead, handing him the other robe as he got up and went to his laptop to work on the software more. She went and checked on her emails, seeing one from her boss:

> *Thank you for the paperwork. I'll get the official word out for the meeting tomorrow.*

Kelly shook her head. She was still stunned. She sent the info to her folks then saw an email from her Dad:

Are you willing to let me put the security alarm in? Just so you feel more secure at the house. I know that you're going to Ireland with him. I'm gonna keep an eye on the house for you and get those little things done. Proud of you daughter of mine. Very proud. Always will be.

Kelly smirked and when Liam came into the bedroom, he smirked. "What?"

"There's the smile."

"Dad just sent me an email. Did you get it figured out?"

He nodded. "They kinda need me back at home. I told them when I'd be back, but it means having to do all of it with a major time difference."

"I could just meet you when..."

He shook his head and kissed her. "No."

"Liam, if they need you to come home, I can come and meet you next weekend."

He shook his head. "I'm not going without you."

"Liam."

"No."

She shook her head. "I can't leave until next weekend at the absolute earliest. You know that."

"I can work on the stuff from here until you can come with me."

"Liam."

"I'm not losing you again. I tried that once Kelly. I tried letting you get on a plane and thought that somehow we wouldn't be apart and I lost you for 10 years. I thought you were dead. I thought I'd lost you completely. I'm not going through that again even if it's for a week."

Kelly looked at him. "Liam."

He shook his head. "I wouldn't make it if I lost you again."

She looked at him again and her eyes were welling up. He looked at her and saw her eyes welling up. He walked straight into her arms and kissed her. "Did you seriously think that I didn't want to get off that plane? That I didn't want to find a way to turn it around so I didn't have to leave? That it didn't kill me when I had to sit there on a plane surrounded by strangers in tears?" He slid his arms tight around her and she shook her head and pushed him away. "With the crap that I've gone through in my life Liam, I figured you forgot who I was and moved on. That I wasn't that damn memorable. That you didn't feel the same way I did. I went to school to get my mind off of you and me. I left my phone at home in a drawer. I didn't even look at it again until I was home after 2 years of school. I didn't get any letters. I didn't even see texts. I didn't get voicemails since they delete after a week. I got nothing. I figured..."

He kissed her. "I figured that you had moved on and forgot all about me."

"I never did. I couldn't."

Kelly nodded. "I know now. I'm not the same person anymore. It's a week Liam. One. I'll come as soon as I can get things settled with work. Go." He shook his head.

"I told my Mum that when I came back, you'd be with me. I'm not coming until you can be on that plane with me."

Kelly shook her head and he tried again to hold onto her. She wouldn't let him. She walked into the bathroom, locking the door behind her and washed the red eyes and puffiness away.

"Kelly." When she didn't reply, he sat down on the bed. She came out a little while later and grabbed her bag.

"What are you doing?"

"Going to the house."

"Kelly." She shook her head, got re-dressed and put her things back into her overnight bag. "Kelly," he said as he took her hand.

"No." She shook her head again, got her laptop and her phone and walked out. He shook his head and went after her, seeing her gone from the hallway. If he'd known that she'd run to the elevator, he would've run after her. He shook his head, cleaned up and got dressed, putting the dress in his suit bag with the other boxes.

"What the hell did I do," he said to himself seeing the bottle of Jameson whiskey gone from the counter. He took a deep breath, made sure he had everything from all the drawers, got his water bottle from the fridge and took his things down to the front desk.

"Sir. Checking out?" Liam nodded and signed off. He got an uber to take him to Kelly's, but when he showed, she wasn't there. He sat down on the back steps and waited. He called her more than once. When she didn't answer, he was kicking himself. He had one option, and it wasn't one that he wanted.

Just as he was about to call her Dad, he heard her truck. He waited. It felt like hours. "What are you doing here," Kelly asked.

"I checked out of the hotel."

"Then go..."

"Kelly, I'm not having this conversation on the beach."

"Why are you here?"

"Because you're home. I'm home. You're my home love, like it or not."

She shook her head and unlocked the screen door, walking upstairs to her bedroom. He brought his things in, following her up the steps. "You're not staying in..."

He kissed her, dropping everything onto the floor. "I'm sorry."

"Liam, maybe you're..."

"What?"

"They need you at work. Go."

He shook his head. "Not without you."

When she went to take the Claddagh ring off, he stopped her. "No."

"Liam, this isn't gonna work."

"Why? Because neither of us made it through that time? Because we both went through hell?"

"Because I'm not gonna be enough. Just go home." He kissed her again, pulling her tight to him.

"What part of you are more than I ever could've dreamed makes you think that you aren't enough love?"

"Liam."

"No."

She tried to pull away and he stopped her. "I'm not letting you exterminate me from your life Kelly. You can't do that. I couldn't."

"It's a week."

"And I thought it'd only be a month or a year. An hour is too long love."

Kelly shook her head and walked away. "Where are you going?"

"I need a sweet tea," Kelly said.

"You need an entire bottle of Jameson's. Sweet tea isn't gonna cut it love."

He took a deep breath and walked downstairs and saw her sitting on the beach. He could feel the rain starting. She was sitting on the sand, curled up like she was trying to fight a demon that she knew was too strong. When he saw that she was almost trembling, he grabbed a towel and walked down to her. "What are you doing love? It's pouring rain."

"Just go Liam."

"Not without you love. Sorry."

"Why me?"

He tried to pick her up and she fought him. "Why me Liam? You were with other people. I know you were. Why me?"

He took her hand and pulled her to her feet, seeing the half-full bottle of Jameson's in her hand. "Because I wanted the girl with the eyes that made me forget everything stupid I ever did. The one that I craved every second for 10 years. The one that made me the man I am. The one who I held every night. I never had that with anyone else. Ever. I didn't want a replacement Kelly. I wanted you. Always you."

She shook her head. "I can't..."

He kissed her as the rain started falling harder as they sunk a little into the sand. He devoured her lips as the rain soaked them both to the bone. He picked her up, wrapping her legs around him and walked her inside, kicked the door closed and sat her on the kitchen counter.

"What..." He didn't want words ruining it. He peeled her shirt off his, her jean shorts, his jeans and every inch of the lacy lingerie that was soaked. He devoured her lips and she tried more than once to break it.

"Liam." He kissed her again, nibbling and licking and kissing down her skin until she was almost squirming in his arms. "Liam."

He looked at her then kissed her lips again. They had sex on that counter. It wasn't pretty or romantic or anything else. It was him reminding her that he would take a bullet for her. That he'd risk anything for her. He climaxed and still managed to walk her into the TV room and lean her onto the sofa, pulling a blanket over them to warm her back up. She grabbed a remote, flipping the gas fireplace on and he kissed her.

"Never ever again," he said.

"I'm not a kid anymore Liam. I can get.."

He kissed her. "If I have to make you forget all of the bad stuff I will. You know that right?"

"Meaning what?"

He kissed her again. "Meaning I'm not letting you get rid of me."

She shook her head, finally warming up just enough. "I never said I was."

"Kelly."

"I never said I wanted to get rid of you. I said if you needed to go back to work, I'd follow once my stuff was cleared up."

"Still not going without you."

Kelly shook her head and went to get up. "Where are you going?"

She got up, grabbed a hoodie from the laundry room and walked upstairs. He shook his head, locked the back door, flipped the gas fireplace off and poured two glasses of the whiskey and walked upstairs. He put them on her bedside table.

"What are you doing," Kelly asked.

"Warming up with my fiancée." She took a deep breath and he slid his arms around her.

"I'm fine."

"So, now you're pushing me away?"

Kelly shook her head and sat down in the chair. He handed her a glass of the whiskey and went and slid joggers on.

They sat there until the rain calmed to a quiet drizzle on the beach. The waves were crashing against the shore, eliminating any trace of them. "Kelly."

"What?"

"I don't want to go without you. I'd like you to come with me. Is that allowed?"

"I can't until the meetings are done next week."

"What about doing video call in's?"

"I can't for these."

"Then we'll leave Friday next week. Overnight flight so your jet lag won't be bad."

"Liam."

"Yes love."

"Can I not just meet you at the airport and fly out on my own?"

He shook his head. "I would really like to be on the plane with you."

She took a deep breath. "Fine."

"Fine what?"

"I'll see if I can move anything up and go from there." He got up and slid his arms around her as she stared out at the water.

"Okay," Liam said as he kissed her neck. She took a deep breath and he knew. This was the woman he loved so fiercely. The woman he would've swam all the way from Ireland for. The woman that he never forgot.

"Come warm up love."

She shook her head. "I'm fine."

"Then kiss me." She took another deep breath and he turned her to face him and wrapped his arms around her, giving her a hug.

"I'm sorry," Liam said.

"I'm used to being alone Liam."

"And I don't want you to be ever again."

She looked at him. "What?"

"I..." He kissed her, holding her face in his hands. "I know that you are used to all of this. You're used to doing everything alone. All of it. You never should've had to."

"Liam."

"We're here love. You have me for the rest of your life. You've had me since that first day. Since that first kiss. I'm not leaving you now."

She kissed him and he hugged her. He grabbed his phone from the bedside table and turned on the song they'd danced to after a pub night when she was a teen. She looked at him.

"What's this," Kelly asked. He smirked and kissed her.

He danced with her like they had all those years before. They weren't quite as drunk as they were that first time, but the sentiment was still there. "Is it weird that I actually kind of remember..."

He kissed her. "The first time I kissed you."

She smirked. "Was that?"

"The night that I slept on the sofa at your hotel." Kelly shook her head.

"I don't even remember."

"I carried you back to the hotel, put you on your bed and went and sat on the sofa then I fell asleep."

She looked at him. "Liam."

"Yes love."

"You know that we can't keep living..."

"I know."

She kissed him and went downstairs. "What are you doing," Liam asked as he turned the song off.

Kelly logged into her laptop, ordered dinner and checked emails. She sent an email to her assistant to see what meetings she had the following week and find out how many of them she could do from Ireland. When she got a reply that she could do the rest after the following Wednesday, she let her know that they'd be leaving Wednesday night and flying into Dublin.

"What," Liam asked.

"We're leaving Wednesday next week."

"You sure?"

Kelly nodded. "So long as no other meetings…"

He kissed her. "Liam, I get that you don't want us apart again. I do. If I have to come back for a meeting, I have to come back regardless of anything else."

He pulled her to her feet, slid his arms around her and devoured her lips. "I get it," he said.

She looked at him. "I can't drop my life because you're scared. You know that right?"

"If you knew love. If you knew how bad things got when I thought…"

She kissed him. "I know. Just breathe. We know better now. I promise you."

He held her face in his hands. "I'm never losing you again love."

Kelly gave him a hug and he snuggled her tight into his arms. "No more fighting."

She nodded and he finally exhaled all the fear. All the worry was gone. The panic had vanished.

Liam sat down on the edge of the sofa and pulled her to him. "What," Kelly asked.

He kissed her. "I love you. I always will. You know that right," he asked.

"Whatever has you this frazzled, just tell me Liam."

"You know that I made mistakes in my past."

"We all have," Kelly replied as he looked at her.

"What Liam?"

"I made one that I couldn't take back."

"Meaning what?"

"I almost ended up being a Dad."

Kelly looked at him and shook her head. "Almost?"

"She miscarried."

Kelly shook her head and tried to stay calm." "Then you should've been a little more careful."

"It happened two years after you left. On the anniversary of your flight home."

Kelly shook her head and tried not to lose her mind. "Liam." He looked at her like his life depended on whether she could forgive his stupidity or not. "Do you know for sure that she did?" When he was silent, Kelly shook her head. "Liam. What if she didn't?"

"I don't know. I would've heard something before now if she hadn't lost it." Kelly went to move away, and he held on tighter.

"Liam."

"I love you. You know that."

"If you have a kid with someone that you don't even..." He kissed her.

"Kelly."

"Find out Liam. End of discussion. I'm not going until you know."

"Kelly." She shook her head and heard the doorbell, then got up and grabbed the takeout. She came into the kitchen, put it on the table and grabbed plates. "Kelly."

"I don't wanna talk about it Liam. After dinner."

She put her food onto her plate, grabbed her chopsticks and sat down. "Sweet tea or stronger," he asked.

"A lot stronger." Liam handed her a glass of sweet tea and sat down with her.

"How on earth do you not know if…"

"I thought you said you didn't want to talk about it during dinner." She shook her head and had her food in silence. "Talk to me."

"About what?"

"Kelly, you can't…"

"What?"

"It happened 8 years ago." She shook her head and got up, drank her sweet tea and got a glass of Jameson's.

"And if she didn't lose it, you'd have an 8-year-old kid Liam. You don't think that maybe you should find out?" He got his phone, sent a text off to a friend and asked if they could find out about whether she had the baby or she actually did miscarry. When his phone rang a minute later, he knew that she was gonna snap at him. He kissed her and answered.

"You're asking that now? Seriously? You spilled the beans didn't you," his friend asked.

"Is that a yes or no," Liam asked.

"I mean, I haven't seen her around in years, but I can find out. She was pretty determined not to be near any of us after that," his friend Ronan said.

"Please," Liam asked.

"Fine. I'll find out. There has to be someone she still talks to."

Liam hung up with him and when he turned around, Kelly had taken her glass and walked upstairs. "Kelly." She didn't say a word. He cleaned up and when he came upstairs, he heard water. He grabbed himself a drink and knocked on the bathroom door.

"What," Kelly asked.

"Am I allowed to come in," he asked.

"Liam." He came in and saw her surrounded with warm water.

"You gonna let me come in with you," he asked.

"Did you get an answer?"

"He's gonna find out," Liam said as he kicked his joggers off and slid into the tub with her.

"You never thought that maybe you should find out before you ran after me?"

He shook his head. "It was a long time ago love. A lifetime ago. I would've found out somehow. I think she did lose it."

"And," Kelly asked. Not 5 minutes later, his phone buzzed with a text:

> *Well, nobody's seen her. I'm gonna ask around, but honest and true, I think she lost it and left town to avoid the memory.*

He showed the text to Faith and she shook her head. "What was her name," Kelly asked.

"Sarah Conor."

She looked at him. "What?" Kelly shook her head, went into social media and searched her name.

"Any of these her," Kelly asked showing him the list. When he saw a photo of her, he clicked it and saw that she had a 3-year-old daughter.

"Well, according to this, she only has one little girl who's just turned three."

"Liam."

"I know." He logged into his social media and sent her a message:

> *Yes, this is way too late for me to ask. I'm sorry. Remember when we were hanging at the pub. Did anything else happen? Just got an odd feeling like maybe you didn't miscarry.*

When he got a reply 15 minutes later, he handed the phone to Kelly:

> *I lost it a week after I found out. Stop reminding me of the past Liam. Go find that fantasy girl you kept complaining about. Surprised you remember my name. You called me Kelly the entire time.*

She shook her head and handed him back his phone and he replied:

> *We're actually engaged. Wanted to be sure you were ok. I royally messed up then. I really am sorry.*

He showed Kelly and she shook her head. "Liam."

"What? You got the answer. What's wrong," he asked.

Kelly shook her head. "Part of me wonders how you ever..."

"What?"

"Nothing," Kelly said as she finished her drink. He tried to calm things down and slide her to him and instead, she got up and left the room. He drained the tub, wrapping a towel around him and walked into the bedroom.

"So, you're now avoiding me," he asked.

"You rubbed her face in it."

"Kelly."

"You did."

"I love you, but you don't understand. After what happened, she was with one of my friends. Two actually. She wasn't exactly all tore up about it."

"Liam, the more crap you say about her the worse you look. You know that right?"

"Kelly, I told you what a mess I was then. It happened. I can't change it. At least I found out whether she did or not. It's done. I doubt I'll see her again."

"Good," Kelly said as he looked over at her. "What?"

"You talking to me or what," he asked.

"Liam."

"Come here."

She shook her head. "I can't believe that I had to tell you to find out." She went to get up and he pulled her back to him, pulling her onto his lap. "And if it were me instead of her?"

"What are you saying love?"

"What would happen if I got pregnant and we didn't work?"

He looked at her. "Kelly."

"Answer the question," she said as she got up.

"I'd never walk away from you."

She shook her head. "And?"

"Don't."

She shook her head and got up. "See what I mean?"

She went to grab her hoodie and shorts and he came up behind her and turned her to face him. "What?"

He kissed her again, kissing her and pinning her against the wall in her closet. "Liam," Kelly said.

"Don't even say it."

"Say what Liam? You walked away from that without looking back. If the roles were..." He kissed her again, picking her up and wrapping her legs around him so they were eye to eye.

One kiss turned into making out then him pinning her arms against the wall. "You're mine Kelly. Mine. Nobody else's. We have a baby; I'm still not leaving even if you lock me out of the damn country."

She knew that his body was reacting. That he was getting turned on somehow even if it wasn't passion. Now, it was carnal need. It was imprinting and making sure she knew that she was his. The kiss didn't break, but the sex was just as passionate and angry. Like it was the first time they'd been together again. Like a man with a need that he needed fulfilled. When her body crashed around him over and over again, he finally snapped out of whatever trance he felt like he was in and his body exploded into her. He kissed her again and let go of her hands.

"Let go Liam." He kissed her with a deep kiss that had her body covered in goosebumps. "Let go," Kelly asked again.

He let go and Kelly slid to her feet, grabbing a hoodie and shorts. "Kelly." She shook her head, walked back into the bathroom and locked the door behind her. He slid to the floor and crumbled. Kelly sat on the other side of the same wall, shaking her head and trying to make sense of the things spinning around her head. She cleaned up, got dressed and left the bathroom, walking downstairs without a word to him, grabbing her phone on the way down. She got down there and sat down by the fireplace, flipping it on. She grabbed her laptop and went through emails, determined to be away from him.

She got her emails done and saw a text from Liam:

Please talk to me.

She ignored it and shook her head. She ordered two more bottles of Jameson's to deliver to the house and took a deep breath. She wrote out ideas that she had about combining the business and building an office in Ireland. She needed something to get her mind off it. She sent the information to Faith and got the delivery a few minutes later. When she heard the squeak of the steps, she shook her head. "Kelly." She ignored him. "Please."

She shook her head. Saying what she wanted to would only destroy any chance of sleep or calm. She got a reply from Faith and was reading through it when he closed her laptop and put it on the table.

"What?"

"Talk to me." She shook her head, grabbed her laptop and put the bag with the Jameson's into the cupboard. She went to turn around and he cornered her. "Talk to me."

"No."

"Kelly."

"Don't. Don't Kelly me. Don't pretend that what just happened is love Liam. It isn't."

"Please."

Kelly shook her head. "Move Liam."

"No."

She pushed her way out of the corner and walked back into the living room. "Kelly."

"Don't."

"Please just talk to me. Please love." She shook her head and sat down in her chair. "Kelly." She took a deep breath and just as she was about to snap, the power went out.

"Great," Kelly said.

He took her hand and walked her into the kitchen. "Liam, leave me alone," she said.

"Candles." She grabbed them out of the cupboard, handed them to Liam and put them on plates, lighting them and putting them in the living room while they waited on the lights to come back on. "Talk to me Kelly. Please love."

"Don't. Don't play that whole crap now. After what..."

"Kelly."

"Don't."

"What do you want me to do?"

"Leave me alone."

"We're in the same house love. Not like either of us can go anywhere."

"Why? Tell me why," Kelly said.

"Why what?"

"Why you never bothered to find out. Why you let it haunt you all these years. Why you tried to get your friends to cover so you never had to tell me. Why you literally think nothing of what happened?"

He tried to sit down with her and she shook her head. "Don't Liam."

"Come sit on the sofa."

She shook her head. "Just say it."

"The day that it all happened, I don't remember any of it. I realized what day it was and went all over the damn internet trying to find you. I couldn't find a photo or a profile or anything. I literally thought for 8 years that you were gone. That you died or vanished somewhere. I had a meltdown every year. That one specifically, the guys took me to a pub to watch a game of some kind and we closed the bar and racked up one heck of a bar tab. I don't even remember how I got to my flat. All I know is that I woke up the next morning with a woman in my bed. I was still mostly drunk. I thought she was you. I slept with her and she left. The only other thing I remember was my boys waking me up at noon with Irish Breakfast. I had a complete meltdown on the floor and didn't leave my room for two days."

Kelly shook her head. "Liam, that doesn't change anything."

"You don't get it do you?"

"Meaning what?"

"I thought you were dead."

"Liam, that doesn't excuse what you did. Not to her."

"I saw her a month or two later and she was in tears. I asked if she was alright and she said she'd been pregnant. That she lost it."

Kelly shook her head. "Liam."

"I was a shit guy. When I stopped going out to the pubs every night, I tried to move on. It didn't work obviously, but I stopped drinking for a while and got healthy instead. I stayed home that day every year. I worked instead. Love, I swear to you, I'm not that guy anymore." She took a deep breath and shook her head. "Tell me what I have to do for you to stop looking at me like that." Kelly got up and went into the kitchen, got herself a drink and grabbed a blanket and pillow off her bed, walking back downstairs. She put both on the sofa, put the drink down on the table, grabbed her laptop and a plate of candles and walked upstairs. "Kelly."

"You're sleeping down there."

He went to follow her back upstairs and she shook her head. "No."

"Kelly." She shook her head, walked into her bedroom and sat down on the bed, reading the rest of the email:

I'll take it up with Dad at the meeting. You lose power too?

Kelly took a deep breath and replied:

Yeah. It's fine. Candles and blankets. See you at the office.

When she heard Liam coming upstairs, she shook her head and finished reading the last of her emails. "Kelly."

"You can't leave the candles lit."

"They aren't," he said throwing the pillow and blanket back onto the bed.

"Liam."

"Not happening. We're talking and then this is done tonight. I don't wanna talk about it again." Kelly shook her head.

"Liam."

He slid her laptop out of her hands, put it on the table and kissed her hand. "I screwed up then. I get it. I apologized to her. It's handled. The guys were trying to avoid it getting brought up so you wouldn't be mad. It's done. We discussed it. Done. I wouldn't do that to you Kelly. I learned my lesson then love. It's not happening again."

Kelly went to get up and he grabbed her hand. "Talk to me."

"That was not about you loving me Liam. That, in that closet, was not about me. It was you getting control back. I'm not a damn toy you can use whenever you want. I'm not doing this. Not this." She took the ring off and handed it to him, grabbed her phone, her laptop, her pillow and blanket and walked downstairs.

She locked up, grabbed a sweet tea, got comfortable on the sofa and went to sleep alone.

Chapter 10

The next morning, Kelly woke up to a mug of coffee on the table, her laptop and cell phone fully charged and Liam sitting on the chair. "Good morning," he said.

Kelly shook her head, took a gulp of the coffee and got up. She went in the kitchen, checked the time and walked upstairs. She grabbed her workout gear, got dressed and tied up her laces, slid in her AirPods and walked downstairs. "We're talking," Liam said.

"Run." She walked out the sliding door and closed it behind her, going for a run on the beach instead. She needed space. Lots of it.

She came back an hour later to see Liam on the deck with breakfast waiting. "Kelly."

She shook her head and he grabbed her hand, pulling her to him. "Eat. Even I know you need to eat."

She shook her head, sat down and ate in complete silence. As soon as she finished, he tried again. "Kelly, please."

"No." She walked inside, cleaned up, then walked upstairs and slid into the shower. She was just about to rinse the shampoo out when he slid in with her. When she opened her eyes, he kissed her. "Liam, you don't get it."

He kissed her again, poured out some conditioner and ran it through her hair for her. "I'm not talking about it love." He kissed her and she shook her head, washing up. "Kelly." She shook her head, rinsed the conditioner out and went to step out when he stopped her.

"What?"

"No more silent treatment."

Kelly shook her head, stepped out and grabbed a towel, putting the other out for him and walked into the closet. She got her dress pants, and top and heels and put them on the bed. She slid her lingerie on, pulled on her dress pants and Liam came out of the bathroom. "We're talking love."

"We don't have time. I have work," Kelly said.

"It's 6:30am. Sit."

"Liam..."

He kissed her. "Sit down so we can talk."

He pulled on boxers and his dress pants and sat down beside her. "I love you. Tell me what I have to do."

"Never in your life ever do that again. You do, I'm gone. Understood?"

"Fine. You accepting my apology?"

She took a deep breath. "I meant it Liam."

"I love you. I screwed up royally. I apologized to her and you. You have the entire story. All of it including the crap details. What else do you want me to say?"

"Nothing." Kelly got up and finished getting dressed.

"Kelly." She shook her head.

"Power came back at 3am. I figured you needed your laptop charged and your phone."

"Liam."

"Kelly, I don't know what to do to fix it. Tell me what you want me to do."

She shook her head. "I need to breathe. Just stop."

He took her hand and pulled her to her feet. "Liam."

"What?"

"What are you doing?"

"No more stupid fights about nothing. My past happened. I can't change it. I wish I could. I wish I could change a lot of things. I've tried. Tell me what you want me to do. You want me to beg, fine. You want me to forget about it, done. If you want me to sleep on the damn beach instead of being under your roof fine. I'm not leaving Kelly. I'm not walking out, I'm not walking away and I'm not leaving you behind." He slid the ring back on her finger and she shook her head.

"I'm allowed to be mad."

"Pushing me away and walking away like that, no."

Kelly shook her head. "Liam, when I'm mad, pushing until I snap isn't gonna work. I need space."

"You walked off yesterday. You left the damn hotel and vanished."

"I came home."

"Walking out on me and taking off isn't fair and you know it. You can't make me leave Kelly. You can't throw me out of your life and think that I'm just gonna go. We have to figure this out without hurting each other."

"Coming from you," she replied.

"Kelly."

"No more Liam. You lie and hide something from me ever again and I'm leaving and not coming back. We're done. Got me," she said.

"I love you. Please love."

"Yes or no," Kelly asked. He nodded. She went to slide her heels on and he took her hand.

"What?"

He gave her a hug. "No more fights."

Kelly nodded.

She slid her heels on and went to go downstairs. "What," he asked.

"Get dressed." She walked downstairs and logged into her laptop, checking emails and saw one from Faith's Dad:

I saw the idea that you had. Worth looking into. Might be helpful for Liam when you two are working from Ireland. Announcement is today. See you at noon. Lunch included and Liam should also attend.

She took a deep breath and Liam came downstairs. "What's wrong," he asked.

"I had an idea last night and Faith already told her Dad. He's looking at having an office in Ireland. Either Belfast or Dublin. Gives you a workspace and gives him a reason to come there."

"Good idea if you stay for a while," Liam said as he walked on eggshells with his words.

"Still mad," Kelly said.

"I know love. I'm sorry." She took a deep breath and he slid the notebook in her laptop bag, sliding her laptop into the pocket of it.

"What," she asked.

"Nothin," he replied. She looked at him. "Put the notebook in your bag."

"Why?"

"Because I don't want any more fights."

She took a deep breath. "You ready?"

"No."

"Why?"

"Stand up for a minute." She stood up and he gave her a hug. "I love you."

"I know."

"Kelly."

"I love you too even if you did royally tick me off last night."

He kissed her. "Come on beautiful. Work is calling."

She stopped and got them coffee and they made their way into the office. "Kelly."

"What?"

"I love you."

"I know. I'm just tired."

"Honestly, I almost carried you upstairs to bed last night."

"I don't know that it would've been a good idea."

He nodded. "That's why I curled up on the sofa with you instead."

"What?"

"It's a super deep sofa. More than enough room for both of us."

Kelly shook her head. "Just so you know, when I'm upset, you need to back away and let me cool off. I don't want to snap at anyone. I just need breathing space."

He nodded and linked their fingers, kissing her hand. "And so you know, anything with you or the slight chance of losing you, I go into panic mode."

Kelly nodded. "Two fights in one night."

"Two that we're never ever having again."

Kelly nodded and they pulled into the parking garage. "Miss Kelly. Up to the third floor. You have a designated spot. Congrats on the promotion," the security guy said.

Kelly shook her head. "Thank you." She made her way up, saw her name on the spot and parked. "This is getting a little much," Kelly said.

"Take the bonus love." They locked up the truck, headed up the elevator and went into Faith's office to see flowers on the desk.

"You," Kelly asked. He kissed her with a smirk.

Kelly looked at the card:

My forever. Congratulations to the most amazing woman I've ever known. – Liam

She went to turn and look at him and he kissed her shoulder. "Had to?"

"After the stupid crap I did last night, yeah."

"Thank you."

"Welcome sexy fiancée," he said. Kelly shook her head and her assistant knocked.

"Morning," Kelly said.

"Morning. So, the meeting is now 12:45. Here are your messages. Mr. Murphy, here are your messages. All work related of course," her assistant joked. "Did you need anything?"

"Did you get that document sent out?" Her assistant nodded. "A little early for a reply, but they did receive it at 5:40 last night."

"Thank you."

"Most welcome," her assistant said as she headed out.

Kelly went online, paid her bills and saw that her account had a few extra zeroes deposited. "What in the world," Kelly asked as she saw the deposit. When it looked like it was a work deposit, she shook her head.

"What," he asked.

"Well, I just got my bonus and my salary increase."

"Then you can get some money for Ireland."

She smirked. "This is insane."

He nodded. "So, I was asked a question by my friends at home."

"What," Kelly asked. "Are we coming to Dublin first or disappearing for a few days alone in Belfast?"

"We can go see your family first, then Belfast."

"Avoiding my friends?"

"For 48 hours."

"Done." He kissed her. "I get it love. I do."

"We can figure out details later." He nodded and kissed her knowing that he'd just won a small victory and not to press for anything else.

"Ask Liam. I can see it on your face," Kelly said as he was silent a little too long.

"Do you want to go and see some of the places that you saw when you were there before?"

"I don't know."

"Other than the inside of our pub."

"I don't want to talk about the pub Liam."

He nodded and kissed her. "Then I'll make sure we have food for when we get there." Kelly nodded and he sat down. Pushing that button was not happening. Not when they were finally calm and speaking again. Him taunting her wasn't gonna happen when she was practically in a suit.

"What," she asked as he sat down and slid her into his lap.

"I love you."

"Love you back. Total pain in…"

He kissed her and she shook her head. "You gonna be able to sit through the meeting and behave," Kelly asked.

"No. You sitting beside me?"

She shook her head. "Wasn't planning on it," she joked.

"Would you?" Kelly shook her head and kissed him.

"We'll see handsome." She kissed him and got up, getting her emails and paperwork under control before the meeting.

When Faith knocked at her door, she smirked. "Good morning Miss VP. Good morning Liam," Faith said.

"Good morning. What's up," Kelly asked.

"So, that idea that you had. How committed are you to it," Faith asked.

"What idea," Liam asked.

"If you want to do it, it'd help with Liam being able to work from there when something's needed or me working from there when I'm in Dublin or Belfast or wherever."

"What are we talking about ladies?"

"Kelly suggested opening an office in Ireland. That way you can work from there if you're in Ireland, we have a bigger connection there plus we can start adding into the UK and Europe with some of the other office stuff we've already been doing," Faith said. Liam looked at Kelly and smirked.

"It's an idea," Liam said.

"I think Dad may be on board, but someone would be taking control of that sector. It's a while off mind you, but I like the idea and so does Dad," Faith said.

"Good," Liam teased.

"I'll see you two at the meeting," Faith said as she headed out with a smirk.

"What," Kelly asked.

"Didn't want to tell me about the idea," he asked.

"It was an idea Liam. Just an idea."

"Kelly."

"What?"

"If they did, would you come?"

Kelly looked at him. "We're not having the what if conversation. Not today."

"You could just never want to leave Ireland."

"And give up the beach? The million- and one-degree humid summers?"

"Are you being sarcastic?"

"Not giving up the beach forever Liam. Your family is there, mine is here. My work is here."

He looked at her. "Negotiation."

"Maybe," she said.

"50/50?"

"Liam."

"Negotiate when we get to Dublin." She shook her head and tried to get paperwork completed. Just as she finished up the first part of what she needed to do; her assistant knocked that her meeting was moved up. "What time?"

"20 minutes. Something about golfing," her assistant teased. Kelly smirked.

"Golfing," Liam asked.

"If you wanna go with them, you might want to tell him," she teased personally hoping for a little time alone.

"You sure you can live without me that long?"

Kelly nodded. "Means I can go and get some stuff done at the house. Get some groceries. Stuff like that."

He shook his head, they grabbed their things and headed to the meeting. By the time they were finished, Liam had plans to golf with Kelly's boss and the guys, and Faith and Kelly were going shopping alone. "Still think we got the better end of that deal," Faith joked.

They headed off, walking around downtown for a while, shopping in a few stores and catching up. "Are you actually gonna marry him though," Faith asked.

"Honestly, we've sorta had world war three already. We knew each other when we were kids, and even then it was only for a week. There's a lot more we have to figure out before that happens," Kelly said.

"Not exactly what he was saying to Dad," Faith replied.

"What?"

"When you came up with that idea, Dad was convinced that you'd be moving there permanently. That's why he changed the contract to include you being there."

"Faith, I know you put that in too."

"I suggested it."

"Honestly, it's been a long time. I changed a lot since then," Kelly said.

"I get it. I went through the same thing when Ridge and I got together. We hadn't seen each other since we finished high school. It was worth it. I got the handsome guy."

"You knew each other since you were babies. A little different. One week alone doesn't make a relationship."

"Three technically. Two now, one then," she teased.

"Woman, would you stop being on his side," Kelly joked as they went and grabbed iced coffees.

By the time Kelly got back to the house, she had groceries, fresh seafood for dinner, and one heck of a worry in her head. Was he actually expecting her to move? She shook her head, got things put away and cleaned up, putting laundry away and emptying the washer. When she heard a car pull in, she looked and saw her ex.

"Not so tough now that the idiot's gone are you," Andrew asked as he walked towards the front door. He knocked and her hands started shaking.

"What," Kelly asked.

"Open it."

"No."

"He's not here to save you Kelly. Open the door or I break it down."

She called the police and told them the situation. "I called the police."

"And you really think my Dad's gonna haul me off?"

"Yeah I do," Kelly said.

"Open the door."

Kelly took a deep breath. "Go away Andrew."

"Beach. Now."

"No."

"Open it."

She took a deep breath, grabbed a pocketknife and opened the door. "What," Kelly asked.

He ran right towards her and had his hands around her neck in less than 3 minutes. "Let go."

"You really think that humiliating me on the beach is a good idea."

"Andrew, stop."

"Telling him to come after..." She saw an arm fly around Andrew's neck and put him in a sleeper hold, knocking him out enough to free Kelly.

"Shit," Kelly said as she looked up and saw Liam.

"Are you alright," Liam asked.

"No." The police showed, hauled Andrew off, and Kelly slid to the floor with her head in her hands and burst into tears. He picked her up and sat her on the sofa as they talked to the officer. As soon as they left, Liam locked up, walked over and picked her up, carrying her upstairs. "Liam."

"We can order something. Just breathe," he said as he slid onto the bed beside her. He curled up with her and wrapped his arm around her as she leaned her head on her chest right over his tattoo. "How was golfing?"

Liam smirked. "I actually beat Emerson," Liam said.

Kelly shook her head. "He's my boss."

"And? I beat him. I haven't played in a year or two and still did well."

"Good," Kelly said.

"And how was shopping?"

"We bought a few things. She got her hubby a few things and I found something for you."

"What?" She handed him the bag. He looked, seeing shorts that would cool him off and he smirked. "Kind of a good idea since it's gonna be kinda hot this week."

"And I'll need it if we're going back and forth." She kissed him.

"Good answer," Kelly said.

"You feeling any better?" Kelly nodded as she was still trembling.

"I hate him. You know that right?"

He nodded and kissed her head. "He's not coming near you."

"That's why I'm worried about going. What happens if he breaks the dang door down?"

"Then your folks and the security that Emerson has staying while we're gone will handle him. We're good love. Nothing's gonna happen. Short of you being surrounded by green instead of blue, we'll be alright."

Kelly shook her head. "Whatever you say handsome."

"You alright?"

Kelly shook her head. "I just don't understand how I let that happen with him. How he thought that was alright." Kelly kissed the shamrock on his chest and he knew she was feeling a little better.

"Alright love. Pick your poison. What do you want for dinner?"

"Chicken."

He smirked. "You coming with me or are we getting delivery?"

"Delivery."

He motioned for her to come closer and kissed her. She slid into his lap and he sat up, pulling her to him. "You okay?"

Kelly nodded and kissed him. "I hate him. You know that right?"

"You and me both. Double actually," Liam teased.

He kissed her again and she shook her head, grabbing her phone. "What?"

"Ordering dinner. You hungry handsome?"

"For a lot of things," he said with a wink.

"Liam."

"You put something not work-related on and I'll order." He slid her phone out of her hand, unzipped her dress pants and she shook her head.

"Fine. You order," Kelly said. She kissed him, got up and got changed and he ordered dinner, adding in peach ice cream. He smirked, went downstairs, got them each a small glass of Jameson's, brought it upstairs and handed it to her as he saw her in the sundress. "Kelly."

"What?"

"What are you doing in that little, tiny sundress fiancée," he asked.

"Cooling off."

"I bet you are."

"What did you order?"

"Chicken, sauce, fries and peach ice cream."

"Nice. Very nice handsome."

"You really okay?"

Kelly nodded as he gave her a hug. "Just freaked out." He kissed her forehead and they headed downstairs and relaxed while they had their drink.

"So, what did you two really talk about," Liam asked.

"Me going to Ireland. Us. The idea about the office there. Shopping didn't really take up much time. We just walked and talked."

"You sure you're okay to come with me?"

"For a while anyway. I still want to be home with my family too."

"I know. All I want is you. If we go back and forth, fine. I just need you."

"And WIFI."

He smirked and kissed her. "You'll have the dang internet alright. We'll be fine love. Promise."

"Why did you put the notebook in my bag?"

"Just had a feeling it was safer there."

"And if I was still mad I could read?"

"Sort of."

Kelly shook her head and kissed him. He snuggled her to him and her phone pinged. "What," he asked.

"Your dinner is on the way."

"I was always keen on dessert first," he teased.

"Well, dessert is waiting," she teased.

He picked her up and slid her onto the kitchen counter. "Liam."

He kissed her, devouring her lips and slid her legs around him. "Liam, don't you dare start..."

He kissed her again. "Start what," he teased.

"You are seriously misbehaving right now."

"Oh love. I only behave in your office. The minute we're through the doors here, you're mine."

"Think so do you," Kelly asked.

He nodded and smirked, kissing her until she was pulling his shirt off. "Fiancée of mine. Are you getting..."

She kissed him, peeled his shirt off, knocked it to the floor and he slid his hand up her legs, sliding the almost nothing panties right off. "They're..."

He kissed her again, devouring her lips until he could feel the goosebumps, her body begging him to touch her and his pants starting to feel way too tight. He was about to slide the sundress up her legs when the doorbell rang. "Don't move."

Kelly smirked and kissed him. "I'm more dressed..."

He kissed her. "Stay there love. I'm not done with you yet."

He went and answered the door, got the food and put it into the microwave. "What are you doing?"

"Finishing dessert."

He slid the dress up her legs and Kelly shook her head. "Liam."

"What love," he teased as she felt his hands start taunting. One brush of his hand against her inner thigh and her toes were almost curling. One touch of his finger against her and he knew she was at his mercy again. He kissed her again and devoured her lips until he felt the waist of his pants go loose. "Kelly."

"Now."

He shook his head. "So bad. Aren't even gonna let me have fun," he teased as he slid a strap from her shoulder and pulled her bra away from what he wanted. He nibbled, kissed, licked and taunted until her body was starting to overheat. "Liam."

"What?" She shook her head and he smirked.

"I did get an A in distracting my woman."

"Distracting?"

He nodded. "Taunting, teasing and taking full advantage. I didn't think you got..."

He kissed her again, devouring her lips. "You are in so much trouble."

"Why," she teased. He kissed her and before she could say another witty response, they were having sex on that counter. Hot, intense, fill me to the brim sex that had her toes curling and her body curving to every thrust. When he picked her up and pinned her to the sofa, they kept going. "You feel too good," he said as her body tightened around him like a coiling snake.

"Liam."

He kissed her again and buried himself into her as his body collapsed into her arms. "Don't move," he said.

"Why?"

"Don't."

Kelly smirked. "And why's that?"

"Not done," he teased.

"With what?" He devoured her lips and his body almost exploded into her.

"One last thing," he teased as he kissed her again and snuggled her tight to him.

"Liam."

"What?"

"Have you finished dessert?"

He shook his head. "Taking a dinner break," he teased. Kelly shook her head and he snuggled her to him.

"Are we," Kelly asked. He kissed her again and Kelly got up. She slid her sundress back on and grabbed plates and their drinks. She slid onto the sofa and handed his plate to him then curled up on the sofa. "What," he asked.

"Nothin."

"Say it love."

"At the rate that you're going, you're intentionally trying to..."

"I considered it."

Kelly shook her head. "Getting very far ahead of yourself there handsome."

"And," he asked.

"That's what you're hoping are you?"

He kissed her. "That's what I know."

"Then you're sleeping on the sofa."

"And you think that's gonna stop us from..."

"Yep."

"We could just..."

"Liam."

"We were getting..." She shook her head and stuffed a Cane's chicken finger in his mouth.

"Stop." He ate the chicken and once she was done, she cleaned up.

"Come," he asked.

"Liam, I'm not having that conversation with you. Not now."

"Not now what," he asked. She looked at him.

"I'm not having that conversation with you. We agreed later. I knew you a week when I was 18. Two weeks now. We can't just jump..."

He kissed her. "I would've done it at the airport. We have our entire lives love."

"And we have a heck of a lot to figure out. What's wrong with us just being together and spending time together? Dating. Living together."

"I want you in my life. I don't want just a damn girlfriend. I want us."

"Liam."

"I want you to meet my friends and family. I want you to come back to where we started. Where we were happy. What's wrong with that?"

"It was a few weeks Liam. One that I knew you."

He slid his arms around her. "Come with me."

"Liam."

"Come."

She shook her head and he walked her outside. "Come and sit love."

They sat down on the beach and he kissed her shoulder. "Liam."

"What?"

"I need time."

"I know love. We have all the time in the world. We always did. We just got stuck apart."

"Liam, that's not what I meant."

"You don't think that you can get engaged officially until we've known each other for years or what," he asked.

"A while."

"While we're in Ireland."

"Maybe."

He kissed her. "Or on the plane."

"Liam."

"Or before we board the plane."

"Liam, stop."

He kissed her. "What if I said that I wanted to take you somewhere?"

"Such as?"

"You'll find out. I was talking to Faith's Dad about it."

Kelly shook her head. "Fine. Faith said we're good to leave Wednesday, but she suggested mid-afternoon."

"Good," he replied.

"What are you planning?"

"You'll find out before we leave," he replied.

"What are you up to?"

"I've loved you since before I knew what love was. I knew then that I didn't ever want to let you go. When I had to, I stopped even thinking clearly. You know that. The only thing that I had that kept me going all of that time was you. Just you. Those eyes, that smile, that feeling that I have when we're together. I would've proposed all those years ago if I could've. I wish I would've love. You know that. Now, I don't want to wait anymore. I don't want us to find just the right time. I don't want us to wait until it's long enough or in the right spot, or the right place or the right world. I want you to marry me. Come with me to Ireland and meet my family.

Meet my friends. I love being here with you. I'd be anywhere if it meant not ever leaving your side again. I'd follow you into hell. Please love. Please marry me."

He looked at her seeing her eyes well up with tears. "Kelly." She shook her head. "Say something love." When she nodded, she could barely make words. "Are you..."

"Yes," she said, stunned that he'd said the words.

"Are you saying yes?"

Kelly nodded and he kissed her and slid the ring on her finger. Somehow, it fit perfectly. "I can't believe that you said yes," Liam said.

"No more secrets." He kissed her. "No more lying." He nodded. "Promise me."

He kissed her again and they ended up making out in the white sand. The same sand that she'd loved her entire life. The sand that she'd played in as a child, that she'd run in, walked in. The sand that she'd wish would wash away her pain when she got back from Ireland that first time. The sand that she spent years kicking when the world threw another curveball at her.

When they managed to come up for air, he helped her to her feet. "Come," he said.

"Where?" He kissed her and walked her inside.

"Liam."

"We're going out."

"I'm not going..." He kissed her and they walked up the steps to the bedroom.

"Liam." He kissed her, picked her up and sat her on the bed.

"What?"

He smirked and she got changed. "Fine, but we're not going anywhere downtown."

"We'll be in town," he teased.

"Are you giving me a hint," she asked.

He kissed her shoulder. "Ice cream."

Kelly smirked. "Walk at Shem Creek?" He nodded.

She finished getting changed and they drove over, parked and grabbed an ice cream together then walked along the path. "Kelly."

"What?"

"You sure you're okay with..."

"We're taking our time with everything else. That's the deal."

"By the way, your Dad says congratulations."

"What?"

He kissed her and snuggled her to him. "I called him when you were getting changed."

She shook her head, grabbed her cell, sat Liam down and they FaceTime called her folks. "Congratulations," her mom said.

"I still can't believe all of y'all were..."

"He wanted to do something on his own. He just wanted our blessing."

"So, everyone is plotting against me now," Kelly joked.

"Congratulations you two," her brother said.

"Seriously? Everyone is there?"

"Long story," her mom said.

"Meaning what?"

"Meaning Hailey is pregnant."

Kelly shook her head. "And y'all were just gonna hold off telling us until after..."

"Yes," Hailey said.

"Congratulations," she heard.

"Where are y'all?"

"At our beach house."

"We'll be over there in a few," Kelly said. They hung up and Liam kissed her.

"What?"

"You sure you really want..." She nodded. They finished their walk, then their ice cream and headed over to her mom and Dad's.

When they got there, they all hugged and hung out and visited. "And how did you end up doing it," Hailey asked.

"Took her to the one place that she'd loved long before I came around. We sat on the beach at sunset," Liam said.

"So, what's next," Hailey asked.

"We're going to Ireland on Wednesday. I don't know how long I'm staying. I don't know how long we're staying." Liam kissed her forehead.

"What about security for the house," her Dad asked.

"Mr. Cartwright offered to have security guard the house. Faith's husband said he'd take care of the security system. I think it'll be fine," Kelly said.

"What are you going to do while you're there," Colin asked.

"Meeting my mom in person, my Dad, my sister and the family then a bunch of my friends are popping in. We're going back to where we met."

They hung out a while longer then headed back. When she let Liam drive, he smirked. "What," Kelly asked.

"Two weeks and she finally lets me drive."

"Just keep your eyes on the road and stay on the right side." When they pulled back into the house, he came around and got her door for her, taking her hand.

"It does look pretty great on that finger there wife to be," he teased.

"Thanks, handsome." She locked the truck and they headed inside, locking up behind them.

"You okay," Liam asked.

"I can't believe she's pregnant," Kelly said.

"You do know that you could be. It could be arranged," Liam teased.

"I bet," Kelly teased as he kissed her.

"Upstairs."

"Drink?"

"Nope." Kelly went and got them each a drink and he grabbed the bottle.

"What," she asked. He took one of the glasses, took her hand and walked upstairs.

"And what exactly are you up to?"

"Finishing my dessert." Kelly kissed him and took a sip of her whiskey.

"Really? You think so do you?" He smirked. He motioned for him to come closer and pulled her to him, sliding his arms around her and pulled her into his lap so she was straddling him. "Liam." He took her glass and put it on the side table with his and the bottle and kissed her. "You got everything you wanted today didn't you," Kelly asked.

SOUTHERN TEMPTATION

"Except one thing." She looked at him.

"Your mom being here?"

"You and I never ever fighting again."

"And what are we fighting about?"

He kissed her, unzipped her jeans and slid his hand down the front. "Liam."

"Mine."

"Nope."

"See, that's the only thing we fight about."

Kelly smirked and kissed him. She went to get up and he shook his head. "Liam."

"Nope."

She slid his hand away from her and got up. "Where are you going?"

"Getting changed for bed." He shook his head and watched her. When she walked into her closet, he shook his head. He kicked his jeans off, slid his t-shirt off and threw it all into the laundry, walking into her closet.

"What," Kelly asked as he watched the lace panties slide to the floor as if it were in slow motion. She slid them into the laundry, slid the lace bra off and he walked over to her. "What," Kelly teased as she turned to face him.

"Right. Like that wasn't to get my attention," he teased.

"Nope," Kelly teased as he walked towards her. She went to grab a t-shirt and he slid his hand in hers, pulling her to him.

"What," Kelly asked. He kissed her, picking her up and wrapped her legs around him and he walked her into the bedroom, leaning her onto the bed.

"What do you want," Kelly teased.

"Dessert part two." He kissed down her neck, nibbling at her breasts and kissing her until her body was almost exploding in goose bumps. He kissed down her torso and nibbled her hip.

"Liam."

He kissed her inner thigh and nibbled then licked and kissed and nibbled at her until she was way past hot. She was way beyond turned on and wet. He kept going until her toes were curling then his fingers continued to taunt. "Liam, please."

"Please what? You want me?"

"Please."

"I haven't even got you warmed up yet."

"Liam." He kept going, probing with his fingers then his tongue then two fingers.

"Come here," Kelly said. He kissed her and nibbled until her body was throbbing around his fingers. He kissed back up her torso and kissed her as her knees slid under his arms. She could've wrapped them over his shoulders by that point, and he slid deep into her over and over and over again. First slow, then hotter, deeper, more intense until her body was climaxing. "Liam."

"Wife." He was almost at his breaking point and he knew it. When he slid to his back, letting her have the control, he could barely even think. It was a whole new feeling. A harder one. A deeper one that rocked every cell of her being.

When he crashed into his release and she fell to his chest, he leaned her back onto the bed and kissed her. "What," Kelly asked.

"I love you."

"I love you back handsome."

"Fiancée."

"Husband to be," Kelly said.

"Say it again." Kelly smirked.

"Handsome?"

"Woman."

"Fiancée," she teased as he kissed her again and nibbled down her neck.

"Say it."

"Husband to..." He kissed her, devouring her lips.

"I love you wife."

"Not yet."

He nodded. "Forever. Mine," he teased.

"You really need to..." He kissed her again and kissed down her neck.

"Liam."

"What?"

"We have to get sleep." He shook his head and looked at her.

"Why are you so quiet," Kelly asked.

"I still can't believe that you said yes."

"You do know that I fully expected that you'd do it in Ireland."

"We could have the wedding there."

Kelly shook her head. "No more rushing everything. I'm right here."

He kissed her again. "Promise me."

"What?"

"Promise me that you never let go and vanish on me."

"Liam."

"Promise."

"If I have…"

He kissed her again. "Promise."

"Liam, breathe. I'm not gonna vanish. You'll know where I am."

He kissed her again and devoured her lips. "Wife."

"What handsome?"

"I love you."

"And I love you. Come get some rest." He kissed down her torso as he slid from her arms.

"Getting cleaned up then we sleep."

Kelly smirked, kissed him and got up. "Where are you going?"

"Pajamas." He kissed her and she grabbed one of his t-shirts, sliding into bed.

Kelly took one last sip of her glass and slid into bed, putting her phone and his on the charger when she saw a text:

You do know she's gonna find out.

She shook her head and tried to ignore it. Liam slid into bed with her and when he slid his arm around her, she brushed him off. "What's wrong?"

"Nothing."

"20 minutes ago we were…"

"Go look at your phone." She took a deep breath and he reached over her to grab it. When he looked at the screen, Kelly got up. "Where are you going?"

She grabbed her pillow and her blanket from the bottom of the bed and walked into the guestroom, closing the door behind her. She curled up on the bed and shook her head. One minute she's in heaven, and the next she's back in hell all over again.

Chapter 11

Kelly woke up the next morning, slid out of bed, grabbed her workout gear and got changed. As she was leaving her closet, Liam blocked her. "What?"

"You go, I'm coming with you."

"Then warm up."

Kelly pushed past him, grabbed her AirPods, got her water, slid her sneakers on and grabbed the house key. She went to close the patio door and he stopped her. "Are you seriously going to take off again?"

"Run or not Liam." He came outside and she locked the sliding door, running down the steps.

"Kelly." She shook her head, flipped her music on and slid her AirPods in, going for a run. When she got half-way finished, he stopped her.

"What," Kelly asked sliding one of the earbuds out.

"You're seriously taking off and avoiding talking to me at all right now?"

"I told you no secrets and I meant it Liam." She put her earbud back in and ran the rest of the way back, unlocked the door and they came inside.

"Kelly, I get being mad, but..."

"Don't," she said. She made something to eat, plated it for both of them and went to walk upstairs.

"Woman."

"Don't. Go ahead and keep your secrets Liam. Enjoy it. I hope they..."

He kissed her. "Sit down."

"No." She shook her head again and walked upstairs. She went into the bedroom, grabbed her skirt, top and lingerie, walked into the bathroom and went to hang it and lock the door when she heard a phone. She grabbed it and saw a message from Liam:

Woman, come down here and eat. I don't want us fighting again.

Kelly ignored it, walked into the bathroom, locked the door, showered, dried off and got dressed, did her hair then had breakfast. Alone. She came out of the bathroom and went to grab her heels when she saw Liam. "Are we talking," he asked.

"No." She walked past him, got her heels and he grabbed her hand.

"What?"

"Come here."

"Liam, I have work to do."

"Wife, sit."

"Liam, you don't get to order me around."

"Sit down so we can end this stupid fight already."

"I have a solution Liam. You broke the damn promise not even 5 seconds after you made it."

She went to slide the ring off and he stopped her. "We aren't having this fight. Not now," he replied.

Kelly shook her head and walked off, put her plate in the washer and left, leaving the spare house key on top of his laptop with a note:

Lock the door before you leave.

She stopped off and got herself a Trenta iced latte and headed into the office, intentionally going early and alone. She relaxed for a while, going through emails then got one from her assistant with the information for the airport. She was pissed. Mad even. She got a bunch of emails done then saw a message from Liam:

We're having this conversation whether it's home or here.

She knew full well that meant that he was either on his way to the office or walking in. She finished going through her emails and was going through her paperwork when he walked in. He put his laptop bag down and looked at her. "What?"

"You walked out."

"And? You know exactly where I was gonna be Liam. It's called a job." He locked her office door. "What," Kelly asked.

"You can't just..."

"What? See a text that proves you were lying? That you kept another secret? What else Liam? Did you tell her to say that she..."

He kissed her. "We're not having that fight again."

Kelly shook her head and got up. "And you think that kissing me is gonna stop me from saying it?"

"Kelly, for once, just stop."

"You're the one that lied." He grabbed her hand and pulled her to him.

"What?" '

'I love you. Please just..."

"Then explain the text Liam. What lie are you gonna come up with this time?"

"We can finish all of this when we get there."

"Meaning what," Kelly asked as she walked off and sat down at her desk to get away from him.

"You can keep changing damn chairs if that's what you want, but it's not gonna change the fact that you have to talk to me."

"Do you want me to find you another office?" He looked at her.

"You're seriously pushing me away all over again?" She looked at him and he could see the hurt. "Kelly."

"What?"

"Do you want me to handle this with a phone call?"

"So, you can get your friends to play along again?"

"Kelly."

"No. Whatever you have to say, think really hard about it. You say something that..."

He kissed her, picking her up and sitting her on the edge of her table. "Breathe."

"Then tell me what the damn secret is that you lied about this time. Another kid? Still married to some..."

He kissed her, devouring her lips and slid her legs around him. "No."

"Kelly, stop assuming that it's bad first off. I'm not destroying our relationship over something stupid. It's literally nothing."

"I don't believe you Liam. I just don't."

"And I'm telling you that I'm not lying about this. It's literally nothing. A surprise party. Period."

"I still..."

He kissed her, devouring her lips. "Stop," Kelly said.

He shook his head. "I promise you love."

"Don't." He kissed her and Kelly pushed him away, getting up. She walked back over to her desk and heard a knock at her door. Liam shook his head and got up, unlocking the door.

"Miss Kelly, everything alright," the security officer said.

Kelly nodded. "Do we have a spare office anywhere?"

"Two doors down. Why," security asked.

"Can we set that up so Liam has an office for today?"

"Yes ma'am," he said as Liam closed the door and locked it.

"Woman."

"I don't want you in here today. I'll get your suite back at..."

He walked straight for her and kissed her. "Get up."

"No."

"Kelly, get up."

"I said no Liam. It's done. I told you before that if you lied to me..."

He kissed her, picked her up and sat her on the edge of her desk. "I didn't do anything. I didn't lie to you, I didn't cheat, I didn't run off and marry some random person and I don't have kids. I have you. Just you. My mom wants a party with everyone there. She doesn't know I proposed. What's wrong with that," Liam asked.

"I don't trust..." He kissed her again, sliding her heels off and pulling her to him.

"When are you gonna hear me? I'm not the idiot guys you've dated Kelly. I'm not about to cheat on you either. The only thing I want is right here in my damn arms." She shook her head and his hands slid to her face.

"When I said I wanted to marry you I meant it."

"I told you not to lie to me."

"It's a party. A surprise party welcoming you back. That's all. If nothing else than we turn it into an engagement party. Just stop love. Stop pushing me away. Stop trying to make me walk out."

She shook her head. "Liam."

"I'm never gonna be that guy you think I am. I love you. I'm not running that risk of losing you so stop assuming that I will."

"Then stop..." He kissed her again, devouring her lips until he knew that she wasn't fighting him anymore.

"Kelly."

"What was..." He didn't wanna talk about it anymore and didn't want her thinking about it. "My friends are ridiculous. Always have been. I tried to get them to stop being stupid about us, but they keep going. Once you meet them, all of that will stop."

Kelly shook her head. "What love?"

"You don't think that all of this happening all the time..."

"The lads who wanted me to be one of the boys. The guys who never got married."

"And?" He kissed her again and went and made sure the door was locked.

"What are you doing?"

He walked back over to her, kissed her and wrapped her legs around him. "Not..."

He silenced her with one kiss that almost made her knees buckle. "Shh."

"Liam." He kissed her again and she felt his hand slide up her inner thigh.

"Wife."

"Liam, what..."

He kissed her again, devouring her lips until she felt her lace panties slide off. He slid them into his pocket, kissing her and she heard the zipper of his dress pants. Kelly shook her head and he nodded, deepening the kiss and pulling her to him as he thrusted into her and they had sex on her boardroom table in her office. They were almost silent, letting their moans fall as they kissed. They kept going until he could feel her tighten around him and he found his release. "No more fighting," he said.

"Then..."

He kissed her again and teased until her body was crashing around him. "Liam."

He kissed her again. "Tonight, all mine. Head to toe," he teased.

Kelly shook her head. "Give them back."

"No."

"Liam."

"What love?"

"Don't what love me." She slid her hand into his pocket and grabbed them, unlocked the door and walked down the hall to the ladies room.

When she came back into her office, Liam had their iced lattes on the table and was going through more emails. "What," Kelly asked.

"Nothin."

"You get any more emails from your so-called friends?"

"The ones who like to cause fights so we can have really good makeup sex? No."

Kelly shook her head. "Remind me to kick a few of them."

Liam slid her into his lap and kissed her. "Nope. Remind me to keep them away from my sexy wife," he teased.

Kelly kissed him and grabbed her coffee. "Still don't like it."

He looked at her. "I love you. Always have and always will, but they were the only ones that helped me through all of it."

"By getting you drunk."

He shook his head. "Not having that conversation love. Not having the fight about them. The book is in your bag. You didn't finish reading all of it."

Kelly shook her head and got up, checking over emails a little more. "Kelly."

"What?"

"Promise me there won't be any throwing people off the cliff situations," he teased.

"Not promising anything."

They got more work done and Kelly's assistant knocked. "What's up," Kelly asked.

"Meeting starts in 10. Last one before the weekend."

"Thank you. What meetings do I have next week?"

"Just one on Monday with Mr. Cartwright. The others I set for call in from home. It's supposed to be a big storm on Tuesday. Wednesday it's an 8am meeting that's a call in as well. I have your papers you need for your flights and the hotel information for the company hotels if you need it. Also, he has a car there and available if you need it."

"Thank you," Kelly said as she handed a file to her.

"What's this," Kelly asked."

"From Mr. Cartwright. Not sure," her assistant said. She opened the envelope and saw a note:

> *You've always been like my other daughter. Go have fun in Ireland and congratulations.*

When she saw the money in the envelope, she shook her head. Now she had a fallback plan. If something went to complete crap while she was away, she at least had her own money. She'd fully planned on getting some so she had it, but now, she didn't need to.

"What's that love."

"Nothin. Just what we need for Ireland. He wants me to look for a location for an office."

Liam shook his head. "And?"

"Nothing," Kelly said as she slid the envelope into the bottom of her purse.

"Love, what are you up to over there?"

She shook her head. "Emails and paperwork. The stuff you're supposed to be doing in your own office."

"But then I couldn't do this," he teased as he got up.

"Do what," Kelly asked. He tilted her chair back and kissed her.

"We have a meeting."

"And?" He kissed her again, she fixed her lipstick and grabbed her phone and laptop, grabbed her papers and headed off to the meeting with Liam.

By the time they were out of the meeting, it was almost lunch. Kelly got the information she needed and the paperwork she had to do while in Ireland and went back to her office to see lunch waiting.

"What did you get?"

"The clam chowder. What about you," Liam asked.

"She Crab bisque. One of my favorites."

"Why are you sitting over there."

"Because I am. I know exactly what you're thinking. Safety behind the desk."

He shook his head and finished lunch then walked over to her. "What," she teased as he turned her chair to face him.

"And what did you think that I had on my very dirty mind love?"

"Not happening in here. Don't start."

He kissed her, leaning over her and tilting her chair back. "Up," he said.

Kelly shook her head. "Come on love."

"Nope. You go get..."

He kissed her again, pulling her to her feet. "Liam."

He hugged her. "Promise me no taking off. No fighting this weekend."

Kelly took a deep breath. "Did I tell you…"

He kissed her again and took her hand. "What?" He sat her on the sofa and leaned in to kiss her. "What," she asked as he kissed her again then sat down beside her and snuggled her into his arms.

"Are you excited to go?"

"After the messages and the drama from your…"

"Kelly."

"I am," she said as she subconsciously wanted to get a hotel suite to herself in case something else happened. They got more work done and he looked at her. "What," Kelly asked.

"Are you actually excited?" She took a deep breath and tried to relax.

"I found a few places for us to go just us. Places I hung out when I was a kid."

"Sounds like a plan. Anywhere exciting," Kelly said.

"Why does it feel like you actually don't want to go?"

"Liam, it's just a lot with everything that's gone on. If they're all determined for us to…"

"I told them that we're engaged. My mum doesn't know and either does my sister. Nobody in my family does. I just told one or two of the lads. They agreed to back off."

"Okay."

"So, we're flying into Belfast."

Kelly looked at him. "Why," she asked.

"Because we need sleep and peace and quiet. Can't get that in Dublin with all the friends and family around. Just you and me off in the cottage."

"Okay," Kelly said as he kissed her forehead.

"I figured you'd be more excited."

"I am. I'm just tired." He kissed her again and looked at his phone.

"It's almost 4. You've been here since 7am love. We can go home." Kelly nodded.

"Dinner," he asked.

"We can..."

"The dress. Go get changed and we'll go."

"What?"

"Back of your door," he said. She looked and saw the suit bag, shoes and lingerie.

"Liam."

"What?"

He smirked and kissed her. "Go. I'll meet you in here." She grabbed her purse and the bags, got changed and came back in to see Liam with a grin ear to ear.

"It's 4pm."

"4:30. Reservation is in a half hour then I get you all to myself wife."

"What's this I hear about wife," Faith asked. Liam smirked and Faith saw her ring. "Holy crap. Seriously," Faith asked as she came in. "When did you pull this off Liam?"

"Long story. She said yes last night when we were sitting on the beach."

Faith smirked. "Of course that's where you did it. Well, congratulations," Faith said as she gave them each a hug.

"We're just gonna head out and get dinner. You good," Liam asked.

"Yes. Just wanted to invite y'all down for a barbecue Sunday. Up to you. Around 7. Ridge wanted to talk to you about the security stuff."

"Sounds good. We'll pop over. I'll bring something for you," Kelly teased.

"The cobbler?"

Kelly nodded. "Girl, thank you. Alright. Go do engagement dinner. I'll see y'all Sunday," Faith said as she headed out and Kelly got her things. Kelly and Liam headed downstairs and the minute the elevator door was closed, he kissed her.

"What," she teased.

"I love you."

"Love you back," she replied.

They got to the parking garage, she put her things in the back and they headed to the restaurant. "Odd question. Why have the big truck? You could've got an SUV or something."

"Never needed more than one vehicle. It's just me."

"Babe."

"I know." He kissed her and they parked. He got her door for her; they locked up the truck and headed into the restaurant. When the hostess walked them to the private dining room, Kelly shook her head. "What are we..."

"Celebrating," Liam said.

He pulled her chair out for her and kissed her. "You do know we didn't have..."

He kissed her again. "Just enjoy dinner. No stress, no crazy people at the door. No drama love."

"And?"

"And what?"

"No texts from the lads either." Kelly kissed him.

Their drinks showed and Kelly shook her head, opting for sweet tea. "Sorta handled," Liam said.

"Meaning what?"

"Your brother took it over to the house."

"So y'all planned all of this without sayin a word to me?" He nodded and kissed her as the waitress came in with their drinks. "What are you up to," Kelly asked.

"Nothin. I thought you needed a night of quiet. No stress, no idiot exes ruining the night."

Kelly kissed him. "Thank you."

"For what? This?"

Kelly nodded. "I may have needed it more than I thought."

He got up, taking her hand and helping her up. "What?"

He slid his arms around her and gave her a hug. "I love you. You know that right?"

Kelly nodded. "I love you too."

He kissed her again and flipped music on. "Liam."

"Dance with me." She smirked.

When she heard a song from when they were 18 come onto the speaker, she shook her head. "Do you remember where," he asked.

"That pub. We danced while the band was playing."

He kissed her. "Honestly, I was still kind of in shock. I have no idea how we ended up bumping into each other, but I wouldn't change a second of the time we had then."

"Except add on about 10 years to it."

He nodded and kissed her. "Very true wife."

She shook her head and kissed him. "Just promise me that we aren't running off to Ireland and getting..."

"I promise."

"And no letting everyone talk us into doing it while we're there."

"You know that my Mum is gonna try hard to get her way," Liam said.

"They have to meet my folks. Big sit-down dinner. All of us. That's the deal."

"So, when do you want to bring them then?"

"Not tomorrow." He smirked and kissed her forehead, finishing their dance then sat down to have their appetizers.

"What are you up to," Kelly asked.

"Romancing you."

He smirked and they had dinner together, had another drink and when they went to leave, an SUV was out front waiting for them. "Really," Kelly asked.

He nodded and kissed her. They hopped in and headed off. When the SUV stopped, they were at the hotel he'd checked into when he first got there. "Liam. What are we doing here?"

"Nothin," he replied as he hopped out. She got her purse and they headed up to the suite. When they walked into a room full of candles and roses, she shook her head.

"Liam."

"I guess you like?"

Kelly shook her head with a grin ear to ear. "What are you up to?"

He kissed her and pulled her to him. "Seducing my wife. Why," he teased.

Kelly shook her head. "The candles are nice and everything, but why?"

He kissed her and snuggled her to him. "I'll give you a hint. Ten years ago."

"Liam."

"Ten years ago today, you landed in Dublin. That's what your ticket said."

"What about my ticket," Kelly asked.

"You had your return ticket. You left the other one in the room you had," he said.

Kelly shook her head. "Liam."

"I kept it. I kept that, I kept the pen from the room, the tickets to the tour bus. I still have the notepad where you wrote your phone number and your email and your address."

"So, either you became a psycho or you're all sentimental."

"Sentimental. I figured the two of us would show our kids someday."

Kelly shook her head and they danced. "I love you wife to be."

"I love you too."

Kelly shook her head and he picked her up. "What," she asked. He walked her into the bedroom and saw rose petals on the bed. "Liam."

"What?"

"You don't have..."

He kissed her again, leaned her onto the bed and kissed her. "I want my wife. That's it. Just you. Always you. Only you."

Kelly kissed him and he deepened the kiss until she was starting to get goosebumps. "Liam."

He kissed down her neck and his hands slid around her, pulling her legs around his hips. "Liam."

"Wife." She shook her head and his hands slid up her legs.

"Did you happen to forget something out of that bag?" Kelly shook her head.

"Not that I noticed," she teased.

"You're so bad."

"I mean, if you want me to put..."

He kissed her and nibbled at her lips. When she heard the zipper of his pants, she took a deep breath. "What," he teased.

"Nothin," she teased.

She went to slide the dress off and he stopped her. "Nope."

"Liam." He kissed her and slid the hem of the dress up.

"What," he asked as he kissed down her neck.

"What are you doing?"

"Nothin," he teased. He unbuttoned the front of the dress as he kissed down her torso.

"Liam." He slid the lace of her bra down, nibbling and kissing and licking until her toes were curling and the heels slid off.

"Mine," he teased.

"Liam." His hand slid up her leg and when she felt his fingers start teasing all over again, she shook her head and intensified everything.

"What sexy wife," he teased.

"You are so very grounded."

"I'll keep it up then."

He nibbled again and she shook her head. "Liam."

"What sexy," he asked.

"I know what..." He kissed her again, undid his dress pants, kicked them and his boxers off and devoured her lips.

"Liam."

He kissed her. "What," he teased as he pulled her legs tight around him.

"What are..." One kiss and she almost melted.

The slow burn was killing her. He did it all intentionally and kissed her like it was the last kiss they'd ever have.

"What's wrong," Kelly asked.

He shook his head and kissed her again as he slid into her, almost taking her breath away. "Wife." Kelly went to say something and looking into his eyes made her speechless. They kept going and he taunted as he coiled her around him. When it got deeper, stronger, harder she almost moaned his name until he kissed her again, muffling the noise. When she felt him slide her on top, she smirked.

"What," she asked as it just intensified everything. He teased as her body throbbed around him.

"Liam."

"Don't stop," he said as he kissed her again and pinned her back onto the bed.

"Roll over," he teased.

"Why?"

She slid to her stomach and they kept going. Harder, faster, more and more intense and then her body climaxed. "Shit," Kelly said.

"You're not done," he teased. She shook her head and kept going with the teasing. Harder was an understatement. Her hands against the wall and him pounding into her until they were both completely spent.

"One more..." Kelly nodded. He grabbed something from his pants and with one move, they were making everything worse. When he found his release, he slid her to him on the bed.

"What," Kelly teased.

"Damn," he said.

"Kinda what I was about to say," Kelly teased.

"Every single inch of this sexy woman is all mine. Forever."

She went to turn and look at him and he smirked. "What," she asked.

"I made a decision."

"Which would be what," Kelly asked as she curled up with him and slid her arm around him.

"Whether we're here or in Ireland or in a box somewhere, I want you with me. I don't care where you need to be. I'll be right there beside you. Forever."

"Good. You better be," Kelly replied.

He kissed her forehead. "Did you like your surprise," he asked.

"Depends. When did you..."

He kissed her. "I wanted to surprise you yesterday. After everything that happened, we needed today."

"Liam."

"We needed tonight."

"You did good with the surprise handsome."

"And if I said that I wanted us to always have date nights?"

She smirked. "Kinda easy to do considering that we have no kids."

"Yet."

"And when we do, we still have them."

Kelly kissed him. "Liam."

"What love?"

"I get it." He kissed her, then the kiss deepened and he leaned her onto her back and kissed her even more.

They spent all night alone in bed making love, making up then making out even more. By the time they got up the next morning, neither of them had any want or need to go back to the beach house. "Breakfast," he asked.

Kelly nodded and kissed him. "Really."

He slid into her arms and her legs coiled around him. "I love you fiancée," he said.

"I love you too," Kelly said as they made love again that morning.

They headed home just after lunch and intentionally went to the market on the way back. He got fresh peaches and a few treats. "You gonna show me how to make that cobbler," he asked.

Kelly smirked. "Something like that."

When they got back to the house, Kelly saw that the door was smashed. Luckily, it wasn't broken or open. "What in the damn world," Kelly said.

They went inside, he locked up and she saw profanities spray painted on the patio window. Kelly shook her head and went to get the cleaner when Liam saw it. "Who," he asked.

"You know who Liam."

"Call the police." She shook her head and he grabbed her phone, calling the police.

Kelly walked upstairs, changed into a bikini and shorts and walked downstairs. "You seriously don't care that he did that."

"He's done it a million times. Every time I told him to go away. Every time I ended up with bruises and kicked him out. Just grab a scrubber and help me clean it."

"And the fact that he tried to destroy your front door?"

"Liam, it can be replaced."

He shook his head and kissed her. "The police are on the way here."

"Liam."

"They're handling it." Kelly shook her head and sat down on the sofa.

"What?"

"Liam, the more you push with the police, the worse he's gonna get."

"Then we find another beach house. One where you're safe. One where you don't have to have eyes in the back of your head. One where you don't have to constantly worry about him showing up."

"This house was my grandmothers. I'm not moving."

"Kelly, your life is more important. What would you have done if it was more than bruises and you ended up in the hospital? What's gonna happen next time he does that and nobody's there to pull him off you? Is he gonna go one step further and..."

Kelly got up and walked outside. She walked down to the beach and started walking.

Kelly got as far down the beach as she could. When she busted into tears and slid to her knees in the sand, she couldn't breathe. He was right. She knew he was right. Walking away from that house was as torturous as when she got on that plane.

She wished she'd been able to turn the plane around. That she hadn't got on the plane at all. That she'd stayed there with him instead of coming home. She could've moved without even a second thought. She could've found a job or gone to school and come home to him every night. She could've had babies already. Had a life without worry that she'd be choked or killed. She could've gone through life with him and never thought twice. Instead, she'd made the biggest mistake ever and come back to Charleston. She took a deep breath and tried to think. He was right. Being at the house, while it had a lot of memories, was part of her past. Maybe finding something else that was a fresh start, more secure, away from the drama from her old life and somewhere they could make memories together was what she needed. She brushed the tears away, took a deep breath and got up. She went to walk back towards the house and bumped directly into her ex.

"Come to your senses?"

"Why? Why spray paint my house? Why try to bust the door down?"

"Because you don't get to walk away from me bitch. Do you know who I am?"

"A man who belongs in jail. An idiot who thinks that putting your hands on me is alright. A fool who thinks that he's so dam hot that every woman would want him. The complete moron who actually thinks that strangling me is gonna change anything. Go back to the hell hole that you came from and dive back in. Leave me alone. My fiancée doesn't want you here and either do I."

She pushed him into the sand and when he got up, he went for her throat. "Let go," Kelly said.

"No. You think you can talk to me like that you little bitch?"

When she felt his hands release a moment or two later, she ran. "Kelly."

She got all the way to Faith's, running right past her place when Liam caught up to her. "Kelly, It's me. Please."

She fell to the sand and Liam caught her. "Baby." He curled her into his arms and sat down with her.

"I love you," he said. She could barely breathe let alone speak. He picked her up and Faith came outside. "What happened," Faith asked.

"I have to get her home."

"Liam, bring her in here."

He shook his head. "Fine. Ridge and I are coming with you," Faith said as he walked back down the beach and got her back to the beach house.

Liam walked inside, laying her on the sofa and felt her holding on tighter. "I'm right here love. I'm not going anywhere ever again."

Faith, and her husband Ridge, showed and Kelly still hadn't let go of Liam. "What in the world happened," Ridge asked.

"Her ex tried to bust the front door down while we were gone last night and spray painted the window. We sorta had a disagreement about what to do and she took off. I went to find her and saw him trying to strangle her. I put him in a sleeper hold and she took off running. She collapsed in front of your place," Liam said.

Just as he said it, the police showed up.

Liam talked to them while Faith stayed with Kelly. When they came over to talk to her, Kelly could barely swallow. "Are you alright," the officer asked. Kelly shook her head. "Alright. Can you write down his name for me," the officer asked as Kelly wrote it down, his address, email and phone number. "Thank you. How long did you know him?" Kelly wrote down the words 3 years. The officer asked one last question. "We're getting you an emergency restraining order and charging him." Kelly nodded. The officer wrote down what he was going to pick him up and charge him with and Kelly added two words that Liam hadn't seen. When the officers took the photos of the damage and left, Liam looked at Kelly.

"Water?" She gave him a look. He kissed her, walked into the kitchen and when he came back, he handed her a half glass of Jameson whiskey.

When she looked over, another guy showed up. "Who," Kelly said trying to talk.

"That's Kellen. One of the guys that Ridge works with. He's handling your security here," Faith said.

Kelly nodded and Liam curled back up with her. "What is he doing," Kelly whispered.

"You're gonna need a new door, security system and cameras. Until the system is installed, are you good with me staying at the house," Kellen asked.

Kelly nodded and Liam wrapped his arms around her. Kelly grabbed her phone and sent Liam a text:

Get the alarm in now. He's gonna come back here.

"How fast can we get the alarm in," Liam asked.

"Gimme 2 hours."

Kelly nodded. "Do you guys want to stay at the house with us tonight? Just so you feel better," Faith asked.

She looked at Liam. "I appreciate the offer. Honestly, I do. I think she wants to stay. If she gets worried, we go to the hotel."

"Just keep me posted. If you guys go to the hotel, tell me. I don't want you worrying," Faith said.

"One thing. If we decide to go to Ireland early," Liam said as Kelly shook her head.

"We can get the meetings available for video call. It's fine," Faith said.

"Alright. Lock replaced and changed to video doorbell. I had one from when we were gonna update them at the beach house," Kellen said. Kelly mouthed a thank you.

"You sure you're okay," Faith asked.

Kelly nodded and curled up tighter to Liam. "Alright. Keep us posted. You need something, call or text okay?" Kelly nodded and Faith and Ridge headed out while Liam watched Kellen set everything up.

When Liam looked over and saw Kelly walking upstairs, he let Kellen know he was staying with Kelly and followed her upstairs. He saw her curl up on the bed and walked into the bathroom, drawing her a hot bath. He lit a few candles and walked into the bedroom to see her in the fetal position on the bed. He walked over to her and hugged her, holding her in his arms. "You need to go to the hospital love."

Kelly shook her head. "Baby."

She shook her head again and he called the officer.

"Mr. Murphy."

"Should she be going to the hospital?"

"Realistically yes. We had 30 witnesses, so he's pretty much screwed. He's in police custody now. I'd say yes. Just for photos of any bruising at all."

"Thank you," Liam said as he hung up with the officer. He looked over and Kelly wasn't in the bed. She walked into the bathroom and slid out of her bikini and shorts and slid into the warm water. He kicked his jeans, boxers and t-shirt off and slid into the tub with her as she curled into his arms.

"Do you want to go this weekend instead of waiting?" Kelly shook her head. "I get it, I do love, but I'm on edge now. You took off and I didn't know where to look until I saw a crowd starting to form. I ran. I haven't run that fast ever. I needed to get to you. I managed to knock him out or he…"

She put her finger over his lips. "I want to take you away from all of this. I don't want you shaking and being scared." She snuggled up to him and kissed him.

"Fine. We talk about it in the morning." Kelly nodded. He kissed her forehead and got her to relax a little. When she started crying again, he shook his head, drained the tub and got a warm towel for her, wrapping her in it and wrapped another around his waist. He picked her up and carried her into the bedroom, sliding her onto the bed and wrapping her up in the blankets. He went to get up and leave and she wouldn't let go of his hand. She pulled him back to her and he kissed her. When she slid over in bed, he shook his head. "Kelly."

She looked at him and he took a deep breath. "Are you..." She kissed him again. He slid into the bed and she slid on top of him.

"Baby," he said. Kelly kissed him. Her throat was still sore, but it was more fear that had closed it off. Recurring nightmares that had replayed in her mind. The fear that he'd find her on the beach and never ever see her alive again. She needed to wipe it out of her mind. Her mind was scattered, scared, terrified, but the rest of her just wanted to wipe the feeling of his hands around her neck away. She needed Liam more than she ever thought. More than she felt. He was the only part of her soul that made sense. When he curled her into his arms and kissed her, that's all she needed and wanted.

He pulled her into his arms and snuggled as best he could. "I think we need to go. We can stay in Belfast for a while. We'll be away from everyone and everything. You can relax and stare out at the water. We can go to the cliffs. Whatever you wanna do love. I just want that smile back. I don't care if I have to hide you away from the world until you're okay." Kelly kissed him and that kiss turned into an even deeper kiss. It turned into making out and somehow, by the time they went to bed that night, he heard the three words that he craved. "I love you."

Chapter 12

The next morning, Liam woke up to the feel of her body against his. "Morning sexy wife."

"Morning," she said with a froggy voice.

"What you doin?"

"Nothin," Kelly teased as he felt her hand around him.

"Really." She nodded and he shook his head.

"Wife." She kissed him and he grabbed her hand, sliding her hands away from him and leaning into her arms. "And what did you want?"

"Nothin," Kelly teased.

He kissed her and her legs slid around his waist. "Babe."

"Mine," she teased.

"Funny," he teased as she snuggled him closer.

"Liam."

"You sure." Kelly kissed him and he smirked, snuggling her to him and he knew. She was back to her old self. He leaned into her and started taunting.

"Mine," he teased as he kissed down her neck then her torso then down to her hip.

"Liam."

"What love?"

"Aah." When he heard that, he knew she was alright. He kept going until he was licking and nibbling and teasing until she was grabbing at him. "I will never ever get enough," he teased.

"Of what?" He didn't have to answer. He let his lips and tongue answer. When he saw her toes curling he made it more intense with two fingers. "Liam."

"Mmm."

"What," she asked.

"You taste too good," he teased as he kept going until her body was overheating, getting way too turned on and ready to pounce on him.

"Liam, please." He kissed back up her body and her legs wrapped tight around him as they had sex. It was hotter, more intense and all passion. It was harder and when they managed to come up for air, Kelly was spent.

"Wife."

"What handsome?"

"Am I allowed to take you to Belfast?"

"I have a meeting on Monday and Tuesday."

"And Faith said to go."

Kelly shook her head. "Liam."

"What sexy wife of mine?"

"I haven't packed."

"That mean you're letting me take you away?"

She kissed him. "Maybe."

"We pack today and leave this afternoon. I don't want us to be here any longer than necessary after yesterday."

"Alright," Kelly said.

He kissed her, devouring her lips again. "Good. Now, what else did you want to do this morning sexy wife?"

"Eat. Not go for a run on the beach. I want to take the cobbler to Faith."

"And pack." She smirked.

"We have to talk to the pilot."

"I'll email them."

He kissed her and smirked. "What?"

"Finally. My dream came true."

Kelly kissed him and she got up. "Where are you going?"

"Breakfast, shower, get dressed, pack, make cobbler. Not necessarily in that order," Kelly said still a little froggy.

"Babe, are you sure your throat is alright?"

Kelly nodded. She went into the bathroom and checked to make sure there were no bruises. She flipped the hot water on, sliding under the stream of water to wash away the stupidness from the previous day. She was just rinsing out the shampoo when she felt Liam's lips on her again. "What you up to," Kelly asked.

He picked her up, leaning her against the shower wall. "What?"

"The officer called while we were busy."

"And?"

"He's being held without bail." Kelly shook her head.

"Down."

"Baby."

"Liam." He kissed her again and she slid to her feet. She washed the shampoo out, put the conditioner in and sat down.

"Baby."

She shook her head. "Don't." She rinsed out the conditioner and he was about to pull her into his arms when she stepped out. She dried off and left the bathroom. "Shit," Liam said as he finished washing up. He flipped the water off, stepped out and wrapped a towel around him and walked into the bedroom. "Kelly." She shook her head. She got dressed, hung up her towel and he looked at her.

"What?"

"Talk."

"Did you think that telling me that when we were about to..."

He kissed her devouring her lips and sat her on the bed. "I wanted to tell you."

"Bad timing."

She got up. "Kelly." She shook her head, grabbed her cell and walked downstairs. She made them breakfast, plated it and started chopping up the peaches for the cobbler. When her phone buzzed, she almost jumped.

"You okay, Faith asked.

"Well, I was gonna call. We are thinking about leaving this afternoon."

"Kinda had a feeling. Liam mentioned that when I called."

"Is it okay though?"

"Dad emailed you. He actually suggested the same thing. Meetings can be on video call. Just get yourself somewhere you feel safer. Kellen offered to keep an eye on the house for you. He can finish the security system updates and stuff."

"Making the cobbler for you too. The least that I could do."

"Girl, you don't have to."

"I'm doing it Faith."

"Alright. We'll pop over after church."

Kelly put the cobbler in and sat down at the table with her breakfast. Liam came downstairs and saw her. "And are you still mad at me?"

"We're leaving this afternoon. Faith's coming over to get the cobbler."

"Babe, I get it was crap timing."

She shook her head and finished her omelet and bacon. "I don't want to talk about it Liam."

He slid her chair closer. "Are you sure that you're up to go now?"

Kelly nodded. "Just know that if I get upset, I'm going to the hotel that..."

He kissed her and shook his head. "No, you aren't love."

She nodded. "Liam, we have a company..."

"I don't care if they have an island. You get upset; you go to the house. No vanishing for a drive or a walk or taking off and going somewhere else."

"Why?"

"Because it's not like here."

Kelly remembered back to when she was 18. Only going out at night when she had Liam with her. Staying in certain areas after dark and avoiding others. "I remember that it isn't Liam. I'm saying that if I need..."

"You have someone with you after dark. We talked about this last time you were there."

"I know." He took a deep breath.

"What?"

"We stick together love. We're gonna be alone just us for a week so we can relax before the family and friends stuff. Short of going to the market in town, we're on our own. Nowhere to really go. When we get back to Dublin, it's another story."

"Fine," Kelly said taking a deep breath.

"What are you cooking?"

She smirked. Not 10 minutes later, she was sliding the cobbler out of the oven.

"That smells so damn good," he said.

"I was gonna offer to make one to bring to your mom," Kelly said.

"Good idea," he teased. She didn't want to talk about going to Ireland. Not at that moment. She just needed to get packed and get through the day.

She let it cool and cleaned everything up, then headed upstairs and grabbed her suitcase. She didn't have many warm clothes but packed whatever she needed. A few nice dresses and heels, jeans, and her lingerie. She threw her toiletry bag in and threw in pajamas. She got her travel charger, her power adapters and all her cords and slid them in her bag. She put everything in, including her jewelry and anything else that could go missing in the house, zipped up her bag and put it by the door. When she heard the doorbell, she came downstairs and saw Kellen, Faith and Ridge.

"Hey. Come on in," Kelly said sliding her suitcase to the side.

"All packed already," Faith teased.

Kelly nodded. "Not much to leave here. Thank you for looking after the house while we're gone by the way," Kelly said.

"Most welcome. Here's the system I got. The door and all the entrances have cameras and motion detectors. You should be secure. You just have to pick the code," Kellen said. He set it up and Kelly set the code.

"Alright. As payment, the warm and barely out of the oven cobbler," Kelly teased.

"I could smell it at the door. Thank you for this," Faith teased.

"Most welcome. I'm making another one to take to his mom. Did y'all want to come sit," Kelly asked.

"We're actually just heading home. You feeling any better," Ridge asked.

Kelly nodded. "Thank you for that last night."

"You're welcome. I guess we'll see you next when you're back," Faith asked.

Kelly nodded and gave her and Ridge a hug. "I'll let you know once we're settled." Faith nodded and she headed out with Ridge.

"Kelly."

"What," she replied as she sat down on the sofa and started going through the last of her emails. When she saw the one from Faith's Dad, she smirked and read through it:

> *Faith told me what happened. I agree with her that it's better for you to get out of town. I have a suite reserved for you at the hotel in Dublin. I also have a car ready for you for when you arrive. Be safe. If you feel the need to leave, go. I left a package on the plane for you in case you need it.*

"What," Liam asked.

"Are you packed?"

"Yes. Are you talking to me now," he asked.

"I wasn't giving you the silent treatment Liam."

He sat down beside her. "I get it. Crappy timing." Kelly nodded. "Alright love. What's next on that long list of stuff to do," he asked.

"Laundry. Beyond that, I have everything done." She slid her passport into her bag, making sure she was covered.

"What," he asked.

"Making sure it doesn't expire this year."

"How long does it take to get a new one with the name change?"

"Liam, we are not having this..."

He kissed her. "Just asking sexy."

"Probably a month."

He nodded. "And when we decide to make it official, you'd have dual citizenship."

Kelly smirked. "And?"

"It means not having to deal with him anymore. If you want to move, we go. You want to go back and forth; we can do that too."

"Can we figure it out when we get back?" He nodded and kissed her.

Hearing the words we get back was enough to put a smile on his face ear to ear. "What?"

"We."

She shook her head. "I love you, but you need to cut back on the Jameson's. You're way too happy," Kelly joked.

"Wasn't just that love. It was you saying getting back. I know that you're worried, but we'll be fine. Always have been."

"Just remember that I do have to get work done." He nodded and got up. "And where are you going," Kelly asked.

"Taking my wife upstairs."

"Not yet there handsome."

"Practicing for when we are husband and wife."

"I bet you are." He took her hand, helped her up and walked her upstairs.

"Liam." He smirked and walked her back to their bedroom.

"What wife to be," he teased.

Kelly shook her head. "No more cobbler making or doing whatever for everyone else. Breathe. Now we can relax," he said determined to make up for his morning choice of words in the shower.

"And what is it exactly that you wanted handsome?"

He kissed her. "I made a decision."

"And what's that?"

He kissed her, devouring her lips. "What if we invited your folks to come in a week or two. After we hang with the family and you meet my friends. What do you think?"

"You want to do it there don't you?"

"We have a chance to get everyone together even if it's only for a few days. What do you think," he asked as he sat down on the edge of the bed and slid her into his lap so she was straddling him.

"And if I said that it's a little much?"

He kissed her. "Then we wait."

She looked at him, seeing how excited he was. "We'll see."

"Kelly."

"Liam, I love that you want to rush into all of it. I haven't even met your friends and family yet."

"All the more reason love."

She took a deep breath. "Fine. I'll ask them, but we have to have somewhere for them to stay."

"Not a problem."

"Fine."

She went to call her Dad and he slid the phone from her hand. "What?"

He kissed her, pulling her tight to him and slid her shirt off. "Liam."

He looked at her as he held her face in his hands. "What love?"

"We need..."

He kissed her again. "We're both packed love. Everything is ready to go."

"And..."

"Are you attempting to avoid being together?"

"No."

"Then talk to me love."

"Liam, we have..."

He kissed her. "We're fine. What are you worried about?"

"What happens when they don't like me?"

"What happens when they do? I love you. My family will. My friends will even if they have an odd way of showing it sometimes."

"Liam."

"Come," he said as he wrapped his arms around her and snuggled her to him. "Nobody is gonna get me to change my mind love. I promise you that."

"I just don't want your friends..."

He kissed her. "You're more important than anything. You always will be love. I waited ten years to bring you home to meet my folks and my friends. I met your folks and a few friends. I just want us..."

She kissed him. "Just anxious."

He kissed her. "They're not gonna bite love. I promise you that."

"Not the point Liam."

"Already engaged. Can't run away now," he teased.

"And who said I couldn't," Kelly teased as he leaned her onto the bed and slid into her arms, wrapping her legs tight around him.

"Now you really can't," he teased as he kissed down her neck. Her shirt slid to the floor, and he peeled his off, throwing it into the laundry bin.

"Liam."

He kissed her. "What love," he teased as he unzipped her jeans.

"You are so bad."

"Very good at distracting you sexy," he said. Kelly shook her head and he kissed her, devouring her lips until he heard her jeans slide to the floor.

"Marry me," he teased.

"Kinda said yes already."

"I know. I still can't believe you said yes."

"You sure I can't change my mind," she joked.

"You're stuck with me for life love. You were when we were 18 and you definitely are now."

"Liam." He kissed her again and snuggled her to him, kicking his jeans to the floor.

"What," she asked seeing the smirk.

"Nothing love." He kissed her again and his kisses trailed down her neck as he nibbled and kissed each breast. When he looked up at her, she was watching him. "What," he asked.

She motioned for him to come closer. He kicked his boxers off, peeled off her panties and knocked both to the floor. "Yes love."

She kissed him. He smirked. "Really," he asked.

"Really." He smirked and devoured her lips. When he felt her finally relax, he wanted her. Just as he was about to take advantage of his sexy wife to be, his phone buzzed.

"I'm not answering it," Liam said as he kissed her and pulled her to him as they started having sex. He was just starting to get going, his phone rang again.

"Liam."

"No." He kissed her again as things just went that much faster. It wasn't making love. It wasn't passion. It was determination to finish what he'd started. When they came up for air and she was throbbing around him, he started getting harder, faster, holding on like she'd kick him out in minutes. When his body crashed into release, his phone went off yet again.

"Liam."

"I swear, I'm kicking someone's backside," he said as he kissed her. Kelly went to grab it and he shook his head. "Don't even think about it sexy."

"Why?"

He grabbed it and saw that his mom had called more than once. He shook his head and kissed Kelly, calling his mom back as she got up.

"Mum," he said.

"Why didn't you answer," his mom asked.

"Because we were outside. What did you need Mum?"

"When are you two coming?"

"We're going up to my place in Belfast for a bit before we come down to the house to see you. A bunch of stuff happened and she needed some time to decompress."

"I get that. I want to see you before the lads do," his mom replied.

"I know. That's the second stop. I promise."

"Your da wants to talk to you."

"Yes mum."

Kelly went and got cleaned up, slid her satin robe on and went and walked back into the bedroom, seeing him in tears. "What happened," Kelly asked silently.

Liam motioned for her to come closer and she slid into his arms. He put the phone on speaker.

"She's right here," Liam said.

"I know how excited you two are to have the wedding you wanted and start your life again but together. Mum and I spoke, and we wanted you two to know that Nan had put money aside for when you two met up again. She wanted to help the two of you pay for the dream wedding. I have the information for you two. She didn't want me to tell you until you actually did it. When you two make it down here, I'll give you the letter and the info. Kelly, I can't wait to finally meet you. He talked about you for so long. We all knew that he'd find you one day. When you get here, let me know. I can pick you up at the airport if you want," his Dad said.

"We have a car coming but thank you. We'll call you when we land."

"Alright love. See you soon," his Dad said.

They hung up and Liam smirked. "And you were worried." Kelly shook her head and snuggled him.

"Liam."

He kissed her. "I love you. I always have and always will. You don't need to keep worrying love. They're gonna love you. Mum is gonna fight for you. So will my Dad."

"Liam, no pressure."

"I know. Breathe."

"Your friends are what I'm most worried about." He kissed her.

"They're jealous love. They will be even more when they meet you."

"And?"

"Wear the black leather pants."

She shook her head. "You are so bad."

"And? Another reason why you love me sexy wife to be."

Kelly kissed him. "You realize that we have to leave in two hours right?"

He kissed her and devoured her lips, leaning her onto her back and undoing her satin robe.

"Liam." He kissed her again. Letting go wasn't an option, and he was never doing it again.

By the time they managed to come up for air, they both had to rush and get the last of their things into their suitcases. "Cobbler," Kelly said.

"What do you need for it?"

"Peaches. Flour, cinnamon, nutmeg."

"Grocery." He nodded and they loaded the bags, headed to the market and went to the airport, walking onto the private plane in comfy sweats. "Can we put these somewhere so I have it for when we land," Kelly asked.

"Most definitely. By the way, you have a ton of peaches. You sure you're gonna need all of those?"

Kelly smirked. "Cobbler," Kelly replied.

The attendant smirked and nodded, putting it into the in-cabin fridge. They got the bags secured and Kelly and Liam curled up on the sofa together. Within 10 minutes, they were taxiing to the runway and were up in the air.

"What do you want to do first," Liam asked.

"Sleep."

"And then?"

"Try and go see a few things. The cliffs. Go drive around and see all the places you love."

"They're all on you," he whispered as Kelly shook her head.

"Seriously. You need to rinse out that dirty mind of yours," Kelly teased.

"That's another reason why you love me sexy."

She kissed him and he smirked. "If you'd like to get a little more comfortable, this does slide out a little if you'd like to lay down."

"What time do you think we'll arrive," Kelly asked.

"4am Belfast time."

"So, in other words 11pm our time," Kelly asked as the attendant nodded.

"Then we probably need sleep," Liam teased.

"I have seafood pasta for you for dinner. You can have it now then get some rest," the attendant asked.

"Sure," Liam said. He kissed Kelly and she shook her head.

"Behave."

"What fun is that sexy wife to be?"

She shook her head and kissed him. "Behave Liam."

"Why?"

"Not my plane Liam. Behave." The waitress brought them dinner and they got their drinks and ate.

"What," Kelly asked as they finished dinner. He shook his head. The attendant brought them blankets and lowered the lights. They finished their drinks and he smirked.

"Liam, I swear, you start something..."

He kissed her and pulled the blanket over them. "What," he teased. She shook her head and he kissed her, she curled up with him and shook her head. "When are you gonna behave?"

"Never."

His hand slid to her backside. "Don't you dare."

He took her hand and slid it to his lap, pointing out how turned on he was. "See what you do?"

"Meaning?"

"It's been like that since we were 18. The only woman that can make that happen." He was turned on and ready to pounce and she knew it.

"Liam."

"Slide them off," he whispered. Kelly shook her head. When she felt his hand slide down the front of her joggers, she went to say something and he kissed her.

"Bathroom." Kelly shook her head and he kissed her again as he got up and helped her to her feet.

When she saw that a privacy curtain and noise block panel was put up between them and the section of the cabin with the attendants, she shook her head. "What are you doing?"

He kissed her again and walked her into the bathroom, locking the door behind them.

"What..." Liam picked her up, sat her on the counter and slid her joggers off.

"Couldn't wait could you?"

He smirked. "Not with you love. Not for a second," he said as he pulled her legs around him and she felt him hard as a rock. "You started it," he teased.

"How?" He kissed her and before she could say a single word, they were having sex in the airplane bathroom. Hot, keep it quiet so nobody hears sex that had her toes curling in her sneakers and Liam even more turned on. He pounded into her over and over again until he found his release and her body was throbbing around him. "So very bad," Kelly teased.

"Like I said. Another reason why you want me so badly," he joked.

Kelly shook her head. "We can't keep tempting fate. You know that right?"

"Brought the box," he joked.

"You are supposed to use them silly."

"Silly? You're calling me silly right now?"

Kelly nodded and he kissed her, pulling her legs tighter around him as she relished that full feeling a little longer. "Like an overheated teenager," Kelly joked.

"You definitely started that then."

"Meaning what," Kelly asked as he cleaned up a bit and pulled his joggers up.

She slid her panties and joggers back on and they made their way back to the bed and curled up together while he told her. "When you were there, I don't even know how to explain it. Having you near me turned me on. Kissing you made it worse. Making out on that bed, it took all the will power I had not to strip you naked and have my way with you."

Kelly kissed him. "Then we'll have to reenact it," Kelly joked.

"Go ahead and say it now. You won't be saying it when we get there."

Kelly kissed him. "Sleep."

"With you around, not really a chance at all," he said. Kelly kissed him and curled up with him, nodding off in his arms, and within a half hour, he followed.

Liam woke Kelly up a few hours later when they were almost back in Ireland. "What," Kelly asked.

"Almost home love." She smirked, kissed him and got up to freshen up. By the time she came back to sit with him, they had to put on seatbelts and were almost on the runway.

Kelly looked out the window to the lush green, the grey of the city and a feeling like she was finally back home, or what seemed like home. "Welcome home handsome."

"Back at ya beautiful fiancée," he replied.

They got to their parking area and saw an SUV waiting for them. "Ready to go to the house," he asked.

Kelly nodded and kissed him. "Is it odd that I'm almost nervous?"

"You and me alone in a cottage without any interruptions? Nope."

She kissed him and walked to the SUV.

"Do we have a car for..." He put the bags in the back and hopped in with her.

"We have my SUV at the cottage. We're fine love."

When they got to his cottage, she smirked and that smirk turned into a smile ear to ear. "Liam."

"Yes wife."

"Closest to my beach house that you could get," she joked.

"I got this place 6 years ago I think. When I decided that I needed to clear my head." The view was beautiful. The beach was nearby, which made it a little easier, and when they walked inside, she smirked.

"Just like home," he teased.

"It is home," Kelly replied as she looked around and he put the bags in the bedroom.

The cute kitchen, the sofa that was the perfect size for the two of them, the porch to sit and have coffee in the morning. It felt like a home, minus the sweaty, humid, overly hot summer weather.

"What are you doing beautiful?"

"Looking at the view," she said as she looked out the window.

"Come with me." He walked her around the rest of the house, showing her the fancy bathroom and Jacuzzi tub, the two extra bedrooms, then the main bedroom.

"Nice bed," Kelly said.

"You okay," he asked.

Kelly nodded. "Just soaking it all in." She sat down on the edge of the bed and he was about to kiss her when her phone buzzed.

"Please don't," he joked.

Kelly kissed him and answered. "Yes."

"How was the flight," her mom asked.

"Good. We just got to his place. We were sorta talking yesterday. When was the last time you two were in Ireland," Kelly asked.

"Years. Long ago. Why," her mom asked.

She put the phone on speaker and let Liam tell them. "Well, Kelly and I were thinking that you should come. It'd give you a chance to meet my family since we're engaged already."

"That would be fantastic," her mom said.

"Two weeks," Liam asked.

"Wow. Okay. I can book..."

"I'll take care of the tickets. I'll email them over tomorrow."

"You don't have to do that," her Dad said.

"Kinda do. My idea, my tab," Liam said.

"We'll see you in two weeks then," her mom said. She hung up with them a few minutes later and Liam leaned her onto the bed.

"Aren't you supposed to call and let..."

He kissed her, sliding her to the pillows. "Liam."

He leaned in and devoured her lips. "Yes wife."

"Food?"

"Already put away. My sister was up here."

"Liam." He kissed her again and snuggled her to him as he pulled her legs around his waist.

"Mine," he teased.

All it took was one kiss. One hot, deep, intense kiss that had her breaking out in goosebumps. "I swear Liam."

He kissed her again and peeled her joggers and panties off, then went for her hoodie and bra. "Wife."

She shook her head and he kissed her again. "You're not cold," she asked.

"Around you? No." She smirked and he kissed her as his kisses trailed down her neck.

"Liam."

"Yes love," he teased as he got to her breasts and teased and licked and nibbled at them until her body was arching against his.

"What are you up to?"

"Christening the bed," he teased as he kissed down her stomach. When he made his way to her hip, she was about ready to pull him to her. When she felt that fullness again, she closed her eyes.

"All mine," he teased as she felt his tongue against her.

"Liam."

"Yes sexy wife to be." She reached for him and he smirked.

"Really? Already?"

She looked at him and he smirked and kept going, sliding his fingers inside the warmth of her core. "You sure," he teased.

Kelly looked at him. "Liam."

"Mm. You taste good," he teased as he kept going until she was almost ready to explode. He kissed his way back up her torso and kissed her, devouring her lips until he was buried deep inside her again.

"You are so not playing fair at all," she said.

"If you can still talk, then it's not enough," he joked as her knees slid to his back.

"Wife." One more all-encompassing kiss and his body gave way along with hers. When he felt her almost shaking, he pulled the blanket up.

"You alright love?"

Kelly nodded and kissed him again. "More," he teased. Kelly shook her head. She didn't let go of him and he didn't dare move from that perfect spot.

"Kelly."

"What," she replied as he kissed her neck.

"You sure I have to share you with the world?"

"Not today," she teased.

"Good answer," he teased. Kelly kissed him and they curled up together.

"Tired," he asked. Kelly shook her head.

"Honestly, I feel better being here."

"Because we're away from the rest of the world?"

Kelly nodded. He kissed her forehead. "That's why I wanted you to come. Especially after that."

Kelly shook her head and went to get up. "Kelly."

"I have to pee. That's it." She got up and made her way into the bathroom, seeing a big tub with a view. She cleaned up a little and got up, washing her hands. When she saw the medicine cabinet open, she opened it a little more. Condoms everywhere, meds and Tylenol. When she saw the meds, she had to stop herself.

"This is insane," she thought to herself seeing Liam's name. All of it was meds to calm anxiety and anti-psychotic. She'd dated enough psycho's to know the drug names. She closed the cabinet and saw the towels. She flipped the hot water on and stepped under the warm water.

She was just inhaling the steam of the shower when she felt arms around her. "See, I knew you'd hop in without me love," Liam said. She turned to face him and he handed Faith her shampoo, conditioner, body wash and sea sponge.

"Thank you."

"Welcome sexy." He ran the shampoo through her hair and kissed her.

"Is it bad that I don't want to let you out of my sight while we're here," he teased.

Kelly kissed him and he rinsed the shampoo from her hair. "What's wrong," he asked.

"Just felt like I needed a shower." He kissed her again and snuggled her to him as she felt his body against her all over again. When she kissed his tattoo with her initials in it, he smirked.

"Now you know why it's right there," he said.

"What?"

"Where you kissed when you were here."

"Liam."

"I would've put it on my neck," he teased.

"You're planning another one aren't you?" He nodded.

"Want something that's us."

"Meaning?"

"You and I do it together." She shook her head and kissed him.

"Maybe start with a decent night of sleep." He kissed her and devoured her lips, leaning her against the cool tile of the wall.

"Liam."

He kissed her again. "Yes sexy."

She kissed him and grabbed her conditioner. She ran it through her hair and felt the sea sponge against her. He kissed her neck then felt his hand against her. "Liam."

"Yes sexy wife." He leaned against her. He kissed down her neck.

"I know..."

She was about to say something and felt him start teasing all over again. "What," he teased.

"Aah," she said as she went up on her tiptoes.

"Come," he said as he sat down on the bench and pulled her on top of him so her back was against his chest.

"What," she teased.

"Please," he teased. Kelly smirked and he kissed her shoulder.

"Please what handsome?" He kept going and when her legs were almost shaking, he slid inside her again and kept teasing. Something was so different, knowing that she could stop watching over her shoulder. That she could stop worrying about her ex breaking in. She could've cared less at that point. Liam had her turned on in ways she never thought were possible.

"I crave you. Every damn second of the day I crave you," he whispered as her body crashed around him from her orgasm.

"Better," he teased.

"Liam." He kept going. And when she actually crumbled in his arms, he kissed her.

"We need sleep," Kelly teased.

"We need to go out."

"Why?"

"Because if we don't, you're not gonna make it out of the bedroom for a month."

Kelly got up, albeit with shaky legs, and rinsed out the conditioner, cleaned up and motioned for him to come closer. "Yes love of my life," he said. She put her shampoo in her hands and washed his hair for him as he picked her up.

"Thank you beautiful." She kissed him and then rinsed the shampoo out.

"You're right. I do feel better," he teased as they stepped out. He bypassed the towels altogether.

"What," she teased as she ended up curled up in the blankets with Liam. He kissed her.

"Promise you won't laugh?"

She nodded and kissed his chest. "I used to dream about this."

"Curled up in bed together?"

He kissed her. "You here in the house with me. Your skin against mine. Me getting hard every ten seconds because you're near me."

She kissed him. "I'm right here handsome." He kissed her again.

"Hungry?"

She shook her head. "I need to ask though. The cabinet was open."

"Kelly."

"When? It looks like it was just filled." He kissed her.

"Liam."

"I told you. I went kinda nuts when you left. I thought that the whiskey could fix it or the Guinness. I finally stopped and flew off the handle every single time someone suggested I got over it. I can't do that. I couldn't. I couldn't imagine losing you for real. My sister probably got it refilled. I went off of everything when I started on the software stuff. I lost my mind more than once thinking that I'd lost you. That you'd died and I wasn't there. I literally thought that I'd get to Charleston and have to find your headstone instead of you." She looked at him.

"Just so you know, I actually had told my parents that if something ever happened that was catastrophic, to find you

SOUTHERN TEMPTATION 349

and tell you. I even put your contact info down." He kissed her.

"You did?"

Kelly nodded. "I never wanted it to be the way it was. I didn't want it to end like that."

He kissed her, devouring her lips and leaned into her arms. "Promise me something."

"What?"

"That you never ever ghost me again."

"I couldn't even if I wanted to. I think you put a gps in the ring."

"Magically I guess."

She nodded and he kissed her. "I don't want us apart again. What about you?"

"What about me?"

"What do you want?"

"To not watch over my shoulder anymore. To actually sleep without..."

He kissed her. "You never have to watch over your shoulder again love. I have your back. Nobody's hurting you again."

He kissed her forehead again and she snuggled in tighter to him.

For once, they just snuggled and talked like they had when they'd first met. "Are you hungry," he asked.

Kelly kissed him. "What are you cooking?"

"Mum said she left us stew to warm us up. What do you think beautiful?"

She kissed him again. "Stew it is."

He kissed her forehead, pulled his jeans on with a hoodie and walked into the kitchen. Fact was, being in Ireland made her feel better. Made her take a deep breath and let the fear go. Whether it was the two of them finding a way to be together, or the fact that she was a good 8 hour plus flight from all her troubles, she knew. She would actually be able to sleep and relax and get her life back to normal. He came back in a few minutes later, handing her a cup of tea. "Thank you." He kissed her.

"Stew is warming up sexy wife. What else did you want to have?"

"Up to you handsome. I'm just relaxing." He smirked.

"About time. He grabbed a sweater from his closet and handed it to her.

"What," she teased.

"Come. You may need the sweater." She kissed him, put her tea on the side table and got up, sliding his warm sweater on and sliding her leggings on. She followed him having her tea and he sat her up on the counter.

"Liam."

He kissed her. "Yes sexy wife of mine."

"Are you happy that we're back?"

"Happy that you're here with me. That I don't have to wonder where you are anymore. I wished a million times over for a moment like this."

She kissed him and he pulled her legs around him. "Like what? Me on your counter while we have your mum's Irish stew?" He kissed her again, devouring her lips.

"I can so turn that into something really dirty," he said.

"You kinda already did about 6 times in the past 72 hours handsome."

Chapter 13

"Are you complaining love," he teased with a smirk and a wink.

"Nope. Just sayin that you really do need to clean out that dirty mind of yours. We..."

He kissed her. "What?"

"We."

"Liam." He smirked. "You need to quit."

He kissed her. "My favorite thing in the world is you saying that word."

"And why is that handsome fiancée?"

"And that's my second favorite word."

"Fiancée?"

He nodded and kissed her, stirred the stew up a little more and gave her a taste test. "That is so good," Kelly said.

"That's why she made it. Sort of hits the spot after flying all the way in." Kelly kissed him and he flipped the burner off and slid his arms around her. "What," he asked. She hugged him.

"It sounds insane. I know. I just..." He kissed her, picked her up and carried her to the sofa, leaning her onto it.

"Liam."

"Yes wife."

She kissed him again. "Are you sure you really want us to go to a big family thing? We can't just hide out for a few weeks?"

He smirked and kissed her, devouring her lips until she was pulling his sweater off of him. "Kelly."

"What?"

"I love you."

"Love you a million times more handsome."

He kissed her again and smirked. "What?"

He slid her leggings off, pulling a blanket over them. "Nothin," he teased.

"Liam."

"Getting you comfortable."

"I bet you are," she joked as she heard his jeans slide to the floor. "You know, I do kinda love this," Kelly said, tracing her initials on the tattoo.

"There's another one that I can get if you want to get it with me."

"Which would be what," she teased as he slid his sweater off of her.

"You can get one with me."

"Of what?"

"Our wedding bands."

She shook her head and kissed him. "Anything else?"

He nodded and devoured her lips. "You tell me what you want me to get and where and I'll do it."

Kelly looked at him. "You're being ridiculous. You know that right?"

"Tell me."

"Liam, you don't need to. This is more than…"

He kissed her. "You tell me."

"Liam."

He kissed her again and she knew he meant it. "You don't have to."

"Tell me where love."

Kelly shook her head and his hand slid between her legs. "Kelly."

"Liam, stop."

"Tell me." He started making it all worse and started getting way past hot and bothered. "Stop."

"What," he asked. When she felt his fingers slide inside her, she shook her head.

"Liam."

"Tell me where love. Tell me and the taunting stops," he teased. When he kissed down her neck and started nibbling and licking and kissing her breasts until she was almost trembling, she shook her head.

"Liam, aah."

"Say it." His taunting intensified until her body was throbbing.

"Liam, please."

"Say it and you can have what..."

She shook her head. "This isn't a game Liam." His hand slid away from her and within seconds, he'd filled her and they were having sex again on that sofa. He couldn't have held on for that long considering the fact that he was more turned on than she was. He held on as long as he could, and when he finally managed to let go, she was almost shaking in his arms. "Kelly."

"Move."

"Kelly, don't." She pushed him away, got up, grabbed the sweater and her leggings and walked off into the bedroom.

He shook his head and went to get up when he heard wheels. "Kelly."

"No."

"Baby."

"No. I'm not..."

"Don't leave." She went to grab her phone and he blocked her, throwing it onto the sofa.

"Don't walk out love. Please." She dropped her bag and walked out the door, grabbing her phone. She went and sat away from the house, away from him. She'd gone through hell before. She'd lost her mind. She'd been used, and now that fairytale happy that she'd had when they arrived was gone. When she saw a glass of Jameson's slide over her shoulder, she shook her head. "I don't want it Liam."

"Then you're gonna need a few blankets. It's not warm love."

"Don't."

"Kelly."

She shook her head. "I'm just gonna stay in a hotel."

"Kelly."

"No. Not after that Liam." She went to make a call and he took her phone. "Give it back."

"No."

"Liam, you can't hold me..."

He kissed her. "Overdid it."

"Once was a mistake Liam. Not twice."

She went to reach for her phone and he shook his head. "Don't go."

"Liam."

"Don't."

"I need to."

"You ran off on me once and almost got killed. The time before that, I lost you for ten years. I'm not losing you again." Kelly shook her head and went to walk away. "Kelly."

"I'm not playing this game with you Liam. You can't force me to do what you want. You can't demand that I tell you where to put a damn tattoo. You can't..."

He kissed her. "Please come inside."

"Liam, I need to go."

"You just got here."

"And I shouldn't..." He kissed her again and picked her up, carrying her back inside. He had neighbors. None that could be that close, but he didn't need anyone doing anything or spreading gossip.

"Liam, put me down."

He walked in, locked the door and sat her on the counter. "Liam."

"Don't. You can't just walk off Love. Please."

"I'm not..."

He kissed her. "Please." She looked at him. "Kelly."

"I'm not staying..."

He kissed her. "We need sleep. You're only..."

She pushed him away and walked off into the bedroom, closing and locking the door behind her. She shook her head, grabbed her hoodie from her bag and curled up in the bed alone. When he knocked a half hour later, she refused to answer. "Kelly, you need food." When she still didn't answer, he grabbed the key and unlocked the door, seeing her asleep in the bed.

He put the Jameson on the bedside table and put the two bowls of stew beside it, sitting on the edge of the bed. "What do you want," Kelly asked.

"Eat with me."

"No."

"Kelly, please." She shook her head and he saw his sweater back in his closet. "That was for you love."

"I don't care Liam. I don't want it." When he saw the ring on the bedside table, he took a deep breath, trying to hold back the anger. It wasn't gonna do anyone any good.

"Come here."

"No."

"Kelly."

"Liam, leave me alone."

"Come here." She sat up and stayed on the opposite side of the bed. "Kelly."

"Don't. Don't think that you can just brush this off. Why don't you go and take one of the damn pills in your cupboard? Maybe it'll help."

He handed her the stew, grabbed her hand and put the ring back on her finger. "Eat."

"Liam."

"Eat the damn stew woman." She had her food in silence. "Seriously," he said.

"Don't."

"Kelly, we're not seriously gonna spend the first day here alone in world war three are we?"

"Depends Liam. Time machine?"

"Kelly, I went too far."

"Damn right you did."

"I'm sorry."

"The first time, fine. Not when it becomes a regular damn power move Liam. Not from you." She got her phone back and glared at him.

"Kelly." She shook her head. "Please." She took the ring back off and handed it to him. She went to get up and he shook his head. "No."

"Liam."

"Don't leave. Please don't." She looked at him.

"I can't keep doing this Liam. I did this at home. He had his hand on my damn throat. He tried to strangle me on the beach. You go too far and try to screw me into submission. What's the damn difference?"

"Kelly."

"No. You don't get to do that. Not today, not tomorrow. Never."

"Please just talk to me."

"No."

"Kelly."

"I'm going home Liam."

"No."

Kelly looked at him. "It was a nice dream."

"Don't do this." She went and slid on her jeans and a different sweater, slid on her Ugg boots and went to walk past him. "Kelly."

"No."

She grabbed her clothes, her suitcase and went to walk out when he grabbed her bags and pulled her to him. "What?"

He kissed her. "Please."

"No."

"Kelly, please. Just stay tonight. We can talk tomorrow."

"Then I'm staying somewhere..." He kissed her again.

"Please love."

"Stop." He kissed her again and picked her up, walking her back to the bedroom. "Liam." He kissed her, devouring her lips and leaned her onto the bed. "Liam."

"What," he asked.

"What part of I'm not staying here didn't you get?"

"Please don't go. Please love."

"This isn't love Liam. What you did wasn't love. It was a week 10 years ago and a week now. You got laid. Congrats," Kelly said.

"Don't do that. Kelly, please. Don't do that. You know dang well it was more. You wouldn't have said yes if it wasn't."

She shook her head. "Temporary stupidity."

"Kelly."

"Don't. Just don't Liam. You love what you thought you wanted. You don't want me. You want someone you can control and boss around. That's not and never will be me Liam. I'm going home."

"No."

"Liam, I'm leaving even if I have to go while you're sleeping." She went to get up and he shook his head.

"Please don't walk away. Don't leave me again. Please."

"Liam, you can't do that and not know that I'm..." He kissed her again.

"Please." She knew that she had no choice. That she'd leave in the car that Faith's Dad had booked, get back on the plane and leave all of it behind. She couldn't face him anymore. She couldn't sit in that chair and pretend that nothing happened, nor could she forget.

"I can't do this without you."

She looked at him. "Liam, you can't force me to do something I'm not going to. You might as well have..."

He kissed her. "Please. Please just give me a chance." He kissed her again and she shook her head.

"Just stop."

"Kelly."

"I'm not staying here Liam. Not after that."

"I'll stay on the sofa."

Kelly shook her head. "You don't get it."

"I can't let you walk out of my life again."

"Then find a way to control yourself and just stop Liam."

"I'm begging you not to leave." She shook her head. "Kelly, I can't lose you. I can't watch you leave and walk out all over again."

"Then don't look."

"Don't leave."

"Or what Liam? Chase me down and do it again? What?" He kissed her and pulled her into his lap. "Don't leave me."

"Liam."

He kissed her again and leaned her onto the bed. "Please."

"Don't."

"Kelly, please."

"Liam, move."

"Don't leave."

Kelly shook her head. "Liam."

"Please don't leave me." She shook her head. She slid out of his arms and got up. "Kelly."

"I said no." She went to grab her bag and he stopped her.

"Stay tonight." She shook her head and pushed him away.

"I'm not playing with you Liam. I said no."

"Stay. We can talk in the morning."

"Why? So, you can do it again tomorrow?"

"Please. Please just stay. I'll do whatever you want. I can't lose you." She shook her head and her eyes started welling up.

"Please love. Please."

Kelly took a deep breath. "I need a minute," she said. She knew calling Faith would be a mistake, calling her folks would be worse. When he nodded and he left her alone with a full bottle of Jameson's, she tried to think straight. She made the decision. She needed to talk to Faith.

Kelly grabbed her phone and called. "Girl, aren't you two supposed to be on vacation? What's going on," Faith asked.

"Fight. Just upset. I don't know what to do, and the instinct is to duck and run."

"What'd he do?"

"He's just... he demanded that I do something then sorta went too far to attempt to convince me to do it."

"The possessive streak. Ridge has one of those. Hell, I have one of those," Faith said.

"It's a little too much."

"You can't just leave because you aren't comfortable. Talk to him girl."

"I did. It's not the first time. Now, I'm just mad."

"What do you really want? Do you want to work things out or do you want to leave?"

"That's why I'm calling you."

"If you're determined to leave, I can get the car to come get you."

"I told him that he can't do that and then it happens again. He won't let me walk out of the dang house. Not like I can walk anywhere."

"Kelly, you can't run from this one. There's nothing that's gonna fix it, and coming back here will just make it worse."

"I just need to get out of here."

"Kelly, do you love him?"

"Not the point."

"Kinda is," Faith said.

"Yeah, I do."

"Enough to work on it?"

"It's like he's..."

"Using sex as a way to make demands? Kelly, I don't want to offend. You know that we've known each other for years. Please don't take this as a slight, but you haven't had a healthy relationship in years. You said so. Yeah, this is a roadblock, but you can't up and run."

"I just don't want this..."

"I know."

"Thank you," Kelly said.

"Just remember that he loves you. Be mad, yell and scream, but you can't take off." Kelly hung up with her a little while later and had her stew. When Liam came in, he saw her still in the bed.

"Tell me that you're staying," Liam asked.

"We're not having this conversation again Liam. Sex isn't a game. It's not your way to make demands. Not anymore."

"Kelly."

"If that's what you want, you picked the wrong person."

"Please."

"For now, I'll stay, but if you pull that..."

He kissed her, leaning into her arms. "I'm not losing you again. I can't."

"I know, but you can't demand something and then use me like that."

"I'm sorry. Really sorry."

"Good. By the way, the stew is good."

He kissed her again. "We eat then go for a walk," he asked.

"Liam."

"We have a half hour. We can either go for a drive or a walk."

"Liam." He kissed her again. "Will you let me go for a walk with you?"

"Do I actually have to?"

"Do you want to go for a drive instead?"

"Depends. Are you gonna stop forcing me into things?"

"Only thing I want is for you to be here. I went too far. I get it."

"Is that why you were taking..."

"Kelly."

"Is it?" He went quiet and that was enough of an answer.

"When..." He kissed her silencing her before she asked the question that he didn't want to answer. "Answer me."

"A long time ago when I was still losing my mind. When I thought you were dead. That's when."

"Liam."

"What?"

"How long?"

"6 years ago. I concentrated on other things."

"Then answer me one other question."

"What love?"

"How many?" He shook his head, got up and did the dishes, putting the rest of the stew into the fridge.

Kelly pulled on her jeans and his sweater, pulled on her Ugg boots and walked into the kitchen. "What was the answer?"

"I don't..."

She looked at him. "You want me to trust you, you have to tell me." "Kelly."

"Answer."

"Enough that I know what I want now. That enough?"

"Over 30?"

He shook his head and cleaned up. "40?"

"Kelly, stop."

"Were they in that bed?"

"No."

"Liam, don't..."

"Nobody was. I bought it when I moved out here on my own."

"If you lie…"

He kissed her, holding her face in his hands. "No more fights. I'm not losing you. We already had one narrow escape. We're not having that fight again, and we aren't starting another. Do you want to come for a walk or go for a drive?"

"I don't want to sit here anymore. We need to go do something constructive."

"We kinda already did sexy wife to be."

"Not that."

"Drive or walk?"

"Drive."

They got dressed, he locked the house up and handed Kelly her phone and purse. "Where are we gonna go?"

"Murlough Bay."

"For what reason?" He smirked and kissed her, opened her door for her and they headed off.

"Liam."

"We're going to the beach so we can relax. Go for a walk like you do at home."

"It's kinda cold."

"It's Ireland. It's never a million degrees like it is at your place."

"How long until we get there," Kelly asked.

"Hour and a half. You want to stop on the way, we stop."

Kelly shook her head and he kissed her hand. "Liam."

"What?"

"Really though. What was the number?"

"Leave it at every time I got near someone, they told me off for calling them by your name. The only one that I didn't, I was beyond drunk."

"How many times Liam?"

"I lost count. There was only once that I didn't use anything obviously." Kelly shook her head. "It was ten years. Ten that I went ballistic missing my girl." Kelly took a deep breath. She had to choose her words carefully.

"Kelly, I'm not gonna break. Just say it."

"And you think that I'm enough for you?"

"Kelly."

"Well?"

"You're more than I could've ever wanted. I just wish we hadn't been apart. That's all."

"You would've still been..." He pulled the car over and kissed her.

"No love. I wanted you. Every single person that came into my life was a temporary fix to a long-term issue. It was like a band-aid on a cut that doesn't want to stop bleeding."

"Liam."

He kissed her and slid his seat back. "Come here."

"No." He kissed her and got her to slide into his lap.

"What," she asked.

Liam kissed her, devouring her lips. "I wanted this. You. Us. That's all I wanted. That's all I ever wanted. Everyone else was literally a distraction. It happened 3 times in the past 6 years. Before that, it was a drunken haze."

"Then you shouldn't be drinking."

"I stopped for the past 4 years. Most I've ever had is a glass or two of Jameson's. I can't tell you why because I don't know why I started drinking and couldn't find my way out. All I know is that I can't be without you. You're the only thing saving my life."

"Why," Kelly asked.

"Meaning what?"

"It shouldn't depend on me."

"Kelly."

"You want to stay sober, then we stay…"

He kissed her. "I'm good."

"Then why does that bottle have a recent date on it?" He took a deep breath.

"Because if something happened and we didn't work, my pain in the butt sister thought I may need them to dig me out of the hole I'd be drinking myself out of."

"And if I'd said no to marrying you?"

He kissed her, devouring her lips. "Liam."

He kissed her again and she felt his hand against her bare back. When the kiss deepened, Kelly shook her head and slid back onto her seat. "Kelly." She shook her head. "Baby."

"If you're gonna drive then drive Liam." He shook his head and turned the car around, heading back to the house.

She was getting mad. She was getting to the point that leaving the house was looking better and better. When they got back, he hopped out, got her door and walked her back inside. "What," Kelly asked.

He got in the door, picked her up and sat her on the kitchen counter. "Are you seriously gonna be mad for what happened when we weren't together?"

"No. All I'm saying is that if you're not gonna drink anymore then don't. I'm fine not drinking."

"Kelly."

She shook her head and slid off the counter and he grabbed her hand. "What," she asked.

"Don't walk away."

"Liam, let go of my hand please."

"Please just talk to me."

"Why?" She pulled away and walked into the living room, sitting down on the chair instead of the sofa.

"Are you seriously avoiding me?"

"Liam, everything is a damn fight. Everything. You get passionate about something and I get jumpy, worried that you're gonna pull that crap again."

He looked at her and sat down on the sofa. "I love you. You know that right?"

"And?"

"Kelly."

"Don't Kelly me. Just don't. What do you want from me Liam? Tell me what's gonna snap you out of all of this." He got up and grabbed her hand. "What?" He walked her into the bedroom and pulled the notebook out of her bag.

"I don't care about the stupid notebook Liam."

"Read it. The end part."

"Liam, say it. I don't want to read it out of a damn journal. Talk." He shook his head and found the page, handing it to her and went and got the bottle of Jameson, handing her the bottle and pouring some into his glass. He couldn't even look at her as she read it:

> *I bought the cottage I always wanted. The one I hoped that somehow I'd be in with Kelly. I'm sitting*

here, in a place where I should be happy. I bought the bed for us to sleep in. I bought the sofa for us to curl up on and watch movies on lazy Sundays after church. I got the kitchen so we could cook together. Everything in this stupid house was for us and I don't even know where she is or whether she's even alive. Every year on that stupid day I look for her. I search for her on the stupid computer and nothing ever happens. This year will be 10 years. Ten of being without her. Of craving and missing her. Of wishing that she was here. The software is working at least and now I have to go to Charleston. Like it isn't bad enough. I have to go to the city that she vanished to. That she disappeared into and avoided me. Every year, I call and it goes to voicemail. I can hear that voice that I wanted, that I craved and needed to hear. All I can hope is that somehow fate steps in. That I see her again. That by some random moment, I am face to face with her. I swear that if I ever am again, I'm kissing her again. I have to. I still have the damn hoodie I leant her while she was here. It still smells like her perfume. I just can't keep doing this. I can't drown myself in whiskey. I can't drink this feeling away anymore. If I don't see her there, it's done. I move on. I find someone else and I sell the house. I can't be there without her. I just can't. I want more than anything to bring her back here and marry her. Relive the happy memories we had and make a lifetime of new ones.

She looked up at him. "Liam."

"That's why I can't walk away. That's why I can't just forget all of this. I told you then that I'd wait. That I wouldn't stop waiting until you came back to me and I meant it. You know this love. I knew the minute I saw you that I wasn't letting go."

Kelly shook her head and got up, taking the bottle with her. She walked outside and sat down on the porch chair. Yeah, it wasn't warm at all. It was cold, and the fact that the rain was starting was fitting to match her bad mood. "Come inside," Liam said.

Kelly poured her glass of Jameson and drank it. "Kelly."

"Leave me alone."

"Babe."

"Don't." She poured another glass and he took the bottle away.

"What are you doing?"

"Come inside. This isn't gonna solve anything."

"And either does that stupid..."

He kissed her, took the bottle and her hand. "Come inside," he said.

"Liam, just leave me alone," Kelly said. He picked her up and she shook her head. "Put me down."

"No." She finished her drink and he walked her inside, laying her onto the bed.

"Liam, why..." He put the glass down and slid into her arms, kissing her.

"What are you doing," Kelly asked.

"Do you even get it?"

"Liam, whiskey doesn't make me forget. That notebook doesn't change anything. All it shows was that you were like a drug addict. You had a damn addiction. That's it. I'm not gonna just go along…"

He kissed her. "Kelly."

"No."

She got up. "What," he asked.

"I'm not staying here with you. I have to go Liam. Don't chase after me, don't make another demand. I'm going to a hotel alone."

He shook his head. "No. Kelly, please."

"All of this was because you have an obsession Liam. It's not love. It never was," she said as she took the ring off and the claddagh ring and put them both in his hands. She got her things, put them into her bag, grabbed her purse and called the driver to come get her.

Liam sat down on the edge of the bed and was crying. Hysterically crying. When the rain started, he slid to the floor. "She can't leave me. She can't. I waited too long for her to come back."

He got up and walked outside, seeing her get into the SUV that had driven them to the house. He ran in the house and got his keys and wallet, grabbed his cell and ran to his car, hopping in and going after her.

She checked her phone and saw that the pilot couldn't come to get her until the following day. She asked for him to come as soon as possible. "Hotel," Kelly said.

"Your penthouse suite is ready and waiting. Is there anything you need," the driver asked.

"A large bottle of Jameson's." They got to the hotel and the driver took Kelly's bags to the desk, got her room key and escorted her to her suite. Luckily it was under Cartwright Industries instead of her name. She walked in and saw two bottles of Jameson's, poured herself a large glass, thanked the driver and locked the door. She walked into the bedroom and saw the oversized tub.

She slid her boots and leggings off, but part of her didn't want to lose the sweater. She shook her head, slid it off, slid her lingerie off and walked into the bathroom, drawing herself a bath. Her phone went off not 20 minutes later. She shook her head and answered.

"What?"

"Which hotel are you in?"

"Liam."

"Kelly, don't. Answer me."

"No." She hung up. She needed to decompress. She needed to calm her system. Taking both of those rings off was the final straw. She knew it. She also knew that if he was face to face with her again, the rings would be back on. When she went into her emails, there was one from the plane attendant:

> *Unfortunately, we can't do a u-turn on the plane. We'll get there as soon as we can.*

Kelly wanted to leave. Even if she had to get on a commercial flight, she wanted to leave. She looked for flights and her phone went off yet again.

"What," she asked knowing full well that it was Liam.

"What hotel Kelly?"

"I'm going home."

"No, you aren't."

"Goodbye Liam." She hung up and almost instantly burst into tears. How in the hell they went from happy and giggling and laughing and playing to that moment was a blur to her. When her phone rang a few minutes later, she shook her head. She saw Faith's name, brushed the tears away and answered. "Hey," Kelly said sniffling.

"What's going on," Faith asked.

"Why?"

"Because Liam just called my cell and woke me up asking where you were."

She shook her head. "I'm at the hotel. I'm coming home."

"What happened?"

"Doesn't matter. I'm coming home."

"Kelly."

"I don't want him here."

"You know he called my Dad right?"

"He told him?"

"I don't know. All I know is that wherever you are, be expecting company."

"I can't do this."

"Kelly, what happened?"

"It's between us. I'm leaving it at that. I'm coming home and getting my life back."

Not 15 minutes later, there was a knock at her hotel room door. She slid out of the tub, wrapped herself up in the robe and walked to the door, seeing nothing through the peephole. It was a given that it was Liam. "Open the door," Liam asked. She shook her head and walked back into the bedroom.

"Kelly, please." She tried to ignore him. When her hands were shaking, she shook her head, pulled her jeans and his sweater on and answered.

"What?"

"Are you letting me in?"

"No." He went to walk past her and she blocked him.

"What do you want?"

"I'm coming in. We're not having this conversation in the hallway."

She shook her head. "You stay on your side of the room then," she replied.

"Kelly."

"Don't."

"You can't just vanish from the damn house."

"I'm going home Liam."

"No."

"I can't do this. It's not love Liam. You've been obsessed for 10 years. Not in love. Not missing me. You're blaming me for your alcoholism, you're putting me on a damn pedestal so high that you can't reach it. It's like you put me on the top of Everest. I can't..." He kissed her, pulling her to him and she knew. Her phone buzzed and she pulled herself away from him.

She looked at her phone:

We're on the way. We'll be back at 3am. We'll get the car to pick you up. Does that work?

Kelly replied with a yes and pressed send on the email. "What was that?"

"Work. Liam, you can't see it. You don't see it. That notebook is all about an obsession. It's not about love. You want to drink, drink. You need help Liam. I can't fix this. I left. I went on with my crap life and ended up in another level of hell in my personal life. We can't get a time machine and change the past Liam. You went insane and I grew up."

He walked over to her and she pushed him away.

"No." He kissed her again and pulled her to him, devouring her lips until she knew she couldn't resist. He carried her into the bedroom, leaned her onto the bed and peeled her jeans off, then the sweater. He peeled his hoodie off, kicked his jeans to the floor and slid into her arms.

"Liam."

"I'm not losing you," he said. He kissed her again, peeling her panties off, slid her bra off and threw them onto the floor with the clothes then kicked off his boxers.

"Liam." He devoured her lips, not letting her up for a moment to breathe. He wasn't losing her. Not like that. He pulled her legs around him and they had sex. When her eyes welled up, he kept going, hoping that somehow they'd find a way back to each other if he just got her back into his arms.

"Aah," Kelly said moaning into his mouth.

"I love you. Even if you don't think that's what it is, I love you," he said as he kept going, nibbling at her lips, her breasts then her lips again. He'd never been so scared in his entire life. He kept going, then kissed her breasts again, nibbling and licking and nibbling even more. "Liam," she said as her body tightened around him and he kept going.

When he realized he'd left a mark, he moved to the other. His body pounded into her over and over again until her body tightened around him again and her nails were digging into his back.

"Oh my god. Liam, stop."

"No." He kissed her again and went faster, harder until her toes were pretzels and her body was crashing around him over and over again. When his body couldn't hold back, he finally exploded and crashed into her so they were as tight together as he could get without crawling inside her.

"Damn it," Kelly said.

"What," he asked.

"Liam, we can't keep doing this."

He kissed her again, devouring her lips. "I'm not losing you again Kelly."

"I'm..." He kissed her again.

"I'm not."

"Liam, I'm going home. You need to fix this crap." He kissed her again and she felt something slide on her hand. "Liam."

"It's your ring. Keep it on."

She shook her head. "I can't do this Liam. You know I can't." He kissed her again and devoured her lips again.

"You don't get to throw me away."

"I never said I was. I said to get help. Talk to someone other than me," Kelly said as she tried to get up.

"Please." She shook her head in response.

She got up, cleaned up and stepped into the shower. She tried brushing tears away, but she barely managed 2 minutes alone. He slid in behind her and saw her in tears. "Kelly."

"Don't," she said.

"Please love. Please don't leave me."

"You think this is what I wanted Liam? It isn't. I wanted to believe that you really did mean it all. That you loved me. I thought the dang notebook was sweet, but the more I read it, the more I saw the obsession. The addiction to something you couldn't have. You screwing every woman near you to get me out of your system was illness. It wasn't you loving me." She stepped out of the shower, dried off and walked into the bedroom, pulling on joggers and a hoodie and staring at that sweater.

She shook her head, went and got a drink and sat down. When Liam walked into the bedroom and didn't see her, he shook his head. He pulled his jeans on and walked into the living room. "Kelly."

"Don't."

"Tell me what you want me to do and I'll do it. Just stay. Please love." She shook her head and her phone went off.

"Yes," Kelly said.

"It's Allison. The attendant from the plane. We're not gonna be able to turn around and be there by three. It's gonna be a day or two. We ended up with mechanical issues. Are you okay if we come on Friday?"

"Fine," Kelly replied.

"We can pick you up in Dublin if it's easier. Just let me know."

"That's fine. I'll see you then," Kelly said determined not to give away who she was talking to.

"This mean you're staying?"

"Liam."

"For a few days."

"Do you not remember me saying that I was going home?"

"Kelly."

"I'm going Liam. I don't even know why I came. Nothing was gonna change no matter where I was."

"Come back to the house."

"No. Just go home Liam. Go hang with your mom..."

"We can go see her."

"Liam."

"She wants to meet you. I know you want to leave. I'm a shit person. Fine. I still love you. She does. Hell. All of us do. Just come and see her with me."

She shook her head. "Go home."

"No."

"Liam."

He shook his head. "I can't leave. I can't be there when you aren't."

She shook her head and guzzled down the rest of her drink. "You wanna stay up all night drinking, fine. You want to drink until whatever's going on is numb, fine. I'm not leaving. I'm not letting you leave without a damn fight."

"Then get your own room. You aren't staying in here." She walked into the bedroom, blocked the door and curled up on the bed.

She could smell his cologne. She could still feel the warmth from where they'd just had sex. "Kelly, open the door." "No."

"Kelly."

"You stay in there; I'm staying in here alone."

"Open the door." She shook her head, brushing the tears away and got up, removing the chair. He opened the door and saw her eyes red and puffy. "Kelly."

"Don't." He pulled her to him and kissed her, brushing her tears away.

"Tell me what I have to do."

"Liam."

"Tell me. Whatever you want me to do, I'll do it. I just can't lose you again. Please."

She shook her head and he slid one finger to her chin, lifting her gaze to meet his. "Please. Please don't leave. Please just stay. You don't want to be in the house, you can stay here. Just stay." She shook her head and he kissed her.

That one kiss was one he wanted to last for a million years. Letting her leave wasn't gonna work. Watching her leave would kill him. Holding on for dear life was his only option. He kissed her again and picked her back up. He leaned her onto the bed and pulled her leg around him.

"Liam, leave it."

He kissed her again. "I love you. You want to call it obsession, but it's love Kelly. I saw a damn therapist when I decided to stop drinking. It's not being obsessed. It's a love that just about destroyed me and ripped my heart to shreds. I can't lose you again."

"You have work Liam. I'm going home."

He kissed her again. "Just stay. Meet her first. Please. Everyone's already there anyway." She shook her head and got up, walking into the living room. She grabbed her laptop and looked at commercial flights. The only option she had was just as bad as waiting for the company jet.

"Please," Liam asked as she closed her laptop.

"I don't want..." He kissed her, picked her up, wrapping her legs around him and walked into the bedroom, leaning her back onto the bed.

Kelly woke up a few hours later in tears. She slid out of bed and checked again, finding a single seat. First class. She had 5 hours before the flight left, which gave her enough time to get there, check her bag and get through security before Liam noticed. When she looked at her hands, the rings were both on her fingers. Leaving it would make everything worse. She got her things, slid them into her bag with her laptop and everything else then left a note:

When you figure it out, I'm gonna be home. Goodbye.

She left the note, quietly slipped out the door and took off, getting an uber to the airport. She got her ticket, checked her bag and got through security with her carry on. She got to the gate and waited. She let the driver know that she was on a commercial flight on her way back and gave him the flight number. Kelly was just taking her seat when her phone buzzed:

Where are you?

She turned her phone on airplane mode and slid her AirPods in. She was way beyond exhausted. She put on an audiobook and fell asleep listening. When they landed 8.5 hours later, she got up, got her bag and was coming down to the pickup area when she saw the driver. "Didn't expect to see you back so soon," the driver said.

"Long story," Kelly said as they made their way to her place.

She turned the airplane mode off and saw 25 missed calls from Liam and 30 texts all of which she decided to read after she got sleep.

Chapter 14

Kelly woke up the next morning to even more texts and missed calls and emails. She was just yawning when it went off yet again. Not even looking at the call display, she answered. "Yep."

"Where in the hell are you," Liam asked.

"I told you I was going home."

"Kelly."

"Goodbye Liam." She hung up and got up, all of a sudden feeling really nauseous. She ran for the bathroom and was sick. Her mind said it was stress or too much Jameson's. Her body said otherwise. She unpacked and saw both bottles that she'd put in her bag. She put everything away, threw in laundry and saw his shirt. The one that still smelled like Liam. The one he'd thrown off when they'd had sex that day. It smelled too good. She threw it in with the rest of the laundry and started the washer then came into the kitchen. She was too tired to clean, but she was hungry. She made breakfast and somehow the smell of eggs made her nauseous all over again.

She was sick again and again all that morning then got something to stay down and went out. Maybe it was because she was in the house. She was in the bed where they'd had sex more than once. That had to be the reason. She took a deep breath, went over to the market and when she came home, she put the groceries away and stared at the pregnancy test that she'd bought. She hoped that she wasn't. That she could just continue on with her life. That she could get back to work. She took a deep breath and took the test, hoping and praying that it was negative.

When she saw the result, she shook her head. "There's no way that's right. No way at all," Kelly thought to herself. She ignored it, throwing everything out when her phone went off yet again

"What do you want?"

"You promised you wouldn't vanish on me."

"Liam, what do you want?"

"You back home?"

"Does it matter?" She didn't mean to be sarcastic, or did she?

"Kelly, answer me."

"Yeah I'm home. You got what you wanted Liam. You wanted to get laid. Congrats on that. Now leave me alone." She hung up and looked out at the water. It had been her respite for too long. When her phone dinged with a text, she was almost afraid to look:

You promised me that you wouldn't vanish on me again. I wake up and you're gone. How do you expect me to react? I'm getting on a flight today. You're not walking away. I love you even if you don't think that I do.

Kelly shook her head. She wanted to avoid the situation. She didn't want him back in her life. Not now. She needed time to decompress and breathe. She needed to wipe him from her system. Not be weak in the knees when he showed up. She shook her head and replied:

And you promised a hell of a lot too Liam. Stay in Ireland. I don't want you here. Not now.

She knew that it would hurt him. She hoped it was enough to deter him until she figured out what a positive pregnancy test meant for her. If it was a false positive, she could deal. If it wasn't, she couldn't hide it for long and he'd know the minute that Faith spilled the beans to him. When her phone went off again, she saw Faith's name.

"Hey," Kelly said.

"You're home?"

"Yep. I don't wanna talk about it."

"Understood. You up for company?"

"I just..."

"He called me twice this morning."

"Fine," Kelly said as she got freshened up and grabbed a sweet tea. Just as she put her glass down, there was a ding at the door. When she opened it, flowers were on her doorstep. 10 dozen red roses to be exact. The fragrance was amazing, but she knew what he was up to. She brought them in and saw Faith.

"He cleaned out the florist I see," Faith teased.

"Aren't you supposed to be at the office?"

"Working from home. What in the world happened?"

Kelly shook her head. "He wasn't in love with me Faith. He was obsessed. I can't..."

"My Dad was the same with my mom. Ridge was the same with me. What's the problem?"

"He was so obsessed that he became a damn unpaid escort or might as well have. He's not well in the head. That's obvious. He handed me a damn journal chronicling the obsession. I saw it. It's not a good thing," Kelly said.

"So instead, you vanished?"

"I went to the hotel. He showed up and demanded to come in."

"The pilot mentioned something about giving you cooling off time."

"And I got a commercial flight home instead." "

I know that things are weird, but you do know that he's flying back here right?"

Kelly looked at her. "What?"

"He's flying back tomorrow."

"What?"

"He said something like, "She can't walk away. I'm not letting her."

Kelly shook her head. "Part of me wishes that he never came back here."

"Kelly, you love him and you dang well know it. You just got overwhelmed. That's all."

Kelly shook her head. "I can't Faith. I can't sit here in all good conscience, pretending that I don't. Of course I love him, but he doesn't know me. He doesn't love me. He loves the old me that was submerged in his life. Not the other way around."

SOUTHERN TEMPTATION

Faith gave her a hug. "Like it or not Kelly, he's not gonna standby and watch you disappear even if that's what you really want."

"Can't you just transfer me somewhere? Anywhere?"

"I can transfer you into the office. That's about it," Faith teased.

Kelly shook her head. After a quick hug, Faith headed off and Kelly slid to the floor. "Please just let him have to stay. Don't let him on that flight," Kelly said silently. She took a deep breath. She knew what she needed to do, especially now. She went outside, locked up and flipped the alarm on and went down to the church.

"Miss Kelly," the pastor said as she came inside.

"Hi. I know it's kinda silly, but I need to talk to someone who isn't gonna be on one side or another."

"Alright," the pastor said as they sat down somewhere private.

"What's going on," he asked.

"Remember a long time ago when I told you about when I went to Ireland?"

"I do remember something about that."

"Well, he showed up here. He had a meeting with my boss about something and we bumped into each other."

"I don't see that that's a problem."

"It wasn't until we ended up dating."

"And?" She told him about the notebook and the things he'd written and told her.

"Part of me doesn't think that it's love. With all of that journal stuff, I think it's more like obsession."

"Kelly, I understand how hard it is to deal with. I do. Just try and remember something. With some people, love is holding onto a feeling or what you'd call obsession. It's an extreme. It sounds to me that his notebook was more of a coping mechanism. It was his innermost thoughts. I understand how it could be off-putting."

"I just...I don't know that we're doing..."

"Miss Kelly, you're worried. I understand that. I also know that you're gonna be alright. What's the concern?"

"He's started getting weird. Demanding I decided on something, and it just felt wrong."

"Kelly, breathe. If you have an inkling that something isn't right, most of the time it isn't. You have that gut instinct for a reason."

"Thank you," Kelly said. The pastor nodded and she took a deep breath and said a quick prayer, then headed back to the house.

When she pulled in, she saw a bag on her front porch. One that looked like a suit bag. One that was all too familiar. She shook her head and walked inside. She went to close the door behind her and saw a hand. "Why are you here," Kelly asked.

"Because you're my damn fiancée. That's why. You vanish on me in the middle of the damn night while I'm naked in the bed beside you. Who does that?"

"Liam."

"No. You promised me you wouldn't vanish."

"And you showed up at my damn hotel. Space would've been good," Kelly said. She went and got herself another sweet tea and he shook his head.

"You can't just vanish like what happened was nothing."

She shook her head. "Why are you really here?"

"Because I'm not losing my fiancée."

"I handed you back the rings Liam."

"And I'm telling you now that I'm not losing the woman I've been in love with for this long."

Kelly shook her head. "What did I say to you?"

"You're wrong. You know it and so do I Kelly. I'm not leaving you; I'm not letting you walk away either."

"Letting me?"

He walked towards her and she shook her head. "No."

"Kelly."

"No Liam." She walked off and tried to avoid him. She would've done anything. He grabbed her hand and pulled her to him, kissing her.

He picked her up, wrapping her legs around him and walked upstairs, leaning her onto her bed. "Liam." He kissed her again, peeling his shirt, jeans and boxers off. He pulled her jeans off and kissed her again. She wanted him, but she was worried. If she really was pregnant, she was in for one hell of a problem.

"Liam, stop."

"What," he asked.

"Having sex isn't fixing..."

He kissed her again and slid her legs tight around him as he peeled off her shirt. It took all of 10 minutes for her to go into worry mode again as the test she'd taken was in the garbage. When she realized that he'd see it, she shook her head.

"What," Liam asked.

"Nothing,"

He stopped. "Tell me."

"Liam why are you here," she said as she slid out of his arms and got up, walking into her bathroom and hiding the test and the box in the back corner of the cupboard. She got up and took a deep breath, sliding her robe on. When she opened the door, he was right there.

"What?" He picked her up and sat her on the bathroom counter.

"Tell me what's going on."

"Liam, why are you here?"

"You're wearing my ring Kelly. I'm not leaving your side. We talked about this."

"And I told you that there..."

He kissed her and snuggled her tight to him. "You can't walk out. I get that you're mad and angry and worried. I do. I also get that you're worried I'm gonna be as crazy as your idiot exes. I'm not. I wrote it so I could get it out of my system. So, I could let it out in a better way. That's it."

She shook her head and he kissed her again. "What?"

"I can't keep doing this. I can't keep being okay with you trying to force..."

He kissed her again and wrapped her legs around him as he slid inside her and kept going, thrusting and trying to screw her bad feelings away. "You really think that I proposed because I wanted this," he asked as it got a little rougher.

"Aah," Kelly said as he pulled her tight to him. When he exploded into her, Kelly looked at him.

"What," he asked as he tried catching his breath.

"You need to go home."

"No."

"Liam."

He kissed her again and pulled her tighter to him. "What," he asked.

"You need to go back."

"Why? For what damn reason?"

"Because I don't..."

He kissed her again. "I'm not leaving you. I'm not walking away."

She tried to squirm away from him but she couldn't. "Why are you so damn determined to get away from me?"

"Because I..." He kissed her. "Because I don't want to keep going through this. You having a tantrum and taking it out on me. You being completely obsessed with..."

He kissed her again and pulled her to him. "What?"

"Don't take them off again."

"Take what off?" She looked at her hands and both rings were back in place. Even the engagement ring that she'd left on the kitchen counter.

"What," he asked.

"You can't just accept it? Move on?"

Liam shook his head. "I never could, and I have no intention of doing it again."

Kelly shook her head and pushed him away. "I don't want you here. You know that right?"

"You're pregnant. Like it or not, I'm not leaving."

"And how in the hell would you know if I was or not?"

"Because I know," he replied. Kelly shook her head and managed to get up. She walked into her bedroom and pulled on joggers and a tank.

"Kelly."

"Liam, go home. Go back to Ireland and find someone else."

He shook his head. "I can't do that and you know it."

Kelly shook her head. "Then leave."

"No." Kelly was getting more and more irritated.

"Liam, I can't keep doing this. I can't keep…"

He kissed her again. "I love you. Why can't you just accept it and marry me?"

"Because you're not in love with me. You're in love with the girl that you knew then. The one that didn't bother fighting back. That let you do whatever you wanted to. I'm not her Liam."

He shook his head. He pulled his jeans on and she walked downstairs. She needed to be as far from him as possible. Not two seconds later, she was running for the bathroom and was sick. Stress didn't help.

When she stepped out, Liam was right there. "Tell me the truth Kelly."

"Move."

"Tell me." He wasn't about to put his hands on her, but he needed to hear it from her. She shook her head and pushed him out of the way. "Just say it."

"Go away Liam. Go back to Ireland, back to your friends and your family and leave me alone."

"You are my family." She shook her head and walked past him, walking outside. At that moment, she didn't care if there was a monsoon. She needed to be away from him. She walked outside and Liam pulled on a shirt, following her.

"Liam, leave me alone."

He walked outside and sat down on the steps behind her. "What," he asked.

"Go."

"No. I told you. I'm not leaving you." She took a deep breath of salty air and kissed her peace and calm goodbye. She got up and grabbed her phone, calling her doctor. "Kelly. What's up," her doctor asked.

"Can I come in today?"

"We have an opening at 1. Why?"

"I think I might..."

"Come in now."

Kelly walked past him, went inside, grabbed her keys and purse and saw him coming outside. She locked the doors and flipped the alarm on and got in the truck. She went to pull out and he hopped in. "Where are you going?"

"To prove that you're wrong." She got to the doctor's office and went in the minute she walked into the waiting room. When he tried to come with her, she shook her head, but he came in anyway. She did the test for the doctor, then got the blood test.

"It may be a little early, but it's best to check," her doctor said.

When the doctor left the room, Liam looked at Kelly. "Talk love. Say something."

She shook her head. "What's the point? You don't listen to me anyway."

"Kelly, please." The doctor came back in a minute or two later and looked at Kelly.

"Well, you aren't gonna be drinking for a while," the doctor said.

She shook her head. "Great," Kelly said sarcastically.

"How far," Liam asked. "Two weeks. Maybe three. It's very early to tell. Just stay as low-stress as possible, no drinking, no coffee. You're good," her doctor said.

"At least I know," Kelly said.

"Come in in 3 weeks. We'll check again and do an ultrasound." Kelly nodded, headed off and walked back down to the truck with Liam grabbing her hand.

"Let go."

"No."

"Liam."

"No." He opened up the passenger door for her and she shook her head and got in. He slid the keys from her hand and hopped in the driver's seat, driving them back towards her place.

"You should've stayed," Liam said. She shook her head. Being in a car with him was making her even more nauseous.

"Liam, why are you here?"

"Because I'm not losing you. I'm not forgetting the past 10 bloody years because you're too stubborn to realize that I love you. You make every excuse you can so you don't have to feel what I know you do. Why can't you just accept it and be with me?"

"Because I know it isn't what you're so damn..." He pulled the truck over and kissed her.

"Get it through your head love. I'm not going anywhere and either are you. We're getting married. I'm marrying the woman I wanted my entire adult life. Don't do this," Liam said. She shook her head and when they pulled into the beach house, she shook her head. He grabbed her hand and pulled her back into the truck as he parked and turned the car off, sliding the seat back and pulled her into his lap. "What?"

He kissed her, devouring her lips and snuggled her to him.

"I don't want to leave, and I don't want you walking out either. Just stay. Be with me Kelly."

"Should've thought of that instead..."

He kissed her and wrapped her legs around him, walked into the house, locking the truck doors and walked up to the bedroom, not bothering to come up for air for even a moment. When she felt her back against the bed, she shook her head and he linked their fingers.

"What," Kelly asked.

He kissed her again and held her tight to him. "I don't want you to leave me. I don't want to lose you from my life again. Why do you automatically think that it's too good to work? That it has to be wrong? I just want to love you Kelly. That's all love."

"I can't do this."

"Kelly."

"Liam, I get it. You're all caught up in the web of all of this. I just can't..."

He kissed her again. "Why are you convinced that me loving you like that is bad?"

"Because I don't want to get hurt alright?"

"The last thing I want is to hurt you. Don't you know that?" She went to get up and he knew he had two options; he either let her up and she avoided him all over again, or he kissed her until she kissed him back. He opted for number 2.

"What," Kelly asked. His hands slid to her face and he kissed her.

"I love you so much it hurts to be away from you. It hurts me inside and out love. I can't lose you. Now especially." Kelly shook her head and he kissed her again, not breaking the kiss but intensifying it. When he felt her legs slide around him, he slid her shirt off.

"Liam," she said as she broke the kiss. He kissed her again and kicked his jeans to the floor. He pulled her jeans off and kissed her again. "Liam, please."

He kissed her again and her arms wrapped around him. When she felt his warmth, she lookup at him. "I want you," he said.

"Liam."

"I want my girl. Am I allowed?"

"Liam."

"Am I?" She kissed him and his arms slid around her as he slid deep inside her to the place that he loved. The feeling of her tight around him and holding on with every ounce of her being. He needed that feeling like she was holding on for dear life. The more he slid in and out of her, the more turned on she got. He went deeper, harder and he felt her nails in his back.

"Aaah," Kelly said sucking in air like she was intentionally not giving him his way. He devoured her lips again and pulled her legs so he could slide in even deeper. He kept going, all the while trying to cherish every single moment in case it was his last. When his body gave way, he fell into her arms and kissed her.

"Don't. Don't tell me to leave. Don't remove me from your life. Please love."

She looked up at him and he devoured her lips. "I can't even get you to leave me alone let alone go away," Kelly said.

"Do you love me?"

"I never stopped Liam. All I said was that you have to know that was how I was…"

He kissed her again. "I'm not letting you go."

"And if all we're doing is ruining what we had?"

"Ruining it, making it a hell of a lot better than it was."

"Liam."

He kissed her again. "I couldn't let go of you. I still don't want to. Please."

"Liam, I don't want to go through it again. I don't want you forcing me into anything. Fine. Some people enjoy that, but I don't. You scared me. You made me…"

He kissed her. "That's not what I was trying to do."

"That's how it felt," Kelly said as she pushed him away and got up.

She went and slid her robe on and walked into the bathroom. She sat down on the edge of the tub and shook her head. "Did you mean that," Liam said as he walked in wearing nothing but his boxers.

"Yeah I did. That's why I left Liam. You told me that when I was here, I picked the wrong people. I did. You doing that felt like another mistake. It still does."

He kissed her, pulling her to her feet. "Please just come back to bed."

She shook her head and brushed tears away. He picked her up and sat her on the counter. "Be with me."

"Liam."

"You don't have to do anything other than love me back. Why can't you do that?"

"Time."

"Meaning what?"

"We knew each other a week Liam. One week. What do you expect me to do?"

He kissed her. "Love me back." He kissed her then wrapped his arms tight around her. "Talk to me love."

She kissed him. "I never said I didn't love you Liam."

"Then what's wrong? Why are you running away from me?"

"Because I'm scared."

He kissed her." You never have to be scared of anyone ever again. Especially not me."

"Meaning what?"

He kissed her, devouring her lips until he felt her legs wrap around him. "Promise me you won't leave me again."

"I said I needed to leave Liam. You can't block me in and hold me hostage while you decide to ravage me every hour on the hour."

"Oh, that could be fun," he teased as his hands slid between her legs and started teasing her again.

"Liam," Kelly said.

"What?"

"I didn't mean it."

He nodded. "I missed that look."

"Which one," she asked as she sucked in air and his fingers delved inside her. When her hand slid to his arm, he smirked.

"What love?"

"What are you up to?"

"Say it."

"What?"

He kissed her. "I love you."

When her body reacted, she kissed him and he sped up the teasing. "Liam."

"Yes wife."

"I love you. You really..."

"What?"

"You need to stop."

He kissed her again. "You want me to stop, tell me." He kissed down her chest, nibbling and licking at her breasts until she was almost curling into his arms.

"Aah," she said as he smirked.

"If you want me to stop, tell me." When his kisses trailed down her torso and landed on her warmth, she held on tighter to the counter's edge. "Kelly."

"What," she teased.

"Tell me if you..." She shook her head and he nibbled, making her legs almost tremble. "You taste too good. Way too good."

When she leaned back, he kept going. "Liam."

"What," he asked.

"Come here." He nibbled a little more and teased until he had her feet on his shoulders, then slid her legs back so he was less than an inch from her and ramped it up even more. "Oh my god," Kelly said.

"More," he asked.

"Liam." He kept going, then kissed back up her torso and let his fingers take over.

"Now, you were saying love."

She kissed him and he picked her up and wrapped her legs and arms around him. He walked into the bedroom and leaned her back onto the bed, kicking his boxers off. She pulled him to her and kissed him as he made love to her again. He couldn't resist her, and at that exact moment, she couldn't resist him either. He wished that they'd talked like this in Ireland. They'd be at the cottage instead of back in the insane sweltering heat.

He shook his head and took a deep breath as he slid inside her. To that warm place where he felt like she was accepting him. Where he deserved that feeling. He started out taking his time, then when she slid her legs tighter around him, he started going harder, faster, deeper. When her nails dug into his shoulders, he leaned down and kissed her as her body tightened around him. "Kelly."

"What?"

"Tell me what you want," he asked.

"With what?"

He kissed her again and found his release. "I'm not leaving. I can't. You know that right?"

"Liam." He kissed her again, devouring her lips. "I don't want to be there without you. I need you. I know that..." She kissed him. "Liam, stop."

"What?" He leaned back onto the bed and slid her to him so she was curled up around him.

"What do you want me to do," Kelly asked.

"I want us to do the tattoo thing."

"And?"

"My mom wants to meet you. I want you to come with me."

"We barely lasted 24 hours."

"Because I was an idiot."

"If I go, I don't want any more reason for us to get in a dang fight. No forcing..."

He kissed her. "Never again. Ever." He kissed her again and snuggled her in tighter.

"I might be able to go..." He kissed her again and pulled her on top of him.

"Tell me and we'll go."

"Liam." He kissed her, devouring her lips and leaned her onto her back, curling up into her arms.

"If we go, promise me that you aren't leaving. That you'll stay."

"Are you willing to give me space?"

"In that little cottage? You sure that's what you want?"

"Liam."

He kissed her, devouring her lips. "You okay going back to Belfast?" Kelly nodded. It's not that she didn't love it there. She did. Just feeling like she was claustrophobic was a little much. Feeling like she was being forced into something was scaring her, but saying it felt wrong. "I just need to be able to have space. No more demands." He nodded and kissed her.

"Only have one request."

"What?"

"Are you willing to do the tattoo with me?"

"I can hold your hand while you do it."

He smirked. "And what should I do?" "Well, it's kinda up to you."

"What if I do something that's about us?"

"Kinda did already handsome."

"That was the kid version," he teased.

"If that's what you want." She kissed him and they curled up together as her stomach and his started grumbling.

"Maybe going there so soon after was too much." Kelly nodded. He kissed her again and Kelly got up. "Where are you going?"

"Food." She kissed him and slid her robe back on, grabbed her phone then walked downstairs. She made one and only one call.

"Did you two make up yet," Faith teased.

"He didn't fly back with your Dad's plane did he?"

"No. Girl, are you two okay?"

"Yeah. For now anyway," Kelly said as she made lobster rolls for them with the leftover seafood.

"And?"

"I wanted to apologize."

"You don't have to. I get it. I've had those fights with Ridge a billion times."

"We're gonna go back."

"Then go get your stuff and head to the airport. I had a feeling."

"Faith."

"Go." She warmed up some butter, pouring it lightly over the top of the lobster and put it into the toasted bun she'd put in the broiler. She went to turn around and bring them upstairs when Liam came into the kitchen shirtless.

"Smells good," he said.

Kelly kissed him. "Not exactly Irish stew, but it's pretty good for here," Kelly said as she handed him the lobster rolls. He kissed her, pulled her into his lap and devoured her lips.

"What," she asked.

"I can't lose you. Promise me."

"I can't promise anything. The future isn't a given Liam."

"Then promise me you'll stay and meet everyone. That if you want to come back, you let me come with you." She nodded and kissed him, throwing him the proverbial bone.

She got them each a sweet tea and they curled up together. "And no drinking while we're..."

"I don't, people are gonna wonder," he said.

"Then limited."

He nodded. "I know that the notebook was too much. I'm sorry," he said. Kelly nodded and kissed him.

"I know why. I just started reading a lot more into it. I kinda had a panic attack."

He kissed her. "No more worrying then." Kelly nodded and kissed him. They had their lunch and Liam looked at her.

"What?"

"Are we going back?" Kelly nodded. She kissed him and cleaned up, then they headed upstairs and he helped her pack.

She brought more, got her rolling oversized suitcase and her carry on with her laptop and charging cords and grabbed the vitamins she'd got from the doc. He kissed her and took her suitcase to the door. She called Ridge and let him know they were flying back out and went upstairs to get changed. She got a reply a few minutes later that he was already on the way. She walked upstairs, slid into something comfy for the flight and Liam smirked. "What?"

"Skirt."

"Liam."

"Skirt," he teased.

She shook her head. "Fine, but I'm bringing my sweats." She threw them in her carry on and within a matter of minutes, the driver was there. She locked up, turned the alarm on and they got in the SUV and went back to the private runway.

They hopped on the plane and the minute they were allowed to get up, his hands were all over Kelly again.

"We're not..." He kissed her and slid her onto his lap.

"Liam. Not..." He kissed her again and his hand slid to her inner thigh as he pulled a blanket around them. She shook her head and he smirked, sliding inside her within a matter of seconds. "Not..."

He kissed her. "Then lay down," he whispered.

"Kind of can't." He smirked and leaned her onto the sofa, curling up behind her as he kicked his jeans off and slid off the lace panties she had on. "You're seriously..." His hands slid under the blanket and the minute he touched her, Kelly's toes were twisted into knots.

"Mine," he whispered as the attendant closed the door between the attendant area and the main cabin. He slid inside her, deeper and deeper until she was almost mewing. Until she was silently moaning and her body was past being turned on. "Now. You were saying something about you can't," he teased as he almost purred in her ear.

"This was..."

"Hot."

"Liam."

When it got harder, faster, more and more intense, her body exploded then again and again. "Mine," he whispered again and let his fingers tease even more. Makeup sex was even hotter that high in the air. When he exploded into her, he kept going, pounding into her until she came again. "And if there's any doubt, wife, it is all yours. Every inch, every drop," he whispered as he kept going and teased her into another wave of orgasm.

They fell asleep curled up together and within a matter of hours, they were back in Belfast and heading to his place. They walked in and he carried her over the threshold. "What are you up to," Kelly asked.

He kissed her. "Nothin," he teased. He got the bags, brought them inside and slid them into the closet in the main bedroom. "Now, before we both conk out, come get some rest."

"Did you tell your mom that I'd left?"

"No. Nobody."

"Liam."

"I knew the pilot couldn't have got back here that fast. I knew you took a commercial flight and the one I took left 5 hours after you left."

"That's how you got there that fast."

"And I'm not about to tell you that I didn't drink, because I was three glasses in when the plane took off."

Kelly shook her head. "And?"

"I called you over and over. I told you. I have you. That's all I want."

"Am I allowed to sleep since someone kept me awake the entire flight?"

"I do love that skirt," he teased.

He got them both some more stew, they ate curled up together on the bed and within an hour, they were both out cold. They got a little sleep, then opted to go for a drive. "Where are we off to handsome?"

"Giant's causeway."

She smirked. "I think I was there."

"A very long time ago wife."

Kelly smirked. They drove and snuggled in the car then when they finally arrived, she was in awe all over again. "And it's not raining. Good sign," he teased.

They hopped out when they could and walked. She was finally calm and serene. No screaming, no fights, no drama. Nothing. They just walked and talked. When they were both getting tired, they headed back, but he handed her the keys. "What," Kelly asked.

"You drive."

She smirked. "You sure?" He nodded and kissed her, devouring her lips then got her door for her. "Liam."

"If you are gonna be here, you kinda need to drive," he teased as he kissed her again. She hopped in and they headed off towards the cottage. When she felt kisses on her neck, she smirked. "Liam."

"What?"

"I can't concentrate when you're doing that."

"Then pull over."

"Liam." He kissed further down her neck then his hand slid around her torso. "Liam, I can't drive if you're doing that."

"What about this," he said as his hand slid under her leggings and down the front of her lacy panties.

"Liam." He kissed her neck and she pulled over. She parked the car and he undid her seatbelt.

He slid her over the console and onto his lap. "What," he teased.

"You start something, you may need..." He kissed her and kept going with the teasing. "Liam."

He kissed her, devouring her lips until he was fumbling and slid her leggings right off. He undid his jeans and she slid on top of him. "You sure," he teased.

She kissed him and he pulled her tight against him as he slid inside her. "Aah," Kelly said.

"Yours. From head to toe, all yours."

"Liam." When she started going faster, he tried stopping her. He didn't want fast and easy. He wanted her body exploding over and over again. He wanted her out of breath and overheated. He wanted her body throbbing until he couldn't hold back. Instead, he was the one out of control. "Turn around," he said.

"Liam."

"Turn around." She turned around and it got ten times more intense and her body practically imploded. "Keep going," he said as his fingers teased and she couldn't even breathe.

"Aah," she said as her body throbbed around him. When he found his release, she leaned back into his arms.

"Don't move."

"What," Kelly asked.

"I need you," he teased.

"For?"

"Sanity."

She went to move and he held on tighter. "Liam."

"Don't move. When she felt that pressure all over again, she leaned back and he started all over again. He came again and her body throbbed tight around him. "Kelly."

"What?"

"I'm marrying you."

"Good to know," she said as she slid out of his arms and slid into the driver's seat.

She slid her leggings back up with a smirk ear to ear. "You seriously need to quit," Kelly teased.

"And you need to kiss your fiancée." She leaned over and kissed him.

"I love you too," she replied. One more kiss and they finished their drive back to the cottage. When she parked, he hopped out, got her door and kissed her, picking her up and wrapping her legs around him again as he leaned her against the wall of the cottage. "What," Kelly asked. He kissed her again and pulled her leggings right off.

"Liam." He kissed her, devouring her lips and they had sex against that wall again. It was hot. So hot they could've burned the cottage down and everything near it. He pounded into her and she didn't let go. When he pinned her hands to the cottage wall, it was even hotter. "Liam."

"Wife." He had one hand holding her hands, the other teasing her into a frenzy. When he slid her to her feet, he kissed her.

"You want to do…"

"We're going inside."

"Why?"

"Because we aren't doing that out here." He thought he was in heaven. The fact that she was willing to bend to his will had him beyond turned on. She grabbed her leggings and panties and he chased her inside. He would've bent her over the counter if she hadn't objected. When he bent her over the bed instead, it was way past hot. His hands teased her as he kept going, filling her in ways that she'd almost craved. He leaned on top of her and when he came up for air, Kelly was almost giggling. "What," he teased as he kissed the back of her neck and got up.

"You realize that you are turning back into a sex-crazed teen right?"

"Only around you."

"Liam," Kelly said as she came into the bathroom behind him.

"Yes sexy wife," he teased as he kissed her.

"What would you think if we went to see your mom and everyone tomorrow?"

"You mean since they're kinda already expecting us to show?"

Kelly nodded and he kissed her. "I'd say that we may have to leave early."

Kelly kissed him. "Then you should probably not keep me up all night."

He kissed her and she shook her head. "Shower," Kelly asked. He smirked and she flipped the hot water on and slid in, if only to clean up a little and taunt the crap out of Liam. She let the water slide down her body and had to admit. It felt better. It felt like she was washing the anger and the fear and the stress out of her body. When she felt him slide in with her, she got a grin ear to ear. "What," Kelly asked.

"Come here."

She turned to face him and he kissed her. "I love you," he said as he kissed her again.

"Love you too handsome fiancée of mine," Kelly teased.

Chapter 15

The next morning, Kelly woke up and went into the kitchen in nothing but his t-shirt and made breakfast. When she felt warmth near her and hands slide around her hips, he kissed her neck. "Good morning handsome," Kelly said.

"Good morning," he whispered as she felt him against her backside. "Liam."

He kissed up her neck then nibbled at the nape of her neck. "Yes fiancée," he replied.

"Hungry?"

"Depends."

"On what," she asked as he flipped the burner off and sat her on the counter.

"On whether we're talking about food or..."

Kelly kissed him and he kissed down her body until her toes were curling and his warm breath was on her, turning her on even more. "Liam."

"What?"

"Don't we have to leave?"

"Nope," he teased as her toes curled even more and he nibbled and licked until her body was almost shaking in his arms. He kept going until his boxers started feeling like they were 3 sizes too small. "Liam."

"Yes sexy wife."

"I need...." He kissed her and peeled his boxers off, taking her on the counter. Her legs wrapped tight around him and her body felt like it was humming a serenade. The feel of his breath against her neck as he kissed her then leaning in and devouring her lips until his body succumbed to the heat between them. "I was wondering where you snuck off to," Liam said, still inside her and kissing her neck.

"Thought you might be hungry." He smirked and kissed her.

"Hungry for other things than food, yes." She shook her head.

"Am I allowed to move," Kelly joked.

He kissed her and smirked. "Depends. Am I cooking?"

"If you want to."

"Dessert was pretty damn good there wife of mine."

"Liam, you are absolutely ridiculous."

"And you love me." She nodded and he went and finished making the bacon and eggs. She made coffee and slid off the counter. Just as she did, the scent overwhelmed her and she ran for the bathroom. He turned the burners off and went after her. "Are you alright," Liam asked.

Kelly nodded and rinsed her mouth out. "Dizzy and nauseous for a minute there," she said.

He picked her up and put her back in bed. "I'll get the breakfast. Just lay down."

"Liam, I'm alright."

"Just let me do this?" Kelly knew there was no reason to fight him on it.

"Fine but only if you eat with me."

He smirked. "Not that kind of eating Liam. I swear, you're like a hormonal teenager."

He kissed her. "Only around the very sexy and addictive wife."

He kissed her again and went and plated breakfast, bringing it all in and curling back up in the bed with her. "I always kinda did love breakfast in bed. Last time we did this, I think we…"

"At the hotel the first time I was here. Waffles if I remember right," Kelly teased.

He kissed her. "And fresh juice. That was a good day," he teased.

Kelly kissed him. "And second favorite?"

"Lobster eggs benedict."

Kelly smirked. "Really," she teased. He nodded and kissed her again, sliding their plates to the bedside table. "Liam."

He smirked. "You feeling better?"

"Depends on what you're up to right now."

"Nothin," he teased as he kissed her.

"Liam, what time are we supposed to be at your mom and Dad's?"

"12 at the latest."

"You realize it's 7:30."

"Fine party pooper," he teased as he kissed her. They both got up, got dressed and put their things together to take with them.

"We should bring her something," Kelly commented as she started getting nervous.

"Already figured out. We can pick the flowers up on our way," he replied.

They loaded up the car and he smirked. "What?"

"You want to drive for a bit," he asked.

"You mean considering what you did yesterday?"

"You did kinda start that. By the way, nice choice," he teased.

"What?" She looked down and realized the dress with buttons up the front gave him free and total teasing access.

"You're driving. You're behaving and driving."

"Good thing we're leaving early then." She shook her head. When they got on the road, he linked their fingers and kissed her hand.

They made it part way and he stopped to refill the gas. "Come," he said.

Kelly kissed him and went over to stand with him. "What?" he kissed her.

"You're driving. I have something I need to do."

Kelly shook her head. "I bet you do," she teased.

"That too," he joked as he kissed her. She shook her head again and he went inside to pay, coming outside with a drink for each of them.

"Thank you," Kelly said.

"Welcome beautiful." He got her door for her, kissing her, and went around to the passenger side. He slid in beside her and directed her back onto the road to get to Dublin. When they pulled into his mom and Dad's, she smirked.

"Kelly."

"Now I'm nervous. Thanks," she teased.

He kissed her. "She already loves you and so does my Dad. Promise." Kelly nodded and took a deep breath. He handed her the flowers he'd bought and they hopped out. He got the bags and the moment they were at the door, his mom opened the door and almost jumped into his arms.

"You're home," his mom said.

"Mum, you remember Kelly," he teased.

"Beautiful. How are you," his mom asked as she gave Kelly a hug.

"Good. Thank you for having me," she said.

"Come on in here. Silly girl. We wouldn't imagine you not staying.

"My old room," Liam asked as his mom nodded. He took the bags upstairs and his mom walked Kelly over to the living room.

"Come have a seat lass."

"Thank you," Kelly said. She chatted with his mom and heard him talking to his Dad.

"Dad, this is my girl Kelly. Love, this is my Dad."

"Nice to meet you," Kelly said. When Liam sat down beside her and slid his arm around her, Kelly leaned into his arms. Somehow, the nerves vanished.

"Well, we have a lot planned. I invited a few of Liam's friends and some family to the pub with us tonight if you're up for a little family visit," his mom said.

"Sure," Kelly said as he snuggled her a little tighter. They all talked for a bit, had some lunch then went to the pub to see all the friends he'd had for years, and a bunch of family he hadn't seen much of. She felt like a fish flapping on land. Nothing to hold onto. Liam had introduced her to a few people, then his sister came in. When she came over to meet Kelly, Liam gave her a look.

"Katie, my fiancée Kelly. Love, my sister Katie. This lad over here is her husband Finn."

"Nice to meet you," Kelly said.

"Well Liam. You did pick a looker here," his brother-in-law said.

"Thank you," Liam said as he kissed Kelly's forehead.

"And what does Kelly do for a living," his sister asked.

"You know that software thing I made? Her boss is the one that bought it. She got a promotion while I was in town," Liam said.

"Vice president," Kelly said leaving out the division so it was easier to explain.

"At least you're engaged to one with a brain this time," his sister teased. They made small talk and once his sister pulled him aside, she excused herself and went outside for some air.

All of it was overwhelming. Way too overwhelming. Cousins, uncles, aunts and then his sister. She thought she'd made it through until one of the random people he knew came outside to see where she was.

"I was wondering where you took off to. You good lass," one of his friends asked.

"Just needed a tiny break. Fresh air," Kelly said. She never had been one for big parties in enclosed spaces.

"If I may, you making it that long in there was a feat in itself lass."

"Thanks. There's just so many people."

"A lot of us were pub friends. Don't worry too much," he said as Kelly saw Liam coming outside.

"Conner," Liam said.

"You did find one heck of a lass my friend. Pretty amazing girl," Conner said as he smirked and headed inside.

"You alright," Liam asked.

"Just needed air. How are you doing with all the friends and family?"

"Since we've already plowed through 5 pints and a bottle of Jameson's?"

Kelly shook her head and knew that she'd get the truth if she asked him something. "Question."

He kissed her. "What?"

"What did your sister mean this time? Were you engaged before?" He shook his head and looked at her. "Liam."

"I can explain."

"Who?"

"Years ago." Kelly shook her head. If she'd been able to run home, she would've.

"When Liam?"

"5 years ago." She shook her head. "What," he asked.

"Nothing. Just wishing that I was allowed to drink right now."

"Kelly."

"Don't."

"Love."

"Where's the key for your mom and Dad's?"

"Not giving it to you. Stay."

"Is she here?"

"Kelly."

"Yes or no?"

"If I said yes?"

"I want the key."

"No."

"Then give me the car keys."

"Kelly."

"You aren't driving anyway." He kissed her and she shook her head. "Secrets. Go figure," she said sarcastically as she went inside and lost him in the crowd. She let his mom know that she was tired and heading back and his mom gave her the key. Luckily, she could walk to the house.

She got there and went upstairs to his bedroom, seeing the king bed and pictures of him as a kid on the walls. Little league, soccer games, rugby awards and awards filled the walls. Nothing but his happy childhood memories. She shook her head, plugged her charger in and slid into joggers and a t-shirt. She washed off her makeup and fell asleep. Leaving wasn't an option. She wanted to, or at least go back to the cottage alone, but it was too far. She curled up, noticing that it was almost 10pm and checked over emails. There was nothing important as she figured, but when she saw an email from Faith, she looked:

> *How in the world is your office this dang clean and organized? Hope that meet and greet the family thing goes okay. I know you hate stuff like that, but hope you at least had a little fun. See you in a few weeks.*

Kelly closed up her laptop and fell asleep not long later. When Liam came in at 2am, he saw her and quietly got changed for bed. When he slid under the blankets, He snuggled to her, feeling the joggers. He kissed up her neck and she semi woke up. "How was the rest of the party," Kelly asked.

"Dull without you. You alright?"

Kelly shook her head. "Tired and kind of nauseous."

"And here I thought you were mad about something."

"I am," she said quietly as he tried to snuggle up closer to her. She came up with a much better solution. When he woke up the next morning, she'd planned some banging around to go with the obvious hangover he'd have.

The next morning, as planned, she banged around a little intentionally giving him a headache on top of his hangover. She walked downstairs and saw his mom cooking. "Good morning," Kelly said.

"Good mornin lass. Come sit. I'm making a special Irish breakfast for you both."

"He's still asleep. I just thought I'd come help. It smells delicious," Kelly said.

"Come have a seat then lass," his mom said. She sat down and poured tea for his mom and herself. "I had a feeling you'd be up early. The boys started in on the pints last night. I almost had to pour Liam out of the car," his mom teased.

"Can I ask something," Kelly asked.

"Sure."

"When I was talking to Katie, she said something about Liam being engaged before."

"It was years ago. He thought that was what he was supposed to do then never went through with it and broke things off with her. You met her. Sara Finley," his mom said.

"When was that?"

"I think he was 18 or 19. Before we knew that he'd met you."

"Oh."

"If you want to ask something just ask Kelly."

"I just keep feeling like there's a secret somehow. Something else he wasn't telling me intentionally."

"He's lived a very colorful life. When he told me about you, he always lit up like a star in the sky. Every single time. He was a mess, I'll give him that, but he loved you. That's why he broke off the engagement and why he broke off the second one."

"When was that," Kelly asked.

"3 years ago," his mom said. She was mad. She knew she had to hide it, but she was really mad.

His mom sat down and had breakfast with her and just as they were finishing, Liam came downstairs. "Morning mum," he said as he kissed Kelly.

"Morning baby boy. I was talking to Kelly and we were talking about the engagements." He looked at her and then Kelly.

"Mum."

"Don't worry. I didn't bring up you not having a gal for 10 years. Didn't bring up that time that you crawled home from the pub because you drank too much Guinness." He shook his head and got himself breakfast and sat down with Kelly. He knew something wasn't right. He knew when she got up and helped with the dishes instead of talking to him that she was ready to kick his backside. When she went to go upstairs, he grabbed her hand and got her to sit with him as his mom went upstairs to get changed for the day.

"Say it love."

"What's the point?"

"Kelly."

"Are we going to your place or staying tonight?"

"My place. Why?"

"How many bedrooms?"

"No, you aren't sleeping in the guestroom." She shook her head.

"Yeah I am."

He shook his head and took a deep breath. "Tell me what happened."

"All that time you were supposedly determined to find me and nothing worked right and you were engaged twice. I guess you left that out of your precious notebook," she said as she got up and walked upstairs, taking out clothes to change into and packing everything else up.

Liam shook his head. "Something wrong," his Dad said as he came in. "Remember when I asked Katie to not bring up the stupid past?"

"Did you think your sister could hold that in with your new lass here? I'm surprised she stayed quiet that long."

"Dad."

"I know. I'll talk to her."

"Then mom just chimed in."

"Have you never told her about it?"

"No."

"Liam."

"I know. I don't want fights. That's all Dad. We've had enough of them."

"She's a good lass Liam. Smart and funny and kind. She was more than you said before."

"Last time I saw her before recently was when we were 18. That little pocket-sized photo was us at 18. I knew then I wanted to be with her. I didn't know what would happen. Honestly Dad, I didn't care about anything else. I couldn't."

"You were engaged to Sally Moore. You walked away and we all knew that it was done, but that's when you vanished for almost a week and a half."

"That was when I met Kelly."

"Ah. Yes, I remember," his Dad said as they finished their breakfast.

"Things were never the same."

"Still, you needed to tell her. She deserved to know son." Liam nodded.

"Refill on the coffee," Liam asked. He Dad nodded and they finished breakfast. When Liam headed upstairs, Kelly was fully dressed and going through emails.

"Are you talking to me?"

"No."

Liam shook his head. "Kelly."

"Just get dressed."

"Come here first," he said taking her hand and walking her into the bathroom.

"What are you doing?"

He closed the door. "Go ahead and yell love." She shook her head and looked at him.

SOUTHERN TEMPTATION

"So, again, more secrets. What did I say..." He kissed her and sat her on the counter.

"What?" He kissed her again and devoured her lips until he felt her kiss him back.

"I'm mad," Kelly said.

"First was before we met. The other I did when I was drunk and was dumped when I called her by your name."

"And?"

He kissed her. "That's it."

"Why did I have to find out from your sister?"

"Kelly."

"And why were you all mad when your friend was talking to me outside?"

"Because he made a bet with one of the guys that he could get you in bed. That's why." Kelly shook her head. "Do you really doubt me? I told you before. The only time I ever..."

"That doesn't mean much Liam. There were 20 girls in there bragging that they'd slept with you."

"Kelly."

"Can we leave?"

"No."

"Why?"

"Because we're not done this stupid fight."

"Then it's done. Happy now? See if you can..."

He kissed her again and kissed her, undoing her jeans. "What?"

He pulled them off. "Liam." He kissed her again, pulling his boxers off and leaned into her arms, pulling her legs around him.

"Not happening."

"Yeah it is." She shook her head and got up. She went to grab her jeans and felt his hands.

"Liam." He kissed her back and pulled the lace panties to the floor, picking her up and sitting her back on the counter.

"Liam."

He devoured her lips, nibbling at them and deepening the kiss until he felt her kiss him back. "No more stupid fights," he said as his hands slid to her inner thighs.

"What are you doing," Kelly asked. He kissed her again. When she felt the fullness inside of her, she was almost out of breath.

"Mine. My wife." She shook her head and he nibbled down her torso, nibbling and kissing and licking at each breast until he felt her body react.

"Fine," she teased as he nibbled even more then kissed her as they started having sex. It was in no way insane, or animalistic or sensual. Now, it was hard, fast, intense and enough to make her body shake in his arms.

"Aahh... Liam." He kissed her again, muffling the moan with his kiss.

"Shh," he teased as they both laughed and he went faster.

"Oh my god," Kelly said as her body climaxed once, twice, three times until he collapsed and climaxed himself. "What," Kelly asked as he leaned his body against her and pulled her tight to him.

"No more fights."

"Liam," she said as he kept going but taunted her with his fingers instead until his body was able to come to attention again.

"Your sister is here," his Dad said knocking on his bedroom door.

"Damn it," he teased. Kelly kissed him and he shook his head.

"You're in for it tonight. You know that right?"

Kelly smirked. "Unless you two go drinking again."

He kissed her. "No more letting my sister cause a rift. Promise," he asked.

"So long as you aren't holding any more secrets."

"Only one, but I'll tell you tonight," he teased.

"One?"

"A dirty one," he whispered. He hopped into the shower and Kelly cleaned up and got re-dressed, sliding his sweater on.

Kelly grabbed her bags, carrying them down the steps to the front room and came in to sit with everyone.

"Drink," his mom asked.

"I'm alright. Thank you. That was an amazing breakfast by the way."

"Well thank you. You remember Katie," his mom said.

"Did you enjoy the party last night," Katie asked.

"It was fun. I guess I didn't realize that the jet lag would hit me so hard. I was just exhausted," Kelly said.

"I'm sorry for that last night. Liam messaged that you were a little upset," Katie said.

"Just interesting hearing the stories."

"And what are we talking about," Liam asked as he came downstairs, hair wet and sat down beside Kelly, sliding his arm around her.

"I was apologizing for last night," Katie said.

"You know, I do know what you were up to. Nice test sister."

"It wasn't a test. I just wanted to make sure she knew everything," his sister said.

"She does," Liam said determined to block his sister from doing anything else to upset Kelly.

"So, where are you two going today," his mom asked.

"We're going to my place. I thought we needed some alone time for a while. We both have a little work to do while we're here."

"What kind of work," his Dad asked.

"My boss wants to open an office here. Add it to the portfolio I'd assume. He wanted me to look at locations that would be convenient for us here."

"So, you're working for him too now little brother," his sister asked as her husband shook his head.

"He wants Faith to run the office, but I'd be working from there maintaining the software I created," Liam said.

"This means you'll be able to come home more," his Dad asked.

Liam nodded. "It means Kelly and I can go back and forth between the two offices as needed."

"And," his sister asked.

"It means that you can spend some more time together," Kelly said.

Talking to his sister was like pulling teeth, and after the cold and calculated responses, Kelly knew that she didn't like her at all. "So, when do you head back to Charleston," his sister asked.

"Probably a week or two. My folks are coming out to see everyone next week," Kelly said. His sister shook her head and got up, walking into the kitchen and Liam followed. All Kelly knew was that the two of them were fighting in a language she didn't know.

When his mom got up to intervene, she saw Liam pissed off. "Kelly, come. We're leaving." His mom tried to stop him and when his Dad got up, she shook her head. She saw his Dad walk Liam back to the kitchen and heard the door close. Kelly walked upstairs, made sure she had everything and came back downstairs to see him grabbing her hand and walking her out the door. He got her door, helped her in and hopped into his side, taking off. "Did you want to tell me what that was about," Kelly asked.

"Not right now." When they pulled into his place, she was almost stunned.

"Liam."

"What?"

"Are you talking yet?"

He kissed her. "Come inside." He got the bags and brought them in with them.

"Talk Liam." They went inside and he showed her around the house, putting the bags into the main bedroom.

"Liam."

"There's a reason why my sister and I don't talk."

"I see that. You gonna tell me what's going on," Kelly asked.

"I'm ready to kick her butt."

"Liam, I get that."

"She's the one that made the damn bet. She bet more than one of those idiots that they could bed you."

Kelly shook her head. "Liam."

"I love you. I do. I don't want your folks to hear her stupid crap."

"Liam, they're not gonna do something stupid. You didn't tell her I was pregnant did you?"

"No. Hell. I wanted to." Kelly looked at him and shook her head, walking upstairs. She grabbed her laptop and was about to tell her folks not to bother. "What are you doing?"

"Why would I want them in the middle of that with her? Give me one reason," Kelly asked.

"Because my parents want to meet them. Is that allowed," he asked.

"Fine. I just don't want this happening again."

"Kelly."

"I don't want them upset."

"Kelly, my mom wouldn't dare. It's fine."

"And what about your sister?"

"She can…"

"Liam."

"She was pretty much told off. I don't think she'll do it again." He took a deep breath. "I promise you. It'll be fine."

"How many Liam?"

He looked at her. "How many of them?" She meant it and she wanted the answer.

"Doesn't matter."

"Yeah it does." He kissed her and she pushed him away. "How many?"

"It doesn't matter love."

"Yeah it does Liam. Answer me."

"My sister invited them."

"I don't care if your sister catapulted to the moon. Answer the question."

"Kelly."

"Fine. You stay here and I'll go back to the cottage."

"Kelly, dammit, stop."

She grabbed her bags, her purse and her phone. "Keys."

"Kelly."

"Keys Liam." He kissed her. "Keys." He picked her up and sat her on the massive bed.

"I'm not fighting about this with you anymore."

"Then answer me."

"It doesn't matter. That's the past and you dang well know it," he said.

"Then answer me."

"Kelly." She shook her head and carried her bags back downstairs, seeing the keys. She grabbed them, walked out to the car, put the bags in the back and got in, starting the car. "Kelly, what are you doing?"

"Leaving." She backed out, pulled up her GPS and made her way back to the road to go back to the cottage. If she hadn't promised that she would stay, she would've flown home. She got up to the cottage a few hours later and went inside. She locked up and put her things back in the bedroom. She didn't need the stress.

When she ran to the bathroom to be sick again, she could barely breathe. She burst into tears. When she went to get up, she saw a single red dot on the floor. She shook her head. "Go figure," Kelly said as she started cramping.

She sat down and was hysterically crying. When she got up, the spot was bigger. She shook her head, hopped into the shower and cleaned up, noticing the blood stop. She called her doctor and, just as she suspected, the doctor said she'd probably miscarried. She took a deep breath, got the bottle of Jameson's and poured herself a glass, curling up on the bed. She nodded off a while later, scared, upset and mad as hell. She knew he wouldn't show. She had the car. The only thing she could guarantee. She had dinner, warming up the last of the stew and curled up listening to an audiobook. When she fell asleep, she was still alone.

The next morning, Kelly woke up and felt an arm around her. She looked and saw Liam and shook her head. She went to get up and he pulled her back. "Liam, let go."

"No."

"Liam, stop." She pulled his arm away and got up, walking into the kitchen. She made herself coffee and poured herself a cup while she made herself breakfast.

"Kelly."

"Go away Liam."

"You took off in my car. Did you think that I wouldn't drive up here?"

"Did you get your girlfriend to drive you?"

"My Dad actually." She shook her head. She took a deep breath and had her coffee.

"You aren't supposed to have caffeine."

"Don't need to worry about it Liam. Gone. Done. Just like the damn..." He kissed her again, backing her up against the counter and sitting her up on it. "Liam, leave me alone."

"No. What do you mean gone?"

"You can take the rings back now. No reason to bother now." She went to take them off and he pinned her hands to the counter. "What?"

"I swear, you drive me insane. You know that right?"

"Liam, go away. I tell you that I want the truth and you lie again. I tell you I want a number and you don't even answer me. Your sister did it to call you out on your crap and you know it. Just go away and leave me alone."

"When did you lose..."

"Last night. Happy now?" She slid off the counter, finished making her breakfast and went and sat down in the chair alone.

She had her breakfast and he walked into the living room. "What?"

"Come here."

"No." She finished eating and went and cleaned up then felt him lean against her and his arms slid around her, resting on her stomach. "Kelly."

"Don't."

"So, now you're just gonna push me aside again."

"You gonna be honest and tell me? All of them? What?" She turned and looked him in the eye and he kissed her. "Stop Liam. Answer the damn question." He picked her up and sat her on the counter. "Liam."

"You don't want the answer."

"Then you aren't gonna be mad when I go home alone."

"You promised me."

"And you promised no more secrets."

"You aren't gonna leave."

"Yeah I will Liam. You promised no secrets, that you'd tell me the truth. You can't even do that. How am I supposed to trust that you aren't gonna break my heart into a million pieces? Trust that you're gonna be there no matter what? How am I supposed to know that I'm not wasting my time with this again."

He kissed her and she shook her head. "Don't."

"Kelly."

"If you're that damn determined to keep your life a secret, then stay. Have fun with it. Maybe you'll find another woman who won't ask you any questions."

She went and had a shower, locking the door behind her, and when she stepped out, he kissed her and leaned her onto the bed. "What?"

"You promised me."

She shook her head. "Move."

"No. Kelly, we're engaged. I promised you then."

"And another lie," she said pushing him away. She got up, got dressed and put everything back in her suitcase.

"Where are you going?"

"Anywhere but here." She went to take her bag and he stopped her.

"Don't do this."

"Don't do what Liam? The only thing that means me saving myself? I've been cheated on and lied to Liam. You won't tell me the truth; you won't answer a damn question without trying to distract me from asking for an answer. That's not a relationship. I'm not a toy that you can play with. Just leave me alone," Kelly said.

She wheeled her bag towards the door and he stopped her. "Where are you gonna go?"

"There's nothing in Charleston for you Liam. Nothing." He walked towards her and she shook her head. He leaned her up against the wall in the living room and kissed her.

"Answer me."

"35."

"All of them?"

"That's what we were yelling about."

Kelly took a deep breath. "And you're still friends with them? You sat in that bar until 2am. You gonna try to convince me that you aren't still..."

He kissed her and picked her up, walking back into the bedroom and leaning her onto the bed. He barely let her up for air for two seconds. "Don't leave."

"Why? Because..." He kissed her again and curled her to him. "Stay. Please love." "Stop lying to me Liam. You know..."

He kissed her, devouring her lips until he felt her kiss him back and she got up. "Where are you going?"

"I can't."

"Kelly."

"Your sister despises me. I doubt..."

"Don't say my folks don't. My parents defended you to my sister and told her to treat you with respect. What makes you think they didn't?" Kelly looked at him. "My mom loves you." "

And everyone else turned it into a dang game. I shouldn't have come Liam. I never..." He kissed her, picked her up and wrapped her legs around him.

He leaned her back onto the bed in the bedroom and pulled his sweater off, then his jeans. "Liam."

"Don't leave me."

"Liam, please." He kissed her again and peeled the sweater off of her.

"Don't go. Stay with me."

"Or what?"

He looked at her. "Kelly."

"You want some, fine. You want me to stay and be here so I'm available when you want it, fine. Don't pretend that's love Liam."

She went to get up and for once, he let her. Kelly got the sweater, slid her Ugg boots on and walked outside, putting her bag by the door. She texted the driver that she needed a ride to the hotel in Dublin and within minutes, got a reply:

Stayed in Belfast last night myself. I'll be there in a half hour.

She sat down outside and looked at the view. When she started crying, she saw Liam. "What do you want?"

"You're actually gonna go?"

"Liam, nobody wants me here. Your friends humiliated me, your sister humiliated me and who knows what else. I'm not staying here."

"Then come with me. We'll go see a bunch of places and get away from everyone."

"No."

"Kelly."

"No."

SOUTHERN TEMPTATION 435

The driver showed and Liam looked at her. "Please," he said.

"I can take you both if you'd like," the driver said. "

Five minutes." He walked into the house, threw his things, his laptop and chargers into his bag and threw it in the back with hers.

"What are you doing?"

"You go, I go." She shook her head and he got in beside her.

When they drove back to Dublin, he shook his head. "The pilot said he'd meet you at the airport," the driver said as Kelly opened the window.

"When did you call them," he asked.

"Last night." Kelly took a deep breath and inhaled the scent. The rain, the green of the land they passed, the salt air as they drove past a few tourist areas. When they got to the Dublin Airport, Liam shook his head.

"Had to didn't you," he asked. Kelly brushed her own tears away and when the car stopped, she got out, grabbing her bag.

"I have it Miss Kelly," the driver said.

She went and hopped onto the plane and curled up alone, brushing away tears. Liam hopped on behind her and messaged his mom that they had to go back. "Are you sure you did," Liam asked.

"No. I do know that I can't do anything until I know. I have to go to the doctor."

"Baby."

"Don't. Just don't Liam."

By the time they landed, Kelly was asleep in his arms. He carried her to the car and they headed back to the beach house. When they pulled in, he gently woke her. "We're home." She shook her head and hopped out, running for the bathroom to be sick. He called her doctor. "On my way," the doctor said.

By the time she arrived, Kelly had been sick over and over again. The doctor checked her out and did a quick ultrasound of sorts. When there was no heartbeat, no sign of anything there, she did an exam. "Kelly."

"I know."

"At least your body fully expelled it. Just take it easy for a week or two alright," the doctor asked.

"We can try again right," Liam asked.

"Later, yes."

"I can't believe this. Was it stress or something," Liam asked.

"I don't know. It could be a billion different things Liam. All we know is that she's lost it."

The next few days, Kelly was miserable. She didn't leave the house, didn't even walk on the beach. Every time he tried to touch her, she pulled away. "I'm not losing you. Not now," Liam said.

To be continued.......

Watch for Southern Seduction coming soon

ABOUT THE AUTHOR

Sue has been writing most of her life, publishing her first book 12 years ago. Now on her 47th novel, she's embarked on a series based in one of her two favorite cities. Opting to do the books in pairs, she's come up with a whole new idea. Not only are they small town romances, but the Charleston series has now increased the spice. Small town, billionaire romances with spice, real romances you get addicted to and characters you can't quite ever get over.

Keep an eye on her socials for updates on new releases, new book ideas, contests and inspiration for her novels.

www.suelangfordauthor.com[1]

Facebook: AuthorSueLangford and SueLangfordAuthor

Instagram SueAuthorGATN

---

1. http://www.suelangfordauthor.com

Don't miss out!

Visit the website below and you can sign up to receive emails whenever Sue Langford publishes a new book. There's no charge and no obligation.

https://books2read.com/r/B-A-FXSR-GWDJD

BOOKS2READ

Connecting independent readers to independent writers.

Also by Sue Langford

Charleston Series
White Sand Romance
Barefoot Billionaire
Barefoot Bodyguard - Charleston Series Book 5
Barefoot Bliss - Book 6 of the Charleston Series
Southern Temptation
Southern Seduction

Watch for more at www.suelangfordauthor.com.

Milton Keynes UK
Ingram Content Group UK Ltd.
UKHW050654260624
444769UK00001B/6

9 798227 060914